A Life of Tea and Sugar

Kayla Danoli

Copyright

Cataloguing-in-publication data
Creator: Danoli, Kayla, author

Cataloguing-in-Publication details are available from the National Library of Australia
www.trove.nla.gov.au

ISBN: 978-0-6454907-4-9 (paperback)
ISBN: 978-0-6454907-5-6 (digital)

Cover design: T A Marshall, Mackay, Queensland, Australia

Disclaimer

This novel is a work of fiction. All characters and events are the product of the imagination of the author. While some of the characters might remind you of people you know, they are fictitious and any resemblance to anyone living or dead is purely coincidental. Although some locations also are real and may seem familiar, the events and where they occur in the course of the story are fictitious.

Prologue

India 1839

"You wanted to see me, Father?"

"Ah, My Girl, yes," Thomas Erskine said. "Come in, come in. I won't detain you for long. I just wanted to tell you that soon you are to set sail for Scotland to live with your Grandmother McGowan. Your basic education has been completed, and you are almost sixteen. Now it is time for you to move to the next stage of your life. Your grandmother has been entrusted with this task; the sooner it begins, the better.

Your passage is booked on a ship sailing for Scotland. It leaves here in six weeks. Miss Crowther's time as governess to children on our neighbouring plantation is ending, and she also is returning to Scotland. She will be your chaperone on the voyage until you are handed over to your grandmother in Glasgow. Over the next weeks, you must devote time to selecting the belongings you wish to take.

That is all I have to say at this time, other than to counsel you to apply yourself diligently to your preparations for the voyage and your new life in Scotland. You may go now."

"No. Why? Why do I have to go away? Why do I have to leave while you and Mother remain here?"

"Such impertinence on your part only serves to confirm how urgent it is for you to commence the next stage of your development. Your grandmother will see to it that you are fit to take your place in society. Now, go and start your preparations."

Sarah almost bowled over her mother, Flora McGowan Erskine, as she rushed from her father's study in tears. "Sarah, Sarah, wait, please. What has happened?" Flora called after her fleeing daughter.

Sarah was heading for her room. Flora allowed her a couple of minutes before following. "Best to let her settle a little before I try talking to her," Flora murmured.

A young serving girl hovered outside Sarah's door. "I'm sorry. I don't know what is wrong. She wouldn't talk to me. She just rushed into her room and slammed the door on me."

"Thank you, Maisie. Go back to your duties. I'll look after things here."

Flora found Sarah sprawled on her bed and sobbing her heart out.

"Come now, Sarah; this is no way to behave. You have managed to upset poor Maisie, as well as me. So, what is all this drama about?"

"Father said I am to leave next week to live in Scotland with Grandma McGowan. He became angry when I asked him why. I don't want to leave here. Why do I have to go? I think I have a right to know why I have to leave."

"Perhaps it was the way that you asked him why that was the cause of the problem. It would have confirmed your lack of understanding of the etiquette required when addressing the head of the household. Maybe if you had asked, 'may I be permitted to know why I am being sent to Scotland', you might have received a different response."

"What difference does it make? It is still the same question."

"Yes, it might be the same question, but it is a matter of appropriate respect and deference that were not shown in the way that you asked your question. Grandma McGowan will guide your tuition in such matters. They are all part of your being *finished* appropriately for your entry into society… and by 'society', I mean Scottish society, not what passes for society here in India."

"This is where I've spent my life. Here is where I want to live. Why do I need to know about Scottish society if I won't be living there? I'll only be there for a year or so while Grandma 'finishes me off', or whatever she is to do, before I'm back here to continue my life in the place I love."

"Time has a way of changing our lives. Let's get you safely back to Glasgow and in your grandmother's care and then see what happens after that."

*****

After sulking and generally being uncooperative, Sarah found she had less than a week to complete her preparations before the carriage with Miss Crowther arrived. It would take Miss Crowther, Sarah, and her parents to the port to await their ship's arrival.

The long, uncomfortable trip to the port had the small entourage arrive late in the afternoon. By then, none of them felt particularly sociable. The rest of the day was spent checking all was in order for the voyage, before Sarah and Miss Crowther joined other passengers to spend the night on board in readiness to set sail on the early morning tide.

Slipping its mooring ropes, the ship headed out to sea, leaving the Erskines waving from the dock. As Sarah watched her parents gradually become smaller and disappear from sight, she wondered about her Grandmother Mary. Is this how Grandmother Mary had felt as the Glasgow docks and the young woman she had been slipped away as she embarked on her adventures as a new wife?

Mary had always been simply her grandmother. Now, as the ship headed out to sea, for a brief few moments, Sarah allowed herself to think of others. But such thoughts and her reflection on the past were short-lived, overwhelmed by her current resentment. There would be plenty of time for such consideration. Without some degree of luck and fair weather when rounding the southern cape of Africa, it would be six months before her ship docked in Scotland.

Heartbroken and not inclined to socialise, the long trip gave Sarah plenty of time to reflect. She either stayed in their cabin or sought out quiet spots on the ship away from the other passengers. There, she let her mind run its course, and wallowed in the emotions almost crushing the life from her. Her mind dredged up everything she had learned from as far back as she could remember.

So much information: details of the McGowan family history and, to a lesser extent, the Erskine family, about her heritage and the family's first years in India. Why feed her all that history when their intent always was to tear her away and send her to a place she had never known – not *really* known? The more she dwelt on it, the more depressed she became.

Her mind kept taking her back to the story of her grandparents' arrival on the subcontinent, their years spent developing the family's plantation, and her own parents' role in the ongoing operation of that plantation. That plantation, the place she loved and called home. That place that no longer would be 'home'.

Her memory wound back the years, driving her deeper into a black hole of melancholia until she was back amongst the times and stories she most loved. Over those boring six months of the voyage, she often wandered back through the stories implanted in her memories.

For the first time, some part of that process caused her recollection of those stories to shift and change a little. Sarah slowly realised those stories she held dear of her parents and her mother's parents were the foundations of her own story. Her current journey into adulthood had at its foundation a wider tale. A story that began long before she was born.

As much as she hated what was happening to her now, her life probably was not so dissimilar to that of Grandmother McGowan's, the woman with whom she would spend the next few years of her immediate future. Sarah was going back, not only in memory, but physically, to where the real story began two generations ago – in Scotland.

Sarah realised her story would not have begun if her Grandfather, Malcolm McGowan, and his wife, Mary, had not gone to India. Had they never purchased their tea plantation, and not employed the plantation manager, Thomas Erskine, who subsequently married the boss' daughter and became Sarah's father.

So, to truly understand her history, Sarah needed to go back and join Malcolm and Mary on their plantation in India early in a tale that would eventually grow and expand into Sarah's own story.

PART 1

India 1820s

Chapter 1

India 1820s

As evening approached, on the small verandah off the side of their sprawling plantation homestead, Malcolm McGowan and his wife, Mary, settled for their customary hour or so of splendid solitude. A ritual that had so quickly become part of their daily life.

Within moments of their becoming comfortable, a young lad of perhaps not more than twelve years, and dressed in his stiff-starched white uniform, arrived with a silver tray loaded with a large pitcher of October Beer and two of the house's finest long glasses. As the McGowans sipped their pale ale in the fading daylight, they watched the workers streaming home from the fields. Soon, their view over the acres of neat rows of tea plants would be wrapped in darkness, and it would be time to dress for dinner.

Malcolm McGowan was among the first managers the British East India Company recruited when it began large-scale tea production in Assam in 1820. But he was from a wealthy Glasgow family, and with family money backing him, his ambition soon reached beyond a managerial position. A McGowan-owned plantation soon became a reality, while their son, Lachlan, remained at school back home in Scotland. On the plantation, Malcolm created a substantial homestead with the help of his wife, Mary, and daughter, Flora, and then added to it over subsequent years.

Their home became a comfortable oasis atop a small rise surrounded by a sea of tea plants, and their lives became easier too. Locals employed as servants in the house and the gardens ensured the place ran smoothly and looked immaculate. Mary's life was now confined to overseeing the running of the house. But Malcolm's life was easier too, since the arrival of his new plantation manager.

The young, fellow Glaswegian poached from one of the British East India plantations was everything the aging Malcolm hoped he would be. Thomas Erskine had taken up the reins the moment he arrived on the plantation. Already trained and *au fait* with tea growing on the Assam plantations, Thomas required neither training nor a period of familiarisation before taking over the responsibility of running Malcolm's kingdom. But something else about Thomas Erskine occupied Malcolm's mind that balmy afternoon as he sipped October Beer with Mary.

"I'm a little concerned about young Thomas Erskine," Malcolm confided to his wife. "He seems to be showing far too much interest in our Flora. Have you noticed anything going on between those two?"

"Between Flora and Thomas…? No. No, I can't say I have. Mind you though, I don't see much of Thomas. He spends most of his time in the fields and away from the house. As for Flora … well, while she has developed into an attractive young woman, she is nobody's fool. She'll not be swept off her feet by some Johnny-come-lately who might be interested in bettering his future through a plantation owner's daughter."

"Was not sending her back to Glasgow as soon as she was old enough the right decision? She is already of marriageable age, and I've seen no prospective suitors queuing up at our door."

"…*Just* of marriageable age, Malcolm. I can't say I've noticed any prospective suitors pitching their pedigrees at her, but she does actively participate in what passes for the social scene in this part of the world. Our daughter is a discerning young woman. I guess, as her parents, we have to trust her judgement."

"That's the point, Mary. What has she had to choose from? Maybe our isolated environment has restricted her choices. I'm concerned she will choose someone she knows from around here because she has no knowledge of what else might be available. Should we talk to her about it?"

"What you mean is, *should I* talk to her about it. I'm inclined to say no. Flora has developed into a daughter we can be proud of, but she is strong-willed. She often has demonstrated her aversion to our interfering in her life's decisions. Any approach by either of us on this delicate subject might push her in the wrong direction – the wrong direction from our point of view, that is."

"You're a wise woman, Mrs McGowan. While I accept your comments as fair and accurate, I will continue to be concerned about our daughter's future. Any young man with half a brain can see she has much to offer, and I don't mean just her beauty."

Mary chuckled but hid it by clattering things about on the tray as she refilled their glasses with ale. Although she hadn't noticed young Thomas Erskine hanging around, she shared her husband's concerns about their daughter's future. Perhaps, being more pragmatic than her husband, she was less troubled by the matter. Anyway, Flora always was her father's favourite. He idolised her from the moment she was born. His concerns were in keeping with the relationship that had developed between father and daughter over the years.

No, she would not raise the subject with Flora anytime soon. Life was too good to waste on lost causes, and if anyone had any influence on the subject of their daughter's future, it would be Malcolm. Sit back and wait, she counselled herself. When – and if – his concerns reach critical levels, he will speak to her … And I will be the pacifist who comes in to smooth her ruffled feathers, and score a few points over Malcolm.

With nothing more to be said, the matter remained 'unfinished business' when they retired to dress for dinner. Nevertheless, uppermost in both parents' minds were thoughts regarding their daughter's future, and the reality that she must soon choose a husband. Mary toyed with the idea of thrusting forward suitors she considered suitable for her daughter. The problem with that idea was where to find 'suitable' suitors.

They did not discuss the matter again, but both kept a keen eye on their daughter and those who showed an interest in her.

About a month later, the memory of that discussion returned to unsettle the parents. A series of forthcoming social events dominated conversation that evening. Everything appeared normal. After dinner, Mary always went to her private sitting room to read or write letters, while Malcolm retired to his study to drink port and smoke his pipe. It was Malcolm's personal time in his private place, and neither wife nor daughter would ever think to intrude … not until that night.

"Father, Thomas Erskine shall arrive shortly. He wishes to speak to you on a private matter. I suggested he come after dinner to speak in your study."

Mary saw her husband draw himself up in his chair and knew it did not bode well. She caught her husband's eye. He looked startled, and not particularly happy. Mary gave an almost imperceptible signal to accept it and not make a fuss, before orchestrating her and Sarah's departure from the dining room.

"Well, I shall withdraw to my sitting room. I intend dealing with some long-overdue correspondence, so I should make a start. Come, Flora, let's leave your father to his drinking and smoking."

"But, Mother, I thought I might…"

"Hush, Dear. I'm sure you have things to be going on with instead of hanging about down here to interfere with the menfolk's business. Come away now."

Minutes later, Thomas Erskine knocked at the front door and was shown into Malcolm's study. "Good evening, Sir," Thomas began. "I apologise for any inconvenience my visit might cause, but I beg a few moments of your time to discuss an important matter with you."

"Aye, well, you're here now, so let's have it out. What do you wish to discuss that is so important and so private it couldn't be done at our regular morning meeting?"

"I've come to ask for your daughter's hand in marriage, Sir. And, while I apologise for any impertinence you might perceive in my request, we – that is, your daughter and I – seek your permission and blessing for us to marry."

"Marriage…! My daughter, Flora, is still a child, much too young to be entertaining such silly notions as marriage. I am…." A noise outside the door interrupted whatever else Malcolm was about to say.

Mary McGowan swept into the room, a wide smile on her face. Through the open doorway, Malcolm glimpsed his daughter hovering outside.

"Good evening, Mr Erskine, and I apologise for my unexpected entrance. *Och noo*, perhaps not so unexpected. Flora is my daughter too. Unlike her father, I know she is not only old enough but also capable of deciding whom and when she should marry. She appears to have chosen you, Mr Erskine. What say you to that?"

Malcolm glared at Mary, who flashed him a smile and ignored him. Malcolm struggled to understand what had happened but recovered enough to find a croaky voice to address their visitor. "Well, man, Mrs McGowan asked you a question. I, too, await your answer."

"I believe it is the wish of both your daughter and me to be married. We wish to create a new life for ourselves, a future together, and one we hope, God willing, will provide you with grandchildren."

"Grandchildren…!" Malcolm's face was so swollen and red, Mary feared he might explode. Nevertheless, she bit her lip to avoid laughing at Malcolm's response.

The situation was saved from deteriorating further when Flora flounced into the room like a man-o-war in full sail and announced, "What Thomas is trying to say, and what this is about is, *we are in love*. We are in love and wish to create a new life for ourselves as a married couple. And, Father, as foreign as it might seem to you, I am old enough to make my own decisions in this regard. So now, how say you?"

Astonished by his daughter's forthright announcement, Malcolm turned his eyes towards Mary. She gave him an almost imperceptible nod, but it took him a further few moments to again find his voice.

"Assuming my blessing is forthcoming, when should this event happen? As you seem to have decided everything else without our input, I don't doubt you also have definite thoughts about that too."

"Nothing definite, but yes, we have thought about it," Flora admitted. "This year's monsoon rains will soon be upon us, and it will become impossible to contemplate holding any such event. A short betrothal of, say, six weeks should see the wedding over before the rains arrive."

Malcolm spluttered, "Six weeks…! No, I can't…."

"Hush, Dear. Flora is right," Mary said. "It is possible to organise a wedding before the rains come. And, once they do arrive, it will be a quiet time on the plantation … and a good opportunity for the young couple to begin adjusting to married life together."

"So they are married – and then what? What of this new life together we keep hearing about?" Malcolm demanded.

"Oh, do stop fussing, Father. None of this will disrupt plantation life in any way. Thomas will continue his duties, and I will continue to help out here as I do now."

"I suppose you plan to start living this new life in this house. How do you see that working for everyone involved?"

"No, Father. We don't plan to live in this house. Thomas is happy and comfortable living in the manager's cottage. As his wife, I shall live there with him."

"Well then," Mary began, "it appears everything has been well thought through. I see nothing more needs to be said or quibbled over. Six weeks is not a long time – and we have a wedding to plan. I suggest whatever needs to be done here tonight be done so we can make a start in the morning on the big job ahead of us."

"Flora, please take Thomas through to the front room," Malcolm said. Once the young couple left the study, he turned to his wife. "By your comments, I take it you approve of this marriage, and I should give my permission?"

Mary nodded and smiled at her husband. "I do … and I think you should go and put them out of their misery now. We both know she has made a good choice and, as you suspected, has taken her time to decide. We brought her up to know her own mind, be independent, and go out into the world as a confident and capable young woman. You like Thomas, so what's the problem?"

"That was before he wanted to marry my daughter."

"There is a lot of you in her, including her taste in men, it seems."

"Come, let's go," he growled.

"Where…?"

"Out to the front room … I have a job to do."

The nervous young couple in the front room watched Flora's parents march in. Malcolm bowled straight up to the drinks cabinet and poured a good measure into four glasses. Then, slowly and deliberately, he turned to face the young ones.

"We need to celebrate the betrothal of my daughter, Flora McGowan, to Mr Thomas Erskine. Here are our best wishes to the young couple and our hope they never regret their decision. To Thomas and Flora…."

Flora raced forward and flung her arms around her father. A bewildered Thomas remained where he stood. Mary went to Thomas and took him by the shoulders. "Congratulations, Thomas … you will get used to him (she jerked her head in Malcolm's direction). We all had to, and he really is a big softie."

By then, Malcolm, disentangled from Flora, strode, hand outstretched towards Thomas. "Congratulations, and best wishes to you both."… And, in a voice barely above a whisper, added, "Know this well, if you ever hurt her, you will pay dearly."

Later, as the parents climbed the stairs together on their way to bed, Malcolm asked, "Have we done the right thing tonight?"

"Of course, and it was the only thing to do. There is a lot of you in our daughter. She knows her own mind and will fight for what she wants."

"Hmm… I see a lot of her mother in her. She knows how to get around me. But she used to be so gentle and compliant, so obedient."

Mary laughed. "Oh, for goodness sake, Malcolm, where have you been for the last decade? It's obvious you haven't noticed she hasn't been any of those things since she was about twelve years old."

*****

A wedding was arranged and, in true plantation style, was a lavish affair. The marriage of Flora and Thomas was celebrated in the plantation's small chapel on the first Saturday after Easter, April 5th 1823. The whole house was a flurry of activity for the six weeks in the lead-up, during which tantrums, outbursts, sulks, and tears, were commonplace, but it was all worthwhile.

Despite the forecast early onset of the monsoons, the day remained dry and sultry as might be expected for the time of year. The house and surrounding gardens were decorated in every imaginable way. The kitchen benches almost groaned under the weight of food prepared for the wedding feast, and the multi-tiered wedding cake, kept in a cupboard under the stairs for the past six weeks and fed Jamaica rum daily, had a powerful smell of alcohol. The cake, if nothing else, reflected the modern thinking of the bride and her mother.

This 'bride's cake' or 'plum cake', to use its common name around that time, followed the latest trend of being heavy, spicy and loaded with fruit. It comprised two tiers that sat directly one on top of the other. And the bride insisted, in keeping with the style set by all the society weddings of the time, her cake should be cloaked in white fondant icing. When the cook received the news, she decided to try her hand on a trial cake before the big occasion.

To her dismay, she found the sultry weather leading up to the monsoon season did not favour fondant icing. It absorbed the moisture from the air and, as it sweated, the dark colour of the cake bled through the icing. Nevertheless, the bride insisted on white fondant icing. As a result, after midnight on the eve of the wedding, the cook and her assistant spent several hours icing the cake.

Then, the big day arrived, and it went off without a hitch. The bride looked beautiful, and the proud groom cut a dashing figure. The chapel was overflowing, and guests had a right merry time at the luncheon that followed. The cake looked stunning and earned the cook a swag of accolades. But then, the celebrations were over, and it was time for the guests to depart.

After disappearing upstairs to change into something more 'suitable', the bride joined her husband, waiting with a carriage hitched and ready to take them away. 'Take them away to where?' was the oft-murmured question among the guests. It was mid-afternoon. The nearest place offering accommodation for the night was at least a day's ride away. Mary chose to ignore the whispered question. She and Flora had agreed a solution weeks ago, and Flora had ensured it was ready for her wedding night.

A small cottage further up in the hills but still on the plantation had been Malcolm and Mary McGowan's home when they first acquired their plantation. It's where they lived until the first stage of the big house was built. Although unoccupied for many years, the cottage remained in good condition thanks to regular maintenance. After cleaning and some additional furniture, the place was an ideal hideout for several days.

With their bags and two large hampers of provisions accompanying them, the couple arrived at the cottage late in the afternoon and were settled in by dinner time. The peace and isolation were glorious after the last few hectic weeks. Flora felt herself relaxing as she soaked up the ambience of the place … and the uniqueness of being somewhere devoid of other people – no parents; no servants; no one else, just she and her new husband.

Flora bid the cabin in the hills a silent farewell on Tuesday morning as they climbed onto the carriage for the trip home ... to her new home in the manager's cottage with Thomas.

Mary had been busy in their absence. The manager's cottage had been scrubbed and cleaned to within an inch of its existence. The larder had been stocked, and Maisie met their carriage on their return.

"Maisie, it's lovely to see you, but should you be here?" Flora asked.

"Yes, Miss. I am now your maid here at this house, as I was before at the big house."

Thomas raised his eyebrows in question at Flora. She sighed. "I see Mary McGowan's fair hand in this. I shan't complain. Maisie has been with me for years. Having her remain with me is a comfort. Nevertheless, I must talk to Mother about what arrangement she has put in place about Maisie's ongoing employment. As our cottage doesn't have servants' quarters, I must discover what mother's thoughts are on this matter."

Mary was a little surprised by the question when Flora caught up with her. "Of course your staff will continue to be accommodated here in the big house. There are more than enough spare rooms here. So, your staff will continue to live here while they work at the cottage for you.

Once the wagon was unloaded, Thomas left Flora alone to settle in while he returned to his duties. Apart from unpacking their bags and the food hampers, there wasn't much else to do, so she sat down to start the thank-you letters to the wedding guests. As was the practice in the big house, Maisie brought an afternoon tea tray at about mid-afternoon and fussed about pouring the tea and placing the cup and saucer within easy reach of where Flora worked.

It was all the excuse Flora needed to take a break from the boring, monotonous thank-you notes she had spent more than an hour writing, and she still had a pile more to do. While she sat sipping her tea and procrastinating about returning to the letter writing, she became aware of the aroma of cooking wafting through the cottage. She rang the bell Maisie had conveniently left on the tray for her. A moment later, Maisie stood in front of her.

"Does my nose deceive me, Maisie, or is there cooking happening in the kitchen of this house?"

"Yes, Miss, the cook is preparing dinner. She didn't talk to you about it first as she thought you would like time to settle in and relax before deciding what to have for dinner."

"That was considerate of her, but I was unaware I had a cook. I assume this is more of my mother's doing and, grateful as I am, I would like to know the identity of my cook."

"Oh, it's Hennie. She has been promoted from assistant cook at the big house, to the cook here at the manager's cottage. She would appreciate a few minutes with you sometime soon to discuss future menus, meal times, and anything else regarding how you want your kitchen to run."

"Of course; how inconsiderate of me not to have talked to her sooner. If she is available soon after breakfast in the morning, please ask her to come to me here."

As Flora watched Maisie's departing figure, she remembered something. "Damn; I intended to go to the big house to see mother after breakfast tomorrow," she muttered. "I don't suppose it matters. I can visit her after I speak with Hennie."

Thomas was later returning from the fields than she expected. She had hoped to follow her parents' example and sit with him for a drink before dinner. But his late return meant dinner was ready to be served at the same time as he arrived home. As he walked in, he announced, "Whatever that is, I hope it's the dinner. It smells divine."

"Dinner is ready to be served, but it can wait a few minutes longer if you'd like to freshen up first."

"I should do that." He turned to walk away, stopped, and turned back to face Flora. With his head on one side, he asked, "Have you amazing talents you've kept hidden from me?"

"Not that I'm aware of or have deliberately tried to hide from you. What particular amazing talent are you asking about?"

"Dinner… I was unaware you were such an accomplished cook."

When Flora managed to stop laughing, she said, "That's because I'm not. Hennie is now our cook and, as I'm to discuss menus with her tomorrow morning, perhaps you should put in your order for your preferred dishes so I might include them in our discussions."

"Oh, I see. I still have much to learn about married life within the McGowan family. I will think about anything I might contribute to the menu discussions."

As they settled into bed that night, both realised they still had a lot to learn about married life and had a long way to go in establishing any form of household routine.

Chapter 2

Despite its slow and, on occasion, tempestuous process, the Erskine household settled into a manageable routine. After they first discussed the matter, Mary managed to refrain from interfering in Flora's household arrangements. While grateful for her mother's generosity in helping her set up home in the manager's cottage, Flora wanted to be mistress of her own home. It was agreed each woman would await an invitation from the other before visiting. Malcolm noticed. He mentioned it to his wife as they sipped their October Beer one afternoon.

"I know I don't spend all day, every day, at this house, but I don't recollect seeing our daughter here lately. Have I missed her visits, or is something amiss?"

"No, I'm unaware anything is amiss, but you are right. Flora hasn't visited for a while."

"Why not? Have you gone to see what's wrong?"

"Flora has her own life now, Malcolm, and we must respect her right to privacy. We observe all the usual social niceties. I don't bowl up to her door without an invitation. Likewise, she waits for an invitation from me before coming to visit."

"Then, what are you waiting for, woman? If nothing is amiss between you, why haven't you invited her over for tea, lunch, or for a chat or whatever you women do when you are together?"

"Don't sell me short, Malcolm McGowan. I have invited her several times, but she has declined to come. Before you ask, Maisie always says the same thing: *Mrs Erskine is busy but would be happy to postpone accepting your offer until sometime in the future*. You are welcome to make what you will of that."

"What is wrong with the woman? You are her mother. Is there something amiss with her marriage? Is she unhappy … or being mistreated? I'll kill the bastard if she is."

"Being her mother doesn't make me privy to what goes on in her home. But, no, I have neither seen nor heard anything to suggest their marriage is negotiating a rocky way forward. Perhaps we should accept our daughter is exercising her independence and right to live her life out from under our wings."

Although he knew Mary's comments made sense, Malcolm remained unconvinced and unhappy about his daughter's apparent distancing of herself from the family. Thoughts in that direction barely crossed his mind before Mary fixed him with a hard look.

"And, Malcolm McGowan, don't go poking your nose where you shouldn't. Don't go questioning Thomas Erskine about the state of his marriage, or you'll have me to deal with afterwards."

"It's a thought that never crossed my mind," he lied glibly, and Mary didn't believe a word of it.

Flora had been married for almost five months the next time she accepted her mother's invitation to morning tea. It was more than six weeks since she last visited the big house. As she was shown into the sitting room where Mary waited, Flora encountered her father in the hallway.

"Hello, Father. Are you joining us for tea this morning?"

"No, I should be out in the… fields … but … on second thoughts, I will join you after all." After dispatching the servant to fetch an extra cup, Malcolm took over escorting his daughter to the sitting room. "Mary, I've decided to join you for tea this morning," he announced as he entered the room. "Look who I found out in the hallway."

"Well, I expected Flora, but you also are welcome to join us." Mary then turned her attention to her daughter. "How have you been, my girl, and how is Thomas?"

Malcolm was stunned. How could Mary sit there making small talk about nothing when there were so many issues to discuss – *major* issues? He was about to head the conversation in the right direction when a hard look from Mary added to his confusion. But, a long time ago, he had learned not to cross his wife when she gave him a clear warning not to. And he also had learned the hard way not to interfere between mother and daughter.

The women chattered on about the manager's cottage, how the staff were performing, whether Flora had heard from any of her friends since the wedding, and how Flora filled in her days. Malcolm's patience was almost at an end. There were questions he wanted answered. At his first opportunity, he *would ask* them. Mary had other ideas.

"Apologies for detaining you, Malcolm dear. I know you planned to ride out to the fields before you joined us for tea. And, all we have done in return is to bore you to death with our women's talk. Please feel free to leave and continue your day." Her meaningful look told him this was not a polite suggestion. He was being dismissed. For a brief moment, his temptation was to defy his wife, but common sense intervened. He obeyed.

As he stomped outside, he acknowledged Mary had won that round, but he was not done yet. Later today, she would hear more about her behaviour.

In the sitting room, Mary heaved a sigh of relief, gave Flora's expanded figure a knowing look, and apologised. "I'm sorry I couldn't get him to leave sooner, but now we are alone, tell me all about it – *woman to woman.*"

Flora twisted her hands together in her lap for a few moments before answering. "It hasn't been good. I expected to be ill, but not so ill for so long. It has settled down now. When the rains were at their worst – and I was at my worst – I couldn't handle trudging through the mud to come to visit. Besides, as every other married woman does, I need to cope with this as the next part of my new life. Every day seems to bring some new learning, and the big one is still to come."

"You should have sent Maisie to fetch me to be with you and help you through this time."

"Thank you, but no, Mother. I am in charge of my life now. Like every new wife, I must learn to deal with whatever comes along. What if Thomas decides to move away from here? How would I cope if I've never learned to do things for myself?"

Although she didn't say so, Mary was proud of her daughter. Flora was right about learning how to make her own way without her mother holding her hand. The conversation then took on a 'baby' focus. Were preparations in place for the baby's arrival? Was a nursery prepared? What about baby's clothes? Had they thought about a suitable nurserymaid? Mary smiled to herself. Malcolm would have been bored to distraction by the topics they discussed.

Her husband had lunch in the field. Mary didn't see him again until their customary drinks at the end of the day. It was cool out on the verandah. The breeze coming up through the valley carried a hint of moisture. As the servant delivered the pitcher of October Beer, Mary eyed it with disdain.

"Perhaps we should have broken tradition and asked for something different today. A steaming pot of tea might have been preferable, given the chill in the air," Mary suggested after her first sip of the beer.

"Are you suggesting I send for tea, or are you happy to stay with the beer?" Malcolm asked.

Mary picked up on the shortness in his voice, and her stomach tightened. Her husband was not himself this evening. She knew she was in for a rough time and searched her mind for a probable cause of his sour humour. She didn't have to think long. She had no doubt it stemmed from Flora's visit that morning. Mary's challenge was to control the situation and ward off the imminent angry scene.

"Thank you for allowing me some time alone with our daughter this morning. It provided an opportunity for a 'woman's talk' with her and to find out why we haven't seen her lately. Although I was trying not to think it, I did wonder if we had offended her in some way, unintentional though it might have been."

"And…? Had we offended her? Mrs McGowan, I would remind you I am neither blind nor an imbecile. I saw her condition. Need I express my anger and disappointment about it?"

"Anger and disappointment…? For God's sake, Malcolm, how can that be your reaction?"

"I knew he was no good when I saw him hanging around our Flora. I should have put a stop to it then. Now, look what it has led to."

"Malcolm, how much beer have you drunk today? You are not making any sense. You're talking rubbish. By *him,* I presume you mean Thomas Erskine … who happens to be our son-in-law. As for his being 'no good', I think he has demonstrated he is indeed up to the job of being a husband and providing us with grandchildren.

Yes, our daughter is with child, and it has not been going well for her until now. Instead of carrying on like some indignant parent whose child has been wronged, perhaps you might stop and think about what this means for us. Flora is about to produce the first of the next generation of our family, and Thomas has played his part in that. Now, perhaps you might be good enough to explain what you see as the problem with that situation."

She knew she had succeeded when she saw Malcolm physically deflate and slump in his chair. He sat for a long moment swirling the contents of his now half-empty glass before avoiding Mary's eyes when he again spoke.

"It is not easy for a father to see his daughter in that condition and know what some man has done to her."

"Why on earth would you be thinking about what happened to her? What this husband and wife do behind closed doors is no more our business than what any other husband and wife might do. If you have trouble minding your own business, think back to your parents. Would they have spent their spare time wondering what we were up to behind our bedroom door?"

A long silence ensued. Although happy to allow it to stretch on, Mary kept a watchful eye on her husband. She knew his silence resulted from his 'resetting his thinking', and she felt confident of a great improvement.

*****

Life returned to what passed for normal. Mary and her daughter visited one another every couple of days. Mary's maid retrieved from storage the few baby's clothes Mary had saved from when her children were born. Pride of place among them was the christening robe in which Malcolm and their two children were christened. She was excited about another generation making use of the robe. All the clothes, except the christening robe, were laundered and mended if necessary before being given to Flora. The christening robe would be presented as a surprise at the appropriate time.

The pregnancy progressed. Where would Flora give birth? Who would be the midwife to deliver their grandchild? On several occasions, Mary tried broaching the subject of arrangements for the delivery. There was no doubt in Mary's mind Flora should give birth at the big house. She mentally prepared a room befitting the event. A midwife was a more complex issue. It couldn't be Mary. She had given birth twice but had never delivered a baby.

On other plantations, the services of an older local woman were called upon in such situations. After many deliveries in their villages, some of these women were quite adept at delivering a baby safely, sometimes even under difficult circumstances. Perhaps, nearer to Flora's time, Mary should talk to the cook, who she was sure would know of a suitable midwife.

The weeks slipped by. Mary was becoming desperate. Although Flora's time was close, she avoided discussing with Mary arrangements for the impending birth. Home again after yet another frustrating visit with Flora, Mary stomped upstairs and flung open the door of the room she had earmarked for the big event.

"There is nothing to do except to go ahead and prepare this room anyway," she told the, empty room. "I can't risk not being ready in time." But a busy week ahead delayed starting before early the next week.

*****

Although it was only yesterday Mary visited Flora, she decided to go to the cottage again to sort things out. Maisie looked … looked how? … Yes, Mary decided Maisie looked 'uncomfortable' when she opened the door.

"Good morning, Memsahib. I'm sorry, I wasn't expecting you. Please come in."

"I was hoping to speak to my daughter. Is she around?" Something was not right. Every other time she visited, Maisie showed her straight through to wherever Flora happened to be.

"Miss Flora is sleeping, Memsahib. She does not sleep well now; only little sleeps, but no long sleeps."

"Is she unwell?"

"No, Memsahib. The baby is keeping her awake."

"Ah yes, I remember what it was like. I'll not disturb her. When she wakes, please tell her I called."

Maisie heaved a sigh of relief as she closed the door behind Mary. Then she took a deep breath before hurrying to her mistress's room. "Your mother has gone, Miss. She s to tell you she called."

"Thank you, Maisie. Is your mother here today?"

"Yes, Miss, she is helping Hennie in the kitchen." Flora's face contorted, and she uttered a strangled scream. "Are you all right, Miss? Can I help?"

"Bring your mother to me please, Maisie… Now! Tell her to bring her basket. When you have done that, fetch towels and sheets from the linen cupboard."

Moments later, footsteps hurried to the bedroom. Maisie, followed by her mother, rushed into the room in time to find Flora writhing in pain and in a lather of sweat. Her mother whispered something to Maisie, who turned on her heel and rushed from the room. Maisie's mother turned to Flora and began mopping her brow.

"Now, Miss, tell me what is happening," she said quietly.

"My baby is coming... that's what's happening. It will arrive at any minute."

"Let's see what is going on before we get too excited. First babies take time to arrive, sometimes as long as a day, or even two days. I do not think… Oh, my goodness; yes, your baby is about to arrive. Where is that girl with those things I asked her to bring?"

Right on cue, Maisie burst into the room as her mother finished speaking. She carried a basin and a heavy-looking pitcher. "The water was recently boiled, but it is only lukewarm now. Will it be all right?"

"It will be good. Put it over there on the little table, please, and then leave us." Maisie went to argue. She wanted to stay, but the look her mother gave her sent her scurrying for the door.

After sending the gardener to fetch Sahib Thomas, their work forgotten, Maisie and Hennie spent the next half hour hovering and pacing. The excitement and tension in the room were almost palpable. All this was new to Maisie. She thought she would burst if something didn't happen soon. Then it did, and everything seemed to happen at once.

The sound of a horse at a flat gallop ended abruptly outside the house. Thomas strode in. "What's happening? Why was I summoned? Where is my wife? Is she all right?"

"Apologies for interrupting your work, Sahib," Maisie began, "but…." Whatever else she was about to say was lost. The indignant wail of a newborn rang through the house… and its squawking continued for a few minutes. "The Memsahib wanted you to be the first to meet your child. It has arrived, but you must wait until you are told it is all right to go in."

A few minutes later, Maisie's mother came into the sitting room carrying a small bundle wrapped in a towel. "Ah, Sahib Thomas, perhaps you wish to meet your new daughter? She had a little to eat and is sleeping now. She will be hungry when she wakes soon and must return to her mother to be fed." She walked over and gently placed the baby in Thomas's arms. "If you would permit me a few more minutes to finish, you can go in to see the Memsahib. She is resting now."

Thomas barely heard her. Mesmerised, he stood gazing at the contents of the tiny bundle. "She is beautiful, so beautiful," he whispered.

Maisie rushed over and eased back part of the towel to see the child. Tears streamed down her face. "Maisie, what is wrong?" Thomas demanded, fearing something was wrong with the baby, something he hadn't noticed.

"Nothing is wrong, Sahib. Everything is perfect, and you are right. She is beautiful."

"And she has good lungs too," Hennie added. "For such a little thing, she made plenty of noise."

Moments later, Maisie's mother again entered the sitting room and spoke to Thomas. "Everything is ready if you wish to see the Memsahib now," she told him before leading him to the bedroom.

When part way along the hall, a thought made Thomas return to the sitting room. "Maisie, does Memsahib Mary know the baby has arrived?"

"Not yet, Sahib… My instructions were to wait until after you saw the baby before I told Memsahib Mary it had arrived. I will tell her now." Thomas nodded and started back along the hallway to where Maisie's mother waited for him.

"The Memsahib is still dozing. The baby will wake her soon enough, but she needs as much rest as possible in the meantime. If you tire of holding the baby, you may put her down in the bassinet over there." Thomas nodded, but he knew there was no way he would ever tire of holding his daughter.

Maisie ran from the manager's cottage and arrived at the big house almost out of breath. Ignoring protocols and training, Maisie rushed in through the front door, nearly colliding with Mary on her way to the sitting room.

"Good heavens, Maisie, why are you rushing about like this?" And then a frightening thought occurred to her. "Is my daughter all right? Has something happened?"

"Please, Memsahib Mary, you should come now. The baby has come."

"Do you mean the baby is coming? Has my daughter gone into labour? We need to bring her here, but nothing is ready. Never mind. We will use one of the other rooms. I don't have anyone to deliver the baby. Oh God, what am I to do?"

"No, no, Memsahib. The baby has arrived. You must come now to meet your grandchild."

"It's here? She has had the baby! Oh God… Has my husband been told? I'll send someone to fetch him. Come, let's go. I can't wait any longer to meet my grandchild." Maisie led Mary into the cottage and directed her to the room at the far end of the hallway.

Without a sound, Mary opened the door and peered in. Flora appeared to be sleeping. Thomas stood beside the bed, gazing down at his wife, and nursing a tiny bundle wrapped in a towel. Tiptoeing in, Mary quietly called Thomas's name. He looked up. Bewildered at first by the sound of his name, his face lit up when he saw Mary.

"Hello, Grandmother. Would you like to meet our gorgeous little girl? Her name is Sarah – or it will be unless her mother has changed her mind. Sarah is the name we had chosen if the baby was a girl." And then it was Mary's turn to have tears streaming down her cheeks as she gazed at the baby in her arms.

"Has the grandfather been told she has arrived?"

"I've sent someone to find him. He will be along soon, I imagine."

"She is so tiny. They tell me she is perfect, but she seems much smaller than I expected."

"You are right. She is. All newborns are tiny, and sometimes first babies are smaller. I'm sure she will soon fill out."

About ten minutes later, the grandfather arrived and was smitten at his first glimpse of the newest addition to the family. Then Sarah started bawling. A couple of squawks brought Maisie's mother rushing to take charge. She knocked but didn't wait for a reply. She marched straight up to the grandfather, removed the bawling baby from his arms, and left him looking stunned.

"She is hungry. It is time for her to be fed. Everyone must leave, please … now." The woman gave a sweeping gesture towards the door to emphasise her words.

The activity in the room woke Flora. Her eyes blinked a few times but remained unfocused. "What's happening? What is that noise?" she mumbled through a parched mouth.

"Come, wake up, Memsahib. Your baby is hungry. You must feed her."

"Wha… Oh yeah… my baby…" Flora still was trying to process the situation when the baby was plonked in her arms.

Out in the sitting room, the three adults, so unceremoniously shooed out of the bedroom, gathered to take stock of the situation. "Can that woman treat us like that?" Malcolm demanded. "Who does she think she is… and who does she think we are?"

"Oh, yes, she has the right," Mary assured him. "Her entire focus is on the baby and its well-being." Turning to her son-in-law, she said, "You mark my words, Thomas, when you appoint your own nursery ayah, you might find her even more protective of her charge. You will have to ask permission to see your child. And, gentlemen, you might be well advised to go about your work for the rest of the day. Mother and child both need time to rest and get to know each other … without interference or interruptions from well-meaning outsiders."

After the men returned to the fields, Mary sat at her desk penning notes informing family and friends of the arrival of her granddaughter. Apart from an air of excitement among the domestic staff, the rest of the day was as normal as possible.

Chapter 3

Difficult Relationships India 1823 - 1829

Later, when Mary and Malcolm retired to the verandah for their afternoon October Beer, both still retained traces of their euphoric state from earlier that morning. While there wasn't a lot of conversation, Mary was concerned when she noticed a dark scowl accompanied Malcolm's silence.

"What's wrong, dear? You appear worried or upset about something," Mary asked.

"I told you he was no good, didn't I? I told you I was unhappy about him hanging around our daughter. He paid her far too much attention, and I didn't do anything about it." Malcolm growled. "Now, I have to accept it's as much my fault as his."

"Who…? Thomas…? What are you on about, Malcolm? What is your fault? Don't spoil a wonderful day by dredging up some spurious feelings you had about your son-in-law."

"They weren't spurious. It proves I had every right to be concerned. Think about it, woman. How long has our daughter been married? Do the maths. It is not yet nine months, and already we have welcomed a grandchild."

"Ooh, I see. No, I hadn't thought about it. But babies do sometimes come early. Perhaps we shouldn't dwell on such thoughts."

"…Not so early – and not without some problem to cause it."

"Well, if you can't leave it be, think back on what your father used to say: *Better to buy a cow with calf at foot than one without. That way, you are sure it can produce.*"

"Mrs McGowan, I do not find such comment at all comforting. I hope you have more constructive thoughts on what we are to do about this."

"For God's sake, Malcolm; …to do about what? Our daughter is married to someone she loves – and who appears to love her. They seem happy and are besotted with their new daughter, who arrived safe and well. For what more could you ask? There is nothing for us to do except refrain from interfering in their lives. Of course, I say that on the assumption you do not wish to find yourself alienated from your grandchild anytime soon."

"Of course not,"

"Good; then let's hear no more about this, shall we?"

While the matter never arose again, Malcolm McGowan's opinion of his son-in-law never recovered. Life continued on the plantation much as before, and the plantation – and the family – continued to prosper. Mary's only disappointment, if any, was that no further grandchildren appeared. She had hoped for a grandson, more for Malcolm's sake than her own. But, although Flora and Thomas's marriage seemed as solid as ever, the family appeared ordained never to become larger.

Sarah, as the only Erskine offspring, grew up very much a part of the world she inhabited. From her ayah to the children she played with, all were 'local'. She developed a love and understanding of the culture of that part of Assam. That was fine until it was time to consider Sarah's formal education. Children of British expatriates in the area tended to be sent back to boarding school in England as soon as they were old enough, in many cases, by the time they were seven years old. Occasionally, daughters continued being home-tutored by an English governess until around age twelve.

What to do about Sarah's education occupied the minds of her parents and her grandparents. Without exception, they all wanted the best possible education and opportunities for Sarah, but the thought of being without her hampered the decision-making. An English governess, Miss Westcott, who came highly recommended by McGowan relatives in Scotland, was hired to preside over Sarah's formal education and training befitting someone of her position.

Everyone agreed the arrangement would last only until Sarah was of sufficient age to be sent 'back home' to boarding school. When that should happen was debated over the years – but always left in abeyance.

Around the same time, another notable event occurred. Flora's brother, Lachlan McGowan, returned to the plantation after fifteen years absence. The younger child of Malcolm and Mary, Lachlan, at the age of seven, was packed off to boarding school in Scotland. Then, from age fifteen, it was considered advantageous he continue his education at various prestigious English establishments. That continued up to and including his poor performance at university.

Then he turned twenty-one. He was still failing university but enjoying a wonderful social life while he was about it. Malcolm decided his son had been indulged long enough. It was time for him to come home and learn the ropes of running a tea plantation. This news was not the birthday present Lachlan wanted. Letters went to and fro, but Malcolm would not be deterred. Lachlan should return home. But Lachlan had one last suggestion that he hoped might delay the inevitable. He wrote his father a persuasive plea.

A friend, who attained his majority around the same time as Lachlan, was given a year-long 'Grand Tour of Europe' to celebrate the milestone. His friend wanted a companion and asked his best mate, Lachlan. Somehow, Lachlan persuaded Malcolm to grant him a similar birthday present. He promised to return to the plantation at the end of his year of adventure.

Twelve months later, Lachlan was back on the plantation for the first time in many years. He struggled to settle back into life at home. It should have been expected. Lachlan was 'his own man' for many years and, during that time, had enjoyed a lifestyle far removed from that on the plantation. Adding to his misery, he was turned over to Thomas to be trained in all aspects of plantation management. He found being a 'trainee manager' humiliating. As the owner's only son, Lachlan felt entitled to a loftier position or at least one with more authority.

It wasn't to be. Some six months after Lachlan's return to the property, his situation was made clear to him in an almighty row with his father. For Thomas, the antagonism between father and son only exacerbated an already volatile situation. Lachlan became sullen and argumentative, ignoring Thomas's instructions, and seeming to delight in treating the workers badly. The plantation's policy always was to treat all workers equally, regardless of colour or culture. Unrest festered among the workers, thanks to Lachlan. Despite Thomas's efforts, it led to the eventual disruption of the harvest.

Neither Malcolm nor Mary was blind to the cause of the situation, but Lachlan was their son. Malcolm blamed Thomas. That wasn't difficult since Thomas had been out of favour with Malcolm for some time. The situation on the property continued to deteriorate and was in danger of becoming a tinder box. There was only one thing to do.

Lachlan was the McGowans' son and heir. Although they were not blind to his shortcomings, the plantation was his home and his inheritance. He had to stay. On the other hand, Thomas was not 'family'; only through marriage. Flora was only a daughter… and, against Malcolm's better judgement, had cast her lot in with Thomas. So she too became expendable along with her husband.

Mary was uneasy. Although she appreciated and understood the crisis which had developed, losing Thomas as plantation manager seemed a drastic remedy. She tried easing into the conversation she wanted with her husband.

"Malcolm, dear, is Lachlan fully trained and ready to take over management of this place? You and I are getting on a bit now. After all these years, I'm concerned you might have ideas of running the place again yourself."

"Our son was given a couple of years to learn the ropes. It might take a few months for me to give his training a final 'polish', but he will be fine. As you say, we are getting on a bit. Sooner, rather than too much later, he must take over the plantation."

"I am aware of this but, if I'm honest, I do not much like the Lachlan we brought home."

"And he does not much like being here." Malcolm chuckled before becoming serious again. "Since his birth, the plan always was for him to take over. That time has come – almost. We gave him a lot of years to obtain a sound education and experience another side of life. Now it is time for him to settle down and take up his responsibilities."

"Once Thomas has gone, where will Lachlan live? Do you see him continuing in the big house with us, or will he move into the manager's cottage?"

"I hadn't given the matter any thought. Perhaps it's a decision best left to Lachlan. Why do you ask? Is it important for some reason I haven't considered?"

She could read her husband well. His tone had become harsh, and Mary knew the signs. She needed to think of some way to diffuse an impending row.

"Nothing to worry yourself about, Mr McGowan," she said, hoping she sounded light-hearted. "My mind had wandered to the domestic staff employed at the manager's cottage. Will they be needed once Thomas and his family have left?"

"Hmm… yes, I see. Our son is a grown man and may wish to maintain his own household. Unless you have concerns with that, I suggest we allow him to decide such matters."

"No, I don't have any *real* concerns…."

"BUT…? Come on, woman, spit it out. What is on your mind?"

"Please don't shout at me, but I have noticed our son has an eye for the young women we employ. Yesterday, I think I interrupted something quite unacceptable he was about to do to one of the younger girls. If he were to continue to live in this house with us, he would have to abide by our rules and standards. Living alone in the manager's cottage, he would be free to do as he pleased with whomever he chose. He would be out from under our watchful eyes."

"Argh, yes. I have noticed his behaviour. Perhaps we should deem the manager's cottage to be unavailable to him. If he should come asking to move in, I don't have to give him a reason."

"When will you tell Thomas his services are no longer required and he has to go?"

"Well, tomorrow seems as good as any other time. I'll give him until the end of the week to be gone."

"That won't do. You may give Thomas notice whenever you see fit, but he must be given time to make plans for himself and his family's future."

"It's only Thomas I want gone. The others can continue to live here, either in this house with us or in the cottage."

"You are not so naïve, Malcolm, as to believe Thomas would leave without his family. There is no way Flora would remain here without him. I half expect Flora will never speak to us again after all this. And, you might as well know, it breaks my heart to know I am about to lose my daughter and granddaughter… and all because your son is both arrogant and lazy."

With her true feelings on the matter made clear, Mary sprang out of her chair and flounced off up to her room, locking the door behind her. After allowing Marry sufficient interval to calm down, Malcolm climbed the stairs and tapped lightly on her door before trying the handle. He was dismayed to find it locked. He knocked louder and called Mary's name – and received no response for his trouble.

This would not do. Mary's assessment of their son was accurate. But he was their son, who was now a man and no longer a boy, and he was due the respect his position warranted. Mary's behaviour was unacceptable and out of keeping with the woman he had married all those years ago. Not only did their son demand respect, but so did he, Malcolm McGowan, as head of the family. Such behaviour could not be tolerated. He began thumping on her door with his closed fist.

After a few such blows, Malcolm glimpsed a figure partly hidden in the shadows. One of the male servants in his starched white uniform hovered in the gloom further along the hallway. "Dear God, what must he think of my performance?" Malcolm thought aloud. It would be the talk of all the domestic servants. By tomorrow, news of it also would spread to the field workers. He knew maintaining respect was fundamental to good management of the plantation.

To regain some dignity, Malcolm straightened up and stepped away from the door. After straightening his jacket and running a smoothing hand over his hair and beard, he turned and stomped down to his study. His composure still in tatters, Malcolm snatched up the neatly folded light blanket lying on the daybed and shook it open. After locking the study door to ensure no servants stole a peek at what was happening, he stretched out on the bed and pulled the cover over him. As his eyelids drooped, he asked the empty room, "Is this what my marriage has come to now, and is my son worth it?" No answers were forthcoming, as an uneasy sleep descended.

*****

Still smarting from Mary's rebuff the previous evening, Malcolm approached his meeting with Thomas in the wrong frame of mind. The meeting did not go well. Thomas became angry and made clear his feelings about Malcolm.

"You disgust me. What sort of man are you; what sort of father? Apart from the fact you have shown me no respect for some years, a father who would turn out his daughter and grandchild in such a way is worthy only of contempt. I would not stay here a moment longer if it were not for consideration of my wife and child. As a husband and father, I must ensure a safe and sound future for my family before they are subjected to any further upheaval. If you have any decency left, you will respect that. As for leaving them here when I depart, that will never happen. Apart from the fact I have more respect for them than to abandon them in such a manner, Flora would not allow me to leave without her and our daughter."

Confronted with the truth, and despite the dangerous level of Malcolm's anger, common sense managed to take over. He turned on his heel and stormed back to the house. The deed was done. There was no more to be said to Thomas Erskine – good riddance to him, and the sooner, the better. But there was plenty more he had to say to Mary. She needed to know he would not tolerate such behaviour in future.

He strode into the sitting room, expecting to find his wife working on her embroidery. The room was empty and devoid of anything to suggest Mary had been there at all that morning. One of the ayahs came in and started dusting and cleaning.

"Where is Memsahib Mary this morning? Has she been here?" he asked the startled girl.

"No, Sahib. I don't think so. I have not seen her today."

"Damned woman," he muttered as he strode out of the room. "Where else might she be?"

A troubling thought crept in from somewhere, although he tried hard to prevent it. He knew, but didn't want to believe, Mary might not be in the big house at all. If he understood anything about his wife it was that she would be with Flora – no doubt trying to comfort her. He had done what had to be done. Surely there could be no question in Mary's mind about that or the reasons for it.

She was an intelligent woman, so why was she behaving this way? He didn't need to ask himself the question. He had the answer. And, he also was aware Mary was disgusted with him. Well, he wasn't going to chase after her or his daughter. He would not go to the manager's cottage. Besides, Thomas might be there. Malcolm did not need to be reminded again today of his shortcomings as a human being. It was important he maintained a strong and steadfast position. He must not give any hint of softening his stance.

Alone in his study with nothing but anger and troubling thoughts for company, Malcolm was startled to see their open carriage rattle around the corner of the house and stop at the front door. He rushed to the window to investigate and saw Mary climb aboard and be handed a small bag by her maid.

"Where the hell does she think she is going?" he growled, almost stunned by what he witnessed.

A few moments later, having persuaded his legs to obey his brain, Malcolm rushed through the house to the front door. It was too late. He heard the carriage move off before he reached the door, and the driver flicking the reins to encourage the team to gallop. The carriage had disappeared when he flung open the door and raced out onto the front steps. Stunned, he stumbled back to his study and flopped into the chair behind his desk.

"What do I do now? What do I do now?" he moaned as he stared at the desktop.

At that most inappropriate moment, with a smug look on his face, hands buried deep in his pockets and without knocking before entering, Lachlan strolled into his father's study. Malcolm slid his eyes up to look at his son.

"So, at last, he is finished, and he and his are leaving. I must interview the staff to decide whether to keep them on after I move into the manager's cottage. It's been too long, but, at last, I can assume my rightful position on this plantation. Of course, I need a proper office in the cottage. Something like this would do," Lachlan said as his eyes slid around the room.

"You arrogant pile of shite! That I could produce such a useless offspring astounds me. Here are a few things you need to get straight in your head before another moment goes by. The list starts with the manager's cottage. It is not available. You will not be moving into it now, or in the future. Now, you would do well to take on board a few other facts, as they will apply to you from this moment forward." Malcolm proceeded to acquaint Lachlan with the reality of his life in the years to come. It did not go down well with the younger man.

He flounced out of his father's study and went in search of his mother, in the misguided belief he would receive a sympathetic hearing from her, and that she might intervene on his behalf with his father. He asked several staff members where he might find her, but none knew. Abandoning his quest, he poured himself a long measure of Jamaica rum, grabbed a book and put his feet up in the sitting room to sulk in comfort. It didn't quite happen that way.

When a tea tray was taken into Malcolm's study, the servant asked if Malcolm knew where to find Memsahib Mary. Her son had been looking for her, and none of the staff had seen her.

"Is that so?" Malcolm asked politely. "And where is Sahib Lachlan now?"

Moments later, Malcolm stormed into the sitting room, grabbed Lachlan by the arm and hauled him out of the high-backed chair where he was dozing. Still holding his son's arm, he dragged him out of the sitting room and to the front door, before pushing him down the stairs. Then, from the top step, Malcolm addressed the scrambled heap on the ground in front of him.

"You are a useless disgrace to the human race. Wanted to go running to your mummy, did you? Oh dear, and you couldn't find her. So, you're gutless as well as lazy… Go out into the fields and pretend to be a manager. God knows – and so will the workers – you are not a manager's bootlace. I have replaced an excellent manager with you… for now. Don't show your face back here until after dinner."

Scrambling to his feet, Lachlan bolted for the stables as soon as Malcolm finished his tirade. He had never been spoken to or treated in this way before. To suffer it now as an adult was humiliating – and frightening. Who was the man who had thrown him out of the house? That was not the Papa he remembered. But, as he rode through the tea bushes, he realised he never knew his father. He went away to boarding school when he turned seven. Before then, he saw little of this man. Malcolm had been in the fields all day establishing the plantation. He left the house before Lachlan arose in the morning and didn't return until after he and his sister were in bed.

Lachlan wished his mother were home. He, too, thought she had gone to comfort his sister, Flora, after she found out they had to leave. There was no way Lachlan would visit the manager's cottage in search of his mother. He had been humiliated enough already today. If Thomas were there, he had no doubt he would be in for another dose of it … and maybe a more physical treatment this time. After all, what did Thomas have to lose?

*****

A surge of relief swept through Malcolm when the carriage arrived, and he saw Mary alight. But almost at once, his relief turned to anger. What did his wife think she was doing? Well, he would damned well find out.

He confronted Mary as she started climbing the stairs to her room. Slapping his hand down hard on the banister railing, he demanded to know where she went yesterday and what she had been doing.

"I went to the port. I've made arrangements. Passages are booked on a ship sailing at the end of next week. Now, even if you intend going to dinner dressed as you are, I plan to freshen up and dress appropriately."

With that, Mary turned and continued up the stairs. When a few steps further up, for a moment, she did wonder where Lachlan might be and whether he would be joining them for dinner. But the thought vanished as quickly as it had arrived. Lachlan wasn't worth thinking about or asking after.

The couple were polite when necessary, but cordial relations were not re-established. A couple of days after Mary's return from the port, Malcolm was alarmed at what he saw as he passed Mary's room. Through the open door, he glimpsed trunks open and spread out around the room. Doubling back, he stood gaping at his wife's room.

"What in the name of God are you doing, woman?" he bellowed. "What is all this nonsense with packing trunks?"

"I told you. We sail in a few days, and I have much to do before then to be ready in time."

"Who is this 'we' you mention? This packing I see happening suggests to me it includes you."

"Of course it does. Surely you are not surprised that I will not stay with someone who treats his daughter and grandchild with such callous disregard, and to witness a son, not worth the air he breathes, making a fool of himself as a manager?"

"I demand you stop this nonsense immediately." Then, in a quieter voice, "Mary, you are my wife. Your place is here with me, as it always has been. I can't believe you question appointing Lachlan manager."

"No, I don't question it. I don't bother myself with the matter. You and your son deserve each other. As for my place being here, that was before… but no longer. Yes, I will remain your wife, but in name only. I will remain Mrs McGowan but in a distant country. There is nothing more to be said. That is how it is to be."

Chapter 4

A New Beginning   India 1829

Mary's announcement was Malcolm's wake-up call to take the first steps towards repairing his marriage. His admission that perhaps he might have handled the situation with Thomas better opened negotiations for a fragile truce. Mary also came to accept that, perhaps, she had been a bit rash and might have over reacted.

Before the weekend, a serious oversight became apparent. Sarah's governess, Miss Westcott, was overlooked in the family's upheaval. Her services were no longer required, but no arrangements had been made for her. Mary discovered Flora also hadn't spoken to Miss Westcott about their evolving situation. She rushed to remedy the situation.

In a meeting with the governess, Mary learnt the governess was considering resigning her position. Her father had died years ago, and now her mother was seriously ill. Miss Westcott felt obliged to return home to care for her mother.

"It's only natural a daughter wanted to be with her mother under such circumstances," Mary said. "How soon can you be packed and ready to sail?"

"I brought little with me. It would take me no more than a day to pack my belongings. Why do you ask?"

"Sarah and her parents sail for Scotland at the end of this week. While it is a sudden arrangement, an extra passage is reserved should you wish to travel with the family."

Miss Westcott was happy to accept the offer and would begin her preparations accordingly. Mary shook her head in disbelief as she watched the governess rush back to her room to start packing. What had she done? No spare berth was booked. Miss Westcott would use Mary's booking for her voyage home.

She could book a berth on the next ship to follow the family to Glasgow. Somehow, Mary knew she would not see Glasgow again any time soon.

As they sat sipping their October Beer, the now customary silence between the couple stretched on a couple of minutes before Mary felt confident enough to speak.

"This morning, I believe I averted a potentially embarrassing situation. Nobody thought to tell Miss Westcott she was about to lose her job with the departure of Sarah. She desires to return to Scotland to care for her ill mother. When the ship sails in a couple of days, she will take my place on board. She will help Flora look after Sarah on the long voyage home and will continue the child's lessons during the months they are at sea."

"Thank you for arranging it. I am pleased you will not be leaving. There is one thing though, do you think it possible normal relations might resume in this house sometime soon?"

"Oh, I think that is possible from about now… if it suits you. But, Mr McGowan, while we may resume normal lives to some extent, what are we to do about our obnoxious, useless son?"

"Now, that is a question I cannot answer. I gave Lachlan a few 'home truths' to chew on, so we will see what effect that has. And I will continue to ride his backside hard every day. Only time will tell how effective any of that is, so we must allow him sufficient time to prove himself.

"And, if he does not? I mean, if, after a reasonable time, he doesn't measure up, what then?"

"Might we leave that bridge until and if we need to cross it?"

*****

The day before the Erskines and the governess were due to depart, the large wagon and the carriage were readied for an early departure next morning. During the day, an array of trunks, chests, and cases, were loaded on the wagon. By evening, both wagon and carriage stood side by side, ready to be hitched up next morning, and two teams of horses waited in the home paddock.

Thomas and his family spent their final night on the plantation in the big house. It was a gloomy affair. Lachlan was sullen and rude from the moment they arrived. Malcolm was compelled to step in to prevent the night's becoming a disaster. He took his son aside as everyone was about to go onto the verandah for drinks before dinner.

"You disgust me. You're behaving like a spoilt child, not a grown man. Do not join us for drinks or for dinner. A meal will be sent to your room. Stay there until everyone departs in the morning. I do not want to see you again before our working day starts tomorrow – and I'm sure nobody else wants to see you either."

Lachlan drew himself up to his full height and was about to argue, but the look on his father's face urged caution. His father was getting on in years, but he was fit and strong. Lachlan knew better than to push him too far. His father might lash out. Lachlan knew his years of the 'good life' had left him soft. He also knew, if his father lashed out, he would measure his length on the floor. Instead of arguing, Lachlan skulked off to his room to sulk for the rest of the night.

Dinner was a sombre affair with little conversation throughout. As Thomas and Sarah headed up to bed, Flora stayed behind to speak to her mother.

"I saw the wagon and carriage were ready for the morning, but we won't all fit in the carriage. Four would be comfortable, but six is too many. Some will have to ride on the wagon. Somehow that doesn't seem right. It will be the last time we're all together for who knows how long. I don't want us to be separated."

"There will be plenty of room in the carriage. Your father and I will not accompany you. For my part, it is the best thing I can do for you. I know I will be unable to control myself, and I do not wish to cause anyone, particularly the little one, any further distress. We will say our farewells here before you leave." Tears welled up in Mary's eyes as she spoke. She did not want to make it harder for her daughter. "Go to your family,

Flora. You must draw strength from each other for the next twenty-four hours to get through this time."

Whether Thomas and his family slept that night is unknown, but the McGowan parents found sleep elusive and struggled to wear a brave face next morning.

"How appropriate… a bleak dawning to a bleak day," Mary announced at her first sight of the morning awaiting them outside.

Mist hung low over the hills, and thick, black clouds filled the sky. "Let's pray they don't have a wet ride to the port," Malcolm murmured in her ear as he wrapped his arm around Mary's shoulders.

The atmosphere was no brighter further along the upper floor where Thomas and his family spent the night. He and Flora looked drained and as though they had not slept. Sarah had been hard to settle before spending the night broken on several occasions by nightmares.

All the family, except Lachlan, sat at the big dining room table for a light but silent breakfast. Even Miss Westcott, who joined them, seemed infected by the same melancholia.

"I fear you will not enjoy a better night's sleep tonight," Mary commented. "Your first night onboard ship is bound to feel strange, but maybe the lack of sleep last night will make for a better sleep tonight." No one responded. Not a smile softened set, stony faces. All too soon, it was time to go. It fell to Malcolm to move people along.

"Time is away. Come. The sooner you are on the road, the sooner you can settle into the cabins that will be your home for the forthcoming months. You and your luggage will board the ship when you arrive at the port. Your ship sets sail at midnight. Its manifest includes a good load of our tea, so some of this place will accompany you all the way to Glasgow. Come now, let's have you started on your way to the port."

No one sprang up in response to Malcolm's urging. It resulted in a reluctant scraping of chairs away from the table and a slow levering of bodies to the upright position. Then they marched in sombre procession, like the condemned to the scaffold, out the front door and down the stairs. A stoic Miss Westcott said her goodbyes and was helped aboard the carriage by Thomas, where she sat rigid and with eyes fixed firmly forward.

A distraught Flora hugged her equally tearful mother for a long moment before Thomas gently unwrapped her arms from around Mary and led her to the carriage. As he helped her on board, another scene developed behind him.

Tears streaming down her face, Sarah raced to Mary and threw her arms around her grandmother. Within a moment, both were sobbing. Mary thought her heart would break when Sarah started screaming.

"I don't want to go. I don't want to leave. I want to stay here, to stay here with you. Don't make me go. Please don't make me leave."

Mary did her best to save the situation by whispering to the child she held wrapped close to her body.

"I don't want to see you go either, Little One, but your place is with your Mummy and Daddy. They need you to look after them – and Miss Westcott. We will see each other again, my sweet. Now, you must be my brave little girl."

Mary continued clutching Sarah to her breast until Malcolm and Thomas prised them apart. Then, while Malcolm kept a firm arm around Mary's waist, Thomas picked up Sarah and handed her to her mother in the carriage. Sobs continued wracking Mary's body as she and Malcolm stood waving until the carriage disappeared.

"Come, my dear. Come inside and try to calm yourself. I think a time like this requires something stronger than a pot of tea, don't you?" Malcolm suggested. Mary nodded, and the young ayah hovering in the background was dispatched to prepare drinks.

After some time sipping their rums in silence, Malcolm was relieved to see Mary, although red-eyed and dejected, appeared in control of her emotions at last. He now felt it safe enough to leave her while he checked on the workers in the fields. Not in the best of moods when he returned at lunchtime, he tried to calm down before joining Mary in her sitting room.

"Have you seen Lachlan at all this morning?" he asked as casually as he could manage.

"No, but he should have been in the fields supervising the workers. I would not expect to see him about the house. Why do you ask?"

"Excuse me, Mary. I've just thought of something I need to check. I'll be back shortly, and then we can go into lunch." Malcolm strolled from the room but, once out in the hallway, rushed to the kitchen.

It took only a couple of questions before he had the answers he sought. They did not improve his humour. As he made his way back to Mary, the lunchtime gong sounded.

"We are summoned to lunch. Shall we go in, my dear?" Malcolm asked as he stooped to help her out of her chair. Conversation was absent until after lunch was served and the ayahs had been dismissed. Lachlan's empty place at the table further darkened Malcolm's mood.

"I see our son is not hungry today. Do you think he might have died up there in his room? Should I send someone to check?" Malcolm asked.

"Isn't it likely he has been detained in the fields for some reason? I'm sure he will arrive soon. He can't be hungry, or he would have returned by now."

"Well now, that's just the point, you see. Lachlan did not come downstairs for breakfast this morning and had not requested a tray. No, hear me out, please, Mary. Although I rode over all the areas where we have workers today, he was nowhere to be seen, and nobody had seen him this morning. Now he chooses not to come to lunch and has not ordered a tray to be sent to his room. Can you understand why I am a little offside about his behaviour? It was bad enough – unforgivable even – that he did not see fit to say goodbye to his sister, and now this."

"Perhaps you were right in suggesting a check on his room, but I would not recommend sending one of the servants. It would be better kept in the family. Perhaps one of us should check on him."

"Good thinking… no point in giving the staff anything more to gossip about. I'll check after lunch."

"Thank you, Malcolm. I was hoping you would go. I don't think I'm up to coping with any more today."

As soon as they finished eating, and after again checking Lachlan hadn't ordered a tray, Malcolm climbed the steps to his son's room. When there was no response to his pounding on Lachlan's door, he returned to his study to fetch the key. Mary felt her stomach tightening as she watched her husband climb the steps again. After hesitating for a couple of moments, she followed Malcolm upstairs.

"Why is his door locked?" she asked as Malcolm unlocked the door.

"I'm about to find out. Please wait out here until I say you may enter."

Reluctant but unsure she could handle unpleasant surprises today, she obeyed and, wringing her hands, waited outside Lachlan's door. While it felt like an hour, Malcolm returned to stand in the doorway a moment later. One look at his face and that tightness in her stomach turned into a pit of snakes slithering about.

"What…?" she croaked.

"I don't know. It's obvious Lachlan hasn't been in his room this morning, and it doesn't look as though he slept here last night either."

"Where else could he be?"

"Wherever he is, it isn't here in his room, and it might help explain why he didn't see his sister off this morning."

"You said he hadn't been in the fields, and now we find he hasn't been in his room. What is going on, and where can he be?"

"Right now, I have no answers for you. I am as confused by our son's behaviour as you are and need time to ponder the situation. I will be in my study if you need me."

"He's hardly likely to have run away from home as a small child might if it didn't get its own way. He is an adult, and adults are more inclined to have a row than run away," Mary thought aloud in the empty sitting room.

She tried recalling her encounters with Lachlan over the last few days hoping she might find some clue there. It was a futile exercise. She knew she must have encountered her son on some occasion – spoke with him at least once during that time – but nothing came to mind. A wave of shame swept over her. So focused on the impending loss of her daughter and granddaughter, she had paid her son scant attention, if any, during the last week. This, despite knowing tensions between father and son were deepening to the point of becoming critical.

"It wasn't all Malcolm's fault," she told the empty room. "Although he didn't show it, he was just as upset about the Erskines leaving as I was, and he has every right to be angry with Lachlan."

At the time, she thought Malcolm's treatment of the lad was appropriate to bring the boy to his senses… to make him accept his position and responsibilities. Was the result quite the opposite? Had they been too hard on him and expected too much of the lad? After all, he knew nothing of plantation life. He had spent so little time there and only as a young child. They should have realised there might be a problem. For fifteen years, Lachlan lived a different life in a different place. He had inhabited a different world, a galaxy away from Assam.

Maybe they should have asked what he wanted to do with his life before hauling him back to the plantation. She guffawed at that thought. There was no chance of that happening. In Malcolm's mind – in both their minds – as soon as he was ready, Lachlan would take over the plantation according to his birthright. Try as she might, she could not recall from any conversation in recent days any hint or clue as to his present whereabouts. She decided to see if Malcolm was having any better success.

"No, my dear, I can recall nothing which might suggest where he is. I have no way of knowing whether it is just Lachlan who is absent or if some of his possessions also are missing."

"Ashamed as I am as his mother to admit it, I don't know what belongings he brought home with him and would be unable to tell if any were missing."

"I should go to check on the field workers again. You never know. Maybe I will find him returned and on the job out there. You were about to say something before I interrupted…."

"Nothing important… check on the workers first. If Lachlan still can't be found after that, come back here. Maybe, if we put our heads together, we might come up with something useful."

"Right… but, Mary, please don't put too much hope on my finding him. I have no positive feelings about what I might discover."

Later that afternoon, after a tea tray was delivered to Malcolm's study, Malcolm and his wife began dissecting every conversation they had with their son over the last week. Their starting point was Malcolm's recent rows with Lachlan.

"Wait, Malcolm, wait. You said Lachlan wanted to move into the manager's cottage once Thomas and his family left. I know you forbade it, but could he have defied you?"

"Given the attitude lately, it is quite possible… anything is possible. Why is it important?"

"Do you think we might stroll across to the manager's cottage? Bring the key." Mary watched a stunned look creep across Malcolm's face as he looked for the key. "What is it, dear? What bothers you?"

"I know Thomas returned the key when they came to spend their last night here in this house. Now it is not here." Pocketing the spare key, he added, "I think I will take that stroll to the cottage, but I'm not sure you should accompany me. It might be better if you waited here."

"Well, that is unfortunate because I *will* accompany you. Shall we go?"

The door was locked. Malcolm raised his eyebrows in question at Mary.

"You have a key. We must go inside to assure ourselves no one is here. For whatever reason, if Lachlan is here, something might have happened to him. Please open the door so I might see," she responded

Malcolm entered but stopped abruptly when only a couple of paces inside. Mary, following close behind, slammed into his back. "What?" she demanded. "What have you found? I can't see." Malcolm moved a little to one side so she could stand beside him.

Dirty dishes and cups cluttered the dining table. In the kitchen, a cupboard door stood partially ajar. While the original open fireplace used for cooking remained in place, a new-fangled (as Malcolm insisted on calling it) cast iron wood-burning stove was imported and installed when Flora and Thomas took over the cottage. A pot with some blackened substance welded to its insides sat abandoned on the brickwork of the open range.

"Flora's staff never would leave the place like this," Mary announced.

"They didn't," Malcolm replied, holding his hand close to the fireplace. "This is still warm. Something has been cooked here today." As he peered at the thick burnt substance coating the pot, he added, "And a competent cook wasn't involved."

"Who is responsible for this mess?" Mary asked. "Nobody should have been here since the Erskines left."

"I believe we both know the answer to your question. I will check the other rooms before I share my thoughts ." Malcolm strode off towards the bedrooms – with Mary trailing along behind. He went first to the main bedroom. There was no need to check further.

Naked, Lachlan lay sprawled across the bed, his crumpled clothes strewn about the floor.

Mary gasped. "Is he alive?"

"Oh, I expect so," Malcolm replied. "At a guess, stone drunk, I'd say. Mary, this is not something a mother should see. Please go back to the house and wait for me there."

"What are you going to do? Don't hurt him… though God knows he deserves a good hiding. Please don't do anything silly, Malcolm."

"Hurt him…? I have no intention of hurting him. But he does owe us an explanation and an apology… and I intend we should have both before the day is out."

After wandering about the house to fill in time, Mary finally settled into her favourite chair in the sitting room. Her embroidery lay in her lap, but she felt no inclination to take it up and work on it. It seemed like a lifetime before Malcolm found her staring unseeing into an empty tea cup.

Startled by Malcolm's return, her embroidery fell to the floor as she sprang out of her chair. She looked past him. Lachlan was not there.

"Relax, my dear; he will be here as soon as he cleans himself up. I know you have been concerned and remain so. But, it is important not to make a fuss over him. It is time he showed us respect, and I intend it starts now. I gave him a few home truths, but there is much more he needs to hear. When he arrives, do not go soft on him. I shall not hesitate to dismiss you from my study if I see any indication of such behaviour on your part."

She blinked and set her jaw, but Mary knew Malcolm was right and his threat was real. Instead of retaliating, she said nothing and followed him to his study. It was twenty minutes later before Lachlan joined them. A more dejected and broken figure Mary thought she had never seen. A small part of her ached for him, but only a small part.

Malcolm delivered a blunt ultimatum. Lachlan stood silent and with bowed head. Malcolm's conditions were harsh, but noncompliance would earn an even harsher penalty. Lachlan had little choice but to accept his father's ultimatum.

Tensions ran high for the next few weeks as both parties fought to hold the dominant position. Then there followed an uneasy truce of sorts.

Chapter 5

Strange New World   Glasgow 1830

To a six year old, the voyage from India seemed to last forever. Sarah knew she did not like boats from the moment she stepped on board the ship. She and Miss Westcott shared a cabin that seemed as small as a hatbox. Miss Westcott took Sarah up on deck for brief periods. Each time wind, sea spray, blazing sun, and the heat, made it an unpleasant experience. And, despite Miss Westcott's efforts to calm her, Sarah found rounding the Cape of Good Hope nothing short of terrifying.

As the voyage stretched month after month, Sarah became increasingly withdrawn and uninterested in her lessons. The governess sought help, but nothing Thomas or Flora tried remedied the situation. Flora became concerned for her daughter, fearing the child might suffer some permanent disability after having to endure such monotonous and uninspiring conditions for so many months. Thomas's mantra of 'only a bit longer, just a few more weeks' failed to reassure Sarah.

Then spirits rose. Tomorrow they would reach Glasgow to start their new lives in a world away from the life they had known.

*****

After farewelling Miss Westcott off to her ailing mother, Thomas went to find a carrier and a carriage. The necessary transport arranged, he rounded up his family and waited while their belongings were unloaded.

Their luggage dealt with, it was time to face the next big unknown: their accommodation and new home until their future in Glasgow became clearer. Thomas gave the carriage driver the address as they scrambled aboard. He felt the tension growing inside him as the carriage made its way through the streets of

Glasgow to the home of a woman he had never met but on whose hospitality he and his family now depended.

Thomas shouted so his wife could hear above the pounding of the horses' hooves and the creaking of the carriage as it bumped along.

"What do you remember of Great Aunt Bess? Before we arrive at her house, what can you tell me about her?"

"She is my mother's aunt and has been widowed for about ten years. She had a son, who died before middle age. Mother and I stayed with her for a few months when we enrolled Lachlan in boarding school. We stayed with her again when it was time for Lachlan to begin his higher education. I think I've always been her favourite – perhaps the daughter she never had.

Since I was old enough to scribble letters to her, we corresponded regularly. Although she is my mother's aunt, she is a few years younger than my mother and seems still in command of all her faculties. While I'm not concerned about the reception we will receive when we arrive, I wish I had more time to warn her of our impending arrival."

"Is she aware we are coming or not? It would be helpful to know what to expect when we arrive."

"I wrote a letter the same day father terminated your employment. Mother sent it when she travelled to the port to book our passages. It might have arrived in the last few days if it was in time to catch a ship. If not, our arrival will be a complete surprise."

Thomas need not have worried. Flora's letter had arrived two days earlier, and Great Aunt Bess had struggled to control her excitement since then. It was apparent the moment the maid opened the door that Bess had imbued almost the same degree of excitement in her maid.

"Oh, do come in. It is wonderful you arrived safe and sound. Madam is in the sitting room. Only moments ago, she said she hoped you would be here today. Come, I'll show you through, and then I'm off to organise tea for you."

Their welcome was everything Flora expected of Bess and more. It was the first time Bess had seen Sarah and, at first sight, fell in love with her. Thomas confided to his wife later, "You might have lost your position as Bess's favourite girl. It seems your daughter might trump you on that score now."

There was no question about it being long-term accommodation. Bess insisted they stay with her in her 'great mausoleum of a house' as she called it. And, since receiving news of their arrival, she had given considerable thought to Thomas's future in Glasgow.

"Now, I know your hurried departure from India didn't allow you much time to think about your life here in Glasgow, but have you given any thought to what you might do here?"

"It's not that I haven't thought about it. I suppose it was more a case of not making any decision until I knew what was available. I will begin finding that out tomorrow. I must secure sound employment as soon as possible to support myself and my family."

"If I may make so bold, I have a proposition for you to consider. Perhaps we might discuss it after dinner this evening. In the meantime, *dinna fash* about how to support your family. I am well enough situated to keep all of you for the rest of your lives, regardless of how the thought of that might distress you. Let's say no more about it until after dinner when we shall discuss my proposition."

The appearance of the maid prevented any further conversation. She reported their luggage had arrived. Some had been taken to their rooms, while the less personal belongings were stored for the time being in a now unused part of the stables.

"Right; well, you have plenty of settling-in to do, and no doubt a good long rest in something that isn't tossing and rolling about will be most welcome. Feel free to relax until you hear the dinner gong at seven o'clock. Come down at six o'clock if you feel inclined to a wee tipple before dinner," Bess said before addressing the maid. "Please show our guests to their rooms and see to their needs."

After a bit of unpacking and a long nap, the Erskines traipsed downstairs to a 'happy hour' before dinner with Aunt Bess.

"Ah, I can't tell you how nice it is to share a wee bevvy with someone at the end of the day. It's a tradition I've maintained since my husband died, but drinking alone lacks something."

"I'm sorry for bringing Sarah along with us, Aunt Bess," Thomas apologised. " I know it's not appropriate, but I wasn't comfortable leaving her alone in a strange house on our first night here."

"She's a bonnie wee child, and it's lovely to have one about the place again. But you are right. She doesn't need to be hanging about with adults who are imbibing alcohol. Did she not have a nanny, or governess, or such like?" Thomas explained about Miss Westcott.

"Westcott, eh? I believe I know the mother well. Was the governess's name Dolina? My Mrs Westcott had a daughter called Dolina. Hmm… not sure how old she would be now."

Thomas shook his head. He had no idea of Miss Westcott's given name. While Thomas spoke, Flora stood deep in thought, her brow furrowed. Then her face lit up.

"I believe our Miss Westcott's name was Dolina. Sarah asked her about it once, and I remember thinking what a wonderfully old-fashioned name it was."

"It sounds as though the mother I'm thinking of is the mother who was responsible for bringing your governess back to Glasgow. The only problem is, my Mrs Westcott is not so gravely ill. Oh, aye, she is getting on a bit and is not as fit and well as she used to be, but she has no serious illness. I spoke to her at kirk last Sunday. She complained about her arthritis bothering her, but that be all."

"We can't be talking about the same person. Miss Westcott wouldn't make up such a story about her mother," Flora insisted.

"Right you are, I suspect. But Mrs Westcott was none too happy when her daughter upped and went off to uncivilised distant shores. She believed – still believes, I suspect – a daughter's place is at home caring for her mother … cheap domestic help if you know what I mean."

"If you are right, that's terrible." Flora's indignation reflected in her voice. "Miss Westcott loved Assam and the plantation and was an excellent governess. Sarah loved her, and I know she already misses her."

"Well, we must remedy that situation," Bess said, adding an emphatic nod. "Your young miss must have a governess, and it seems no one would be better suited than Miss Dolina Westcott. It can be arranged."

What Bess intended wasn't clear to Flora, but Flora wasn't sure she liked the sound of it. But then, Thomas added his thoughts to the conversation.

"It would be good for someone to take charge of Sarah when she is at home, but we intend enrolling her in a local school as soon as possible. We believe she would benefit from being amongst other young girls instead of being educated at home alone by a tutor. So, if we find a suitable academy for her, a governess would have nothing to do for much of most days. Is it worth employing one?"

"*Och*, spoken like a true man… with no idea of caring for a child," Bess chuckled. "There is more to it than keeping a child company when it is at home. My thinking is, in the first instance, Miss Westcott would live here and again take charge of Sarah while we explore enrolling her in school. Miss Glendenning runs an academy for young girls close to here.

It is a small institution, which she runs at her residence with the assistance of one other young woman, and she has a limited student intake. Perhaps she devised her selection criteria to ensure only a small intake."

"Do we know the selection criteria, and if there is a waiting list of potential students?" Flora asked.

"Well now, 'selection criteria' might not be the correct term. From what I hear, it's more like the level of fees she sets that ensures few parents of young girls apply to enrol their daughters."

"That is not encouraging information," Thomas said. "We cannot contemplate applying to enrol Sarah until I find employment, and then only if it pays well enough to afford Miss Glendenning's fees."

"Don't be too hasty with such negative thoughts," Bess told him. "Let's investigate the situation with that academy first before abandoning the idea. If we take the positive view, we will endeavour to have Miss Westcott live-in to care for Sarah, as I suggested earlier. Then, if Sarah is enrolled with Miss Glendenning, the only difference would be Sarah's absence at school during the day. So, any hours Miss Westcott has spare while Sarah is at school, she could spend with her mother … who I know isn't an invalid and doesn't need full-time care."

Flora, taken aback by Bess's words, was lost for a suitable response for a few moments. It appeared Aunt Bess was used to being in charge and having her own way, but was what she was proposing at all possible? Was it right to make such plans without first consulting Miss Westcott… and her mother? Bess didn't appear to see it as necessary and seemed confident Mrs Westcott would endorse the arrangement. And, was there a hint of optimism in Aunt Bess's comments regarding the possibility of Sarah's being enrolled in Miss Glendenning's academy? At last, Flora found her voice.

"I suppose the best we can do is to ask Miss Westcott whether she might be interested in such an arrangement. Oh, and that would have to be after we first established that your Mrs Westcott is our Miss Westcott's mother."

Thomas nodded his agreement before adding his thoughts. "Yes, let's find out about Miss Westcott first, as she, or someone similar, is needed now. Then, perhaps after we know about my future employment, we might explore the possibility of enrolling Sarah with Miss Glendenning."

The two women murmured their support for his approach before Thomas added to his comments.

"Perhaps we all overlook one important aspect of all this," Thomas suggested. "Not only have I yet to secure employment, but what I might earn from any employment I do secure might be insufficient to employ Miss Westcott, let alone pay Miss Glendenning's fees. We have no income at this time. Employing a governess will soon deplete our financial reserves. While the arrangement to return Miss Westcott to the fold sounds wonderful, maybe we should wait until I have established a definite income stream and are able to pay her."

"Did I not tell you not to *fash* about money?" Bess demanded. I will be paying for Miss Westcott – and I would consider it an honour to do so. Let's hear no more about any of this. Thomas, as promised, you and I are meeting after dinner. Try being a little less gloomy until then."

When Flora took Sarah to bed, Bess took Thomas to the study. Although Bess's husband was long dead, his presence lived on in what obviously had been 'his' room. The essence of the man lived on in the furniture, the books, and even in the pipes still resting in the pipe rack.

"Now, Thomas, I am not sure how familiar you are with the story of our family." Thomas shrugged and shook his head. "Right. Well, I will give you the short version of only what you need to know. I was the youngest of my family, and the only one of my era still alive, while Flora's mother, Mary, is the only one of the next generation still living. So you see, there are not herds of us running around.

Now, back to my short story… I made a good marriage when I was still quite young. My husband, from a reasonably well-off family, was an astute businessman. Together, we built up an exceptional business and were early players in the sugar industry in the Caribbean. We stayed with sugar and built up quite an enterprise here in Glasgow. It remains a major entity here. Since my husband's death, I own it."

"Is there no other close family? I thought there was a son."

"Aye, we had a son, who was never blessed with even a hint of business sense… was more interested in 'adventure' than learning the business. He wanted to live on our sugar plantation in the Caribbean rather than be here learning to run the company. In hindsight, it probably wasn't a bad thing he went to live there. He wasn't bright and wasn't energetic. If I'm honest, he was lazy and indulged … and I suspect that's much as Flora's brother, Lachlan, is today."

"That's probably an accurate assessment of Lachlan."

"Well, I said this was to be a short story… So, to cut it short, our son embraced life in the tropics to the fullest, but it was not kind to him. A combination of lifestyle and the tropics saw him dead before he turned forty. He never returned from the Caribbean. Then, after my husband died, I inherited his share of the company, and I now own and run the whole show … with the assistance of an excellent manager." Bess paused before asking, "So, Thomas, what do you know about sugar?"

"Ah, well now, that will be another short story. Nothing… I know nothing of the sugar industry other than Glasgow is a major port for its importation."

"Good; I like honesty –especially in a man. It is so often missing in men when they are trying to impress me. As you undoubtedly have noticed, I have clocked up a few years now, and none of us knows how many more we may have left. Your wife and her mother are my only remaining living relatives, and her mother is a wee bit older than me. In the normal order of things, Mary will likely depart this mortal coil before me. That then would leave Flora as my sole remaining family member. While she is unaware of it and will remain so until I drop off the twig, she will inherit everything I own here and in the Caribbean, when I go.

So, young Thomas, it's as well you have returned to Scotland. You now will have time to learn all there is to know about the sugar industry and my whole empire before you have to join your wife in running my enterprise. Your education can start tomorrow if that sits well with you."

"Do you intend to tell Flora about your plans, or is it to remain a secret?"

"Best not to worry her about it at the moment. When the time comes will be soon enough. I doubt Malcolm McGowan will leave his daughter anything when he goes, not while he has a son around to inherit everything. And a right disaster that will be when it happens."

"Bess, after all you already have done for us, this is a most generous offer. But I need to know what your suggested employment involves. For me, the big question is whether I am up to the job. I spent the last however many years managing a tea plantation. I haven't seen too many tea plantations around Glasgow."

"Of course not. Your job in the past was about managing employees, ensuring the business of running a plantation happened as it was supposed to. Your work here will be much the same – with a difference. Here, you won't be dealing with the savages of India, but it won't be any easier dealing with the horde of burly, contrary Scotsmen I employ."

"The plantation workers are not savages. They are beautiful people and good workers. All they need is respect."

"And I suspect that a bit of respect and a firm hand are all my employees need to keep the wheels of my enterprise turning as smoothly as they should. The job is not about growing or making sugar. It's about managing the men who handle the product when it arrives here in Glasgow. And also there will be tea. So, what do you say? Have I found myself a new Operations Manager?"

"What about your existing manager? I know you think highly of him."

"Aye, I do. He was a young man when he started as an assistant to my husband. Then, when I inherited the business, he stayed with me to run the show. He is excellent, but he is my 'money man'. He negotiates all the supply and distribution contracts and ensures payments arrive when expected. But he is not much at managing the workers. In all fairness to him, he doesn't have time to see to the workers as well as manage the money."

"How have you managed up until now? Who has looked after the workers?"

"Ah, well, there has been a procession of men of various ages who tried. The last one managed to antagonise the workers to the point of almost inciting a riot. Need I say he is no longer in my employ? I appreciate you might want time to consider my offer, but I would welcome an answer as soon as possible."

"If I possessed a few more details of the job, I believe I could settle the matter of my employment tonight."

As their discussion of Thomas's employment was drawing to a close, Bess threw in one more surprise. "As you are aware, Flora was a big help to her father with running the plantation. She ran the office for him. Once Sarah's situation is settled, I fear the days will drag on for Flora. When I notice a sign of that becoming the case, I shall suggest she might like to assist my manager with some of his work. It wouldn't need to be full-time, of course; just a few hours whenever would suffice, I should think."

"And I suppose it never occurred to you that this might provide an opportunity for her to 'learn the ropes' of running the enterprise in preparation for when she has to take on running the it herself. You are a crafty woman, Aunt Bess."

Their discussion of Thomas's new job continued for about another ten minutes before Bess called it a night.

After Bess went up to bed, Thomas spent a few minutes going over in his mind everything they had discussed. He needed it to be all straight in his head before he faced Flora. She would have questions, and he needed to have answers, the 'right' answers, to give her.

He checked on Sarah before joining Flora in their room. Before he had time to shut the door behind him, Flora gave way to her raging curiosity. The question-and-answer session began.

"What did Bess want to talk with you about that she didn't want to discuss with me? I know I had to see Sarah to bed after dinner, but I would need to be blind and stupid not to realise Bess did not intend I should be part of your conversation. Am I permitted to know the details now, or is it to remain a secret from me?"

"There is no secret. Bess wanted to offer me a position in her enterprise. She knew I probably would balk at the offer in the first instance and wanted to ensure we could discuss the details carefully and calmly before I made my decision."

"So, what was the position, and what is the outcome of your discussions and deliberations?

"Tomorrow, I begin my employment as Bess's Operations Manager."

"I'm not too happy about our being treated as a 'charity case'… the poor relatives for whom some respectable means of support is required."

"That is not what this is about. Bess needed someone to manage her workers. She believed my previous experience suited the job."

"And what about you? Do you think you're suited?"

"Yes, I do. It was my decision, and I would not have accepted the position if I did not believe I could do the job."

Flora mulled over all Thomas had told her as she waited for sleep to come. She felt her concerns slipping away. Maybe this was the right job for Thomas, and maybe it was the great start to their new lives they needed.

Chapter 6

New lives

Launching their new lives proved stressful for Thomas and Flora. Sarah was least affected, but the changes bewildered even her.

On his first morning, Bess carted Thomas off to meet her manager. Thomas was dreading the meeting and the new unknown world ahead. His state of mind had him nervously twisting his hands together in his lap for the entire ride. Bess noticed. As they neared her building, she scolded Thomas.

"You will have no skin left on those hands if you keep that up. My manager does not bite. No one you will meet today has ever attacked one of my staff. These days, we here in Glasgow are quite civilised – even polite on occasion. Relax and just be yourself. After all, everyone wants to see the real you, not just someone on their best behaviour for the occasion." Then adopting a steely countenance, she added, "Rest assured, should anyone try to attack you, I will defend you." With that, she brandished her furled parasol like a sword.

The mental picture of this pint-sized, elderly woman in the *en Garde* position ready to defend him was enough to ease his tension. He laughed aloud and dropped Bess a mock salute.

"Thank you, Ma'am, but I believe I am big enough, old enough, and sufficiently prepared, to fight my own battles. Of course, a few 'sacred cows' could be slaughtered in such skirmishes." They were both giggling as the carriage drew up in front of Bess's building.

"Come now, Laddie. I'll take you to Michael. I think you'll like him, and I'm sure he will be delighted to meet you."

Michael was bewildered by his boss' unexpected appearance in his office and intrigued by the young man with her. But Bess was right. Thomas took an instant liking to the man behind the large oak desk and relaxed in his presence. Some of that was soon replaced by discomfort.

"Good morning, Michael, my good man; apologies for barging into your office at this hour, but I come bearing a gift to atone for my rude interruption. Allow me to introduce Thomas Erskine, your new Operations Manager. Thomas, recently arrived from India, has *extensive* experience managing a tea plantation, including its vast tribe of workers."

While all Bess said in his introduction was true, hearing it made Thomas squirm. It had a different effect on Michael. His face lit up, and he bounded out from behind his desk to grasp Thomas's hand.

"Welcome aboard, Sir. I *cannae* tell you how welcome you are. But enough of this standing around jabbering. Let's show you what you have taken on here, shall we?"

"If it's all the same to everyone, I might leave you gentlemen to get on with it without my hanging about," Bess announced as she headed for the door.

Thomas's induction began with a tour of his new workplace and introductions to 'leading lights' from among the various work gangs he would manage.

"Aye, that went well," Bess murmured as her carriage moved off. "Now for the Erskine womenfolk – and starting with young Sarah, I think."

"Oh good, you're back," Flora said as Bess strode into the dining room. "I just sent Sarah upstairs to fetch the stuff for her lessons. Establishing her daily routine is important to prevent her from falling behind. Is there a small room we might use as a classroom instead of working in Sarah's room all day?"

"You could set up in the library. It's a pleasant room but sees little use these days. There is good natural light, and Sarah might like to use one of the small tables as her desk. Come, I'll show it to you."

Bess led them into a cavernous room lined on three sides with expensive-looking books. She drew back the drapes at the far end, allowing daylight to flood in to bathe a small table and its surrounding area. She ran her hand across the table to check for dust and seemed pleased her fingers remained clean.

"What about this then? Will it work as a classroom for Sarah?"

"Such a magnificent room… yes, thank you, Aunt Bess. This is a perfect classroom. But I warn you; I am tempted to explore some of those books."

"The books are there to be read. They probably would appreciate your disturbing the dust on them."

"As lovely as this will be as a classroom, it's possible it won't be for long. My priority is exploring schooling for Sarah, starting with Miss Glendenning's, I think. Once she is attending school, I don't imagine she will need a classroom here."

"Ah, yes, Miss Glendenning and her academy for young girls… Enquiries in that direction should begin as soon as possible to sort out Sarah's ongoing education. Remember, we also must talk to Miss Westcott about moving-in here."

"Do you know Marie Glendenning well?"

"I can't say we are close friends or that I know her well, but we are acquainted."

Flora felt disappointed. She had hoped Aunt Bess was close to Miss Glendenning and might exert some influence when enrolling Sarah in the academy. Her disappointment nudged back to life a concern Flora had managed to hold at bay during their discussions about Sarah's education: if Sarah was accepted into the academy, would they be able to afford the fees? Better she aired her worry before the matter progressed further.

"Maybe we should wait a while, a few weeks perhaps, before approaching Miss Glendenning. I can continue Sarah's lessons in the meantime, and if Miss Westcott is available, she could pick up from where she left off. I don't imagine a short period of such arrangement will affect Sarah's future."

"Nonsense… Sarah needs to be settled into a routine as soon as possible. Anyway, there is no guarantee a vacancy exists at the academy to enable Sarah to enrol. We might have to wait. I don't understand your inclination to delay this matter."

"It's my concern about the fees. Thanks to your generosity, Thomas has a job providing regular income. But it is too early to tell if there will be enough money to cover all our immediate costs, let alone trying to meet school fees."

"What costs? I know it's a long while since I was not long married and was bringing up a child, but I am unaware of such worrying costs, as you mentioned."

"We need to purchase a home, furniture, a carriage, and employ one or two staff. While we have some money put aside, it won't stretch far enough to cover everything and still leave a little left over. Our cash reserves need building up before we commit to extra expenses such as Miss Glendenning's fees."

"All this talk about money is becoming tiresome. Indulge an old woman, please, Flora. Let me tell you a story. I married well. My husband was a successful businessman whose death left me well-off. On his death, I inherited everything and have done even better over my years at the helm. In short, Flora, I have pots and pots of money, and no one to spend it on, no one to help me enjoy it in my old age. Please allow me to enjoy some company again in this big old house and allow me to fuss over the youngest generation of my family."

"Oh, Aunt Bess, I'm sorry. I didn't mean…."

"Hush now... I haven't finished. As I explained to Thomas – and he seems to have overlooked mentioning to you – as part of the salary he receives as Operations Manager, I will pay Sarah's school fees. Might you see yourself clear to allow an old woman this small indulgence at this late stage of her life?"

With her emotions in turmoil, Flora wrapped her arms around Bess. Flora tried to explain as her tears dripped onto the woman's shoulder.

"I never meant to offend you or to appear ungrateful. We never imagined such kindness and generosity. I feel embarrassed about arriving like some charity case on your doorstep, uninvited and without notice. In addition, now you have created a place for Thomas in your empire to provide us with an income."

"That's rubbish, my girl. Having just farewelled one, I needed an Operations Manager. Thomas was a gift that could not have arrived at a better time. It's grand to have company in this house again after all these years on my own, and the staff enjoy having people to fuss over. I promise not to interfere in your lives or your child's upbringing. So, unless you can't stand my company, please say you will continue to stay here."

The ensuing conversation lasted about half an hour and mainly involved Bess giving Flora a vague idea of the extent of her wealth and how she achieved it. As the discussion came to an end, Bess had one last message for Flora to contemplate.

"Flora, I am not a McGowan, and I am not your father. I come from the other side of your family, and I suspect we are a different breed from the McGowans. You will find my approach to family, kinship and other similar matters far removed from your father's. In my side of the family, females are as important, and afforded the same rights, as male members. That's not something I've introduced. It's how it's been for generations with my lot.

Now, shall we make a quick trip to Miss Glendenning's academy before lunch?"

Marie Glendenning was busy with her students when Bess and Flora arrived but welcomed them into her office about fifteen minutes later. Their meeting proved a cordial affair and allowed Flora to develop an admiration for the teacher, a fact she commented on during their ride back to the house.

"What an amazing woman... so friendly and approachable, but underneath she is a resolute woman with a strong sense of purpose. Apart from what she would gain from her lessons, I believe Sarah could benefit from being around Miss Glendenning. I'm disappointed there is no opportunity for Sarah's immediate enrolment in the academy."

"We knew that was a possibility, and Marie was encouraging. She said a vacancy might occur in a month or two, and she noted Sarah's name should that happen."

"Now, the matter of Sarah's schooling is dealt with, do we talk to Miss Westcott?" Flora asked

"Yes, but not today." Flora's eyebrows shot up in surprise.

"You surprise me. I anticipated we would talk with Miss Westcott this afternoon."

"No, I doubt that's wise. We would need to talk to her at home today and would be unable to talk privately with Dolina. Her mother would be there and would do her damnedest to scuttle our plans. She would not want to lose one minute of her unpaid help's time."

"So, how else do we talk to Miss Westcott?"

"Well now, I wager the daughter will accompany her mother to kirk on Sunday. That's when we will pounce. While I engage the mother, and possibly another couple of women in serious conversation, you take the daughter off to a quiet corner to put our offer to her. Perhaps she will be unsure and nervous at first, but by now, she probably has realised she came home under false pretences. If you prosecute your case well, that can work in our favour."

"I'm not sure I'm up to the task."

"You are, my dear, and practice between now and Sunday will ensure it."

True to her word, practise they did. But, in between times, tutoring Sarah kept Flora busy. All too soon, it was Saturday night, and the first week of their new life was over. When in their room after dinner, Flora aired her growing concerns.

"Thomas, are you sure the job you accepted in Bess's enterprise is right for you?"

"Yes, of course it was the right decision. Why do you ask? Does something about the job bother you?"

"I don't know what to think, but I am concerned. You look so tired and worn out at the end of every day. I am concerned for your health. If you explained that the job is too much for you or not to your liking, I'm sure Bess would understand. You could search for something more suitable."

"Thank you for your concern, but it is unfounded. The job is perfect, or will be once I master it. Everything is new and different. Even finding my way about the place is challenging, and there is much to learn about the business. Nevertheless, my primary concern is the men, all the workers employed at the warehouse and the port. I feel confident, except for one or two. They are all good workers, but bad habits have developed. It results from poor management in the past. I fear it will require a good measure of time and patience to right the situation."

"But you are spending such long hours at work every day. They are much longer days than were required on the plantation. I fear for your health if it continues for too long."

"I'm sorry. I would have spoken to you earlier had I realised my late finish every evening was troubling you. I stayed behind for a while every evening to learn about the business. When I accepted the position, I knew nothing of the sugar industry, and there is much to learn. The little I have learnt is fascinating, and I desire to know more."

"Perhaps you should approach Bess. She probably has extensive knowledge of the industry in the Caribbean and still owns a sugar plantation there. You might find it more comfortable and relaxing if she shared her knowledge with you in the library or her study of an evening."

"Sound advice, Mrs Erskine, and advice I will act upon at my first opportunity."

"Will you accompany us to kirk tomorrow?"

Thomas grinned. "I suspect it is expected and not an option."

Flora giggled. "Oh yes, I fear regular church attendance is another new habit we must embrace in our new life. It's not that we didn't attend church on the plantation by choice. Our chapel had no regular services, and it was too far to travel to the nearest church."

"For me, my Faith is not a chore. I live by and practise it daily, and I hope our daughter develops a similar dedication to help guide her life."

Thomas's words were not news to Flora. From the outset of their relationship, she realised his belief was strong, but she hadn't realised how strong. Nevertheless, Flora was determined

Sarah should be free to decide what was important in her life once she was old enough to do so.

Separating Dolina Westcott from her mother proved more difficult than Flora imagined. The ever-resourceful and persuasive Bess eventually dragged the mother over into a debate she was having with another couple of older women, and dropped Flora a meaningful wink as she did so.

Without hesitation, Flora shepherded Dolina to a quiet corner. "Miss Westcott, if you could spare me a moment, I have a proposition to put to you."

When she heard Flora's proposal, Dolina's eyes lit up for a brief moment. Then her face crumpled, and she glanced in her mother's direction. She was disappointed she couldn't accept the position Flora offered, as her mother would never allow it.

"She doesn't look too ill or incapacitated, your mother, I mean," Flora said as she also glanced across at Mrs Westcott. "Does she need looking after? Is she incapable of managing without you as her fulltime slave?"

"No. I admit I was brought home under false pretences. My mother is well, and capable of looking after herself, but she would never agree to such an arrangement. She won't let me leave home again."

"It seems you must have stood up to her once before, or you would never have come to India. You could do it again – if you wanted to accept my offer." Flora saw Dolina shake her head, and realised she needed to play what Bess called a 'trump card'. "It isn't so difficult, Miss Westcott. All you have to do is to decide if you wish to look after Sarah again and, if you do, tell your mother straight out how it will happen."

"Yes, yes, I know, but I have another idea. Sarah won't be starting school until Miss Glendenning has a vacancy. Perhaps, in the interim, I might spend the day with Sarah while I live with my mother and be at home with her in the mornings and evenings. Then, when Sarah joins Miss Glendenning's academy, I could move in to live with you. Once Sarah goes to school in the mornings, most days, I would go back to look after mother until Sarah returns in the afternoon. How would that suit you?"

"Sounds like a reasonable compromise, but will your mother accept it?"

"Oh, she will… or, as you suggested, she will be on her own, fulltime, again."

"How soon might we implement this new arrangement?"

Dolina shrugged. "There is nothing to be gained from procrastinating. I will inform mother tonight and resume tutoring Sarah tomorrow – if that suits you."

"Excellent; I look forward, as Sarah will too, to having you join us tomorrow. Perhaps we should rescue your mother. She is looking a bit desperate over there."

As they started towards the other group of women, Flora, with a grin across her face, dropped Bess an almost imperceptible nod – mission accomplished – and Bess flashed Flora a smile.

That night, Flora broke the news to Thomas about Miss Westcott and was disappointed when he didn't display a similar degree of enthusiasm about it. She questioned his reaction.

"I am pleased Miss Westcott has agreed to take charge of Sarah again. But it raises some concerns about you. What will you do all day here in this big house now Miss Westcott will be looking after Sarah?"

I'm sure I will find plenty to do, and if I should find myself at a loose end, I'm confident Bess will remedy the situation."

*****

Contrary to shared doubts, the arrangements agreed with Miss Westcott at church that Sunday morning were implemented the following day. Dolina Westcott arrived every morning and spent the day overseeing Sarah's lessons before returning to her mother in time to prepare their evening meal. Two months later, when Sarah enrolled in Miss Glendenning's academy, the arrangement with Dolina Westcott reverted to the original plan. Miss Westcott moved in to live in Bess's big house with her charge, and during the days when there was nothing to do for Sarah, Dolina went home to help her mother.

Although everything appeared to be going well in that regard, Bess noticed Flora was becoming increasingly unsettled, restless even. Sitting in her office reviewing recent import figures one night, Bess realised Flora was bored. And why wouldn't she be?

This young woman who lived a full and busy life from when she was a young girl was now reduced to spending her days reading and embroidering. The thought of it made Bess shudder.

"Faced with a similar life, I probably would throw myself off a bridge instead," she told her empty office. "So, what's to be done about it?" she asked the universe.

By morning, Bess believed she had the answer and a potential plan. Once breakfast was over, and Sarah was off to school, Flora retired to the sitting room to spend the morning there. Bess seized her opportunity. After allowing Flora to settle, Bess marched into the sitting room.

"Flora, dear, what is that you're working on?"

"Eh? This…? Oh, it is nothing special, just another piece of embroidery. I don't know yet what I might do with it when it's finished."

"Well now, this won't do, my girl. You can't be sitting around here all day doing things that have no purpose. I can't have you here doing nothing when I am in need of a part-time assistant for my manager."

"I wasn't aware you needed an assistant for Michael. I haven't heard you mention it, but I suppose it has nothing to do with me anyway."

"Surprising you should believe that. I think it should interest you. It would be a great help to me if you could see your way clear to find a few spare hours each week to assist Michael in running my empire. I wouldn't want it to become a chore, but it would be a help to me, and to Michael."

"Of course I'll help, if Michael will have me. It is the least I can do after all you have done for us since we lobbed up on your doorstep. I don't know how much help I might be though as I know nothing about your business."

Choosing to ignore Flora's final comment, Bess just nodded sagely. "Stuff and nonsense, my girl; there is nothing new in what we do. Stuff comes in; stuff goes out. Money comes in, and we spend money. It's as simple and ordinary as it is in most businesses. Apart from that, Michael has the patience of a saint and will be an excellent teacher."

"Thank you. I suppose I could talk to Michael about the position and what he might expect of his assistant."

"Good; well, don't just sit there. There is no time like the present. Come on. Let's go and get you started with Michael."

A few minutes later, with the two women on board, Bess's carriage rocked and creaked as it sped through the streets on its way to the headquarters of Bess's empire.

Chapter 7

A working life

Bess noted with a degree of satisfaction how, in an amazingly short timeframe, life in her home settled into a comfortable routine. Sarah went to school every morning, and Miss Westcott went home to her mother… Thomas left for work early every morning… and after only a few short weeks, Flora also went to work most days.

Although she intended Flora spend only a couple of hours some days helping the manager, she now spent at least four hours every day working with Bess's manager, Michael. As Bess strolled around her garden, she told the universe it was 'a most satisfying situation'. Not only was Flora's daily boredom overcome, but Flora was learning the ropes and would be well-equipped to run Bess's enterprise when the time came.

Flora and Thomas spent their days in different parts of the business and rarely encountered one another between breakfast and dinner. Although Flora enjoyed her new life and was kept busy, it was overshadowed by her concern for Thomas.

He was coming home late again, sometimes after she had gone to bed. She could not convince herself that he still found something new to learn about the business. After gentle attempts to broach the subject with Thomas failed, Flora opted for a more direct approach. She waited until an ideal opportunity presented itself.

"Thomas, I am concerned about the hours you're keeping at work. Sarah and I hardly spend any time with you now. I know your responsibilities are considerable and probably weigh heavily on your shoulders, but is it necessary to spend half of every night at work?"

Again, Thomas tried dismissing Flora's concerns and became angry when Flora was determined to discover what kept him at the warehouse for so much of his life.

"No, Thomas, don't try to dismiss me again as you have done every time I tried to discuss this with you in recent weeks. Either you tell me what is going on, or I will enlist the aid of both Michael and Bess to find out. Now, will you tell me what keeps you away from your family most nights, or do I take my concerns elsewhere?"

"All right, I will tell you, but promise not to talk to Bess or Michael about it." Flora shrugged but agreed. "Please don't be angry, but it is not work keeping me back late at work."

Was her worst nightmare coming true? Flora felt as though the air had been knocked out of her, and she feared her legs would buckle under her. She eventually found her voice.

"So you have found something more interesting – more pleasurable – than the company of your wife and daughter in the evening? What does this mean for the future of this marriage?"

"What's this nonsense about the future of our marriage? Argh… No, it's nothing like that. All right, I'll tell you, although I wasn't planning on telling you just yet. I'm not spending the time at work. I'm studying. Before you ask more questions, please try to remain silent while I explain. Just give me a moment to work out where to start."

There was no question of Flora's remaining silent. Stunned, the power of speech had deserted her. She sat stonily silent as Thomas paced the room. Finally, he stopped and turned to face his wife.

"It is not that I am unhappy in my present position or that I don't appreciate the generosity afforded us since our arrival in Glasgow. It is about something else. The explanation you seek originates in India, at the port where we spent some hours before sailing for Scotland.

While you, Miss Westcott, and Sarah settled us into our cabins, I spent some time wandering around the dock and met and talked with a man with an interesting tale to tell. Alexander

Duff was a missionary from the Free Church of Scotland sent to begin his work in India. After a few days with friends in Assam, he was on his way to his new post in Calcutta. Duff was one of the first missionaries sent to India to live in a village and spread the word of Christianity. His story was fascinating. I was in awe of what his work might achieve. It grabbed me and refused to let go."

"So, how does this explain your late nights and your neglecting your family?"

"I was coming to that. I was drawn to the idea of becoming a missionary in India, but I had to complete a course of study to qualify. My time in India and my knowledge of its people considerably reduced the amount of study required. In about another month, I should complete my studies."

"And then what happens? We say 'thanks Aunt Bess's as we pack up and head back to India? Where in India are we likely to end up?"

"I have no answers to the many questions you must have, but can tell you we are unlikely to move back to India in the near future. A suitable opening for a missionary needs to occur before one can be sent out there. There are others ahead of me awaiting appointments. All I can tell you is there will be late nights for the next several weeks until I complete my studies. Then, life will return to normal, and for the foreseeable future, we will continuc here."

"As your wife, I believe it should have been discussed with me before you made any serious move to become a missionary. Yes, I would like to return to India at some time, but I don't want it to be any time soon. There is our daughter's education and her future to consider. And, I wish to be consulted about where you might be sent. There are places I would not want to go, nor allow my daughter to go either. Had you considered any of those things before embarking on this selfish journey?"

"Well, as my wife, I expected you would respect my decisions, follow me in whatever I chose to do, and go with me to wherever I was sent. Was I mistaken?"

"Now you ask? Yes, you were mistaken. Regarding your decisions, I will not blindly comply with any you make affecting my life and that of my daughter without having been involved in shaping those decisions. I will simplify that for you. You will go alone if you receive word of a posting tomorrow, next week, or next year. I will not accompany you, and I will not allow my daughter's life to be disrupted by such wild schemes."

"You are my wife, and I expect…."

"Yes, I am your wife, but that might remain in name only if you follow through on this matter."

He allowed Flora what he considered sufficient time to cool down before going up to bed, but he found himself locked out of their room. Flora refused to answer the door. Aware he risked waking the household if he continued trying to persuade her to open the door, Thomas returned to the library to spend the night on a couch.

Flora did not appear for breakfast, and nor did Miss Westcott or Sarah. Flora asked for breakfast trays to be sent up to Sarah's room for the other two while she waited for Thomas to leave before going down for breakfast. Bess noted the empty chairs at the breakfast table.

She gave Flora a shrewd look when she appeared in the breakfast room. One look was enough for all Bess needed to know.

"I had a long and happy marriage," Bess told Flora. "Although I have been a widow for a considerable time does not mean I don't remember what it was like for a marriage to encounter a rocky patch. Is there some way I can help to remove the boulders from the pathway of your marriage?"

"No, I don't believe anyone can help. Thomas has developed set ideas about a wife's role in a marriage and how she should behave. I don't agree and will not comply. No, Aunt Bess, don't interrupt. Let me finish. While you might be stuck with my child and me for longer than you imagined, Thomas will likely not trouble you for too much longer."

"*Dinna fash* about living here. I hoped you would still be here when I dropped off the twig – all of you. But I will be happy with however many choose to stay," Bess told Flora as she wrapped an arm around Flora's shoulders. "And remember this, my girl. From experience, I can assure you, when two people love and respect each other, these things do blow over."

"If only that were true in our case. I fear it is not. I have just realised Thomas does not respect me, and I now wonder about that other part of it too."

"We will see about that. But right now, I'm concerned about whether I'm about to lose the best operations manager I ever had. Maybe you should tell me about it, or as much as you can without divulging anything too private for my ears."

Michael had the office to himself that day when Flora didn't show up for work. He thought it odd. She always told him if she would be coming in late the next day, or not at all. She hadn't said anything. When he went in search of Thomas to ask about it, Thomas was busy supervising the unloading of sugar from a ship. He continued in ignorance until just before lunchtime when Bess made a brief unscheduled visit. Bess's explanation that *something had come up and Flora might not be in for a day or two* only added to Michael's intrigue, but he knew better than to ask her – or Thomas – for details.

Things remained icy in the Erskine household for several days, resulting in a complete lack of communication between husband and wife. Although tempted to intervene, Bess restrained herself. After all, what could she do – apart from maybe bashing their heads together? What eventually righted things between the couple remained a mystery to Bess, but she was content just to be happy it happened.

With the domestic crisis apparently resolved, life resumed a smooth routine. Sarah excelled at school, Flora spent almost all of most days helping Michael, and Thomas had the warehouse running smoothly after a few skirmishes with some rougher-type employees. Nevertheless, the thought that one day this wonderful, structured life could end was never far from Flora's thoughts.

What would she do if Thomas announced he had a posting to India? She wouldn't allow herself to dwell on it. Life was sweet, so why turn it sour? She lived with that philosophy for the next eighteen months.

Thomas seemed tense, nervous perhaps, at dinner one night. With no opportunity to discuss it with her husband during dinner, Flora had to wait until they went up to bed. Flora's stomach tightened as the hours slipped by. By the time they climbed the stairs to their room, it had become a squirming mass. She had no doubts whatever troubled her husband would not be good news for her either.

They barely had closed their bedroom door behind them when Flora stopped and spun around to face Thomas.

"Right, Mr Erskine, what is on your mind tonight? I know it will be bad news, so let's have it out and deal with it, shall we?"

"I'm not sure I would call it 'bad' news, but I did receive some unexpected news today. I was offered a missionary position."

"How can that be anything other than bad news? At least, from Sarah's and my point of view, it is – and maybe from Aunt Bess's as well."

"Please wait until you have all the information before jumping to conclusions. The position I was offered was to go as a missionary to China."

"China…! There is no way I will be going to China, and nor will our daughter. If you accept the offer, you will go on your own."

"Flora, please; I had hoped we might at least discuss the matter first. But as you appear to have firm convictions on this matter, I won't waste time telling you the details of the offer. No, please wait. I haven't finished yet. I have no desire to go to China. From the outset, I made it clear I was interested only in a posting to India. I reminded them of that by return post today and turned down their offer of China."

"So, am I supposed to be pleased you are not going to China? Isn't it just a matter of time before they find an opening for you in India, and we will have this conversation again?"

"Are you still reluctant to even consider moving back to India? I don't understand why. You were born and grew up in India and loved the life and the people there. Why do you now fight me at any mention of returning to India? Perhaps if I could understand your reasons, I might be in a better position to ease your concerns."

"You have misinterpreted my situation. It is not that I loved all of the country or its entire population. A small part of India was my home, and that small part is inextricably tied to my family, my friends and the people I grew up with there."

"Would you be more inclined to discuss a posting with me if it were to a location somewhere in Assam?"

Flora took a moment to consider her answer. "No-o, I don't think so. I have no home there anymore. I am estranged from my family – or they chose to abandon me and mine in favour of my useless brother. Nothing remains there for me except the happy memories from my previous life on the plantation. Returning to any part of India holds no attraction for me. If anything, the thought of it reopens the wounds that caused us to relocate to Scotland."

The new rift in domestic harmony, while not as intense as the previous bout, continued to disrupt the household for a couple of weeks before subsiding to linger just below the surface. But, while no longer hostile, the couple's relationship remained strained for the next couple of months … until Thomas received another letter to reignite the problem. This time, it became more of a skirmish than a war.

In their room after dinner, Thomas broke the news to Flora. "Today, I received an offer of a posting as a missionary to Assam. They await my reply and would require me to set sail for India within three months."

He didn't say more. Instead, he stood silent and gazed at his wife, waiting for her reaction and the inevitable row that would follow. Nothing happened. Flora stood unmoving like a stone statue, her face an emotionless mask. Even her eyes did not harden and flash as they usually did when she was angry. After a few moments of nothing, no reaction whatsoever, Thomas felt he had no option but to encourage some response from Flora.

"So, Mrs Erskine, how do you feel about my offer? I must reply by tomorrow's post, so I need your response. If I accept the position, are you prepared to accompany me or not?"

"I must think on it. All I will say now is that I am not happy about it, regardless of what I might choose to do."

Thomas did not get a response that night or the next day. It was a week later before Flora announced that she and her daughter would accompany Thomas if he chose to accept the posting. Stunned, Thomas stood motionless for a few moments. It had been too simple. He expected more to come, sure Flora would have more to say, and it probably would include a list of conditions that would have to be met. But nothing more was forthcoming. Flora flounced off to prepare for bed.

Unconvinced about Flora's agreeing to accompany him back to Assam, he held off accepting the missionary position for a few more days. The couple never mentioned Thomas's posting again, but various activities he noticed suggested Flora was preparing their belongings for the return voyage to India. He went ahead and accepted the posting, agreeing to embark for India in three months from the date of his acceptance.

Now committed to the venture, it was imperative the arrangements for their departure be discussed and put in place. Two nights later, Thomas asked Flora to cut short their after-dinner drinks with Bess to allow them time to discuss their future together.

"Flora, dear, it is time we planned for our return to India. When I accepted the posting, I agreed to leave here three months hence. I suspect there are many things to put in place before then, and I wish to discuss them and any concerns you have. Would tonight be a good time?"

"Of course we should talk about such matters; tonight is as good as any other time. Is there anything in particular you want to discuss?"

"Perhaps we should start with your thoughts on this matter. Although you agreed to return to India with me and to accept the life of a missionary's wife in a village somewhere, it is obvious you are not happy about it. Please tell me what is bothering you?"

"Yes, I suppose you have a right to know. My original position regarding this missionary business has not changed. I never anticipated being a missionary's wife, and I'm still unhappy about the prospect. Nevertheless, I have agreed to accompany you and will honour that undertaking. But, in case you think I have changed my position and now embrace the prospect of a missionary's life, I have not. I am returning to India not for the sake of this marriage, but for my mother's sake."

"Your mother…? What does she have to do with anything? I thought you and your family were estranged. Now it appears I was wrong."

"My mother and I have corresponded regularly since I arrived in Scotland. It will come as no surprise that my brother is a disaster as a plantation manager. My father, whom I have little respect for since our departure from the plantation, has returned to a more active role in running the place. He is an old man and my mother fears for his health. My concern is for my mother. Being nearer to her means, somehow, I may be able to assist her in supporting my father. Although I don't know where we will be stationed in Assam, it will be closer to home than Scotland. For no other reason have I agreed to return to India with you."

"While I don't have all the details yet, I can't guarantee the village I am sent to will be near your family's plantation. My stipend as a missionary will be low, not much above a pittance. Flora, I doubt it will provide for your travel to the plantation."

"Perhaps not, but I have put aside a tidy sum since I have worked for Bess. I will not hesitate to use that money to facilitate visiting the plantation whenever I deem it necessary. There is something else you should be aware of when discussing our future.

While the life of a missionary is what you have chosen for yourself, it is not a life I wish to be a part of now or in the future. I appreciate the work missionaries do, but it is not something I wish to be involved with, and I would hope there is no expectation a missionary's wife will become involved in her husband's work."

"Thank you for your honesty. I have to admit your comments cause me grave concerns regarding our future. While I have not seen anything to suggest a wife should become involved in her husband's work, I believe there is an expectation she would assist in his efforts to improve the lives of the villagers."

"Well, what is done is done. I agreed to accompany you, and I will. Then we shall see what happens. But I give you fair warning that, if I am unhappy with the life you offer in a village somewhere, I will not hesitate to move with my daughter to my family's plantation."

*****

Tears flowed freely down the faces of the three females involved as the Erskine family prepared to board their ship for their voyage to India. Flora was on an emotional rollercoaster from the moment she agreed to return to the subcontinent. There was resentment of Thomas for his harebrained idea of becoming a missionary, guilt at leaving Bess in the lurch after all she had done for them, and excitement at seeing Flora's mother, Mary, again. And a touch of apprehension was also mixed in there, apprehension about facing her father again.

Of course, Bess was disappointed when Flora broke the news of their departure. She also knew Flora was torn between wanting to stay in Glasgow and her need to be near her mother. Although she did not say anything about it to Flora, Bess was proud of the hard decisions Flora made and her reasons for them. If nothing else, it confirmed for Bess that Flora was the right person to inherit Bess's empire – when the time came. And Bess had no doubt that, when the time came, Flora would bolt back to Glasgow to pick up the reins and drive the enterprise Bess and her husband had worked so hard to establish.

It hadn't worked out so badly for Miss Westcott in the end. What would become of Dolina once Sarah left and she no longer needed to live-in at Bess's house concerned everyone. It was fortuitous Mrs Westcott chose the week before the Erskine family were due to depart to have a major stroke. Dolina Westcott did not have to worry about how she would fill in her days after that – looking after her mother was about to demand all her time and energy.

Thomas wasn't such a bad bloke Bess told herself. Sure, he had acted selfishly and inconsiderately towards his family, but he had done the right thing by her. Thomas had sorted out the 'heavy' end of her enterprise and weeded out the troublemakers. He made sure everyone was adequately trained to do their jobs well, and he ensured his replacement was up to the job before he handed it over.

But it was time for the family to board the ship, and soon they were waving goodbye to a forlorn Bess standing alone on the dock. As the ship slipped its moorings, Flora drew a deep breath and took a moment to brace herself for the six-month voyage ahead.

Chapter 8

Return to India

The voyage from Glasgow to the subcontinent took six months, thanks to innumerable violent storms encountered during the latter half of the trip. All the Erskine family succumbed to seasickness, further straining family relationships. No thought was given to Sarah's education for some weeks. A collective sigh of relief went up when their ship made port.

"It will be so good to be on firm land again," Flora told Sarah as they stood at the railing watching a bevy of workers make fast the ship's moorings. But the voyage was only the beginning. Worse was to come.

Sarah, drawn and pale from so much time spent in their cabin and being ill, looked up at her mother but didn't respond. Her mother noted Sarah appeared unmoved by their arrival in India. Flora saw Thomas amongst the first to leave the ship as soon as the gangplank was lowered. She took her daughter back to their cabin to prepare to disembark. They soon returned to the railing to scan the dock for Thomas.

Flora's pulse quickened when she couldn't see Thomas among the milling crowd below. Sarah, sensing something was amiss, asked where her father was.

"He had to find the man with the wagon to take us and our belongings to our new home. He is down there somewhere taking care of things for us." Flora hoped she sounded more confident than she felt.

Something was not right. Thomas had been gone too long. There was still no sign of him on the dock, and no wagon was drawn up to the ship in readiness for their belongings. Flora's grip on the railing tightened.

"Mummy, are you all right?" Sarah asked in a little voice.

"Of course I'm all right now we have arrived. Why do you ask?"

"Your hands are a funny colour. They are almost white."

Flora eased her grip on the railing as she smiled at her daughter. "Maybe it's because I've been holding onto the railing for too long. Come, let's take a walk to see what else is happening on board."

As they neared the gangplank area, Flora spotted Thomas pushing through the crowd on the dock beside the ship.

"Look, down there, Sarah. Your father is coming back. We should be off here soon and starting the next stage of our journey."

"Daddy looks angry."

Although she, too, had noted Thomas's set face and frequent use of his elbows to barge through the crowd, Flora thought it best not to say anything to frighten Sarah. She settled for a safer alternative.

"Let's wait in our cabin. It shouldn't be too long before we are heading to our new home."

Only moments after they returned to their cabin, Thomas strode in. His face told Flora all she needed to know: something was seriously amiss with the arrangements for their departure to Thomas's new mission. She allowed Thomas to speak before she asked questions. He didn't waste time before doing so.

"There has been a significant change. Alexander Duff has changed my posting. I am now being sent to a location in the same area as your family's plantation."

Before Thomas could continue, Flora demanded, "Is that so terrible? If your business is about saving the people, those near the plantation are as worthy of saving as others."

"It is more complicated than a change of address. The residence available to me is a tiny one-room shack fabricated from local materials and big enough to hold a narrow cot and nothing else. There is no cooking facility. I am expected to eat with the local families."

"Where are Sarah and I supposed to live?"

"I am told there is no provision for a wife and child as they did not think you would be accompanying me. And, as it is a new mission in a new area, they don't provide more than I have described until it becomes clear the posting will succeed."

"Yes, I can understand their thinking, but it doesn't answer the question regarding Sarah's and my accommodation. What's to be done about us? Paying to stay somewhere would soon expend our saved funds, and you've already admitted your stipend is nothing more than a pittance."

"Duff agreed to put us up somewhere tonight and will have a wagon collect our belongings later today or first thing tomorrow, but that is the extent of the assistance he will provide."

"Thomas, we need to discuss this further. Let's take a stroll in the fresh air while we do so." Flora gave a slight jerk of her head in Sarah's direction as she spoke. Thomas nodded his understanding. An almighty row was about to occur, and it wasn't something his child should witness.

"Perhaps a stroll might be good. Sarah, please remain here in our cabin while your mother and I take a turn around the deck. We shall return soon."

They were barely out of Sarah's earshot when Flora unleashed her anger to reacquaint Thomas with the folly of his harebrained idea of becoming a missionary.

"For the life of me, I cannot understand whatever possessed you. Your Faith might be strong, but you are not even particularly religious – never have been in the time I've known you – and yet you decide to devote your life to doing God's work. As you are well aware, I never wanted this life for our daughter or me, and I will no longer humour you by staying with you while you establish your new life.

Please return to our cabin to look after Sarah while I go ashore to arrange tonight's accommodation for me and my daughter. When I return, you will be free to leave for your new posting with what few personal possessions you can take with you."

Stunned for a moment, Thomas was too slow to respond. When he went to do so, Flora had strode some distance away. Telling himself there was no point in racing after her, he dragged himself back to their cabin – and Sarah's inevitable question about the whereabouts of her mother. It was more than an hour later when Sarah's question was answered. Flora strode back into their cabin. Ignoring Thomas, she spoke directly to Sarah.

"Sarah, dear, have you packed all your belongings?" The bewildered young girl nodded. "Good. Come then; we must make our way down onto the dock."

Moving to peer out the cabin's porthole, Flora continued, "Ah yes, the wagon is alongside, and our belongings are being unloaded. Thomas, you and your Mr Duff have arranged transport to your new location. Perhaps now is the appropriate time for you to take up those arrangements."

"Please explain what is happening here, Flora. Where is the wagon you mentioned taking our belongings, and will they be kept safe?"

"Perfectly safe, Thomas, but time is fast away. Come, Sarah. Pick up your things, and let's be on our way."

"What about daddy?"

"Your father will leave the ship in his own good time. Our wagon will be loaded soon. We must be on it when it is ready to leave."

As she finished speaking, Flora shepherded Sarah and her small case out of the cabin. Thomas grabbed Flora's arm as she swept past him.

"What is all this nonsense about boarding a wagon, and where do you think you are taking our child? What arrangements have you made, Flora?"

"I am going home, and I am taking my daughter with me. They are not expecting me, so I have no idea what our reception will be. I suspect it will not be the most joyous welcome home, but I doubt they will turn us away. Mother will see to that, I think."

Having said her piece, Flora turned on her heel and marched out the door to a frightened-looking Sarah. Grabbing Sarah, she set a brisk pace to the gangplank. Thomas rushed after them. In the time it took for him to make sense of what happened and pursue them, Flora and Sarah were too far ahead for him to catch up. Stepping up to the railing, Thomas took a quick look at the dock below. Sarah was seated on the wagon. As Thomas watched, Flora climbed aboard, and the wagon moved off.

"They are gone, lost to me now, possibly forever. What have I done? My wild ideas of becoming a missionary, and lack of sensible planning, have lost me my wife and child." Thomas was a pitiful sight as he stood by the railing, murmuring to no one and shaking his head in a distracted manner.

"Are you right there, Sir?" one of the crew asked as he cautiously approached Thomas. "Can I help you with something? It is time for everyone to leave the ship. Sir, you must disembark soon."

"Yes. Yes, of course. I'll collect my belongings from my cabin and be gone. And I must find the man who came to collect me before he abandons me."

*****

A somewhat bewildered wagon driver exchanged few words with Flora on the journey to the plantation. He remembered the shock among the workers the day the plantation manager, Thomas Erskine, said farewell. And he remembered the tears shed by many when the owner's daughter, Memsahib Flora – now Mrs Erskine – and her young daughter said goodbye. Many would be pleased to see Memsahib Flora and the young girl returned. But he thought it strange that, when he left for the port with a wagon load of tea, nobody mentioned collecting the woman and her daughter from the ship.

Only a couple of bags of supplies for the plantation left ample room on the wagon for their belongings. Lulled by the rocking of the wagon, Sarah soon fell asleep slumped against a bag of potatoes. Flora was pleased. With Sarah sound asleep,

Flora was free of Sarah's constant questions about where they were going and why her father wasn't with them.

A long trip lay ahead of them. It would be dusk when they arrived at the plantation. With every mile travelled, Flora's stomach grew tighter until its squirming mass became a huge lead ball. So much stuff swirled around in her head, she couldn't focus on how her unexpected arrival might be received. Those thoughts she did manage to grab hold of as they flitted through her mind did nothing to ease her tension.

If she were honest, she would acknowledge that the thought of facing her father again terrified her. He had thought so little of her, he had no hesitation in abandoning his daughter and granddaughter. How would he react now when she returned without her husband? From when they were to be married, her father had made it clear he disliked Thomas. Malcolm McGowan would now consider his assessment of Thomas Erskine well justified.

Flora accepted chances of a happy homecoming were remote. But what about Sarah? How would she be received? She was Malcolm and Mary McGowan's grandchild. If not overjoyed to welcome her home, would they at least be happy to see Sarah again? Although such thoughts were unhelpful, they continued to dog Flora until they turned onto the plantation.

"Not long now, Memsahib. How does it feel to be home again?" the driver asked as they rode between fields filled with rows of tea plants.

"Oh, how I have longed for this fresh air, its quiet peace, and the sight of so much greenery."

Ahead, the big house loomed up before them, its sight ending Flora's euphoric moment. Then another stray thought elbowed its way to the front of Flora's mind: something was not quite right about the plantation. She pushed the idea aside. As they started up the track to the house, Flora roused a grumpy Sarah, who sat up rubbing her eyes and demanding to know where they were.

Surprised staff rushed out to the wagon. It was not supposed to be so heavily loaded, and it was not supposed to pull up at the front door. Maisie shrieked with joy at the sight of Flora perched high on the wagon, and tears tumbled down her cheeks as she rushed to help Flora down.

"Thanks, Maisie, but please help the little one down first. She has been asleep and still isn't awake properly."

Moments later, Malcolm McGowan, shouting about why the confounded wagon was parked at the front door, stormed down the front stairs and out to the wagon. "What's the meaning of this?" He demanded of the driver as he made a sweeping gesture over the wagon. As he did so, Flora stepped out from behind the wagon to respond to her father.

"If you want to shout at someone, it should be me. It's not the driver's fault. He stopped here. At least he was gentleman enough to rescue a distressed woman and her child. Shall we go inside to discuss the matter? *Pas devant…* and all that…"

The racket going on outside brought Mary McGowan to her front door to investigate the cause. Before Malcolm had responded to the challenge, Mary yelped and rushed down the stairs, pushing Malcolm aside as she went past. She was sobbing as she wrapped her arms around Flora and Sarah.

A plaintive little cry came from Sarah. "Grandma, you're squashing me. I can't breathe."

"Oh, I'm sorry. Come on inside. After you freshen up, you can tell me all about what fortuitous event returned you to me."

On her way past, she addressed the wagon driver. "Please take the wagon around to the back and unload the supplies for the kitchen. Leave everything else on board and put the wagon under cover for the night. We will sort things out and unload it in the morning."

Malcolm watched slack-jawed as Mary took charge of the situation. There was nothing left for him to do. The driver had climbed back onto the wagon and was on his way to the kitchen. Mary ushered their two guests up the stairs and into the house, leaving Malcolm alone on the driveway.

After the two freshened up, Flora asked Maisie to look after Sarah while Flora went to talk to her parents. Maisie was delighted with her new task. Maisie and Sarah chatted excitedly as Flora headed for the stairs and whatever might await her downstairs. Mary heard her coming and waited for her daughter at the foot of the stairs.

"We agreed you should join us in our evening ritual of a drink before dinner. Come through to the balcony and take in the view as you relax with a drink."

"Relax, mother…? I doubt that is likely to happen – not if Father has any say in the matter anyway."

"You might be surprised. And I thought you knew better than to jump to conclusions."

"I do, but I know my father well. I doubt there has been time since our arrival for you to placate him on our behalf." Mary chuckled but didn't respond.

As soon as the young lad in his starched white uniform finished fussing with the tray containing their pitcher of beer and glasses and was out of earshot again, Malcolm launched into the conversation he wanted to have.

"There are a few questions requiring answers, not the least of which is how long you plan to stay here."

"That rather depends on how long you are prepared to allow us to stay."

Mary could restrain herself no longer. "This is your home. Of course, you may stay as long as you wish. I welcome having you around again. And I know your father needs and would be grateful for your help with the plantation. It also will give us a chance to reacquaint ourselves with our granddaughter and watch her grow up – even if only for a short while. Isn't that the truth, Malcolm?"

Her husband responded with a reluctant grunt before moving on to his next question.

"Your entourage appears to be missing a member. In other words, your arrival is notable for being one family member short. Where is your husband? Should we expect him to descend upon us soon as well?"

"No. You may rest easy on that account. Argh, it's a long story, but one you both should know. Please allow me the courtesy of not interrupting until I tell it."

Over the next few minutes, Flora rolled out the story of Thomas's decision to become a Presbyterian missionary and of his appointment to a village somewhere in the surrounding region. At various stages of the story, Flora observed her mother shake her head, and a look of disgust was plastered to her face as the story progressed.

"So, because he did not want you with him, he returned you to us? I am pleased you are here safe and well, but I am not sure I condone the reasons for it."

As Mary finished speaking, Flora glanced at her father. His face was set, dark and stone-like, while he nodded his agreement with Mary's comments.

Again, Flora was forced to dole out more details of the 'new life' Thomas had given them. This time, they were details of the debacle that occurred at the port and the discovery that Thomas's posting made no provision for wife and family.

"So, you see, it was good fortune that, when I went in search of accommodation for Sarah and me, I found the plantation's wagon at the port. I admit to not giving it too much thought before rushing to the driver to arrange for us and our belongings to be on the wagon when it returned here. I apologise for the lack of forewarning, but I was desperate to put a safe roof over my daughter's head. I apologise if our arrival has caused you any inconvenience or upset."

"Tut, tut… there is no need for such stuff and nonsense, my dear. This is your home and always will be. It is where your daughter was born, so it will always be her home too." Mary ended her words with an emphatic nod.

"Well, now we know the why and wherefore regarding your arrival," Malcolm began, "but we still don't know how long. Is there an answer to that question?"

"Yes, there is," Flora said tentatively, "but I don't think it is the one you want to hear. You see, the only answer I can give you is, I don't know. If I'm honest, at the moment, I'm inclined to stay forever. Who knows how I might feel as time passes?"

"Daughter, am I to take it you consider your marriage to be over?" Malcolm murmured. The look on his face suggested the idea pained him.

"It may be. I don't know how Thomas feels about our separation. I am so confused by everything. I can't give you a straight answer."

"If I may make a suggestion, Flora dear, perhaps we should plan on your stay here being a long one and make arrangements accordingly. Do you have any thoughts on what those arrangements might be?" Mary asked.

"Is the manager's cottage occupied at the moment?" Flora asked. Malcolm and Mary shook their heads in unison. "Good; well, depending on how it suits you, perhaps Sarah and I could set up home again in the manager's cottage… and, please, may I have Maisie back to help me?"

"Of course, you may move into the manager's cottage if you wish, and it will be staffed appropriately. You will see to it, won't you, Mrs McGowan?" Malcolm asked his wife.

"Yes, of course, if you think you will be happy there. I admit I am a little disappointed you won't be here in the big house with the rest of your family. Now, what about Sarah's education? We need to find a suitable governess. Hmm… and I think I might know one. I'll look into it before I say more. First thing in the morning, I will have your belongings moved into the manager's cottage, and you will need to supervise that. In the meantime, you and Sarah will spend tonight in the big house."

"Don't be disappointed, mother. I'm sure I will be here every day to take care of the office work for the plantation just as I did before I was married."

Discussions then became light and general. Flora watched her father relax, and the evening became like 'old times'. It was inevitable their conversation should move to focus on the plantation and about how things were with it. At one stage, Flora's comment caused a few moments of heavy silence.

"Maybe my memory plays me tricks but, as we came up the track today, I thought the place looked different. I don't know whether it looked 'tired' or somehow a little 'unloved'. But it wasn't as I remembered it."

"The whole place is on the verge of ruin," Mary snarled, breaking the silence that followed Flora's comment.

"Steady on, Mrs McGowan," Malcolm said soothingly. "Things are not as bad as your mother paints them, Flora, but the place does need a lot of work to return it to its previous standard. I am an old man now, and I can't seem to manage everything needed and when it's required. The place has slipped. Although production is unaffected, I don't imagine that will remain the case for much longer."

"Well, I am at your disposal. I can take on the work I did before, but I also learned new skills while working in Aunt Bess's empire. Now, I am capable of doing much more."

"What we really need is a good plantation manager," Mary spat at Malcolm, "and it is way past time we did something about it, and before running the place kills you."

"But I thought Lachlan….," Flora began.

"…Lachlan is the plantation manager?" Mary tried finishing Flora's sentence. "He is in name only. He was useless when he replaced Thomas and has learned nothing since, not even how to do an honest day's work. And where is your son tonight, Mr McGowan? Come to think of it, where has he been for the last couple of days? And does his absence have anything to do with the missing keg of rum I heard staff murmuring about?"

The dinner gong curtailed further examination of Lachlan's shortcomings or the state of the plantation.

Chapter 9

Lachlan & the plantation

After breakfast, Flora left Sarah in her grandmother's care while she and Maisie went across to supervise unloading the wagon and setting up the Erskines' possessions. In no time, the cottage looked as it had before the fateful events of about three years ago. Missing only were kitchen supplies. Once finished setting up, Maisie went to the kitchen to deal with the matter of the supplies for the cottage.

On her way to the front door after a final inspection, Flora paused and slid her eyes over every inch of the lounge room. Then, with a final nod of approval and a wide smile, she went to have morning tea with her mother.

Mary and Sarah were in Mary's sitting room. Maisie arrived and took Sarah, leaving the two women alone and free to discuss whatever topics they chose without fear of interference from anyone. Flora wasted no time in sending their conversation in the direction she wanted.

"Mother, I gleaned from last night's comments that Lachlan is not shaping up well as a plantation manager, but your comments about his absence intrigued me. What is going on, and where is he likely to be?"

"They are important questions, but ones I cannot answer with any certainty. As you were aware, your brother was unhappy about being brought back here. He did not want to return and fought hard not to become a plantation manager. It appears he went out of his way not to learn anything about the job from Thomas while apprenticed to him, and he has defied your father in every way possible since Thomas left."

"Well, none of that is news. It was obvious to some of us Lachlan would never make a plantation manager. Is it down to his lack of endeavours the place looks a bit rundown?"

"In the main, it is down to Lachlan. Your father has stepped in to try to fill Lachlan's shortcomings in managing the workers and the plantation in general, on top of trying to run the business side of it. It's too much for him, and I worry about his health. Having you here, even for only a short while, will take some load off him."

"As I indicated, mother, I now know more about running a business than I did before, thanks to Aunt Bess. I am capable of taking on more of the work here than before. But what about Lachlan's absence and the missing rum….? Last night, you sounded as though you might know more than you said."

"If only that were true. I don't *know* anything, but it doesn't stop me speculating. It's not the first time your bother has disappeared. Over the past years, there have been numerous occasions, sometimes with serious consequences. But that's another story. It does not answer your questions about Lachlan's current absence."

"Do you have any idea where he might be?"

"I've almost driven myself mad thinking about it, but I've come up with only one possibility: the cabin in the hills, the one where you spent your honeymoon. It's the only possibility and the only place we haven't searched."

"So, he escapes without telling anyone he is not going to be around to attend to his duties, and he remains absent until found and returned to the fold. Is that what happens? And this time, a keg of rum went missing at about the same time as Lachlan. Has anyone checked the cabin in the hills?"

"No, not yet. And yes, it is likely he has taken the rum. In the past, he was always drunk when found after going missing. He required a couple of days of 'drying out' before being able to return to work. I fear he will drink himself to death."

Although tempted to question whether that might be such a bad thing, Flora bit her tongue. Regardless of what a waste of a life Lachlan was, he was her parents' only son and her only brother. Should his untimely death occur, it would cause untold grief to those left behind. Flora decided to risk airing an idea.

"Mother, forgive me for this, but would it be so terrible to allow Lachlan to take charge of his own life, to spend it wherever he wished, doing whatever he wanted?"

"My belief is that would be the best thing that could happen. It would be in everyone's best interests. Once he was gone, your father could employ a proper plantation manager again." Mary heaved a disappointed sigh before continuing. "It's all well agreeing that should happen, but it would break your father's heart. He accepts Lachlan will never make a plantation manager, but he is not yet able to consider casting his only son adrift."

"Right; I do understand how hard that might be. But, in the meantime, Lachlan needs to be found – and likely dried out as well. What are your plans for the rest of the day?" Mary shrugged. "Well, why are we sitting here when we could be on our way to the cabin in the hills? If we leave now, the round trip won't have us back here until dinner time. What do you say to that?"

"Let's go… I'll have a cart brought around. If Lachlan is there and is in the condition I expect, I will not risk putting him in one of the good carriages. He can go in the back of a cart."

About half an hour later, as Mary and Flora climbed aboard the cart, Maisie and Sarah waited to wave them off. Maisie would care for Sarah while they were gone, and Mary had organised a hamper and a demijohn of water from the kitchen to take with them.

Soon after midday, they stopped in a shady clearing beside the track for a quick bite of lunch – and to give their backsides a brief respite from the cart's rough ride. After about fifteen minutes, they resumed bouncing along the track to the cabin.

At about two o'clock, they entered the clearing surrounding the cabin. Behind the cabin, a small cart with its shaft resting in the dirt was beside a yard occupied by a lone horse.

"That poor horse looks distressed," Flora said as they pulled up beside the cabin. "I can't see that it has any water. Should we deal with the horse before we go inside?"

After finding a pail, filling it from the hand pump at the back of the cabin, and leaving it for the horse, the two women stood at the cabin's front door. They paused to take a couple of deep breaths before Mary flung open the door and they marched inside. A stench greeted them. It was strong enough to have both ladies reach for their handkerchiefs to cover their noses. There was no need to search for the source of the smell. It originated from right in front of them.

Lachlan McGowan lay spreadeagled on the floor of the small living room. Naked except for a pair of britches, he looked filthy, his hair matted and unruly. A further inspection of the scene caused both women to gag. Overlaying the smell of rum was the unmistakable stench of urine and faeces. A closer look at Lachlan's trousers confirmed the origin of the offending odour.

"What do we do now?" Flora wailed. "He is disgusting."

After a moment's thought, Mary responded. "He needs a good hosing off. Let's see if we can drag him outside to the water pump."

With one woman on each arm, and after manipulating his dead weight through the narrow backdoor, Lachlan was dragged outside. Mary grabbed a pail resting against the rear wall and marched over to the hand pump.

"Flora, I saw another pail inside. Please fetch it."

Once Flora returned with the second pail, Mary delivered the message they both dreaded. "Right; now we need to have these trousers off him. No point trying to clean him up with those still on him."

They removed Lachlan's last piece of clothing amid much coughing, gagging, and shallow breathing. Mary carefully gathered it up and, with it held out in front of her, strode to the edge of the clearing before flinging the trousers into the bushes. While she dealt with the offending britches, Flora had pumped water to fill each pail.

Then, they worked in rotation filling their pails and sloshing their contents over Lachlan, who lay on the grass, oblivious to everything. After each had thrown a couple of buckets of water over him, it was time for the next stage of the exercise.

"Please lend a hand, Flora. Now we've washed the front of him, we need to roll him over to wash his other side. We should drag him across the grass, away from the slop we have created."

With much grunting and sweating, the women rolled a wet, slippery Lachlan onto his front on a dry patch of grass. Then the bucketing resumed. After another couple of pails had been filled and sloshed over him, Mary deemed her son clean enough. He remained out cold.

"I don't understand how all that cold water didn't bring him out of his drunken state," Flora said as she stood looking down at her brother. "What do we do with him now? We don't know when he might return to the land of the living, and we can't stay up here all night. We didn't tell anyone where we were going. There will be a hue and cry if we don't return home tonight."

"While he dries off a bit out here on the grass, I'm off to search for another pair of trousers for him. Surely he brought a spare pair with him. We can't take him home like he is."

They found other britches in the cabin. "Although in dire need of laundering, they are far better than what he has on now or what he wore previously," Mary announced. "Let's see if, between us, we can manage to put these on him."

It was a struggle made worse by the fact that Lachlan remained wet. After expending more effort, they managed to restore his decency, at least in part. The major part of the operation was still to come. They had to take him home.

The easy part was positioning the cart next to the body. The almost impossible task was somehow loading Lachlan into the cart. Not about to be defeated at this late stage, the women positioned themselves on either side of Lachlan. Then, grabbing him under the arms, they dragged him into a sitting position against the rear of the open cart.

"That was easier than expected," Flora announced, "but I have reservations about our ability to achieve the next part."

"Somehow, he has to go into the cart. Lacking anything better to use, we will have to summon up whatever brute strength we can manage." Mary wished she felt as confident as she sounded, but that was the truth of the matter. They had to take Lachlan home.

Between them, they managed to lift him just enough to have his head and shoulders up on the cart. After that bout of exertion, the women stepped back to take a few deep breaths.

"Which end do you want to take?" Flora asked her mother. "Do you want to take his legs to lift and push, or do you want to climb up onto the cart to lift and pull?"

It was decided Mary would deal with the legs while Flora went onto the cart to lift and drag him on board. Their first tentative attempt to move him achieved nothing more than grunts from the women.

Flora stood up and stretched her back as she eyed her lump of a brother. "Right, mother, take a couple of deep breaths before we give it one more almighty try."

This time, their effort achieved more success. They now had most of Lachlan in the cart. Only his legs dangled over the edge.

"One more mighty heave-ho should have the rest of him up there too," Mary told her daughter. "If you're up to it, let's get on with it."

Success at last…. Exhausted, the women paused for a minute. But Lachlan was in the cart and ready to be taken home. Mary fetched a blanket to cover him, while Flora collected Lachlan's few possessions from the cabin and stowed them in the cart alongside their owner.

"What about the other horse and cart, the one Lachlan used?" Flora asked. "We can't leave the horse here with no one to look after it."

"Do you think you could manage the other cart by yourself?"

"Despite spending the last couple of years in the city, I still can manage a horse and cart. Mother, you head off home. I'll close up the cabin and follow you when I'm done here."

"No, let's hitch up the other cart before I leave. Oh, and we should check how much is left in that keg of rum. If it is not too heavy to lift, we should take it back with us."

A little over half an hour later, Flora waved her mother off before locking the cabin's doors and climbing aboard her small cart. The remnants of the keg of rum accompanied her home.

At the little clearing where they had stopped for a quick lunch, Mary stopped and waited for her daughter to catch-up.

"Mother, are you all right? What has happened?" an anxious Flora called as she approached the clearing.

"I'm fine. I wondered if you might like to stop for a short break."

"It is getting late. If you are up to it, we should push on."

"I'm fine, and it suits me to keep going. At least at home, there will be others there to unload our 'cargo', and we won't have to worry about it."

Before following her mother on the last leg of the trip home, Flora gave her brother's horse a drink of the water from the demijohn they refilled before leaving the cabin. She was concerned for the poor animal. After receiving inadequate care while at the cabin, she hoped it would survive the journey she now asked it to make.

Their return met with mixed reactions. As they drew their carts to a stop in front of the big house, Malcolm strode down to meet them.

"Where the hell have you been, and what in God's name have you been doing all day?" he bellowed as he came down the stairs.

By the time he finished speaking, he was beside Mary's cart. "And what the hell is this you have in the back? Christ, is that a body?"

"No, not yet, it's not, but it might be by the time we've finished with him. Perhaps, instead of standing there shouting at me, you might like to organise some men to remove your drunken son from this cart and take him upstairs."

"What? Lachlan…?" Malcolm reached over and pulled back the blanket for a better look. "Good God, where did you find him? And is he just drunk – or something worse?"

"Malcolm dear, perhaps we might leave our discussions until later… when we are inside and might conduct them in private."

"Yes, of course, and apologies, my dear. I'll round up a few chaps to deal with the situation. And you, my girl…," he said, turning his attention to Flora, "what surprises have you brought home for us?"

"Nothing more exciting than a partially drunk keg of rum... perhaps someone might take care of that as well?"

Shaking his head, Malcolm strode off to organise the necessary muscle power. As he did, Mary heard him murmur, "What is the world coming to? Women haring around the countryside on their own…."

"Come inside, Flora. We have about enough time to freshen up a little before dinner, and you might even have time to squeeze in a goodnight kiss for Sarah," Mary suggested.

As the two women came down the stairs a short while later, they saw four plantation workers exiting the front door. Malcolm stood waiting until the women descended the stairs before addressing Mary.

"Lachlan is in his room. It probably will require a thorough clean when he finally emerges from it again."

Mary cleared her throat before announcing, "About our Lachlan, Mr McGowan… we need a long, hard chat about that lad." The dinner gong curtailed any further comment Mary intended.

"Aye, the time has come," Malcolm agreed, "but it must be postponed now until after dinner."

Dinner was a mostly silent affair. The women were tired after their outing and their exertions. Malcolm sat dark and menacing as he dealt with his thoughts about his son and the actions of his wife and daughter.

Once they had eaten, the trio adjourned to Malcolm's office. Malcolm remained standing as the women commandeered the most comfortable two chairs. As soon as they were seated, he launched the discussion they knew would happen that night. As Malcolm was about to speak, Flora spoke up.

"Before we discuss anything else, I should warn you that Lachlan might need to be checked for injuries. I suspect he lost quite a bit of skin off his back when we dragged him into the cart," she warned.

"Humph," Malcolm snorted. "That will be the least of his problems before I'm finished with him."

But that wasn't the end of it. Malcolm wanted to know how and where they found Lachlan, and he wanted chapter and verse, not just an executive summary of the women's day out.

"Perhaps this is something for the parents to discuss and not one requiring my involvement," Flora suggested.

"I'm not so sure of that," her father growled. "I want all the details – and not just one side of the story."

"Oh, for goodness sake, Malcolm, you will have the whole story from me. There is no point in this conversation if it is not open and frank. But Flora is right about not being a part of it.

Flora, my dear, today was a big day. Take the opportunity for an early night and go off to bed. Sarah is already asleep upstairs, so let her stay where she is for the night. You should stay here again too. Move back to the manager's cottage tomorrow."

Alone at last, the McGowans prepared for what both parents knew would be a difficult discussion that must result in a planned course of action regarding their son's future. Mary led into the conversation they had to have.

"Malcolm, we may begin as soon as you sit down. Whatever else we achieve tonight, we must make a firm decision about Lachlan. He is desperately unhappy here… and so is everyone else due to his being here. So, what are we to do, Mr McGowan? What are your thoughts on the matter?"

"A simple life is all I want. I had hoped that, in my old age, my only role would be to oversee the operation of the place, but that's not the case. I've had to take on managing the place again. That would be enough in itself, but constantly having to clean up messes Lachlan creates is almost an impossible job for one person."

"If I understand you correctly, it sounds as though removing Lachlan from the equation still would leave you with a major workload but a manageable one."

"Yes, Mrs McGowan, that about sums up the situation."

"Well, Malcolm, the other concern we haven't discussed so far is how to proceed if Lachlan were to be removed. If he were gone from here, you would be free to employ a proper plantation manager again… and not have to run the place yourself. How say you to that?"

Reluctant to offer an immediate answer, Malcolm bounced up out of his chair and began pacing to room. Mary allowed him about a minute of indulgence before calling him to order.

"Come now. This is supposed to be a frank and open discussion. It is not a time for ducking the issues – especially unpleasant truths. Do sit down so we may thrash this out sensibly. And, first, you might respond to my question."

"All right, yes... as you suggest, if Lachlan were no longer in the way, I could employ a manager to ensure the proper running of the plantation. And, yes, my role then could revert to oversight of operations."

"Right, Malcolm, let's stop dancing around the real decision we both know is required: what to do with Lachlan? Do we continue to allow him to lie about the house drunk every day or help him to have the life he wants?"

"That is the crux of the matter, isn't it? The difficulty is in knowing what the life he wants looks like."

"We could try asking him. Once we know, we might be able to work out how we may help him achieve it. Of course, we should be prepared to be unhappy – even horrified – by what we discover."

"And then what? How do we proceed if we are completely against what he puts forward?"

"We talk some more. Along the way, we would hope to guide him towards a worthwhile future. Regardless of how those discussions might proceed, we must accept that, in the end, it is his life, and he is free to choose how he lives it."

"So, Mrs McGowan, when do these meaningful conversations with our son begin?"

"As soon as he is sober enough to be capable of coherent thought and speech. How say you to that, my husband?"

"Let it be so…."

Chapter 10

Changes

Lachlan's 'drying out' took a couple of days. The first time Lachlan fronted for breakfast again, Malcolm decided it was time for the conversation the parents needed with their son.

Although Mary thought it was 'men's business', something conducted man-to-man, and should not involve her, Malcolm disagreed. In the end, Flora was the only family member unaware of the outcome until her father's announcement at dinner.

As Flora considered her invitation to dinner, she became uneasy. It was not a family birthday or other anniversary of any note, and she could think of nothing to have prompted the invitation. She concluded she would have to wait until dinner to discover the reason. Until then, she would endeavour to ignore the tight, squirmy feeling in the pit of her stomach. After all, it wasn't unreasonable for her parents to insist on her joining them for dinner on occasion.

The first course barely arrived at the table when Flora caught her mother give her father an encouraging nod. Malcolm immediately reacted. Tapping his knife on his plate to gain attention, he then made a show of clearing his throat before delivering his announcement.

"No doubt we all have noticed Lachlan has not joined us. He is not late. He will not join us tonight as he is preoccupied with his packing. Tomorrow, Lachlan will board a ship bound for England. It will be his first step in establishing a new life elsewhere. We wish him well in that new life." His message delivered, Malcolm promptly took up his cutlery and began eating.

Flora felt her lower jaw sag. Startled, she looked at her mother, who was inspecting the contents of her plate and didn't acknowledge her daughter. A heavy silence filled the dining room briefly until Flora regained her voice.

"So, what happens now?" she croaked. "Father, do you intend to run the plantation by yourself?"

"Hush, child," her mother murmured. "This is not a sudden decision; your brother will have a much happier life elsewhere. Everything is in hand for the future of this place. Do not bother your head about it."

"Your mother is right. There is nothing to concern you in this matter. It was the best decision for everyone. But, we do need to talk about your future… and the whereabouts of that supposed husband of yours."

"Not tonight, please, Malcolm," Mary demanded. "Those matters are for a different time and place."

"Don't fuss, mother. I understand how confusing you must find my present situation, as do I. But I agree. Neither tonight nor tomorrow will be the right time. There are other matters of higher precedence."

No further questions regarding the state of her marriage were forthcoming over dinner or during the quick drink she shared with her parents afterwards. Nevertheless, Flora knew she must face their questions soon. What answers could she give that wouldn't cause unnecessary alarm? Searching for those answers kept her awake well into the wee hours of the morning.

Despite feeling below par in the morning, Flora ensured she and Sarah gathered with the rest of the family and staff to see Lachlan off to begin his new life. It was impossible to gauge Lachlan's emotional state as he bade everyone farewell and shook his father's hand before climbing aboard the wagon for the trip to the coast. Lachlan's insularity was nothing new. He was sullen and moody during the brief time she spent with him since he became an adult. He shut out everyone and everything, and today was no exception. He behaved as expected, with no indication of his feelings about leaving his home forever.

Once Lachlan departed, everyone attempted a 'normal' life, although what constituted 'normal' was difficult to define. As the wagon carrying Lachlan disappeared from view, Malcolm immediately left to oversee work in the fields. Staff returned to their duties, and Flora and Sarah hurried back to the manager's cottage to begin Sarah's classes for the day.

Mary had fussed about finding a suitable governess for Sarah. Flora opposed the move, believing they were unlikely to remain long at the plantation. Time flew by. They were still there… and with no indication for how much longer. Some days, continuing Sarah's education seemed a burden. On such days, Flora asked herself what else she would be doing if she didn't spend her days with Sarah.

If she had some indication of how long they would remain at the plantation. If they had some word from Thomas…. Weeks slipped by with nothing heard from her husband. Despite her best efforts, every so often, one niggling question would make its presence felt. Where exactly was Thomas? Had he abandoned them? Was the story about no suitable accommodation just a ruse to jettison wife and daughter? Had he intended they should end up on the plantation and in the care of her parents?

Those questions were never more troubling than when she joined Mary for morning tea a few days later.

"Flora, dear, don't think I'm prying, but I am concerned about what's happening with you and your marriage. Sarah's education requires many hours. Shouldn't we think about a governess for her? Your father demands so much of your time now to help run this place. I don't want you run ragged trying to keep up with everything you need to do.

Perhaps the first thing to consider is how long you will likely remain here. If only for another couple of weeks or so, endeavouring to find a governess would be pointless."

"How long we will be here is more than I can say; more than I can guess at even. I appreciate the questions and concerns our presence causes and the inconvenience should father employ a plantation manager. But I don't have answers to put your mind at rest – or mine.

I've received no word from Thomas, and I don't know the location of his village. I tell myself it is to be expected given the unknowns he faced in his new calling, but I don't mount a convincing argument. I share your unspoken concerns about the state of my marriage, not the least of which is whether it still exists or not."

"Right; then we should move forward in the most positive way we can, given the uncertainty of everything. I will begin finding a governess for Sarah today. Who knows how long it might take to find someone appropriate? But it will take even longer if we don't make a start."

Finding a governess proved easier than either woman imagined. Two weeks later, Miss Carter arrived to take up her position. Flora's reservations regarding Sarah's acceptance of Miss Carter evaporated five minutes after the new governess arrived. She and Sarah hit it off almost immediately. After a 'handover' to the governess, Flora had spare time on her hands… and the dilemma of how to utilise it.

Malcolm saw no problems with Flora's new situation. He had more of the administration of the place to handover to her and wasted no time in doing so. Flora relished being in an office almost full-time again. Although careful not to make radical changes that Malcolm might notice, slowly, she introduced new approaches to the administration function – ways she had learned working with Michael in Aunt Bess's empire.

Her father would not approve of changing how things were done for the best part of a century. The other advantage of spending so much time in the office was that she could have morning tea with Mary, who seemed to welcome the company. Flora had to admit life was sweet, except for one thing.

It was three months since they returned to the plantation… and since she last spoke to Thomas. As each day became a week, and the weeks turned into months, Flora's conviction that Thomas had abandoned them increased. The trouble was that with each passing day, it became less painful. So, at the end of three months, along with her questions, her hope and pain also disappeared.

No further comment regarding Flora's marriage was forthcoming for some time until the mail arrived late one day. It included a letter for Flora. She recognised Thomas's handwriting. Her stomach tightened, and she felt light-headed. Collapsing into the nearest chair, she sat staring at the envelope lying on her lap for a couple of minutes.

"To find out what it says, you have to open it," her mother said quietly. "I'll be in my sitting room if you need me."

"No. No, please don't leave, mother. Stay with me while I read what he has to say."

To be available but not too close, Mary drew the nearest chair a little closer to flora and eased down into it. Alert for any hint of trouble or stress, Mary's eyes never left Flora as she tore open the envelope and extracted one small sheet of paper.

"Oh, my God, can this be true?" Flora exclaimed.

Mary bounced up and rushed to her daughter's side. Tears were streaming down Flora's cheeks when she looked up at her mother.

"He hasn't abandoned us. He is coming here to see us... but it will be a short visit," Flora read aloud to her mother as she scanned the note clenched in her hands.

"Only a short visit, eh? And after how long?" Mary demanded. "Flora, I know this sounds almost too good to be true, and maybe it is. Does he provide other details about his impending visit, such as when it might occur?"

"Yes… yes, there is a little more. Thomas has arranged a ride on a wagon that will come through this way in about three weeks. Then, about three or four days later, he will catch the wagon again on its way back. I know that's not long, but it is wonderful news. I don't know how I will contain my excitement until he arrives. Perhaps we shouldn't tell Sarah about his visit until just before he is due. Both of us shouldn't have to endure the agony of waiting so long."

Mary agreed but avoided further comment. It was different that evening when she shared the news with Malcolm. His initial response was a surprised lift of his eyebrows, but a worried look soon replaced it.

"What are we to make of this development, Mrs McGowan? Please share your thoughts on this matter. As you have had a while to consider it, I'm sure you have developed a few ideas by now."

"If only I knew what to make of it, I would feel more relieved than I do. Such a short visit after such a long time might not bring good news. Perhaps Thomas's visit might confirm all our doubts since Flora returned."

"You think he is coming to confirm the end of their marriage? Hmm… it's a possibility, I suppose. He always was a gentleman. The least a decent man could do is to front up, tell the truth, and do the right thing by his wife and child."

"We shouldn't jump to conclusions, but I am fearful of his motivation now in coming here. Nevertheless, his decision to come here, knowing he must face you again, took a brave man. Let's allow him a hospitable welcome until we ascertain his intentions."

"That's asking a lot of me, Mary, but in fairness to all involved and in deference to your wishes, I agree to at least wait before judging Thomas, and won't react to his presence until then."

"Malcolm, we both know Thomas is entitled to feel hostile towards you. Your treatment of him was unfair and uncalled for, not just at the time of his dismissal, but from when he married your daughter. You made a disastrous decision we both knew wouldn't work and handled it badly. Admit it. We both knew appointing Lachlan as plantation manager was inviting disaster."

"What's done is done and can't be undone."

"No, it can't be undone… but you could try making amends." After delivering her final barb, Mary flounced off, leaving Malcolm to think about it over a rum or two.

*****

The clock, the calendar – everything – appeared to move in slow motion, and the next three weeks became the slowest, longest period Flora had ever known. Although the exact day of Thomas's arrival was unknown, Flora was determined not to mention the big event to Sarah until a day or two before he might arrive. It had been a struggle, but now she had to prepare Sarah to see her father again. After carefully planning the event, Flora was stunned by Sarah's response.

Later, Flora told her mother she expected Sarah's memory of Thomas to have diminished and would require the child's memories to be rekindled. That proved not to be the case. Thomas was alive and well in his daughter's memories. But Sarah's response to news of his imminent arrival troubled Flora.

Sarah nodded in response and then continued with whatever she was doing. Uncertain the child comprehended the situation, Flora explored the matter further with her daughter.

"Won't it be lovely to see Papa again?" A half-hearted nod in response. "Aren't you even a little bit excited about his visit?" It scored a shrug this time. "Don't you want to see your father again?" At last, Sarah put down what she was doing and looked up at her mother.

After appearing to give the matter a moment's thought, she replied, "I suppose it will be nice for you, and that will please me. Papa won't be here long, so it won't make much difference to my days before he is gone again. But, yes, I suppose it will be nice to see him."

Recounting the incident to Mary reduced Flora to tears. "What am I to do, mother? How am I to fix this mess – and preferably before Thomas arrives?"

Mary took her time responding. "I suppose Sarah's reaction was to be expected. Her father has never been a significant part of her life, not while you were in Glasgow or since your return here. His life necessitated his leaving home each morning before Sarah was awake and returning late in the evening after she was in bed. And, since you moved back here, he hasn't been around at all.

No one is to blame. It's just the way life is. The way life has to be sometimes. I fear 'fixing' the situation will have to wait until you and Thomas are together full-time again. Then, the crucial thing will be to have Thomas become more of a presence in his daughter's life. That might not be what you want to hear, but I believe it is the reality of Erskine family life. In the meantime, I suggest you wait to see how Sarah reacts to Thomas's arrival."

"Yes, I suppose I was asking too much to achieve anything in the next few days. Oh, I wish I knew when Thomas would arrive. I hate waiting without being able to plan anything."

Flora didn't have long to wait. Following a restless night spent worrying about her daughter and her husband, a wagon rumbled through the plantation just before lunchtime, depositing Thomas in front of the big house on its way through.

The noise of an unexpected wagon had Flora rushing to the office window. A glimpse of the wagon's passenger caused a strangled yelp. Mary, in her sitting room, heard the sound and came running. She almost had the wind knocked out of her by a tearful Flora rushing to the front door.

"What's happened?" Mary rasped as she tried regaining her breath. It was pointless asking questions of the figure racing along the hallway. Instead, Mary gathered up her skirt and galloped after her daughter.

When Mary reached the front door, Thomas already had Flora wrapped in a firm embrace. She paused to enjoy the site of the happy reunion for a moment before calling down to the couple below.

"Take him home, Flora dear, to clean up and rest for a while. We will expect you both at dinner this evening. Welcome back, Thomas. It's good to see you again."

As soon as Mary finished speaking, Flora disengaged herself from Thomas and, taking him by the hand, led him to the manager's cottage. The wide smile almost splitting Mary's face was determined to remain plastered there for some time.

Later, a somewhat tense Thomas accompanied his wife to the big house for pre-dinner drinks with her parents. Unsure of her father's reaction to Thomas but determined not to let it show, Flora became increasingly nervous as they climbed the stairs of the big house.

Neither of them had cause for concern. The drinks were a cordial, unusually informal affair, followed by a pleasant dinner. As usual, once dinner was over, the two couples adjourned to Malcolm's office. After about five minutes, Mary took matters into her own hands.

"Come, Flora, perhaps we should leave the men to do whatever men do after dinner. Besides, I'm sure you want to check on Sarah before long. So, gentlemen, we will leave you to your own devices."

Flora thought to object, but her mother had anticipated such a reaction. As she finished speaking, Mary wrapped an arm around Flora's waist and shepherded her towards the door. Once outside in the hallway, Flora complained about being made to leave her husband alone with her father.

"Hush, child. There are bridges to be mended, and that will be no easy task if there are spectators. Now is the time for those two men to be alone with each other and, hopefully, to clear the air between them. I know being here and dealing with your father cannot be easy for Thomas, but this is not an easy time for your father either. He knows he has much to apologise for, and it will not be easy for him to do so."

Dejected but hopeful, Flora walked back to the cottage alone. Although it wouldn't change anything – wouldn't turn back the clock – she would be relieved and happy if the air were cleared between the two men in her life. She dared not hope her father and Thomas might rekindle the good relationship they shared before she married Thomas, but peace between them would be wonderful.

Thomas, claiming tiredness after his long journey, did not linger long over any 'men's business' that night. It was only about ten minutes after she left the big house when Thomas followed his wife back to the cottage.

Later, as he lay luxuriating in the novelty of crisp, clean sheets and a wonderfully soft mattress, his mind wandered back to the conversation between him and his father-in-law and the invitation Malcolm issued:

Well, no doubt you'll be wanting to see the place again. Straight after breakfast tomorrow, join me for an inspection of the plantation.

Keen to see the place again but unsure of accepting the invitation, Thomas had tried for a 'diplomatic no-thank-you':

While I would enjoy a ride over the place with you, I have no desire to upset Lachlan. He is unlikely to take kindly to my intrusion into his world.

Malcolm would not take no for an answer. After receiving every assurance it would not bother Lachlan, Thomas agreed to meet Malcolm at the stables the next morning. He hoped Flora hadn't planned anything for tomorrow. While he didn't want to upset her, he did want to look over the property.

An anxious Flora met him when he returned to the cottage for lunch. "How did your morning go, Thomas? Was everything as you expected? All went well with father, I hope."

"There were no problems. I quite enjoyed the morning, meeting old friends and inspecting the plantation. Yes, it was a most enjoyable few hours. Now, tell me about your morning and Sarah's education."

His clever segue moved the conversation away from his morning and onto family matters. For her part, Flora was happy to explain her now expanded role in helping her father run the plantation and how it required her to spend quite a bit of every day in the office. Sarah's education was also something Flora was happy to discuss at length. The new governess, Miss Carter, had proved capable of educating their daughter as they wanted.

From the outset, they had agreed that, although their only child was a girl, her education should not be restricted or constrained by that fact. Her education was not to be about those 'frilly' things girls are taught. As her mother had, Sarah was to have a 'proper' education that included literature and mathematics, and all the other subjects usually the preserve of boys.

"How do we manage to pay for Miss Carter's services?" Thomas asked. "And, I suppose I should ask how we are managing to pay for food and lodgings here on the plantation."

"No money changes hands. My mother insisted on paying for Miss Carter. My labour pays for the rest and also earns me a small stipend. So, in case you were thinking we are once more living on the charity of others, that's not how it is."

Although Flora tried to steer the conversation back to Thomas, he seemed reluctant to discuss his work. But Flora persisted. She wanted to know how Thomas's position as a missionary suited him and how soon they might join him in his village. Although coy about everything, he managed to answer all her questions… but, as she discovered later, without providing any actual information.

After Sarah's lessons finished for the day, Thomas spent the rest of the afternoon with her until it was time to dress for dinner with his in-laws. To his surprise, the morning spent with Malcolm had been pleasant, but Thomas remained wary of encountering the 'other side' of Malcolm, that last impression he had of his father-in-law before their departure for Glasgow.

Would tonight prove another pleasant interlude, or would he regret having accepted the dinner invitation?

Chapter 11

A New Job

Dinner was pleasant enough. As usual, as soon as it was over, the diners retired to Malcolm's office. While the other three made themselves comfortable, Flora remained standing.

After everyone settled, she announced, "If you will excuse me, I would like to return to the cottage. No, Thomas, please stay. Sarah seemed a little unsettled tonight. I want to check she went to bed without causing Miss Carter or Maisie too much grief. If all is well at home, I will return."

As Flora left the office, Malcolm opened the conversation he was determined to have, and flora wondered whether leaving Thomas alone with her parents was the right move.

"So, Thomas, how is this new venture of yours? Is it as you expected?" Malcolm asked.

"No, I wouldn't say that. It was not one of my wisest moves. More than that is best left unsaid."

"I'm sorry to hear that, although I'm sure the lack of appropriate accommodation for your family hasn't helped," Mary said. "What's to be done about it? Do you have any thoughts on how to improve it?"

"Ah well, I don't want Flora to find out about it, but I have taken steps to improve our future together. I have given my notice and will relinquish my post soon. In attempting to do the 'right thing', I gave them plenty of notice before I leave the village."

"How will that make your future any more secure than it is now?" Malcolm demanded.

"That is why I do not want to tell Flora about it yet, not until I have positive news for her. I have been letting it be known about the area that I am available for a suitable job on a plantation, one that provides acceptable accommodation for my family."

"How is your quest progressing so far?" Mary asked quietly.

"Nothing yet… but it is early days."

Malcolm hadn't dared hope the conversation would produce these results. He seized the opportunity.

"Given you won't comment further on your current employment, Thomas, perhaps you might share your thoughts after our ride this morning," Malcolm asked.

"I found it was a most pleasant interlude. Thank you for the opportunity to see the place again and to speak to old acquaintances."

"Good, good, but what about the plantation…? Do you have any comments to offer about it?"

"Well, I don't wish to be rude, but since you asked, I thought the place looked a little… tired… yes, I think 'tired' is the right word for it.

Please accept I mean that as an observation, not a criticism. And I was not casting aspersions on Lachlan or his ability as plantation manager. I have no wish to upset the lad, although I suspect my presence here is upsetting enough for him."

"Yes, 'tired' is a good description of the place's appearance. And there is no need to worry about Lachlan. Lachlan is no longer plantation manager and is unaware of your presence here."

"Uhmm… I hadn't caught sight of Lachlan since I arrived and thought… well, he might be sulking. After all, I did break protocol by not seeking the plantation manager's permission before setting out this morning."

"I repeat, Lachlan is not the plantation manager, and he does not know of your presence because he is not here. Lachlan no longer lives here and is no longer part of this family. So, you are not guilty of breaking protocol this morning. I invited you to join me."

"That's true, but it is still the prerogative of the plantation manager… oh, are you the manager? Are you telling me you are trying to run this place single-handed?"

"Age is a terrible disappointment. I am an old man and not as capable as I once was. I was misguided enough to think I could manage, especially with Flora helping me. But I accept I was wrong in making such a presumption."

Throughout their conversation, Malcolm's eyes remained firmly fixed on the diminishing contents of his glass. Finished speaking, he slowly lifted his eyes to dart a glance in Mary's direction. At the edge of his peripheral vision, Thomas thought he saw Mary make a slight movement in response to her husband. Might it have been a gesture of some sort? But now Malcolm's eyes were locked on Thomas.

"As I said, I am an old man, and now accept I cannot run this plantation by myself. I require a steady, experienced plantation manager, and recently began searching for a suitable candidate.

You seek a position on a plantation, and I need a plantation manager. How would the plantation manager's job here suit you?"

"Are you offering me my old job?" Thomas spluttered.

"I believe we are, Thomas," Mary confirmed. "And while we accept that, after all that has gone before, you may wish time to consider the offer, please may we have your answer before you depart again?"

"Thank you, Mrs McGowan. I could not have put it more succinctly," Malcolm told his wife. "My wife is right. While I know it doesn't allow much time, I would appreciate your answer – or at least some indication from you – before you leave again."

"Well, while you refill my glass, perhaps I could give the matter some thought."

With no effort to hide his surprise at the request, Malcolm took Thomas's glass and made a fuss of refilling it, resulting in the process taking longer than usual. When he handed it back, Thomas sniffed the rum's aroma and took a long sip before returning his attention to Malcolm.

"Of course, there remain some finer details to discuss; however, at this juncture, I can say I am more than a little interested in your offer. Perhaps I should clarify my position before we proceed further. Because of the undertaking I gave

Mr Duff of the Church Missionary Society, I would not be free to take up a new position for a further month. Then I would have to wait to catch the next wagon coming this way. Does that affect your offer?"

"I'll send a cart to collect you. Tell me where you are located and how soon – at the earliest – I might send it. If those finer details you referred to relate to your conditions of employment, you will find little has changed except for a small increase in your remuneration." As he finished speaking, Malcolm extended his hand to Thomas, who clasped it firmly.

From her position on the sideline, Mary asked, "Excuse me, gentlemen, but have we reached an agreement? Thomas, does this mean you have accepted the plantation manager's position?"

"Yes, my dear. You witnessed us shake on the deal," Malcolm confirmed. "Now we just have a couple of those finer details to sort out."

"And to tell Flora," Mary added.

"Ah, yes. I would prefer you left that to me – probably tomorrow morning," a beaming Thomas suggested. "Perhaps I should take my leave now to see how the situation is in the cottage. I am concerned my visit might be causing Sarah's unrest."

*****

Flora was beaming when she skipped into the office that morning. As soon as Flora arrived, she bounded over to her father. Planting a kiss on his cheek, she murmured, "Thank you, Father," before rapidly retreating to her desk.

"You're early this morning, my girl. I half expected you would want to spend what little time you have with your husband rather than coming in today."

"The thought of spending the day with Thomas was tempting, but we decided to give Sarah a day off from her studies instead for Thomas to spend time with her. I think it will be good for them to reconnect again."

"Well, you have the office to yourself until lunchtime. If you change your mind, you are free to return to the cottage. It's just as important for the whole family to reconnect."

Tempting though it was to leave, Flora remained in the office until lunchtime but couldn't bring herself to return afterwards.

After dinner that evening, the two women left Malcolm and Thomas to finalise arrangements for Thomas's return to the plantation. Having given the matter careful thought during the day, Thomas told Malcolm, "Three weeks from today… If you could arrange for a cart to collect me, then I shall start work here the following day."

It took only a few more minutes to finalise the details before the two men agreed an early night was in order. On his way out, Thomas stopped by Mary's sitting room to collect his wife after the two women had spent the intervening time sipping tea and admiring Mary's latest embroidery efforts.

Not wanting to intrude on what might have been 'women's business', Thomas called to Flora from the sitting room doorway. "Come, Mrs Erskine, we have much to discuss and plans to make. If you would excuse us, please, Mary, I will take my wife home."

Two days later, Thomas was gone again, and Flora had to put aside her own emotions to help Sarah again cope with the loss of her father.

*****

Although it felt like a lifetime, three weeks took the usual length of time to pass, and they did so without any unexpected disaster or drama. But the time passed, and late one afternoon, the sound of an approaching cart had Flora up out of her chair and rushing to the window.

Aware of how anxious and impatient his daughter and granddaughter were for Thomas to return, without alerting the rest of the family, Malcolm dispatched a cart before first light to collect Thomas. The driver was from the same village where Thomas was stationed. The lad would spend a few hours with his family before leaving early the next morning to return to the plantation.

Everything went according to plan. The cart made good time. Malcolm suspected it departed a lot earlier than intended to return so early in the afternoon. For Malcolm, life felt so-o-o good again. Not only did he have an excellent plantation manager to ease his workload, but his daughter's shriek of excitement at the sight of the cart was a bonus.

The following day was as though the last three years hadn't happened. Thomas was up early and rode out to take charge of the workers, and a smiling Flora was at her desk at her usual time. For a few minutes, Malcolm was at a loss to know what to do with himself… but only for a few minutes. His daily routine from the time before he sacked Thomas soon slipped back into place, and he was busy again, but in a way more befitting his advanced years.

As Malcolm and Mary sipped their pre-dinner drinks a couple of weeks later, both were in a reflective mood. Maybe the sounds of the wildlife as evening settled over the plantation fostered the quiet moment. A whisper of cool night air sneaking across the verandah dislodged a tendril of Mary's tightly coiffed hair. She heaved a sigh as she patted it back into place.

"What is it, my dear? Are you all right?" Malcolm asked quietly.

"Oh, yes, I'm fine. I was thinking how our life is so perfect again. Would you agree?"

"So perfect, I feel as though I've shed at least ten years of my age since Thomas's return. And our daughter is positively blooming now she has her husband back."

While she agreed, a thought had lurked in a dark corner of her mind for the last few days. Mary knew she must discuss it with her husband, but this evening was not the time. There was no point in ruining a few blissful moments of thanksgiving by introducing the realities of life. Another time would suffice; some other time when a more suitable opportunity presented itself. Although the thought lingered, the awaited opportunity did not arise. Then, a few weeks later, other news pushed it from her mind altogether for a while.

*****

Maisie rushed from the manager's cottage to the big house and went straight to Mary's sitting room. She knocked tentatively at the door.

"Excuse me, Memsahib Mary, but Memsahib Flora asked me to tell you she would not be at work today. She told me to tell Sahib McGowan, but I didn't like to disturb him."

"Thank you, Maisie. Has something happened at the cottage? Is Memsahib Flora or Sarah ill?"

"Uhmm… I was told just to say Memsahib Flora would not be at work today."

"I see. Thank you, I will let the Sahib know."

After Maisie left, Mary sat for a few moments to ponder the situation before heading to Malcolm's office.

"Well, it's about… oh, it's you," Malcolm said as he looked up to see Mary enter the room. "I had hoped it was Flora. There are some urgent matters I want attended to today and, wouldn't you know it, she decided to come in late today."

"My, my, aren't you quite the grump, and for so early in the morning too. Your urgent matters might have to wait – or you might have to take care of them yourself. I've just received word that Flora won't be coming in today."

"What's this all about? She's always here, every day. I hope this isn't a sign of things to come because her husband has returned."

"Malcolm, I'm not having this conversation with you right now. I have other important things to do."

"Like what?"

"Like why our daughter isn't at work today. So, if you will excuse me…."

Mary flounced out of Malcolm's office and headed for the front door. Her concern strengthened as she strode to the manager's cottage. Malcolm was right. It was so out of keeping for Flora not to come to work. Something serious must be amiss.

A flustered Maisie met Mary at the cottage's front door. Although reluctant to answer Mary's question regarding the whereabouts of Memsahib Flora, Maisie eventually mumbled a response.

"In the bedroom, Memsahib; she is not well today… but I was told not to disturb her." The pleading in Maisie's voice was unmistakable.

"That's fine, Maisie. You don't need to disturb her. I can make my own way to the bedroom."

At the bedroom door, Mary paused to knock lightly before pushing open the door.

"I said I did not want to be disturbed," an angry Flora shouted.

"Perhaps you did, but not to me. Now, what seems to be the problem here today, and why wasn't I sent for directly?" Mary demanded.

"Please don't fuss, mother. I'm just not feeling well today."

"Not well, how? Is it something you've eaten, or is it from something you've caught?"

Flora heaved a sigh of resignation. "If you really must know, mother, I think I'm pregnant."

"Pregnant…? Oh, that's wonderful. Are you sure that's all it might be?"

"Fairly sure; I remember it well from last time. I had given up hope this might ever happen again. Now I'm almost not game to believe it is true. Am I likely to be so sick for as long as I was with Sarah?"

"It's hard to say, my dear. Babies are all different – we are all different – but the result makes it all worthwhile. I take it you don't want this to be common knowledge yet?"

"Oh God, no; it is far too early to have people start watching my waistline. You may tell father if you think it appropriate."

"As you probably won't spend too much time in the office over the next few weeks, perhaps I should tell him."

*****

Much to Flora's surprise, it didn't last as long, and she wasn't as sick as the first time. Between her work in the office, Sarah and Thomas keeping her busy, the months slipped by without anything mention-worthy occurring… until the last month.

Flora found herself constantly exhausted. Her back ached, and sleep happened in bursts of about an hour's duration. She wanted it to be over, but she knew she had a couple more weeks to wait. Hennie's mother was again on standby for the birth. In case the baby decided to come early, the chosen midwife started spending every day at the cottage. And she had moved in with her daughter, Hennie, to be close-by should the baby decide to come during the night.

In the wee hours of the morning, about a week before he was expected, John entered the world. As both the child's great-grandfathers were named John, there was no difficulty or argument in choosing a name for the family's newest member.

Life soon settled back into its measured routine, and baby John continued to thrive. It was time for Mary's conversation with Malcolm that she had avoided for far too long. As they sat sipping their pre-dinner drinks in the still twilight, Mary eased into the discussion she wished to have.

"Malcolm, the arrival of a new member of our family has me thinking about our generation speeding towards the end of its term on this earth. It is a part of life. The thought doesn't bother me. But what happens after we are gone? What happens to this place?"

"What is it you really want to know, Mary?"

"The family tradition for almost a century was for everything to be handed down to the male heir of the following generation. We had intended, on your death, everything would go to Lachlan. Is this still how you see it happening?"

"I must confess to not giving the matter any thought in a long while. As you say, we intended to leave everything to Lachlan. I now need to devote thought to this matter. I am sure Lachlan will get nothing. I meant it when I told Thomas that Lachlan was no longer part of this family."

"Does that mean everything will go to Flora instead?"

"Possibly, but there is another new male in our family. Perhaps the inheritance might skip a generation, and everything should go to young John."

"But John is not a McGowan. He is an Erskine."

"Ah, yes, I see your point. Maybe we should look at what can be done about that. Do you have a problem with John's inheriting everything? You're not still favouring Lachlan, are you?"

"No. That answers both those questions. I initiated this discussion to have both of us think about what we want to happen when we are gone. I would like us to think on it for a while before revisiting this matter. What do you say to that, Mr McGowan?"

The dinner gong curtailed further discussion. Malcolm said as they stood to go to dinner, "You're a wise woman, Mrs McGowan. I don't know where I would be without you."

A couple of months later, the matter of inheritance raised its head again, and then only in a related way. An itinerant minister would conduct a service in the plantation's chapel the next week. Such visits only occurred two or three times a year, and Thomas and Flora planned to take advantage of this one to baptise John.

"Why do they have to wait for the minister?" Malcolm asked Mary when he heard the Erskine's plan. "Thomas is a missionary or something. Couldn't he do it?"

"Perhaps he could. But as the child's father, he has a different role in the ceremony."

After thinking about the forthcoming baptism, Malcolm insisted the Erskines come to dinner the following night. After dinner, Malcolm herded them all into his office. Barely allowing them enough time to settle in their chairs, Malcolm began his campaign – without too much preamble or finesse.

"How do you feel about a name change?" he asked Thomas and Flora. "I'm thinking your surname should be changed from Erskine to McGowan."

There was no way Thomas would entertain the idea and said so. Flora agreed.

Disgruntled but not defeated, Malcolm offered another suggestion. "Well, at least consider the young lad's name being John Erskine-McGowan." It met with no more approval than his first suggestion.

About ten minutes later, a breakthrough was achieved. The baby would be named John McGowan-Erskine. Although unsure why this was so important to her father, Flora knew him well enough to suspect a bigger issue was behind the move. But her agreement was tentative until she knew more about Malcolm's motivation. Nevertheless, it was enough for Thomas, and he finally agreed to the child being given a hyphenated surname.

Mary, who was also not privy to Malcolm's thinking, suspected it had to do with future inheritance issues. She confided her suspicions to Flora soon after the baptism. While she still didn't quite understand the rationale behind the name change, she accepted it might be beneficial in the future.

Then the Erskines and the McGowans settled back into the pleasant and well-practised ebb and flow of plantation life, which they enjoyed, undisrupted by any major events, for the best part of another year.

Chapter 12

Death and Growing Up

After baby John's baptism, life settled into a constant pattern of work interlaced with family time, providing a reasonably relaxed and stress-free environment. But, when everything is going so well and everyone feels confident about their world, something usually upsets things. And life on a tea plantation in Assam was no exception.

Six months after John McGowan-Erskine's baptism, Malcolm requested Thomas and Flora join him and Mary for dinner. Of late, such invitations were for special occasions, and an invite to dinner at the big house was not commonplace. Although unaware of any 'special occasion', from the moment the Erskines arrived for dinner, they knew this was no ordinary dinner invitation.

They sensed a certain tension about the place. As they sipped a pre-dinner drink, Flora cast her mother several glances but detected no indication her mother was worried or stressed.

As soon as the staff departed after serving the first course, Malcolm announced, "I would appreciate it if we didn't dally too long over dinner tonight. I have news to discuss with you. As soon as we finish our meal, I ask that we adjourn to my office."

Intrigued by Malcolm's announcement and almost on cue, all four chairs were pushed back from the table. No one rushed, but a smart-paced, orderly procession proceeded to Malcolm's office. Flora was relieved her father didn't waste time and moved straight to the matter he wished to discuss.

"Today, I received some news I must share with you all. It is unfortunate I have to divulge it so soon after a pleasant meal.

In today's mail was a letter from the English High Commissioner to Egypt. Its contents were particularly distressing, but I will come straight to the point. Our son and brother, Lachlan McGowan, is dead."

Mary took a deep breath before wringing her hands together in her lap. "Please, Mr McGowan, may we hear the details of this matter?" she whispered.

"I will share all I learned from the letter. It appears Lachlan and his friend Richard took time off from working in Richard's family's business. Like so many of today's young men, they went to Egypt for adventure. Although details are sketchy, they were returning to town from an archaeological dig somewhere in the desert when an unexpected severe sand storm occurred.

The party of four, Lachlan, Richard, and two Arab guides were caught in the storm in a flat area of the desert affording nowhere to take shelter. A week later, when they had not returned to the dig site as arranged, the alarm was raised. Searchers discovered the beasts the group rode being cared for by a group of Bedouin in the area. The four bodies were found two days later. Both Lachlan and Richard were buried in Egypt.

It pains me to share such details with you, but it is best to know the facts and try to adjust to the reality of the situation."

"Malcolm, when did this happen?" Mary demanded. "Had we known sooner, we might have attended the funerals and taken care of any outstanding business relating to Lachlan's life."

"Today's letter was the earliest we could know of it. The High Commissioner wrote as soon as they identified the bodies, but Egypt is far from here. The tragedy that claimed our son and brother occurred some months ago. Such are the vagaries of communications we live with here in the hills of India.

It will take us some time to deal with this matter. I propose we raise a glass now in honour of Lachlan and then call it a night. I don't doubt none of us feels inclined to socialise tonight."

Flora maintained a brave front while comforting her mother, but later in the manager's cottage, her stoicism evaporated.

Floods of tears and bouts of sobbing began. After Thomas managed to comfort her a little, they sat side-by-side in their darkened sitting room as Thomas listened to his wife pour out her heart.

"He had such promise but turned out to be such a waste of a man. My only hope is the new life he began in England, and his and Richard's work were what he looked for in his new life… that he found happiness and contentment in the different world he created for himself.

My feelings about the manner of his death are jumbled. Part of me takes some comfort from his dying doing something he wanted to do and probably enjoying the excitement. But another part of me finds the whole manner of his death too tragic to comprehend."

Thomas held her close and murmured, "We must try not to judge him and take comfort in the belief he had, at last, made the life he wanted for himself. He spent so little time here, he had no connection – no true heartfelt connection – to this plantation. Perhaps your father's actions finally allowed Lachlan to pursue his happiness."

Although she knew they were the truth, Thomas's words were little comfort. But she knew she must believe those words if she were to remain strong to support her mother in her grief. Amid the grief and turmoil of emotions, one thing remained clear to Flora.

"No matter what happens after this, my children will not be sent away to school while they are young. Perhaps when they are older and might wish to attend higher education, the time will be right for them to leave here for some defined period. It is not because I don't want to be separated from my children. It's because I do not want this family torn apart by some similar situation again.

I need your support in this matter, Thomas. While I do not know your thoughts on this issue, I promise I will fight to my last breath to prevent my children from being sent away."

After reassuring her he shared her thinking, Thomas calmed Flora enough to go to bed. Flora, though restless, slept through to morning, while Thomas spent a long while waiting for sleep to come before waking again only a couple of hours later. Although he shared Flora's determination not to educate the children in Scotland, he was concerned about achieving the standard of education he wanted for his children if they remained on the plantation.

Time, the great healer, gradually returned life to normal following Lachlan's tragic death, and no further family upheavals of any significance occurred for some time.

*****

Life flowed along smoothly for about two years, until just before Sarah's twelfth birthday. It occurred during pre-dinner drinks on one of the few occasions lately when the Erskines dined at the big house. Malcolm threw the 'stone' that created the ripples.

"My diary tells me your Sarah is soon to turn twelve. What arrangements have you made for her to return to Scotland to continue her education?"

Thomas fidgeted on his chair while he tried to think of a suitable – non-inflammatory – response to Malcolm's question. Flora had no trouble answering.

"She won't be going back to Scotland. Sarah will continue her education here on the plantation. We will consider the rest of her future once her education is complete." Flora saw Mary wince as she delivered her reply.

Malcolm almost choked on his drink. "Not going back to Scotland… I've never heard such nonsense. Of course, she needs to be sent back – if not to Scotland, then somewhere else. What is this nonsense about keeping her here? Oh, I suppose this is her father's fancy thinking, is it?"

"No. It has been my intention for some time, and Thomas agrees. Before you continue, father, remember your daughter's education. I was not sent back to Scotland at the tender age of twelve, so why should I impose something different on my daughter? Are you suggesting that, by not sending me back to school, I am illiterate and poorly educated? And, before you answer, I suggest you remember who runs your business for you."

The debate raged for some time but, by the night's end, no doubts remained in anyone's mind that Sarah would not be sent away to school. Although the matter was never discussed again with the McGowans, Mary did try to broach the subject a few months later. Flora shut her mother down as soon as she realised the conversation her mother was trying to initiate.

"I told you, Sarah is going nowhere any time soon. And whether she leaves here at some time in the future will result from an Erskine decision and not because McGowans think it appropriate."

As a result, Sarah's thirteenth birthday came and went with her still 'at home' on the plantation. Although no one said so, it probably was true that everyone secretly preferred it was where she should stay. So, life continued unchanged for a few years longer. The only real innovation as far as the children's education was concerned was the engagement of a dedicated, highly-qualified teacher to take charge of educating both Erskine offspring.

*****

About twelve months later, when everyone felt settled and as one with their world, the winds of change again rippled the surface of their tranquil pool.

Malcolm was grumpy and offside with everyone and everything of late. Flora noted he arrived in the office looking haggard most days. She wondered if he were not sleeping well, but wouldn't dare enquire. But Mary noticed he looked 'grey', and that look was becoming a permanent fixture. Although well-tanned, Malcolm's leathery complexion had taken on a grey tinge, and he no longer looked fit. His face looked pudgy somehow. While what they saw concerned both women, neither felt courageous enough to broach the subject of his health with Malcolm.

Although it took the best part of a week, Mary persuaded Malcolm to accompany her to the port when she went shopping. And although it was a tougher fight, she convinced him to see a doctor while they were there. With everything agreed, she wasted no time in organising their trip.

Mary's shopping did not take long. After all, she didn't have much to do. The whole trip was a ruse to have Malcolm visit their doctor. So, her bit of shopping complete, Mary trotted along to the doctor's rooms to see if Malcolm was still there or wandering around the town trying to find her.

As she walked in, Malcolm was called in to see the doctor. Mary told him she would wait for him. Selecting what appeared to be the most comfortable chair in the waiting room, she sat and took out her embroidery to help while away the time until Malcolm's return. A surprisingly short time later, the doctor invited her to join her husband in his examination room. He didn't waste time or mince his words.

"I'm pleased you were able to join us, Mrs McGowan. You need to hear what I have to say, and I dare say you will be responsible for ensuring your husband does as I tell him. Malcolm, you need to slow down. A period of complete rest is required in the first instance to put you back on your feet again. Then, once your health has recovered, you need to take things easy, avoid unnecessary stress, and rest each day.

Follow those rules, and you will be around for a few years more. Ignore my advice, and you might not be around for much longer. I have prescribed a tonic for you. It should help to have you on your feet again in no time."

Malcolm wanted to hear none of that, and assured the doctor he had never before heard such a load of rubbish. Mary noticed her husband's face reddening and knew she must intervene to prevent an unpleasant situation.

"Tell me, Malcolm McGowan, when did you obtain your medical degree?" she demanded. "There is no argument to be had here. You have not been well for some time, and it has been obvious to those around you. You have been given an ultimatum:

do as you've been advised, and you will be around to enjoy our company for some time. Ignore the doctor's instructions, and you will not see your grandson grow to adulthood."

Taken aback by Mary's forthright comment, Malcolm spluttered as he tried for an appropriate comeback. But Mary was not about to put up with any further nonsense. She reached across and snatched up Malcolm's tonic prescription before slipping her hand under Malcolm's arm and hauling him to his feet.

"Thank you, Doctor. We'll be on our way. Come, Malcolm. The doctor has other patients to see, and you have a prescription to collect before we head home." Still holding onto his arm, she dragged him out through the waiting room and onto the street.

Once they were out on the street, Malcolm began a vehement protest. There was nothing wrong with him. How dare Mary behave this way? How dare Mary intervene in something which was none of her business.

"None of my business… and how did you come up with that idea? You are my husband of many years now past. That makes it my business. And, as I have no desire to become a widow anytime soon, that also makes it my business. I have no doubt you will do your utmost to make the lives of all those around you completely miserable in the next little while. But, Malcolm McGowan, I assure you, regardless of the quality of your behaviour, you will comply with the doctor's instructions. And you will continue to be my husband for years to come.

So there is no doubt on your part, be assured I am not about to put up with any nonsense from you, and you are about to undertake a period of complete rest. Now, my dear, you have the duration of our journey home to come to terms with those facts… but come to terms with them or not, that is what *will* happen."

When Mary was in such a frame of mind, Malcolm knew better than to argue. He lapsed into a sullen silence for the trip to the plantation.

It was late when they arrived home. Malcolm attempted to go straight to his office. Mary had other ideas.

"No, you don't. The new regime begins now. You will not go to your office. You will go upstairs to freshen up and rest until it is time for pre-dinner drinks. I do not want to see you down here again until then. Now, go upstairs."

Flora, who stayed late in the office to know the outcome of Malcolm's visit to the doctor, heard her mother issuing instructions to her father. She waited until she heard Malcolm open the bedroom door before venturing out to speak to her mother.

"My, my… aren't we living dangerously this evening?" Flora asked her mother in jest. "But, I have to say I'm impressed that he did as he was told. Either the pair of you had a monumental row on the way home, or the doctor's news was not good. I'd be happier if it were the former rather than the latter."

"There is no need for concern, my dear, but it might mean running the office alone for a while. The doctor prescribed complete rest until your father is on his feet again. After that, he will need to take things easy and relax more."

"Relax! He doesn't understand that concept. He will never do that."

"Oh yes, he will, and I intend to ensure he does."

After giving Mary a nod of understanding, Flora took her leave. Nevertheless, she knew she was in for a restless night. Flora had no problem with running the office on her own. She knew she was more than capable. It was the battle ahead for her mother that bothered her. And she knew her realisation that her father was old and in poor health would weigh heavily on her for some time to come.

Implementing the new working arrangement proved not as troublesome as some feared. Malcolm spent only a couple of brief periods each day in the office, filling in the rest of his day with long rides around the property and long afternoon rests. Whether it was due to lifestyle changes, the doctor's prescribed tonic, or a combination of both, was a mystery to Mary.

Regardless, after only a couple of weeks, Malcolm's greyness disappeared. Nevertheless, she was determined he would not return to his old lifestyle, and she ensured he didn't.

About six months later, as they went onto the verandah for their regular pre-dinner drinks, Malcolm announced he had a serious matter he wished to discuss with Mary before dinner. As if to not allow his courage to evaporate, as soon as they settled, Malcolm launched into the discussion he wished to have.

"I have become nothing more than an ornament around this plantation. No, don't interrupt me until I'm finished. The place runs well without me, although I know there is an increased workload on my plantation manager as he undertakes my work as well as his own. Between Thomas and Flora, they have taken on board everything I used to do. I am redundant now. And, no, that does not bother me anymore.

If I'm honest, I admit I found it difficult to accept that fact for a while. Now, I am comfortable with it and wish to capitalise on it."

"Your picture of your life here is a bit shy of the truth, I suspect," Mary began, "but perhaps you should explain what you mean by *wishing to capitalise on it*."

"Think about the other side of our business, the handling of our tea once it arrives in Glasgow. At the moment, we rely on others to distribute it in the best way possible and obtain the best price for our product. For some time, I have suspected those we rely on in Glasgow are not as wholly committed to our best interests as I would like."

"This is not the first time I've heard you allude to your concerns about the Glasgow end of our business. But, so far, I am unable to determine where this conversation is leading. I suspect it's to do with tightening up the Glasgow end of the business, but how you propose to do that eludes me."

"My presence is no longer required on the plantation. Thomas and Flora are more than capable of running this place, and I suspect they might even do it better than I did. I could continue to contribute to the business in a meaningful way if I were located in Glasgow.

So, Mrs McGowan, the purpose of this evening's conversation is to ask you to consider relocating to Glasgow. It would involve a major change for both of us, and not one easily contemplated, but I do ask that you give it serious thought."

Surprised by the direction their discussion had taken, Mary found herself at a loss for a response to Malcolm's request. But, for a brief moment, she had perhaps felt something… a hint of excitement.

"I give you an undertaking, I will consider all you said, and I will take my time about it. Something that occurs to me is the amount of work required before a move to Glasgow is possible, should we agree to move. There are many arrangements to alter, and new arrangements to put in place, for successful operation of this plantation, not just for the coming years but for future generations. I will also consider such matters before I give you my answer."

Dinner that evening was a silent affair. Mary's mind was too preoccupied with all the ifs and buts associated with Malcolm's proposal, while Malcolm continued questioning himself about how he really felt about the prospect of such a monumental change in his life. So, after only one quick drink after dinner, the McGowans settled for an early but restless night.

It was a week later, again over pre-dinner drinks, before Mary resurrected the subject of Malcolm's proposed relocation to Glasgow.

"Well, Mr McGowan, you asked me to consider moving to Glasgow. I confess to mixed feelings about such a move. We have spent so long here and not in Scotland. Nevertheless, we've always thought of Glasgow as 'home'. But, after much thought and several sleepless nights, I offer you my support for your proposal. As you said, the younger ones are capable of running this place. It is time for us to think about how best we might assist them. Glasgow might be the answer.

We have matters to deal with and things to put in place before we commit to a firm date."

"What things …? I can't see how it will be a difficult transition here on the plantation."

"Thomas will take on overall responsibility for the place, but will need a plantation manager to assist him. The Erskines will need to move into this house to free up the manager's cottage for the new plantation manager. And, you need to give serious thought to your will. As it stands now, in the event of your death, everything was to go to Lachlan. Now that can't be. Lachlan died intestate, so it's not as though the terms of his will could apply. I don't presume to tell you how to deal with this situation, but I insist you make a new will as soon as possible… just in case something happens to you.

And it is time we included Thomas and Flora in our planning. They might have valid suggestions that could influence how this matter progresses."

"Right... as usual, Mrs McGowan, you are right about what needs to be done. May I have a few days to have matters straight in my head before we involve the Erskines in our plans?"

Chapter 13

The new Order of Things

Once the decision was made, it took surprisingly little time for the necessary arrangements to be in place and a date set for the McGowans' departure for Glasgow.

Thomas and Flora would run the plantation as stand-in owners. A new plantation manager, Royston McFarlane, a single man with an impressive record in such positions, was employed to take over that role from Thomas. The Erskines moved into the big house, leaving the manager's cottage vacant for the new incumbent. That was the easy part. The one remaining matter to deal with proved harder for Malcolm.

On his demise, he wanted the plantation to remain in the family. Although Flora was his daughter, and a McGowan, she was now an Erskine. Bequeathing the planation to Flora was simply another way of leaving it to Thomas. As her husband, as soon as the property became Flora's, Thomas would assume control of it. It was the way of things, but it was not what Malcolm wanted for the property already handed down through a couple of generations of the McGowan family.

Between Mary and the family's solicitor, and after much debate, a workable solution was achieved. After Malcolm's death, the plantation would be left to Thomas's son, John McGowan-Erskine. As it was likely John would still be a child when he inherited the property, Malcolm's will included a special clause:

Should said John McGowan-Erskine remain a child at the time of his inheritance, until such time as John McGowan-Erskine attained his majority, his parents, Thomas and Flora Erskine, would continue to manage and be caretakers of the property until John McGowan-Erskine attained his majority and assumed ownership in his own right. In the event Thomas Erskine should die before John McGowan-Erskine assumes ownership, his mother, Flora Erskine, will continue to maintain the manager/ caretaker role.

With everything then in place for them to exit the plantation, and not to allow Malcolm time to dwell on it, Mary ensured it wasn't long before they boarded a ship for Scotland. The day before the McGowans sailed, the Erskine family accompanied them to the port. Both families overnighted at a hotel before the McGowans boarded their ship the next morning.

It was an intense, stressful night. Everyone's emotions ran high. Malcolm, in particular, was uptight and sullen as he struggled with knowing leaving the place where he had spent his whole life would be for good as he was unlikely ever to return to Assam.

On the dock next morning, during those last tearful farewell hugs, as Malcolm wrapped Flora tight in his arms, he whispered to her.

"I know you will take good care of the place, my girl, but please take good care of yourself too. You have always been my most precious possession. I don't think I could stand to lose you, or see you hurt in any way. Remember: there is always a place for you and your children with us in Glasgow."

Then it was time to go. Malcolm led a sobbing Mary up the gangplank and onto the ship as a sobbing Flora, surrounded by her family, waved them goodbye. To avoid further stress, as soon as the mooring ropes were dropped, Thomas rushed his family into the carriage and headed home. The heavy prevailing silence made the long trip seem even longer than usual.

Their arrival at the house just as twilight descended had staff rushing to deal with the horses and carriage, the luggage, and ushering tired children upstairs to freshen up. Dinner proved no more pleasant than the trip home. Afterwards, when everyone headed up for an early night, Thomas lingered a while in his office.

Over a nightcap, he reflected on the last couple of days and his feelings about the departure of the McGowans. Despite his differences with Malcolm over the years, he felt a tinge of sadness about their departure, and in the tacit knowledge Malcolm probably would not have much longer on God's earth. But there also was another emotion, an even stronger one. It was a feeling of freedom, as though a weight had been lifted from him. And that was information he would not be sharing with his wife.

The Erskines' respective management responsibilities kept both Thomas and Flora busy. It helped with the transition to a McGowan-less life on the place and avoided the possibility of a long adjustment period. The governess and teacher also recognised the benefit of keeping busy at such times and ensured the Erskine offspring did not sit moping over the absence of their grandparents.

A few weeks later, as the Erskines continued the tradition of pre-dinner drinks on the verandah, both were in a reflective mood.

"Life seems to run along so smoothly at the moment, I half expect it to be a false belief everything is wonderful. I find myself waiting for the inevitable disaster that I'm sure is waiting to descend upon us," Flora admitted.

Thomas nodded sagely. "Aye, everything is rosy right now. The plantation is doing well, and Royston is an excellent plantation manager. On my ride this morning, I noted the place again now looks as good as it ever did. Let's enjoy what we have, and not cultivate any misgivings or dark thoughts. Whatever the future holds for us will arrive soon enough."

*****

Flora's dreaded disaster lurking in the wings took its time to materialise. About fifteen months after her parents left, the letter bringing the dreaded news arrived.

Mary wrote of Malcolm's deteriorating health. The doctors were honest but pessimistic about his condition, and she feared their prognosis that he had less than twelve months to live was accurate.

Although they all knew Malcolm was not well when he left for Glasgow, Mary's letter knocked the breath out of Flora. Alone in the office, she sat stunned, staring at the letter she clasped in her lap. That's how Thomas found her when he returned to the house for lunch.

Unable to find the words she needed, she simply handed Thomas Mary's letter before dissolving into tears. After a quick scan of Mary's information, Thomas took a moment to consider the situation before commenting.

"You will want to head for Glasgow to see your father and support your mother. According to this letter, you have no time to waste. We have a load of tea on a ship leaving the port the day after tomorrow. I'll send someone to book a passage for you on it.

Start packing now and put in place anything you feel necessary for the time you are away. We will leave for the port tomorrow and stay until the ship sails.

Perhaps it would be best not to take the children with us. They don't need to suffer another emotional farewell so soon. You should spend time with them this evening to prepare them for the goodbyes when we leave for the port first thing in the morning."

For Flora, the rest of the day was a blur. As they were about to go to dinner, she stopped and held on to Thomas.

"I can't go, Thomas. I really can't. I can't leave everything that needs doing here left undone for maybe as long as twelve months."

"Yes, you can, and you must. There will be no argument on this matter. Your passage is booked, and you will be on that ship when it sails. Now, come. Dinner awaits us."

He knew his wife would be away for longer than twelve months, but did not think it wise to point that out to her. He thought more about it after dinner when Flora went to spend her last evening at home with the children. In reality, he knew it would be at least eighteen months before he saw his wife again after she left.

The whole family took some time to return to their normal routines after Flora's departure but, over time, came acceptance. While Thomas had more than enough to keep him busy and prevent him dwelling too much on his wife's absence, the task of keeping both Erskine children occupied all day every day fell to their teacher and their governess, Miss Carter.

It didn't take Thomas long to realise Miss Carter's time with the children was confined to early mornings and evenings. With the children at their lessons during the day, Miss Carter looked for things to do to keep herself busy. Thomas wondered whether that situation might provide a solution to another problem.

Since Flora's departure, he had attempted to run the place on his own and acknowledged he had managed quite well. But some of the routine office work was behind schedule as he had found precious little time to devote to it. Perhaps Miss Carter might be adept at basic bookwork and spend some time helping him in the office each day. He resolved to discuss it with her after lunch.

Soon after broaching the subject with her, he discovered Miss Carter welcomed the opportunity to fill in her days, but she had some reservations.

"Although I am not unaccustomed to bookwork, it is some time since I was engaged in such duties. As I am unfamiliar with the systems in place here, it might take me a little while to become competent and able to render meaningful assistance."

Given Thomas's assurance he would provide whatever assistance he could, Miss Carter suggested they implement the new arrangement the following day. They agreed she would spend three hours each day in the office, but acknowledged that time might increase once she became comfortable in the role. Thomas felt proud of himself that evening as he wrote Flora a letter apprising her of the new office arrangements.

His euphoria was short-lived when another thought slammed in from the field. As he slid the letter into its envelope, the rogue thought made him pause. How would Flora react to news of this arrangement? Although he couldn't imagine any reason for her to be unhappy, the little voice in his head advocated caution.

"Is it possible she might not be happy about it?" he asked his empty office. "Surely she could find no fault with my actions and should feel relieved the office work will be kept up-to-date."

It didn't matter how hard he tried to convince himself Flora would not – could not – find fault with his arrangements with Miss Carter, the little voice in his head kept warning he was on dangerous ground. Although still none of the wiser about what possibly could upset her, Thomas decided ignorance might be a safer bet. It might be safer if Flora were to remain unaware of the new arrangement – at least for the moment.

So, almost four months after Flora left, and while she remained on her way to Glasgow, a new era began in the big house. In truth, her new life on some days left Miss Carter feeling exhausted. While Thomas's limited knowledge of her duties amounted to 'the governess looked after the children when they were not at their lessons', her position demanded much more. She was responsible for ensuring the children's rooms were kept neat and tidy, and their clothes laundered, pressed and mended as required. Granted, she did not do the actual laundry herself, she had to ensure it was done and to a satisfactory standard. Any mending was her responsibility, and a growing, active young lad generated plenty of it.

There also were 'rest days' – usually one day each week – when the children attended no classes. On those days, it fell to Miss Carter to provide stimulating activities for her young charges. These often included a bush walk or a picnic – sometimes accompanied by a swim in the creek for young John. And then there would be more clothes to launder and mend.

Despite her other commitments as the family's governess, Miss Carter proved invaluable in the office. The envisaged three hours rapidly increased to at least five hours per day. Miss Carter loved every moment of her new life. It allowed her to use her brain and apply her intelligence.

She relished being seen as something more than just a nursery maid. And she knew Thomas valued her assistance and her opinion. He sought her advice, opinion or thoughts on various matters with increasing frequency. She told herself their relationship had become 'close', and she revelled in her self-assessment of her position as being vital to the running of the plantation. And, the bonus was that Mr Thomas Erskine was a handsome, good-humoured boss.

As the weeks passed, the occasional dark cloud would hover over her existence for a few minutes. She loved her life, being important, and proving she had a brain and knew how to apply it. But how long would this life continue? She had no doubt it would not continue once Mrs Erskine returned to the plantation. So, how long might she be able to enjoy her new role? Although she tried avoiding it, the answer wasn't too difficult to work out.

Flora Erskine would be gone from the plantation for at least twelve months: a voyage of six months to Glasgow and a further six months for the return voyage. But how long she might spend in Glasgow with her ailing parent was unknown. Miss Carter doubted that the lady of the house would immediately turn around to come home again once she arrived in Glasgow. She took some comfort in her calculations that she had at least several months to enjoy her new lifestyle.

Frequently, Thomas also pondered Flora's likely return to the plantation. Despite his almost overwhelming feeling of guilt on occasions, he still had not told flora of the new office arrangements. Yes, he questioned his motivation in withholding the information, but somehow always managed to justify it.

After she arrived in Glasgow, Flora and Thomas exchanged letters weekly, providing ample opportunity for him to advise her of Miss Carter's new role – but he hadn't. And flora didn't indicate how much longer she might remain in Glasgow. Sometimes at night, as he lay alone in their bed, the pain of her absence was almost unbearable. Somehow, after such occasions, in his next letter to Flora, he managed to prevent himself from demanding to know when she would return. After all, her letters all spoke of Malcolm's deteriorating health and how the end was drawing ever nearer. Thomas realised it was not a time to ask his wife such questions.

*****

The event they all dreaded, but Thomas secretly hoped for, occurred about two months after Flora arrived in Glasgow. Malcolm finally succumbed to his worsening health. That same day, Flora penned a note of his death to Thomas. She spoke of spending some time to help her mother adjust to her life alone, but did not indicate how long that might take.

Six months after the event, Thomas learned of Malcolm's death. Having read Flora's letter again, he slammed it down on his desk. "So why isn't she home yet?" he demanded before considering the matter.

Of course, she wouldn't be home yet, he told himself. To be here now, she would have needed to depart Glasgow on the same ship as her letter, and she had made it clear she would be staying on for some time with her mother.

"How long?" he demanded. "How long does it take to settle an old woman who has been expecting her husband's death for more than a year? Malcolm's death could come as no surprise. Surely everything was in place for after he was gone."

Miss Carter, coming along the hallway on her way to work in the office, paused at the sound of Thomas's raised voice. Loath to interrupt when he had someone with him, she waited in the hallway, unintentionally eavesdropping on Thomas's angry soliloquy. Once she realised he was alone, Miss Carter rushed to the office.

"You sounded angry. I'm sorry, but I heard you as I came along the hallway. What has happened to upset you? Can I help in some way?"

"No, there is nothing to be done. The matter will sort itself out in the fullness of time."

Although Thomas intended that should be the end of the discussion, Miss Carter's curiosity had been aroused. From what she heard, she believed Thomas's anger was directed at his absent wife. Fair enough, she thought. The woman left him to cope alone for far too long. It's as well he's had me to help him. Right now, I see in front of me a man in desperate need of more of my help … and help is what he shall receive.

After a little judicious coaxing, Miss Carter had her way. Thomas opened up about Malcolm's death and Flora's letter.

"After everything that's happened, I know it's only right for my wife to see her mother settled again before she leaves, but some indication of how long that might take would be useful. Oh, forgive me, Miss Carter, this should not bother you. These are the moanings of a restless man. Work is the best cure for this. Shall we get on with it?"

Now she knew what had upset Thomas, and that knowledge upset her. If Mr McGowan had died, his daughter, Mrs Erskine, would likely be keen to return to the plantation as soon as possible. It was likely she'd already booked her passage … or could be on her way back already. These thoughts settled like a lead blanket over Miss Carter, making it difficult for her to concentrate as she tried to work on the ledger.

Jessica Carter was not ready to relinquish her position in the plantation's office. In truth, she would never be prepared to relinquish her position. Apart from the work being engaging and sometimes challenging, it involved at least some time every day alone in the office with Thomas Erskine.

If only that woman would stay away a bit longer, she thought as she slammed the ledger closed, *I'm sure I could win the prize.*

Such thinking left Jessica Carter dejected for the rest of the day. She was sure her boss was warming to her, not just as his assistant, but as a person. A woman who was here, helpful, and concerned for his well-being – and available. Yes, she was almost certain he was beginning to see her as more than just a bookkeeper.

Her big question now: how to step up her campaign to win the prize in whatever time might be available? Although unsure how to go about it, one thing was clear in her mind. Mr Thomas

Erskine would receive 'extra special' attention henceforth from today.

Over the next few weeks, despite her unstinting efforts, her campaign appeared to fail to gain traction. With each passing day, success seemed less likely, and then the almost insurmountable impediment to her conquest occurred.

"She's coming home," Thomas shouted as he brandished the single-page letter. "My wife is coming home. Uhmm, when did she write this letter?"

Then Thomas fell silent while he read Flora's letter again and devoted a few moments' thought to its contents.

"Hell! She is already on her way home. If my calculations are correct, her ship should dock at the port in about three or four weeks. I must go to the port to confer with the harbour master about her ship's arrival."

"Oh, that is good news," Jessica Carter chirped, hoping her voice did not betray her true feelings.

All the while, the little voice in her head screamed, No! No! No! She had lost. Her campaign was over. As her quest had been unsuccessful after so much effort for so long, she surely had to accept defeat. Nothing was to be achieved in such a short timeframe before the lady of the house returned. Then the next big question made its presence felt: what would become of her once Mrs Erskine once more took control of the household and the office? Miss Carter didn't have to give the matter much thought to realise her days at the plantation were fast drawing to a close.

Early next morning, Thomas left for the port to confer with the harbour master. Unsure she could maintain her pretence of excitement at Flora's impending return, Jessica Carter went down to breakfast late. Thomas had already left, so she didn't encounter him at breakfast or in the office that day. But, other than feigning illness, she would have to sit with him at dinner that evening.

All day, she strived to conquer, or at least control, her feelings of hatred, anger and disappointment. After all, there had never been any doubt Mrs Erskine would return and, if she were honest with herself, there was never any indication Thomas was so lonely he might stray from his marriage vows.

Chapter 14

Changes

Three weeks later, Thomas paced the dock as Flora's ship tied-up. Waiting for her to come down the gangplank seemed to last forever but, at last, she was there with him, and he wrapped his arms around her. It took a while longer before her luggage was unloaded onto their carriage.

"Right, now we are off to the best hotel in town for dinner," Thomas announced as he urged the horses on. "Then we will spend the night in their best room before returning to the plantation in the morning. How does that suit you, Mrs Erskine?"

"It sounds wonderful. The thought of sleeping in a bed that's stationary all night is almost enough to make me swoon. Are the children here at the port too?"

"No, no, no… tonight is our time. Tomorrow is for fussing over our offspring – but not tonight. Besides, I want to hear about your time in Glasgow and how things were when you left. Perhaps the children don't need to hear some of that. Share the appropriate bits with them later."

"How have you managed all the routine office work without me? I expect to spend some time bringing everything up to date, but being involved again will be good."

"Well, you might be in for a surprise. You might find everything is done, with no catching up necessary. So, you should be able to ease back into life on the plantation without any fuss and bother."

"How did you manage that? How did you keep everything up to date when you didn't understand most of what I did?"

"Ah well, that's where Miss Carter came in handy. Her role as governess diminished after we hired a dedicated teacher for the children. While she remained a necessary part of the household, she had spare hours every day. I put her to work in the office. Initially, for only two or three hours each day, but it increased to occupy all her spare time. She has done an excellent job. I believe she enjoys the work, and not just because it occupies her spare time."

"Hmm, I see. Well, I will look into that as soon as I settle into my normal routine again."

"Is it your intention Miss Carter will not continue in the office now you are home again?"

"I see no reason for her to continue in the office, but I will review her position and workload before making any decisions."

Miss Carter did not figure again in conversations. It might have been due to Thomas's careful focusing of discussions on the present Glasgow situation.

"That you felt it safe to come home suggests your mother is coping well without Malcolm. How are things in Glasgow, and will she be all right on her own?"

"My mother is made of stern stuff. It doesn't matter how well you understand the situation. Nothing prepares you for the final outcome. She did take my father's death hard when it came. They had been married for a long time and were devoted to one another. But, ever the strong, intelligent woman, my mother was more than capable of embracing a new opportunity.

Aunt Bess, who is a handful of years younger than mother, suggested mother should move into Bess's big, rambling, old house with her. She suggested they would be company for one another and could keep an eye on each other over the coming years."

"Your mother agreed to such an arrangement?"

"Oh, aye, but it took her a day or so to think it over. Once she accepted that moving in with Bess offered merit for both women, she started moving home immediately. I felt compelled to stay with them until I was sure both women had settled into their new way of life and were not encountering undue stress. Then there was nothing more to keep me in Glasgow, and I was on the first boat home.

Tell me about the children. How have they been in my absence, and have there been any major issues?"

"They are fine. Of course, they missed you, but everyone kept them occupied and busy the whole time. It seems to have worked. I'm assured their studies haven't suffered in your absence. Sarah has blossomed into quite the young lady while you were away."

"Ah, yes, Sarah… I'll need to talk to you about her, but I'll leave it until I've settled back into plantation life and had time to assess that situation."

Thomas was keen to pursue Flora's comment further, but she refused to be drawn on the matter. There was nothing for it but to allow conversation to move away from the family and onto the plantation, particularly the continued performance of the new plantation manager, Royston McFarlane.

*****

Flora's return was greeted with all the fuss one might expect after such a lengthy absence. Several evenings later, over their pre-dinner drinks on the verandah, Flora admitted settling back into her old life had been a hectic few days. A matter at the forefront of her mind nagged at her. But Flora decided against discussing it with Thomas for a while.

Although Miss Jessica Carter had attempted a warm welcome home for her boss, Flora felt it was a long way from genuine. There had been a flash of resentment during a discussion of how Miss Carter filled in her days during Flora's absence. The young woman emphasised how helpful she had been to Mr Erskine by keeping the office up to date.

"Thank you for that, Miss Carter. But, now I am home again, you will not need to go into Mr Erskine's office again."

"No, I didn't expect it would be any other way."

It wasn't the words that bothered Flora, as the venom in their delivery. Flora chose not to make an issue of it at the time. But it brought to mind something else she became aware of almost as soon as she arrived home. And Flora noticed it again that night at dinner. Yes, she had a couple of important matters to deal with, but both needed to be handled with care and after sound planning.

About five weeks after arriving home, Flora deemed the time was right to tackle those matters with Thomas. And what better time to do it than over pre-dinner drinks when they both were relaxed?

"Thomas, Sarah is about to turn sixteen."

"Ah, yes, I know her birthday is in a few weeks. Did you have something in mind for it?"

"Yes and no; I'm inclined to hold a party, although it is only a sixteenth birthday. But my concern goes beyond Sarah's birthday. According to her teacher, she has completed her formal academic studies and done very well. She now needs to move into the next stage of her life, that of being a young woman… a young eligible-for-marriage woman."

"Surely she is still too young for such thoughts?"

"Not at all, my dear. I'm not suggesting Sarah should be contemplating marriage yet. Before then, she needs to be appropriately 'finished' and made ready to enter society where she is likely to meet the 'right' man to choose for her husband."

"Finished! Yes, I know what it means, but I struggle to apply this conversation to our young daughter upstairs in her room. Nevertheless, I agree it needs to happen if she is to meet and marry the kind of man we want for our daughter. Is Miss Carter the right person to deliver the next stage of our daughter's training?"

"Good heavens, no… definitely not. And there is no suitable 'society' here for her to enter."

"You appear to have given the matter some thought. Perhaps you should share those thoughts with me."

"What I am about to share with you is not hard and fast. While it is my best thinking on the matter, it is open to discussion." Thomas nodded his understanding, and Flora continued. "I think Sarah should be sent to her grandmother in Glasgow. My mother and Aunt Bess will ensure Sarah is properly prepared to take her place in Glasgow's society. And, as those two women already are part of that society, introducing Sarah into it should pose no problems."

"I don't welcome the thought of sending our daughter away. After all, we didn't send them away to school so we could keep them here. We wanted them to know and appreciate the life we have here, and not end up as Lachlan did."

"There is no argument from me, but Sarah is a young woman now. What are her chances of making a good marriage if she remains here? It's more than wanting her to find a good man. I want her to marry someone who can offer her the lifestyle she deserves and is accustomed to from living here."

"Argh, I share your thinking. I want the best possible marriage for our daughter. Sending her back to Glasgow is likely the only way to ensure that. But what about Miss Carter? If Sarah is gone, is it appropriate for her to remain here as governess to John?"

"No, John needs a man to guide him. I know he is still young, but these are his formative years, and I would feel more comfortable with a man to guide him. What about the teacher, Gerard Stanley? Might he consider the more expanded role of teacher and carer?"

"The only way to find out is to discuss it with him. Should I wait until you have the necessary conversations with Miss Carter before I speak to Gerard?"

"Ideally, our conversations should be simultaneous, but that won't be possible. You know the man better than I do. Would he keep quiet about our plans if you discussed them with him now?"

"Only one way to find out, I suppose: sound him out about keeping secrets before we tell him anything. How soon do we deal with Sarah's side of this matter?"

"How about tomorrow? While you talk to Sarah about her forthcoming new life, I will break the news to Miss Carter. Now I think on it, and provided she agrees, Miss Carter might chaperone Sarah on her voyage to Scotland. How does that sit with you?"

"When do you envisage all these changes coming into effect? Implementation is likely to be delayed, maybe for as long as twelve months. It will take at least that long for you to send a letter to Scotland and receive their reply."

"We discussed the matter before I left Glasgow. Both mother and Aunt Bess agree this is in Sarah's best interest and now await my advice about when it will happen. The party for Sarah's birthday is in two weeks. My thinking is to allow approximately a month for Miss Carter and Sarah to gather the belongings they will take with them."

"Six weeks then… all the more reason to have those difficult conversations tomorrow, book passages, and send a letter to Scotland as soon as possible."

First thing next morning, Thomas spoke with the teacher, Gerard Stanley, about taking over both full-time care and education of young John. Thomas had expected some resistance and was amazed when Gerard jumped at the idea. After the finer details of the arrangement were discussed, Gerard agreed not to mention the new arrangement until after other changes became general knowledge.

After Gerard departed, Thomas murmured, "Now, if only the next one is as easy and goes so well, I will be a happy man,"

At ten o'clock that same morning, as arranged, Thomas sent for Sarah at the same time as Miss Carter met with Flora in Flora's sitting room. By the time Maisie found Sarah to tell her Thomas wished to speak to her, Flora's conversation with Miss Carter had ended. It was over when Jessica Carter refused to stay another six weeks and then chaperone Sarah to Scotland. She told Flora she would leave as soon as she could book a passage, and would travel to the port the following day to arrange it.

Flora rushed to Thomas's office and was relieved that Sarah had not yet arrived. She relayed Miss Carter's response.

"What do we do now?" Thomas asked. "We don't have a chaperone to accompany our daughter."

"All is not lost, my dear. Miss Crowther, the governess on the neighbouring plantation, will soon return to Scotland. I'm sure she would welcome the invitation to look after Sarah on the voyage. I will book both their passages. We should proceed as though that is what will happen."

There was a knock on Thomas's door a few minutes after Flora left.

*****

Then Sarah's memories wound forward to reach that fateful day and the events that led to her being on board the ship and on her way to Scotland. Tucked away alone in a quiet corner on deck, Sarah could not stop her memories. They rolled on despite her struggle to bring them to a halt, to forbid them to progress further. But her memory paid her no heed as it revisited the events of that fateful day and the brief meeting with her father in his office.

"You wanted to see me, Father?"

"Ah, My Girl, yes. Come in, come in. I won't detain you long. I just wanted to tell you that soon you are to set sail for Scotland to live with your Grandmother McGowan."

So began the difficult conversation. Thomas chose to deliver the facts as succinctly as possible, leaving no room for doubts or arguments. The information provided, Thomas wasted no time wrapping up the meeting with his daughter.

"That is all I have to share with you at this time, other than to counsel you to apply yourself diligently to your preparations for the voyage and your new life in Scotland. I have nothing more to say. You may go now."

Sarah remembered having other ideas and demanding to know why she was being sent away. Flustered by being challenged, Thomas adopted an even harder line as he again dismissed her.

"And that brings me to where I am today on this ship on my way to a life I do not want," she told the waves rolling by as she stared out from her secluded corner of the deck.

But Sarah's memory was not done yet. It continued its journey along the path she had set for it to revisit memories formed from information gained after the events of that fateful day.

*****

After Flora McGowan Erskine was almost bowled over by her daughter as she rushed from her father's study in tears, she stuck her head into her husband's office before running after her fleeing daughter.

"It went well, I see," Flora threw at her husband, who was pouring himself a good measure of rum after the confrontation with his daughter.

Flora didn't wait for Thomas's answer, turning on her heel instead to race upstairs after their daughter.

Their conversations that morning resulted in Thomas and Flora's plan undergoing a few modifications over the following days.

The first was the matter of a chaperone for Sarah on the voyage. After Miss Carter refused to accept any part of the proposal put to her, that afternoon, Flora went across to the neighbouring plantation for a discussion with Miss Crowther.

Unlike Miss Carter, Miss Crowther wasted no time accepting the offer, and the suggested timing of their departure suited her. Flora promised to go to the port the next day to book their passages. Between Flora, Miss Crowther and Miss Crowther's employers, agreement was reached for Miss Crowther to stay on in her present position until it was time to leave to join the ship.

A second part of the original plan fell by the wayside when Sarah refused to have a birthday party and claimed that, if her mother went ahead with organising a party, she would not attend. Flora feared that she would attend … and make a terrible scene to embarrass her parents while she was there.

"Right, my dear, there will be no birthday party," Flora murmured after her daughter delivered her ultimatum and stormed out of Flora's sitting room.

Over pre-dinner drinks that night, the parents compared notes on the day's events. Flora told Thomas of Sarah's potential boycott of any birthday party they might organise. "I think it would be best to scrap the party and, as there won't be any reason for delay, maybe we should bring her departure forward instead of waiting until a month after her birthday. I now favour a departure date about two weeks after she turns sixteen."

"I agree. I can't see the need to delay the inevitable for any longer than necessary – as long as it suits Miss Crowther. I don't know when it happened, but our daughter has become a petulant handful."

"Don't worry about it. Between them, mother and Aunt Bess will soon knock that out of her. They will ensure our young lady realises life doesn't always behave as you wish, and you must make the best of it.

When I book their passages to Scotland tomorrow, I will aim for a ship departing in about a month."

"Will such an earlier than planned departure suit Miss Crowther?"

"Yes. Miss Crowther has a flexible arrangement with her present employers. I suspect all parties involved will be happy to see the deal completed. I will have an interesting trip to the port tomorrow. Miss Carter also ordered a cart for tomorrow to take her to catch her ship. When I decided to travel to the port tomorrow, I cancelled her order and asked for a carriage for both of us instead."

"As you say, it will be an interesting time, and a silent one, I should imagine. I can't see Miss Carter being in a communicative mood after all that's been said and done. You appeared relieved when she announced she would leave immediately. Was your decision to terminate her employment influenced by something else I wasn't aware of?"

"You might say so… and I don't doubt you were unaware. From the moment I arrived home, I sensed Miss Carter resented my presence – resented my return and bringing to an end her time in the office. I am not blind. I saw how she looked at you over dinner and whenever you were around. It was clear to me she had designs on you. She wasn't needed once Sarah went back to Scotland, and it was best Miss Jessica Carter left before she made a fool of herself over you."

"Good God, woman, are you suggesting she might have had improper thoughts about me?"

"No. I'm not suggesting anything. I'm *telling* you she had improper – carnal – thoughts regarding you. Better she leaves now than hangs around much longer."

Stunned, Thomas agreed it was best Miss Carter left as soon as possible, but admitted he had never sensed anything Flora described.

Next morning, Miss Carter was surprised when a carriage instead of a cart rolled to a halt in front of the big house. She was about to take the driver to task for his mistake when Flora bounced down the steps a shouted a cheery 'good morning' to the driver as he climbed down to deal with the luggage.

"Oh, I see," Jessica Carter stammered. "I take it this carriage is for you. I ordered a cart."

"There won't be two rigs going to the port today. The carriage is for both of us. Our driver has almost finished with the luggage. Climb aboard so we can leave as soon as he is done."

Ah yes, Thomas, you were so right, Flora thought as she followed an angry Miss Carter up into the carriage. It would not be a pleasant trip. And, as he predicted, it was notable for the heavy silence that prevailed the whole way.

Flora was away from the plantation for the next two days, booking the two passages and dealing with a couple of other minor matters while at the port before heading home again. Although on a wagon that brought a consignment of tea to the port for shipment instead of in a comfortable carriage, her trip home was more relaxed and enjoyable. But her first task on returning to the big house raised Flora's stress to extreme levels once more.

Now there was a definite date for Sarah's departure for Scotland, Sarah needed to know so she could prepare for it. As Flora half expected, her conversation with Sarah did not go well, but Flora was prepared to endure only so much of the girl's venom. When Sarah paused momentarily to draw breath before delivering her next tirade, Flora gave rein to her anger.

Her mother's anger in full flight was something Sarah had never experienced before, and never wanted to experience again. After delivering a few 'home truths' and her disgust at Sarah's behaviour over recent days, Flora flounced out of Sarah's room. A few steps outside the door, Flora stopped and marched back to the door, which remained open.

"As you seem unable to conduct yourself in any way resembling an adult, you are not welcome to dine with us. With Miss Carter now gone, you will be eating and doing other things alone in your room until you leave for Scotland or until you amend your demeanour." Having delivered her message, Flora flounced off again and bounded down the stairs.

She encountered Maisie as she reached the bottom of the stairs. "Maisie, please arrange for Memsahib Sarah's meals to be delivered to her room until further notice. And, Maisie, I suggest you don't pay her too much attention for the next little while, not until she develops some manners and learns to behave properly."

PART 2

Scotland 1840

Chapter 15

A Different Life

It was mid-1840 when Miss Crowther handed Sarah over to her grandmother waiting on the dock at Glasgow. Despite Miss Crowther's best efforts to help Sarah see the potential of her new life in Scotland, Sarah remained hostile to the whole idea.

Leaving Sarah to finish packing and tidying their cabin, Miss Crowther rushed from the ship for a quick word with Mary McGowan before returning to collect Sarah.

"Ah, Mrs McGowan, it's good to see you again. I'll bring Sarah to you shortly, but I felt compelled to warn you she still does not favour this change. I apologise in advance, but I can't guarantee her behaviour will be acceptable. I must return to our cabin now as I only left her on the pretence of dealing with some paperwork."

A porter was collecting their luggage when Miss Crowther returned to their cabin. A sullen Sarah stood outside the door. Immediately the porter departed, Miss Crowther dragged Sarah inside.

"Young lady, I have put up with about as much of your nonsense as I can take. In a few minutes, we will make our way down the gangplank, and I will entrust you to your grandmother's care. The change to your life is not my fault, and nor is it your grandmother's. Neither of us deserves such disgraceful treatment. I have tolerated it as part of the job entrusted to me by your parents.

Your grandmother has no reason to accept the rubbish you have dealt me since we left India. And, as you will be spending your next few years in her care, I suggest you think carefully about how you behave in future. I suspect any bad behaviour now will severely impact your future life. Do you not understand any of that? I am not only disappointed in your behaviour, but also disgusted. Don't make your grandmother feel the same way. You may live to regret it. That's all I have to say, but I suggest you give it thought on our way down to the dock.

Stunned by Miss Crowther's words, Sarah managed no more than a nod when Miss Crowther added, "Right, shall we go now?"

Her message delivered, Miss Crowther strode off toward the gangplank. A little slow to realise what was happening, it took Sarah a few moments to rush after her chaperone. At the top of the gangplank, they paused to peer down at the dock. Miss Crowther made a show of searching for Mary McGowan in the crowd below.

"Look, there she is. There's your grandmother. Can you see her?

Of course, Sarah recognised her grandmother. Mary McGowan was the woman waving a fur muff at them. Pulling up the collar of her coat and holding it tightly about her neck, Sarah followed Miss Crowther off the ship and onto the dock.

Mary, tears streaming down her face, ran forward and wrapped Sarah in a tight embrace. Another woman emerged from the crowd and hurried to where the small group was clustered.

"Aunt Bess…! Oh, this is too much for me to take in," Sarah croaked. "I can't tell you how wonderful it is to see you both again."

While the two women fussed over Sarah and commented on how grown up she was, Miss Crowther went to supervise the luggage as it was unloaded from the ship. Bess rushed after her.

"That is my driver by the carriage over there. Point out your luggage, and he will load it… yours too, Miss Crowther. Tell him where you wish to be taken, and we will drop you there on our way home."

"It is most kind of you to offer, but I don't want to take you out of your way."

Bess was adamant about it and, as it turned out, they would pass Miss Crowther's address on their way home. "So, my dear, nobody is being put out by it. Just point out the luggage to the driver. We will be on our way as soon as it's loaded."

After bidding farewell to Miss Crowther when they dropped her off, it was on to Bess's big house and being fussed over by staff for the remainder of the day. Mary outlined the next stage of Sarah's life at dinner that night.

"You have been enrolled in Miss Faulkner's Finishing School for Young Ladies. You start tomorrow and should be well advanced by Christmas. You might have covered some of the material you will encounter through the efforts of your governess.

The broad-based year-long course equips a young woman of a certain station with the necessary knowledge before entering society. It covers manners, etiquette, languages, art, music, ballroom dancing, and appropriate dressing for various occasions."

"If I already have done some of these things, why do I need to undertake this course?"

"Regardless of what you have done in the past, it is not all you need to know. My job is to make sure you go out into the world well-equipped with such skills, some of which might not carry much importance in plantation life. Miss Faulkner's school offers you a wonderful opportunity, and it was no easy matter persuading her to take in one extra student. She only agreed as a special favour to me and her long-time friend, Aunt Bess. We hope you appreciate this opportunity."

Grandmother was right, Sarah told herself as she prepared for bed that night. I should be grateful for what everyone is doing for me, but I hadn't thought my new life would include returning to school. "But how else would I fill in my days?" she asked her pillow as she settled down for the first night of her new life.

*****

As she crawled into bed one night after four weeks of being 'finished' at Miss Faulkner's school, Sarah spent the brief time before sleep arrived reviewing her studies. While there were some subjects she did not enjoy and struggled to meet the teacher's expected outcomes, others she quite enjoyed.

Sarah was proving a better than average artist and, on a fine, warm day, she enjoyed nothing more than taking her easel outside to paint the garden and the surrounding landscape. French was another subject she did not think she would enjoy, but she excelled in it. Her rapid mastery of the language astounded both her teacher and Aunt Bess, who was fluent in French. How to behave and how to speak to whom were 'boring' aspects of the course. But Christmas was nigh, and that focused everyone's attention on another subject: dancing.

Miss Faulkner made sure her students understood the significance of the Festive Season: *Christmas was coming, and that meant balls and parties aplenty*. And balls and parties meant 'dancing' and lots of it on many nights. So the students spent many hours learning the dances they would be expected to know on such occasions, and the appropriate etiquette expected of them at such functions.

Mary's focus was on appropriate attire for the various functions Sarah would attend. There needed to be a very special 'introduction to society' gown and at least one more for subsequent occasions. Time was running out. Mary knew she would pay a premium for the work and almost have to beg the seamstress to make the outfits in time for the round of social occasions.

While they were 'her' gowns, Sarah soon learned she had little say in their fabric or design. It was a case of Mary and the seamstress conferring and fussing over such details. Sarah learned how the gown would look as its production progressed. She also learned there was to be a 'first big occasion' which required a 'special' gown. What that meant was a mystery to Sarah, but all she could do was to go along with whatever was required of her – and that seemed to involve endless boring fittings.

Although she didn't share her thoughts, in Sarah's opinion, the 'special' gown was all right and would be easy to wear. It was an all-white creation in the French empire line style in vogue now for some years. Featuring a high waistline, tight short sleeves, and long tubular skirt, the gown's only decorative feature was a pattern worked in gold thread around the hem.

Sarah was less impressed with the second gown Mary commissioned – a lot less impressed. It was created from many yards of some pale green, light – almost film-like – fabric, and featured a heavily boned long bodice ending in a peak well below the waistline. Its short puffed sleeves were slashed to reveal their different coloured lining fabric. The voluminous shirt was made from yards of fabric pleated in some intricate way to produce its required bell shape.

Apart from the boned bodice barely allowing her to breathe, the most alarming feature of the gown was its off-the-shoulder style. Her protests about the bare-shouldered look met with disdain from the seamstress and Mary.

"This gown is in the latest style now taking Paris by storm. In it, you will be the belle of the ball," the seamstress told her, and Mary echoed her comments.

It was obvious there was no point in making any further fuss, but Sarah was determined to establish what her grandmother's planned social calendar held for her. After dinner that night was an ideal opportunity for the conversation Sarah wanted to have. And, later, she would wish she hadn't.

Aunt Bess and Mary couldn't conceal their excitement as they outlined the social occasions Sarah would attend over the December-January period. With careful questioning, she soon realised the same people appeared to be attending most, if not all, of the events Mary listed. Mary and Bess seemed particularly excited about the first of those occasions: Douglas Wallace's Christmas ball to be held the week before Christmas.

"Who is Douglas Wallace, and why would I be invited to his ball?" Sarah demanded. "How does he know I even exist? Anyway, I don't remember receiving an invitation, so I couldn't have accepted it."

"Don't be silly, girl," Mary rebuked her. "Surely you have covered such matters in your classes. Of course, you didn't receive a direct invitation. It would have been inappropriate for Mr Wallace to invite you in that way. As my granddaughter and ward, you are included in my invitation, which I accepted on behalf of both of us. Although I think it unnecessary, I would point out you are under age and all the rules regarding minority apply. Apart from that, it would have been inappropriate to issue you an invitation when you have yet to enter society. This ball will mark that occasion."

"Is that why I'm to wear that virginal white gown on which the seamstress is presently completing the gold embroidery? ... Because it is to be my 'first time?'"

"That is a deplorable thing to say!" Mary snapped. "And not words or thought fit for a young lady. Despite everyone's best efforts so far, Sarah, you appear to have learned nothing about manners or how to behave in general. Here is something you need to think about, and I mean think long and hard about:

Such behaviour as you have displayed on numerous occasions since your arrival is rude and unacceptable. In the past, it might have been tolerated, even overlooked by your parents, but it will no longer be tolerated here. My job is to turn you into the young lady your parents wish you to be and to introduce you into society so you have every chance of making a good future life for yourself. I do not intend to fail this task. My advice is to stop acting like a spoilt four-year-old child and start acting like the grown-up you are to become. A warning comes with this advice: if you do not amend your ways, life here in Glasgow will become difficult for you, and returning to India because you don't like it here is not an option.

Sarah bolted up to her room to sulk for the rest of the evening. During the night, she appeared to give Mary's words some thought as she had been urged to do.

A contrite Sarah appeared for breakfast the next morning to apologise to both Mary and Bess. After stressing how grateful she was for all they had done for her and promising to adopt a more acceptable demeanour in future, she attempted to explain her recent behaviour.

"None of this was my idea. I wasn't consulted. Nobody asked me if this was the future I wanted for myself. I was perfectly happy on the plantation and, like my mother before me, I'm sure there would have been opportunity to meet an ideal husband had I remained there. All my friends are there. All the people I know and love are there. I miss them, all of them, and I feel lonely here. Oh, I'm not suggesting you are not good company, but I need the company of young people, and to be able to live a young person's life."

Bess stepped in before Mary could respond. "I'm sure at some stage of our lives, everyone in this room has felt that way. The good news is, we were not allowed to go our own way and, back then, 'going our own way' before we were adults would have been nothing short of folly. Both your grandmother and I have had wonderful full lives. That would not have been possible had we been allowed to do as we pleased when we were teenagers."

After Bess's comments, Mary took a moment before speaking to rethink her intended response. Her contribution then took the conversation along a different line.

"I heard what you told me, and it made sense. Since you arrived, you have been afforded little time to settle in and get to know people. But I can't help thinking about the other girls attending Ms Faulkner's school. Isn't there anyone amongst your classmates you've become friendly with?"

"Well, yes, I suppose I have become friendly with one of the girls. Her name is Jane McCabe. She also lives with her grandmother here in Glasgow and has done so since she was quite young. I understand her parents are overseas somewhere, and it was safer to send Jane back here to live."

"Of course… Yes, I know Mrs McCabe. We serve on a couple of committees together. She is a lovely lady and an astute business woman. Her son and his wife are either in the Caribbean or the Americas, running the family's plantation. I've met Jane and see her at kirk."

"Perhaps we could invite Jane to tea. What do you think, Bess? Could you arrange that with Mrs McCabe?" Mary suggested.

"Having Jane come to tea would be great, but you don't need to arrange it through her grandmother. Jane manages her own social life. She is free to go almost wherever she likes. Of course, Mrs McCabe's maid, or secretary or whatever she is, always accompanies her. She isn't allowed out on her own."

"That sounds unbelievable," Mary exclaimed. "How old is Jane?"

"She's just a couple of months older than I am. Most of the girls at the school are allowed the same freedom. Jane's grandmother doesn't go with her for ball gown fittings. The maid goes with her, and they go shopping afterwards. I think the woman who goes with Jane is in her late twenties, so quite close to Jane's age," Sarah said with a triumphant toss of her head.

"Is this correct?" Mary asked Bess. "You know Mrs McCabe. Is she likely to allow this?"

"I'm afeared times have changed since we were young girls, Mary. And yes, I assess Maude McCabe to be a modern thinker." Bess looked almost apologetic as she answered.

Bess had no doubt Mary would struggle to accept today's liberal approach to bringing up young girls, but Maude McCabe was on the boards of a couple of leading girls' schools and would be aware of current trends. If she were honest, Bess would admit she found Mary's approach to looking after her granddaughter a bit archaic. She dared voice her opinion – but only after Sarah left them alone.

"Mary, you may tell me it is none of my business, but I think you are a bit too protective – a bit too 'old-fashioned' – in your guardianship of Sarah." Bess saw Mary stiffen as she delivered her bombshell. She continued despite the blast she expected.

"I agree there remains a need to protect our young women from some of the things life might throw at them, but the world has changed. Today's challenge for today's parents and guardians is to ensure their charges are adequately equipped to take their place – and perhaps make their mark– on an ever-changing world stage. You will do more harm than good if you insist on cossetting Sarah too much.

She is an intelligent and capable young woman who is likely to make a good marriage in the future. She needs to have experienced life sufficiently to make a good choice when the time comes, and she will need your support transitioning to married life."

"Are you suggesting I should 'loose the reins' a little?"

"Aye, Mary, it is what I'm suggesting. You have a golden opportunity to be a part of Sarah's life as she moves to the next phase of it. …Better she remembers you fondly for allowing her to gain the knowledge and experience to make the best decisions for her future."

Mary admitted she wasn't comfortable with the advice, but accepted it was something she should devote some thought to before it was too late. As Mary made her way up to her room, she decided to endeavour to sit down with Mrs Maude McCabe to update her thinking on bringing up young women.

*****

Although she wasn't immediately aware of it, Sarah's life underwent a subtle change over the next couple of weeks. Mary did not accompany her when she went for the final fittings of her ball gowns. Instead, Jane and her chaperone collected Sarah and they visited the seamstress together.

It proved a rewarding experience. Jane went into raptures over both Sarah's gowns before asking about her slippers to match.

"What slippers…? What are you talking about?" Sarah stammered. "Of course, I have shoes to wear, but what are these slippers you're talking about?"

"Oh, Sarah, I see I need to take you in hand. You can't wear your normal boots with gowns such as these. They need special satin slippers to peep out from under those skirts. Has your grandmother not mentioned having matching shoes made for you?"

A confused Sarah could only shake her head.

"Right then… you have an allowance, don't you?" Jane asked, and Sarah nodded. "Good. As soon as we finish with these fittings, I'll take you to my bootmaker. Ask the seamstress for a scrap of material from each gown, so the bootmaker will know the colour and fabric to use for the slippers."

After her routine visit to her business office, Bess returned home to find Mary pacing the sitting room. The look on Mary's face made Bess catch her breath.

"What disaster has occurred? Quickly, Mary, tell me what has happened."

"I've made a serious error of judgment; that's what has happened. I allowed Sarah to go for her fittings with Jane and the chaperone, and she still has not returned. I knew leaving the house without me was wrong, but I allowed it to happen anyway. Where can she possibly be after all this time?"

"For goodness sake, Mary, *dinna fash* yourself like this. Their chaperone is a capable, level-headed woman. She will not allow the girls to do anything silly. But, Mary, they are young women. Young women like shopping. Like as not, they went into town after finishing with the seamstress."

While she knew everything Bess said was true, *knowing* it and *accepting* it was different. What would Flora think if something had happened to her daughter? One thing was sure: she would never forgive Mary for allowing it to happen. Mary's dark thoughts were interrupted when Bess announced, "Come now, Mary. Tea is served."

They had not long sat down with a large pot of tea when Bess heard a carriage pull up and rushed out to meet it. She returned a couple of minutes later.

"Look what I found outside," Bess said as she returned to Mary. "Let me introduce you to my guests… I thought it might be nice if they joined us for tea after their busy morning."

With that, Bess ushered in Sarah, Jane and their chaperone. "Thank you, tea would be wonderful right now," Jane told Bess.

"Right, now what exciting things have you done this morning," Bess demanded. "Come on; tell us about it to help brighten our lives."

"Oh, grandmother, I have had the most amazing time," Sarah gushed. "I can't wait to tell you all about it."

"We can't wait to hear all about it, can we, Mary?" Bess replied… and, with raised eyebrows, she gave Mary a knowing nod instead of a verbal I-told-you-so.

Chapter 16

The Social Scene

Sarah stood admiring herself in the full-length mirror, any recollection of her earlier 'virginal' comment now erased from memory. She murmured, "So this is what grown-up looks like."

Her simple white empire-line dress fell gracefully to allow just the toes of her white satin slippers to peep out from under its hemline. A couple of white artificial roses tucked into her upswept hair, and a small white satin purse dangling from a ribbon around her wrist completed the image in the mirror.

A light tap on her bedroom door ended her few moments of quiet introspection.

"May I come in?" Mary asked as she poked her head around the half-open door.

"Of course, come in."

"And me too," Bess chorused as she followed Mary into the room.

"What do you think?" Sarah asked her audience as she executed a dainty pirouette. "Is this acceptable for tonight's ball?"

Tears streamed down Mary's face as she attempted to answer, but she was so choked up, the words didn't come.

"You look beautiful, my dear," Bess replied instead. "Is this the same little lass who lived here with her parents all those years ago? My, oh my, what a stunning young woman you have become."

When Mary finally found her voice again, her heartfelt comment almost reduced Sarah to tears. "How I wish your mother were here to see her daughter now. It is an image – a moment – no mother should be denied."

Minutes later, a nervous Sarah with Mary and Bess were on their way to the grand home of Douglas Wallace for his Yuletide ball. Many were already there, and the array of finery on display was stunning. Sarah cast an eye down over her gown that she had thought amazing so recently and now wondered whether it was up to standard for the event.

After being announced, the trio entered the Wallace mansion's grand ballroom. Sarah stuck close to Mary, barely lifting her eyes as they wove through the crowd. Although she followed resolutely without a murmur, Sarah wanted to shout, "Where are we going? Why can't we find a quiet spot and stand there for a few moments?"

Then a familiar voice was calling her name. "Sarah, Sarah, you have arrived. When you weren't here, I thought something might have happened, or you had pulled out. I'm glad you are here now though." Jane was yelling as she made her way through the noisy crowd to meet Sarah.

"Come; let me introduce you to a few of the younger generation so you don't have to hang about with the oldies all night." Then, almost as an afterthought, she added, "Good evening Mrs McGowan. I'm just borrowing your granddaughter for a while to introduce her to some of the other girls." Before Mary could utter a word, Jane dragged Sarah into the crowd.

Bess chuckled. "That one has you pegged, Mrs McGowan. She knew better than to allow you time to object. Now you can relax. Sarah will have a great evening and make new friends, something she has had little chance to do since arriving in Glasgow."

History would show one of the 'new friends' Sarah made that night was their host's elder son, Robert Wallace.

As Sarah and Jane wove their way through a particularly rowdy group of young men, one member detached himself from the group and stepped out in front of Jane.

"Good evening, Miss McCabe. It seems forever since we last spoke … and who is this gorgeous creature with you tonight? I don't believe we've been introduced."

"Robert…," Jane shrieked. "It's good to see you again. When did you return?"

"Two days ago…." Then, placing his hand to hide his lips, he added in a mock whisper, "I hoped I would be too late for this *ceilidh,* but it appears the gods had other ideas. Still, there are compensations to be had." He slid his eyes in Sarah's direction as he finished speaking.

Giggling, Jane made the sought-after introduction and explained, "I've known Robert since we were both children living in the Caribbean, so we go back a long way. Robert still lives there on the family's plantation." Then turning to Robert, she asked, "Will you stay long in Glasgow this time?"

"I'm not sure. It rather depends on what father has in mind for me to do while I am here, but I am sure it will be at least two or three months."

Further conversation was curtailed when the musicians struck a loud chord to gain everyone's attention. It heralded Mr Douglas Wallace's arrival on the stage with the band. His speech of welcome mercifully was short and to the point. After thanking everyone for attending, he wished everyone a pleasant evening and a Merry Christmas before being replaced on the stage by another gentleman who appeared to be the Master of Ceremonies for the evening.

In a loud, strident voice, he announced, "Gentlemen, take your partners for…."

The musicians began playing a familiar tune, and Robert focused his most disarming smile on Sarah. "Miss Erskine, would you do me the honour, please?" he asked as he offered her his arm.

It was the start of what would later be a blur of memories of dancing, laughing, talking and meeting new people. Above all, Sarah would remember it as *a wonderful night.*

Towards the end of the evening, Mary was surprised when she heard Bess murmur, "My, my; that's the fifth dance for the night."

"What are you on about, Bess?" a confused Mary demanded.

"Have you not been watching? Oh, I am surprised at you. I thought you were more attentive – like a hawk watches its prey attentive." The look on Mary's face told Bess Mary was short on patience. "As you don't seem to have noticed, that is the fifth dance Mr Robert Wallace has had with our Sarah. And, I would say, he looks a touch smitten."

"Smitten? With Sarah… no, she is far too young for such nonsense."

"We shall see about that."

Alerted to a possible situation, Mary's eyes never left Sarah for the remainder of the evening. Although nothing untoward occurred to bring Mary rushing to Sarah's side, Mary noted Robert Wallace never strayed more than a couple of paces away from her granddaughter.

For the rest of the night, the question foremost in Mary's mind was whether this was something she should worry about. As she drifted off to sleep, Mary told herself it was only one evening. Everything had been innocent enough. And it was kind of young Mr Wallace to help make Sarah feel welcome and not isolated among strangers. When Mary shared her thoughts on the matter with Bess the following day, Bess somehow managed to suppress her laughter and simply nodded in false agreement with Mary.

The Wallace ball was only the start of a long round of social events that continued to almost the end of January. The three women in Bess's house found their calendars well-marked after receiving a stream of invitations to various events, from morning teas to more lavish occasions. The next major event was the Lord Provost of Glasgow's annual Christmas Eve ball.

Sarah would wear her new pale green ball gown to the event, but several other major events to which they were invited were scheduled in the weeks after Christmas. As the invitations flowed in, Mary confided to Bess that Sarah couldn't be expected to wear the same gown to all of them. More gowns were required and quickly. Between them, the two women hatched a plan to deal with the perceived situation within the limited timeframe.

Of course, they would continue to engage the same seamstress who made Sarah's first two gowns. She would be asked to produce one more gown as quickly as possible. Another seamstress, whom Bess had discovered recently and had proved more than competent, would be asked to create another of the required gowns.

Their plan would see Sarah spending some time just about every day visiting one seamstress or another. But, as Mary told Bess over a pre-dinner drink a week later, "Introducing a young woman into Glasgow society is an expensive and time-consuming undertaking."

"Ball gowns were never a cheap acquisition," Bess admitted, "but Sarah's collection will see her appropriately attired for some time to come."

The Lord Provost's ball was Glasgow's gala occasion of the year. Although still a little uncomfortable about displaying so much bare flesh for the first time in her pale green off-the-shoulder gown, Sarah was stunned by the image smiling back at her from her mirror.

Her nervousness almost overwhelmed her when they arrived at the ball. For a brief moment, Sarah wondered if she might manage to dive back into the carriage and be taken home again. Her two 'chaperones' prevented such nonsense by taking her by the arms and hurrying her into the hall.

"It was the dress that was the problem," she later told Jane. "I felt as though I was half undressed." Jane dissolved into laughter. "Yes, yes, I know it was ridiculous. It only lasted until we were inside the hall, and I saw what everyone else was wearing. There were bare shoulders – young bare shoulders – everywhere."

"And of course, young Mr Wallace was there again to help take your mind off your shoulders," Jane teased her. "How many dances did you have with him that night?"

"Uhmm… well, quite a lot, I think."

"Oh, I think Robert Wallace managed to snare all but a couple of the dances. You could do a lot worse than that one, you know. How do you feel about the young man?"

"Jane, that's a ridiculous thing to suggest. I've only met him twice. Although I admit, he is a personable enough young man, and he does know how to flatter a girl."

"Not bad looking either," Jane added with a wicked grin.

*****

The social events rolled on through January and saw all Sarah's gowns pressed into service on more than one occasion, including the original plain white one. After its first wearing, that one underwent some enhancement. Large, handmade roses adorned each puffed sleeve, while others were strategically placed throughout the gold embroidered design at the hemline. It was further enhanced by a bright red velvet ribbon added to the empire line. It ended at the centre front in a large flat bow with tails that trailed a long way down the skirt.

It did not go unnoticed by Mary or Bess that young Mr Wallace seemed to attend all the same events and was particularly attentive to Sarah.

"Bess, what do you know about Robert Wallace?" Mary asked over tea one afternoon. "I know he comes from a substantial family, but what about the lad himself?"

"I wouldn't become too concerned about his attention just yet. Robert runs the family's plantations in the Caribbean and isn't often seen in Glasgow these days. I've heard his visit on this occasion is to deal with some matters relating to the family's business interests. As the eldest son, he needs to be informed and involved in whatever happens in that regard, especially now his father, Douglas Wallace, is getting on a bit and might be looking to hand over the reins soon."

"I just hope his intentions are honourable while he is here in Glasgow, for however long that might be. Do we know how old he is?"

"There was a lavish 21st birthday party a couple of years ago, so I suppose he would be about 23 or 24."

"He doesn't have a wife tucked away somewhere in the Caribbean, does he?"

"Not to the best of my knowledge... no, not an official one anyway."

"That is not the most reassuring information. Nevertheless, I fear I should alert Sarah's parents to the possibility of a youthful infatuation."

"Hers or his…?" Bess asked with a giggle. "Mary, were you never young, or perhaps I should ask if you even remember being young once. If you feel you must mention your wild suppositions to Sarah's parents, then you must do so, but please don't apply false 'fact' to whatever you tell them. Nothing can be gained from concerning them about something that might be nothing more than figments of two old women's imaginations."

Regardless of Bess's comments, Mary felt obliged to mention it to Flora, and was surprised by the response she received by return mail:

As I recall, the Wallace family are a well-placed entity in Glasgow and has well-managed enterprises in both Glasgow and the Caribbean. Sarah is now of marriageable age and could do a lot worse than Robert Wallace, if the situation should develop along those lines. Should such eventuate, please advise as soon as possible so we can arrange to be in Glasgow for the event.

Some of Mary's questions were answered a couple of weeks later when Bess received an invitation for her, Mary and Sarah to join the Wallace family for dinner. The two women went to great lengths to ensure Sarah's outfit on the night was the most appropriate possible.

Dinner was a wonderful occasion with interesting conversation, plenty of laughter, and not a hint of pretension on anyone's part. And the young Mr Wallace, who would be home for most of the year to deal with various business matters, appeared never to take his eyes off Sarah. All the while, Sarah sat with a shy smile plastered on her face and blushed whenever she saw him watching her.

Over a night cap after Sarah had gone to bed, Bess suggested, "Mary, if you haven't mentioned young Mr Robert Wallace to Sarah's parents yet, I would recommend you do so. I believe the time is right now to speak with some authority on the matter – as opposed to being able to air mere suppositions."

About a week later, Bess received a note from Robert Wallace. He begged her indulgence in a meeting with him, at her office preferably, to seek her advice on a personal matter. Bess dispatched one of her staff with an immediate reply: she would be pleased to receive him at her office in the city at ten o'clock the next morning. Then, it was all Bess could do to wait patiently until the appointed time for their meeting.

While Robert didn't indicate the matter to be discussed other than it was personal, Bess was intrigued. It was not impossible to imagine it might be about Sarah. If that were the case, should Bess alert Mary to the meeting? Common sense finally prevailed after having sacrificed sleep in considering the question. In the end, Bess decided to err on the side of caution. What if it had nothing to do with Sarah? She would worry Mary for nothing. But, the main reason she elected not to mention the meeting to Mary was because Mary would also demand to be in attendance, and Bess was not about to betray Robert's confidence in that way.

Next morning, as Bess prepared to go to her office, Mary suggested she might accompany Bess as she had nothing better to do that day. It took some quick thinking and something a bit removed from the truth to persuade Mary to find something else to occupy her time.

Bess arrived nervous and early for their meeting. Robert arrived on time and appeared equally nervous. After the usual pleasantries, Bess took charge.

"Well, Mr Wallace, you requested this meeting, so perhaps we should discuss whatever it was that brought you to speak to me."

"I'm aware what I have to ask you may seem a little indelicate. The problem that confounds me at the moment is who to talk to as Sarah Erskine's official guardian, whether that be her grandmother or her parents."

"Perhaps the answer to that depends on what you wish to speak about."

"Ah, yes, I suppose that is the case. I wish to ask for Sarah's hand in marriage. And I know that, under normal circumstances, I would approach her father directly for his permission to marry his daughter, but does that still apply? I mean, now that her grandmother appears to be Sarah's guardian while she resides in Glasgow, is it Mrs McGowan I should approach?"

"Aye, I do see your dilemma. What does Sarah say on this matter? I assume I am correct in thinking you have discussed marriage with her … though goodness knows when you have had time enough alone to do so."

"Of course, we have discussed it, and she has agreed to marry me. My problem now is how to proceed."

"Hmm… perhaps due to the unusual nature of the situation, an approach to Mrs McGowan in the first instance might be in order. Mind you, I can't guarantee she will feel sufficiently authorised to grant such approval. Nevertheless, as you say, Mrs McGowan is Sarah's guardian while she is in Glasgow. Speak to her first, and then we shall see where it goes. Of course, I'm sure you are aware that, should she insist you obtain Sarah's father's permission, the process will be lengthy.

As an aside to your main concern, may I ask where you envisaged the marriage might take place?"

"Here in Glasgow… Why do you ask? Where else might we be married?"

"Sarah might prefer to be married at home – a long way from Glasgow. And that would bring with it a whole host of other complications to consider. Has Sarah given any firm indication of her preference?"

"Well, we have discussed the matter, and she always speaks of the wedding as being here in Glasgow."

"Right then, Mr Wallace, it appears your next move is to approach Mrs McGowan regarding Sarah's hand in marriage, and the sooner, the better. To help facilitate the matter, I'm inviting you to tea tomorrow afternoon. Sarah and I will likely be in attendance but, as soon as we have taken tea, I shall spirit Sarah away to allow you to speak with Mrs McGowan privately. Shall we say four o'clock?"

As she rode home after meeting with Robert Wallace, Bess thought aloud in the empty carriage, "What have I done? Have I set the young lad on the right path or given him false hope? Too late to worry about it now. First things first, I need to work on Mary to ensure the lad at least receives a civil hearing."

Bess needed every minute of the more than 24 hours she had to work on Mary before Robert arrived. Although reluctant to see it any other way, Mary eventually conceded that Sarah was old enough to marry and seemed to have chosen Robert Wallace. As the time for Mary and Robert's meeting approached, Bess admitted later she was almost reduced to praying Mary wouldn't revert to her original thinking at the last minute.

Then Robert arrived and tea was served. Afternoon tea proved a formal and stilted affair. Once tea was over, Bess suggested she and Sarah might take a stroll in the garden. Sarah was having none of it. She was determined to be a part of the subsequent meeting.

While the staff cleared away, Mary dealt with the Sarah situation. Taking Sarah aside, Mary delivered a few stern words that left Sarah in no doubt that she would be going outside with Bess. The matter dealt with, Mary returned to the others who had chatted amiably in her absence and announced, "Bess, Sarah wonders if you might like to take a stroll in the garden with her."

Problem solved. As Bess and Sarah left the room, Mary focused on Robert.

"Now, Mr Wallace, what brings you here to talk to me today?"

Long before the meeting ended, Bess and Sarah had enjoyed as much of the garden as they could handle for one day, and Bess, with a grumbling Sarah in tow, retired to the library to await further developments, or at least for Mary to join them there.

After whiling away more than half an hour reading a book without absorbing any of its contents, Sarah jumped in surprise when Mary and Robert appeared in the library doorway.

"Mr Wallace is about to leave. I've brought him along to say goodbye," Mary announced.

Formal goodbyes were said all round, but Bess noted Robert could barely hide his excitement or control his smile when he spoke to Sarah. The grumbling and sulking were a thing of the past as a beaming Sarah joined the other women to wave Robert on his way. But, given her earlier behaviour, Mary made her wait until after dinner before discussing the reason for Robert's visit.

"Mr Wallace has asked for your hand in marriage. What are your thoughts on the matter? Are you inclined to accept his proposal?"

"Yes, oh yes. Please say you gave approval for us to marry."

"I hope you realise this is a most irregular situation. Under normal conditions, Mr Wallace would need your father's approval. Nevertheless, as our circumstances are different, I am empowered to grant approval for the marriage. Of course, since meeting with Mr Wallace, I have penned a note to your parents. You must remember your father does have the right to veto the marriage if he sees just cause."

Sarah flared in response. "I'll elope if he does!" Mary gave her a hard look. "I'm sorry. I didn't mean that. It's just that I would be broken-hearted if he did intervene to prevent my marrying Robert."

"Well, on the assumption he won't veto it, we have a lot to do if you are to be married soon after Christmas." Sarah rushed over, threw her arms around her grandmother, and thanked her before both women wiped away tears of joy.

The next few months flew past in a blur. Apart from having to arrange the actual wedding event, there was the invitation list to develop and invitations to be produced. The wedding's coinciding with Hogmanay shortened the invitation list considerably. Invitations would be sent only to family members and very close friends. The many others who would arrive after the wedding feast and enjoy the dancing until the clock struck midnight would be invited by Douglas Wallace to participate in his Hogmanay celebrations.

And there wasn't just Sarah's attire for her big day to organise. There was a whole wardrobe to prepare for her to take with her into her married life. Both Bess and Mary knew no matter how much attention they paid to every possible detail, there was likely to be more to do – and changes to be made – once Flora arrived in Glasgow… And Flora and Thomas would not arrive until the end of November.

Chapter 17

The Wedding

The date was set: December 31 – New Year's Eve – to coincide with the Wallace family's Hogmanay celebrations. The marriage would be celebrated in the Wallace family's small chapel on their estate.

Despite all the planning and monitoring of progress, December became a nightmare for most of Bess's household. The bride's mother required a new gown for the occasion, and insisted on checking all the arrangements already in place met with her approval. Predictably, some changes were made, and a few new initiatives added.

Thomas also needed a new outfit for the occasion. For him, visiting the tailor was an ideal opportunity to escape the house and the constant wedding hurly-burly. Douglas Wallace, the groom's father, aware of Thomas's situation, helped by frequently inviting Thomas to the Wallace house, and inviting Thomas to accompany him on an inspection of the Wallace empire's operations in Glasgow.

Sarah had assumed the wedding would allow her to meet her future husband's siblings. At a combined families' dinner a few days before Christmas, she learned Cameron and Cecile Wallace would not attend the wedding. Robert pointed out that, with his absence in Glasgow, his brother, Cameron, had to remain in the Caribbean to manage the family's plantations there, and his sister, Cecile, had to oversee the household staff.

After the dinner that night, as she lay in bed, Sarah reflected on all that had happened since Robert first sought her hand in marriage. Although Sarah had thought to be married at Christmas, Mary wasted no time in changing Sarah's thinking.

"Christmas is not a popular time for weddings in Scotland. There is no Christmas holiday, which means most people cannot get away to attend. Hogmanay, New Year's Eve, remains Scotland's most important festive occasion, even in 1841.

Although Queen Victoria might be fast making Christmas Day the important festive occasion in England, for Scots, Hogmanay is still almost the only time of the year when extended families have a few days to gather and enjoy the festivities."

She remembered Mary's final comment on the subject, a statement that allowed for no further discussion:

So, Sarah, you are to be married on 31 December 1841. It will coincide with Hogmanay and be a grand event with all of Glasgow's social elite in attendance. Our priority must be to give thought to your wedding gown. Of course, we must involve Aunt Bess in such planning. She is more familiar with the tradition and the latest fashions.

Over morning tea the next day, Sarah was summoned to join Mary and Bess in planning *The Wedding Gown*. Naïve as she was, Sarah was under the misguided impression it would be a simple matter, but the often heated debate raged for some time – between Mary and Bess. They appeared oblivious that it was Sarah's gown they were discussing … and, as she was at the table with them, she was available to contribute to the conversation.

Having been excluded from the debate for as long as she could suffer, Sarah slapped her hand hard on the table. The sound stunned her two companions into silence.

"I know you both mean well," Sarah began, "but this is *my* gown for *my* wedding. Do you think I might have some say in this matter?"

"Apologies, my dear," Bess said quietly. "You are quite right. We have been going on about the gown for far too long, when it is a simple matter requiring little if any, argument.

You are marrying into the Wallace family, one of the most affluent families in Scotland. We have more than sufficient resources to ensure your wedding gown reflects your class, and suitability to become a Wallace family member. A coloured gown would suggest we could not afford a better gown for you.

Therefore, you will have a white gown of the finest fabric available, and it shall have gold embellishment – nothing too ostentatious mind … just a little discreet gold embroidery perhaps. And, of course, it will follow the same style as your recent ball gowns. That style is still at the pinnacle of fashion.”

“She will need a cloak,” Mary threw in as soon as Bess finished speaking.

“Aye, she will. Perhaps a well-lined blue velvet cloak with a fur-trimmed hood…?” Bess suggested.

Sarah remembered being left speechless by the turnaround in the conversation that had the two women agreeing on what she should wear to her wedding. They still hadn’t sought any input on the matter from Sarah but, as she didn’t have any argument with their final decisions, she didn’t question anything they proposed. For weeks afterwards, Sarah seemed to spend most of her days with the seamstress, who suggested a slightly shorter hemline – better for trudging through the snow!

The idea of a short skirt did not appeal to Sarah, so she argued against it. But the matter was settled. She was much relieved to discover ‘shorter’ meant a hemline that stopped just below her ankles instead of allowing only her toes to peep out from under it. But what about that *trudging through the snow* comment? Why would anyone expect her to trudge through snow? Exhausted by everything to do with her gown, and reluctant to display her ignorance, Sarah elected not to question the mention of snow. She told herself it was unlikely to be of any consequence and not worth a second thought.

*****

While the lead-up to Christmas was frantic, by contrast, although it adhered to something of a traditional format, Christmas Day almost was a non-event. Of course, there was the usual attendance at the morning church service, followed by a more indulgent lunch than usual. But, between church and lunch, there was another tradition Bess instigated some years ago to honour. Stepping between Flora and her daughter as the family made their way to the carriage after church, Bess linked arms with the two women.

"Now ladies, we have an important task to do and, this year, you can help me and Mary attend to it. Every year on Christmas Day, I distribute fruit and sweet treats to the children in the poor house. Since her return to Glasgow, Mary has helped me, but this year, with the four of us on duty, it should be done in a flash." Then, Bess looked across at Thomas and added, "Thomas, you and John needn't worry. You have the privilege of staying cosy by the fire in the house while we are out and about distributing the gifts."

Once back at the house, the two male members of the party followed Bess's suggestion and settled in beside the fire in the library, while Bess took the women through to the kitchen.

"Those four baskets on the table are full of goodies for us to distribute to the children in the poorhouse. Three are full of fruit, and one with little sweet treats. If you each pick-up a basket, we will take them out to the carriage and be on our way. The sooner we have it done, the sooner we can thaw out in front of the fire along with the men folk."

The children rushed out to meet them as soon as they arrived. As the three women, each armed with a basket of fruit, handed each child a piece from one of their baskets, Sarah followed behind to give each child a sweet treat from her basket. No child missed out, and emptying the baskets did not take long. Then the women scrambled back into their carriage, thankful for its scant protection from the elements. But they were a subdued, gloomy group as they settled in for the ride back to Bess's house.

As soon as her teeth stopped chattering, Sarah drew in a long, audible breath before uttering in a broken voice, "What a pitiful existence. It seems obscene to return to what we have waiting for us after what we witnessed this morning."

"Aye, it is depressing," Bess agreed quietly. "But we should take some comfort in the knowledge that, for a brief moment or two, we brightened their little lives by giving them something they otherwise would never have."

"It will be wonderful to have people around the table to help lift our spirits over lunch. I am looking forward to having all my family included in those who might join us this year," Mary added with a sigh.

But there were only six people at the Christmas table that year. In past years, Bess often invited a friend or two, or her business manager, Michael, to join her for Christmas lunch. That year, only the residents of Bess's house sat at table.

Although staff had tried their best to create a joyous atmosphere throughout the house, their efforts either went unnoticed or fell flat as far as the family was concerned. Christmas Day 1841 was a distraction… an unwelcome pause in an otherwise hectic program … an imposed intrusion to be endured in the lead-up to the big event set down for a few days hence.

To compound the less than festive atmosphere in the dining room, Thomas insisted on proposing several toasts as lunch progressed – and as he became increasingly drunk. His final effort ended the meal when he spoke of it being the last Christmas the Erskine family would spend together. Later that week, their number would be reduced by one with the loss of their daughter, Sarah. By New Year, she would be a Wallace, and no longer be an Erskine, no longer a part of his family.

His words caused the women to reach for their lace handkerchiefs, and for Sarah to sob uncontrollably. Ignoring those around her and unable to contain her anger until a more appropriate moment, Flora acquainted Thomas with his lack of sensitivity and any other shortcomings she could remember. Within moments, the table was deserted, everyone having absconded to their respective rooms to deal with their emotions in private. The upshot was dinner that evening was a brief, heavy affair completely devoid of 'good cheer'.

For the first time in twelve months, Sarah questioned her relationship with Robert Wallace. It wasn't so much that she questioned marrying Robert. It was the fact she would be leaving the Erskine family – her family – behind her for good. Of course, she realised and relished the notion she would become Mrs Robert Wallace, but that night, it felt more like she would be losing her identity.

The more she thought about her forthcoming marriage and all that would follow, the greater her emotional turmoil became. If she hadn't cried herself to sleep, she might have spent the entire night awake. It was no surprise to Sarah that she looked a long way from her sparkling best the next morning. She expected comments at breakfast.

She needn't have worried. No one at the breakfast table that morning looked any better than Sarah. And, thanks to his insensitive comments that caused everyone a rough night, Thomas found himself virtually ostracised for the next couple of days.

All the women in Bess's household were busy leading up to Sarah's wedding on December 31. The flurry of activities helped them forget Thomas's *faux pas* at dinner on Christmas night. Nevertheless, keen to avoid the wrath of the 'petticoat brigade' again, Thomas kept his head down and concentrated on entertaining and keeping his young son, John, out of trouble.

*****

The days slipped by, and the last day of the year had arrived: New Year's Eve. The 31st day of December 1841 was not only Hogmanay but also Sarah and Robert's wedding day. While recent weather had been cold, the morning of the wedding was bitterly cold, with a heavy snowfall overnight and more expected sometime during the day.

Douglas Wallace had offered Sarah a room in his mansion to use as a dressing room before the ceremony. His offer was politely refused. Sarah, Flora, and Mary insisted the time before the ceremony should be spent at Bess's house. At about eleven o'clock that morning, Thomas and John, resplendent in their new outfits, were sent off to the Wallace residence to join others in awaiting the bride's arrival at the private chapel on the grounds of the estate where the marriage would take place at noon.

"Isn't it a bit early for Father to be on his way to the chapel?" Sarah asked as she heard his carriage pull away.

"Perhaps…," Bess replied with a knowing nod. "Better they are sitting in a chapel than getting in the way here. This morning is about 'women's business', and men would just be underfoot."

About half an hour after Thomas and John departed, a further two carriages drew up outside Bess's house. Their arrival caused a flurry of activity in the front room of the house as the women prepared to follow the men.

After the inevitable dose of motherly fussing and the shedding of a few tears, Mary, Bess and Flora donned their heavy outer garments, climbed aboard the first carriage, and set off for the Wallace estate. Sarah and her best friend and maid of honour, Jane, remained in the front room.

"If you plan to go through with this marriage, we do have to go out there and brave the elements," Jane chirped. "Shall we go… or are you having second thoughts?" Then after a giggle, she added, "I was going to say 'or have you gotten cold feet', but I realised 'cold feet' are the next episode in this story."

Jane was right. After carefully negotiating the slippery front steps and a few plodding steps through the snow to the carriage, the driver helped the two girls on board.

"My boots are sodden already, and my feet are freezing," Jane complained but received no comment from Sarah.

She swivelled around to look at Sarah and was disturbed by what she saw. Sarah had half turned to look over her shoulder at Bess's house, already fading into the distance. Jane also noticed the tears welled-up in Sarah's eyes. This would never do. As Sarah's maid of honour, she couldn't allow Sarah to arrive at her wedding red-eyed from crying. It was supposed to be a happy occasion.

"Don't look back," Jane said as she took Sarah's hand. "Today is not for feeling nostalgic. It's about being happy and excited. Focus on what is in front of you, where your exciting new life lies. Look straight ahead. Robert is waiting for you. There is no turning back now."

"Oh, I know, Jane, but it all seems such a big step now that it's happening. I will no longer live in that house with Grandmother and Aunt Bess. I will no longer be an Erskine. Everything from my entire life is being left behind. While I know everything you said is true, I feel a deep sense of loss right now."

Sarah sniffled a bit and gathered herself together a little before continuing. "Jane, you are a little older than me, already 20 on your last birthday. What about your future? Is there some eligible bachelor I am unaware of lurking in what lies ahead for you? And I suppose the big question is where you intend to spend your future: here in Glasgow with your grandmother or your parents on their plantation?"

"So far, there is no potential partner in my plans. Oh, I am aware my family have been making sure a few 'suitable' suitors come my way. While they might be suitable from my family's point of view, to date, none has excited me. As for where my future lies, I guess the answer is 'who knows', but I do know I don't plan to leave Glasgow in the foreseeable future."

There was no time to continue the discussion. The carriage was drawing to a halt in front of the Wallace mansion. Sarah shook her head in disbelief.

"Didn't anyone tell the driver the wedding was in the private chapel and not the big house?" Sarah squirmed forward on her seat to reach out and bang on the side of the carriage to attract the driver's attention.

"Sit back, Sarah," Jane ordered. "This is where we were supposed to be delivered. Are you not aware of how the event is to progress?"

"All I know is that it is usual for the bride's family to host the marriage of their daughter. But Douglas Wallace offered the use of the chapel when he learned Aunt Bess considered her ballroom inadequate for the occasion. Has there been a change of plans? Is the wedding not in the chapel? Are we to be married in the Wallace mansion instead?"

Before Jane could fully explain, the driver opened the carriage door after knocking politely to interrupt the girls' conversation. "Ladies, we have arrived. May I assist you to alight?" he asked.

As she hauled Sarah to her feet, Jane said, "Come on, Sarah, all will be revealed as we go along."

They found not only the driver, but also James, Robert's long-time friend and best man, also ready to help them alight. As they made their way carefully across the short distance from the carriage to the front steps of the house, Robert rushed out onto the top step.

"Perfect timing," he announced. "We have about another minute before we need to move off."

"But the carriage…," Sarah whispered to Jane as she watched their carriage depart from the house.

"Shush," Jane murmured. "All is well, as you will see when we gather on the top step."

After checking his fob watch, Robert told James, "Right; we are all here, and it is time. I'll tell him we are ready to go."

James spun on his heel and came back to stand beside Sarah. "Jane, if you stand in front of us, Robert will return in a moment. He has gone to organise the piper."

"What is happening?" Sarah demanded. "And why aren't we at the chapel?"

"Ah, I see you are unfamiliar with our Scottish tradition. Let me explain as concisely as possible in the time we have before we move off." Before continuing, he moved a little to one side and pointed to a pathway recently cleared of snow, but now wearing just this morning's flurry of snowflakes.

"The piper will lead us along that pathway, across the little bridge over the frozen ornamental pond, and onto the chapel. Robert and Jane will follow the piper, and you and I will fall in behind them. It is the Scottish tradition being observed to the letter. And, on our way back to the house after the marriage, we will cross the pond again to assure the newlyweds of good luck from having crossed water twice."

"We have to trudge through the snow?" Sarah couldn't believe she had heard correctly.

"Aye, but it is not far to go. And the skirl of the pipes will have your blood up so you won't notice the cold."

Although she doubted that would be the case, another development was far more concerning. As the piper's first notes reverberated through the house, Robert rushed back out to join them on the top step. But his interest wasn't in Sarah. Instead, he took Jane by the arm as the piper marched out and stood in front of Robert and Jane. There he paused for a moment before piping his way down the steps.

Robert waited until the piper had descended about three steps before he and Jane stepped down to follow him. As Robert moved off, James took Sarah's arm and moved to the edge of the top step.

"We will wait until they go down a couple of steps before we follow," he told Sarah.

"Why am I with you and not with Robert?" Sarah demanded. "It's nothing personal, James, but it is Robert I'm marrying."

"That's true, but you are not yet married. It would be most inappropriate for Robert to lead you into the chapel. He and Jane will be first into the chapel and take their respective places in front of the communion table while they wait for me to bring you to them. Now, please do shut up. It is time for us to follow the others. All will become clear as we go along."

The two couples followed the skirl of the piper like children following the Pied Piper. Sarah let go of James' arm to free both her hands to hold her skirt a little higher. Her boots were sodden long before they reached the little bridge over the pond, and her feet were frozen. She did not fancy having a cold, soggy, wet hem flapping around her ankles for the rest of the day.

And so, they followed the piper up to the chapel door. There, they paused for a few moments. The piper changed tunes before moving off again. James held Sarah back as Robert and Jane followed the piper into the chapel and up the aisle. Just before they reached the communion table, James nudged Sarah and took her arm.

"Now it is time for you to take your place for the big event."

The chapel was small and intimate. Its limited seating capacity meant only close family members and a handful of close friends were invited to witness the marriage. Nevertheless, the place was so packed, a handful of men had to stand at the back.

John, Sarah's brother, in his brand new livery, stood to attention to one side of the aisle and close to where Robert waited. With the most solemn dignity, he held before him a small satin cushion, which Sarah remembered seeing her grandmother making. As James led Sarah past John and on to her respective place in the line-up in front of the communion table, James snatched up the ring from John's satin cushion and shoved it in his waistcoat pocket. Duty done, John dived back onto the front pew beside his father.

While the minister cleared his throat and welcomed the congregation before commencing the main ceremony, Sarah's eyes were drawn to the unusual object on the communion table. The silver Quaich glinting in the flickering candle light intrigued her. But the minister had launched into the marriage ceremony, and Sarah's attention returned to why she stood in the chapel that day.

Then the simple ceremony was over. Robert and Sarah were pronounced man and wife, and the minister brought forward the silver two-handled Quaich containing a small measure of whiskey and handed it to Robert. After both sipped from the cup, it took only a few minutes for the formalities to be over. Sarah and Robert, arm in arm, led everyone out of the chapel to where a line of carriages was drawn up.

"Is one of those for us?" Sarah asked.

Robert laughed. "No, my love, we will return to the house the same way we left it. And, as we cross the pond again, we will cross water for the second time today to ensure our marriage is blessed with good luck."

For a brief moment, Sarah wondered whether ice constituted water but, knowing so little of Scottish customs, she elected not to query it.

Chapter 18

Stress and Tears

The pathway wasn't suited to heavy traffic so, one by one, the carriages collected their passengers and took the long circular driveway to the big house. The snow had deepened over the preceding couple of hours, so the trip to the house was slow and careful.

"Now I suggest we occupy a pew and wait in the chapel where it is a bit warmer," Robert announced. He ushered Sarah into the back pew on one side of the aisle while James guided Jane to the opposite bench.

"How long do we need to wait here?" Sarah asked as the minister approached them.

"Well, that depends on how long it takes to have everyone inside and settled, but it could be half an hour or so by how slow those carriages are moving."

While the minister chatted to them, James kept a watchful eye on proceedings at the big house. It was some time later before his first report.

"The last of the carriages is unloading its passengers now. There seems to be a degree of fuss and bother happening. Oh, I see… one of the elderly passengers, a woman, almost fell over in the snow."

Sarah went to stand, but Robert stretched out his arm to prevent it.

"I thought we would now be on our way to the big house once everyone else was there," she hissed at him.

"Good God, no. Most of them won't have made it into the ballroom yet. They will still be handing over personal belongings to staff on duty in the lobby and greeting people they haven't seen since last year. No, we need to allow them at least half an hour to be in the ballroom and find a drink before we even think of heading over to join them."

Although not keen on the thought of doing battle with the snow again, Sarah thought it might be preferred, if the alternative was another half hour of listening to the minister drone on about nothing of interest. Nevertheless, as wait she must, Sarah slumped back beside Robert on the pew and affixed a polite smile as the minister continued to drone on about what a year it had been in his parish.

Perhaps the freezing weather and snow were somehow at fault, but time seemed to pass slowly today. Long before James indicated half an hour had elapsed since the last passengers arrived at the big house, Sarah had begun to squirm and fidget with impatience. It was supposed to be her big day. Why did she have to sit there bored for so much of it?

At last, James announced he thought it time to make a move. After a couple of moments of consultation between the two men, they stood and extended a hand to their respective partners.

"Right then, let's away to the house to join the others," Robert announced.

"But look, other carriages are arriving now," Sarah observed. "Do we now have to wait for those people to go inside before we can leave here?"

"No. Further carriages will continue to arrive until sometime this evening. The later ones will not be wedding guests, merely other family friends and acquaintances invited to celebrate Hogmanay."

After Robert again thanked the Minister, the foursome fell into position with James and Jane behind Robert and his bride. The piper who led them to the chapel suddenly reappeared. The first Sarah knew of his presence were the opening notes he played as he took his place at the head of the short procession. Something dangling from James' right hand caught Sarah's attention.

"James, why do you have the silver Quaich? Shouldn't it remain in the chapel?" The others smirked before James replied.

"This is your Quaich, yours and Robert's. It doesn't belong in the chapel. It is yours to keep as a memento of today. I'll leave it over at the big house so it can be packed with your other belongings going to the Caribbean."

Then, with heads bent against the flurry of snowflakes swirling about them, the piper led them out onto the pathway – and the now ankle-deep snow. Sarah felt the dampness of the snow seep through her shoes and stockings, and the pain as her feet began to freeze. Still, they maintained sedate and dignified progress to the bridge over the ornamental pond, where they paused again for a few moments.

"This is your second crossing of water today, my friends," James reminded them. "So, your future happiness is now assured." But that wasn't the end of it.

Sarah hoped they would now be on their way again, on their way to somewhere warm and dry where her feet could thaw out. But her hopes were dashed when she realised Robert had other plans.

It was a surprise to all of the other three when Robert announced he had one more duty to perform. With exaggerated aplomb, he moved to stand beside the bridge's handrail. After digging in his pocket, he brandished a coin aloft, before tossing it in a shiny arc over the railing and onto the frozen pond below.

"There… Now we are doubly assured of good luck and a long and happy marriage," Robert told them.

"What's that all about?" James demanded. "I'm not aware of any such tradition."

"Perhaps that's not surprising. It's not a Scottish tradition. It's one I picked up overseas but has much the same intent as our tradition of crossing water twice today."

"Aye, well, if we are done with traditions, shall we continue to the big house?" James asked.

No reply was required. The moment James asked the question, the piper resumed playing. With heads once more bent against the snowflakes and cloaks held tightly around them, they followed the piper to the big house.

Again they paused for a few moments on the top step before entering. During those moments, there was much smoothing and straightening of clothing and shaking free snow accumulated on their trek. But, as they did so, the piper changed to a different tune and moved off into the hall. The couples fell into position behind him.

At the entrance to the ballroom, another brief pause occurred. In that short interval, Sarah observed a flurry of activity in the room.

"What's happening? There appear to be many more people than were at the chapel."

"Because the chapel is so small, only a select group of family and friends could pack into it. The rest of the wedding guests have joined us here. As evening falls, more people will arrive for Hogmanay celebrations tonight."

When activity in the ballroom ceased, the piper and his entourage moved forward. They marched the length of the room to the top table at the far end. Sarah realised the activity she had witnessed earlier was the guests moving out of the way to provide the bridal party with a clear passage to the table. The guests, who had socialised while awaiting the wedding party's arrival, now formed two groups, one along each side of the ballroom, to create a clear central passage through the room.

Platters of oatcakes already adorned all the tables. Then, once everyone settled at the tables and the requisite few official words were said, the rest of the wedding feast came out. Mini beef parcels, pieces of haggis, bowls of taties and neeps, were placed on tables, and eating began.

Sarah's boned and tightly fitted gown soon warned her no more than a few judiciously selected morsels were all she should enjoy – if she wished to continue to breathe. From her vantage point at the top table, she observed most of the guests suffered no such restriction. And the eating –accompanied by whiskey and rum –continued for some time. When the platters were empty, all appetites appeared satiated, and no guest appeared in danger of starvation, the party developed into a loud and somewhat boisterous affair.

After a few more speeches, Sarah thought all traditions had been honoured, and she could relax and enjoy the remainder of the evening. Her assumption was premature and wrong. One last tradition remained.

The musicians, grouped off to one side of the top table and silent until then, came to life and struck up a lively tune.

"It's time for the Grand March, my dear," Robert whispered as he bounced up off his chair. Then, extending his hand, he bowed to Sarah. "Shall we, Mrs Wallace?"

With suitable dignity and aplomb, Sarah allowed herself to be led out to the centre of the ballroom… and the dancing began. After the bridal couple twirled around for a few moments, their attendants, James and Jane, joined them on the floor. Both sets of in-laws soon followed. A few moments later, it became a free-for-all as the rest of the guests chose their partners and made their way onto the floor.

All wedding-related traditions dealt with, Sarah relaxed. With the 'stuff of weddings' over, the arrival of more guests heralded the start of Hogmanay celebrations – and with plenty food and drink to help them flow smoothly.

Dancing, eating and drinking continued with the only quieter moments for the arrival of the haggis. After it was piped into the room and the Address to the Haggis delivered, the rowdy good time resumed until the clock was counted down to midnight. A deafening cheer went up as the clock struck twelve. It was silenced when loud banging on the front door broke through the noise of the party.

"Pray, answer the door, if you will," Douglas Wallace commanded a footman conveniently waiting by the front door.

A well rugged-up young man entered. Another loud cheer went up as he removed his head covering to display a mop of unruly black locks that matched his beard and moustache.

"What's that all about?" Sarah whispered to Robert. "Who is the visitor? By the way everyone cheered him, I assume he is someone important."

"Oh, I have no idea who he is, but he is important." Robert saw the confused look spread across Sarah's face and rushed on to explain. "Do you not believe in *First Footing*?"

"I've no idea what you are talking about," she replied more tartly than she intended.

"Aah, I see. Well, a dark-haired man crossing your threshold soon after the start of the New Year ensures good luck for the whole of the coming year."

"So, is he a friend of yours who I am yet to meet?"

"Good Heavens, no... it is important that he be a stranger. The head of our household staff would have gone out and found an acceptable stranger for the role. After he downs his dram of whiskey, he will receive his shilling as he leaves, his duty well done."

"Do we also have to find a dark-haired stranger to First Foot our threshold to bring us good luck for the year?"

"Might be a bit difficult at the moment... as we don't have a threshold for anyone to cross. We will have to borrow some of the Wallace family's luck to take to our threshold in the Caribbean."

"Of course, how silly of me. But, Robert, will we not have our own threshold later tonight? I mean, you're not planning to spend tonight in the big house, are you?"

"No, we certainly are not spending the night here. In fact, it is time for us to quietly slip away and allow the rest of this mob to get drunk without us."

Holding hands, the couple wove through the crowd to the front door. There James and Jane waited with the couple's cloaks ready for them to grab on their way out to a carriage waiting at the foot of the stairs.

"Right to go then, Sir?" the driver asked as Robert helped his wife on board.

"Yes, thanks. Let's be away from here before anyone misses us."

"Where are we to spend the night, Robert?" Sarah whispered. "Wherever it is, I'm pleased it is not in the big house with all those other people who look like they might party until dawn."

Robert chuckled. "Good God, I wouldn't dare risk spending the night there. We would be sure to have unwelcome visitors at some point during the night. No, we will spend tonight and the rest of our time until we board our ship in the estate's gillie's cottage."

"Won't having us there be inconvenient for him? Or have we turned him out of his cottage for the next several days?"

"We no longer employ a gillie here on this estate. Once the hunting part of the estate was sold off, one wasn't needed here. So, our man relocated to our other estate in the Highlands, where he still has plenty of game and visitors to look after."

Although knowing nothing about what to expect, Sarah couldn't help thinking a 'cottage' might be a much lesser beast than where they normally lived. Such thinking had her depressed by the time the carriage drew up in front of the cottage. She was in for a surprise. From outside, it looked as good as the manager's cottage the Erskine family had lived in on the plantation before moving into the big house there.

Inside, it was clean, tidy, and well-appointed. Staff had been busy there during the evening. A fire on the grate had warmed the place for their arrival, and a bunch of heather in a large vase occupied a low table in the sitting room area.

"Oh, this is just perfect. Thank you, Robert."

"It was my pleasure, Mrs Wallace, but I might remind you we do have one more wedding tradition to be getting on with tonight," he murmured in her ear… and she felt the heat rise up her throat to her face. Sarah had no doubt her face would be bright red.

A further surprise awaited Sarah in the bedroom when she found most of her belongings neatly stowed there. Who had packed her things, and when had they managed to do it without her noticing?

*****

Pots and pans being rattled about in the kitchen woke Sarah next morning. The aroma of breakfast wafted through the house. Staff on loan from the big house had started work early today, and the fire had been stoked to ensure the place would be warm for the couple when they ventured out from under the covers.

Over breakfast, Robert announced he had important family business to see to at the big house and could be gone for most of the day.

"Am I required to be involved?" Sarah asked.

"No. My father and I have business matters to discuss. As they don't involve you, there is no reason for you to accompany me to the big house."

"What am I supposed to do? Do you expect me to remain here alone all day, and if so, what am I to do with myself?"

"You have many thank-you letters to write. Now might be a good time to make a start on those. I will have someone from the big house bring you a list of the names. If you would prefer to spend the day preparing for our departure, you might ask for a carriage to take you to Aunt Bess's house. It is up to you how you fill in your day. But I would remind you we have plenty to do before our ship sails for the Caribbean next weekend. The sooner you start on those things requiring your attention, the less stress and panic there will be as the week draws to an end."

Soon after, Robert was on his way to the big house, and about twenty minutes later, a footman arrived with an envelope containing the list of names requiring thank-you notes. Sullen but accepting of the situation, Sarah fetched her writing material and set to work. Her only brief respite from the monotonous chore was a mid-morning tea break. By lunchtime, a polite note to each of the names on the list awaited dispatch.

Around noon, the concerned cook approached Sarah. "I apologise for interrupting your work, Madam, but I have had no instructions regarding today's luncheon requirements. Will you be in for lunch, and is Mr Robert expected to return to eat here?"

"Oh, I do apologise. I had forgotten all about conferring regarding meals. I will be in for lunch, but Mr Wallace might not be free to return. Perhaps we might plan on something light: soup, perhaps if possible in the time available."

Robert did not return for lunch, so Sarah sat alone to partake of a bowl of thick, hearty soup and a lump of freshly baked bread. Then, with nothing better to do and feeling desperate, she called for a carriage and went to spend the afternoon with her family.

While the women at Bess's house fussed over her, excited discussion of various aspects of the wedding filled most of the afternoon. Thomas remained aloof from such conversations, preferring to sit alone with his dark thoughts instead. Later, he confided those thoughts to Flora.

"So far, I am not at all impressed with young Mr Wallace's behaviour as a husband. What man leaves his wife alone to fend for herself in a strange place when they have been married for less than a day? Perhaps we should have been more circumspect in considering his request to marry our daughter. Already I am concerned about his treatment of her, and soon I will not witness how he treats her nor be there to intervene if she needs me."

Flora struggled to keep a straight face while treating Thomas's comments with the gravity and respect they deserved.

"Aye, I understand your concerns. But Sarah is a resourceful young woman now, and she must become used to planning her days and making a life for herself within the confines of her marriage … just as every other woman must do at such a time. Nevertheless, I, too, have a major concern."

"Well, out with it. I'm sure it will be something that also concerns me."

"Perhaps not, my love. I am concerned that Robert Wallace has gained himself a father-in-law after the same style you inherited when you married me. You are concerned because you love our daughter, just as my father's concerns were from his love for me. While my father's concerns were unfounded, they did create an incredibly difficult situation in our marriage. Mr Erskine, *I do not want to see the same thing blight my daughter's marriage.* So, I suggest we allow the young couple to sort out their marriage without our interference."

"I'll have no choice. Robert is about to spirit Sarah off to the other side of the world, where I won't know what her life is like. But I do hear what you are saying."

"Good; then I'll just make one last comment before the subject is closed: perhaps it is a good thing they will be on the other side of the world and away from us."

*****

Days tumbled over one another in a continual stream of activities. Flora took Sarah shopping for 'essential items' Sarah would need in her new home, and basic wardrobe additions befitting the lady of the house. For Sarah, the week slipped away too quickly. Before she had talked to Robert about anything, it was Friday morning.

Robert was so busy finalising family business matters before their departure, the couple's only time together was at breakfast and dinner each day. Over those days, Sarah's feeling of dread became almost unbearable. There was excitement at the prospect of spending more time with her husband, and of a grand adventure in a new land. Her feeling of loss at being torn away from everything familiar and those she loved outweighed any feelings of excitement.

Friday evening proved hardest when Bess hosted a dinner party for both families as a farewell gesture. It was a grand occasion: wonderful food, drink, and the best company. Beyond that, it was notable for the wet eyes that occurred throughout the night. Everyone appeared happy for the party to continue, and it lasted much longer than expected.

At almost midnight, Robert suggested it was time to go. It was as if no one heard. No one made a move. Another ten minutes elapsed before Douglas Wallace stood and invited the others to do likewise.

"Tonight has been pleasant, and as much as we would wish to delay tomorrow for as long as possible, it is past the time for Mr and Mrs Wallace to be on board their ship and settled in before sailing on tomorrow morning's tide."

"Will we be able to go on board at this hour?" Sarah whispered to Robert.

"Yes. It is one of the Wallace's ship. They know to expect us whenever we arrive."

Tears flowed freely down all the women's faces as the two families stood huddled together just inside the front door of Bess's house. With stiff faces and staunch to the end, the men said their farewells. Robert managed to drag his wife out of her mother's arms and down the steps to their carriage. Sarah sobbed inconsolably all the way to the docks. Robert couldn't comprehend the depth of his wife's emotion, and couldn't help thinking this was not the promising start to the next phase of their lives he had hoped for.

Sarah only picked at her breakfast, but conceded later that the standard of food served surprised her. She admitted to herself it was the best food she had ever tasted on board a ship and, if nothing else, that should help ease shipboard life for however long it took to reach their Caribbean destination.

Such thoughts triggered another realisation: she still didn't know how long the voyage would take, or what to expect when they reached their destination. Now was not the time to explore that. The ship was preparing to sail, and Robert insisted she accompany him up on deck.

There they were. All the members of Sarah's family clustered together on the dock as they waited to wave the young couple on their way. More shouted goodbyes and tears occurred as the gangplank was drawn on board and the mooring ropes were slipped.

As the dock and those still clustered on it faded into the distance, Robert took Sarah's arm and eased her away from the railing.

"We are on our way to start our new life together. Come; let's go below to discuss our hopes and dreams for that new future."

PART 3

The Caribbean 1842

Chapter 19

Discovery

Never having dealt with anything like this before, Robert stood bewildered in their cabin. With no idea what else he could do, he stood beside his wife, patting her head and murmuring 'there, there'. The soul-wrenching sobs subsided to sniffles, but Robert remained at a loss as to what to say or do. When the sniffles eased to occasional sniffs, Robert felt it safe to speak.

"Talk to me, please, my dear. Tell me what has upset you so. I thought you were excited and looking forward to our new life, but it seems I was mistaken."

"I do want to go with you to the Caribbean, and I am excited about what our new life might be like. But leaving everything and everyone I know and love behind in the knowledge I might never see them again was so painful. And suddenly, I am frightened."

"Frightened? I know of nothing that should frighten you but, if you explain, maybe I can help ease your concerns."

"It's just the not knowing, not knowing where I am going, what it will be like, who will be there, or what will be expected of me. The plantation is home to you. It's where you spent most of your childhood and adult life. But I don't know what it is like or what to expect."

"Ah, I see how remiss I have been in not discussing this with you sooner. Still, all is not lost. It means the conversation I thought we would have this morning needs to be more in-depth than planned. But I will need your guidance in this matter. Tell me where you wish me to begin."

"Oh, well, I don't know where to begin. Suppose we start from when we arrive on the island and progress from there.

Perhaps, make it a like a travel itinerary: the trip from the port to where we will live, what our home is like, and who will be there to meet us. Is that too much to ask or too difficult to achieve?"

"Not at all; it makes sense to tell it as you suggest. So, let's make ourselves comfortable. Then I will map out your travel itinerary for you."

A few minutes later, the young couple were seated comfortably on opposite sides of a low table, and refreshments had arrived. Soon, Robert was explaining every step of the way once they arrived on the island.

"You probably will find it a pain, as the rest of us always do, having to hang around at the docks for our belongings to be unloaded. A wagon will be positioned to receive our things as they are unloaded, but we need to supervise the process to ensure nothing is overlooked somewhere in the hold."

"Yes, I'm sure I would feel more confident if I checked everything as it was unloaded. Then what happens? Do we climb on the wagon with our belongings and head for the plantation?"

"Good God, no. It would be a dreadful trip on the wagon, and not the best way to introduce you to the paradise that is to be your new home. A carriage also awaits us. The man who brought it to the port could drive us home, or I could send him back on the wagon with our belongings, in which case, I would drive us back to the plantation. What do you say to that?"

"I think I would prefer you drove me home. How long will it take us to reach the plantation?"

"Right, that's one thing decided: I will drive us back to the plantation. As for how long the trip will take, we also need to consider something else. How the next stage plays out depends on the time we arrive at the island. If it is anything other than at first light, we will overnight at the port before heading for the plantation next morning. Don't worry. We often use quite a good hotel there."

"Oh, that's disappointing. I was looking forward to seeing the place soon after our arrival. Why do we have to spend the night at the port if we arrive any later than first thing in the morning?"

"It's a full day's travel from the port to the plantation – and then a little further to our home. Once we leave the port, there is nowhere along the way for us to overnight. We would need to keep going through the darkness and arrive after everyone else had gone to bed. No, if we can't make an early morning start, we will spend the night in a hotel at the port."

Sarah nodded her understanding of the situation, but nothing masked her disappointment. "I see, and I accept that, however it happens, I will have a full day's travel before I see my new home. Tell me about what I will see along the way."

This was something Robert had never done before; never had any reason even to give it a thought. Now, he had to describe for Sarah the scenery they would encounter, and his commentary needed to be both exciting and interesting. Not an easy task, he thought, given the sameness of much of what they would see along the way. Nevertheless, he promised she would be familiar with her new surroundings by the time they reached home.

He continued outlining how the journey would wind through the countryside until it reached the plantation. "Then, we are close to home. There is a long, gravel driveway snaking up a low rise to end at our front door."

"Tell me about the house. Is it made of brick or stone, and how many rooms does it contain?"

"Uhmm… Let me see. It's constructed from both brick and stone, but also from timber. It's a big place with lots of verandahs with doors opening onto them to catch the prevailing breezes. How many rooms? I don't know. I've never counted them. Suffice to say, there are a lot. We will not be cramped for space."

She looked alarmed and, for a moment, Robert was nonplussed. What had he said to alarm her? All was soon revealed.

"Am I expected to look after all those rooms, to keep them clean and tidy? Why would we have so many rooms? Will we have a lot of visitors who stay at the plantation? And, will they expect me to cook for them?"

When Robert finally stopped laughing, he attempted to set her mind at rest. "Of course not. We have servants – a whole flock of them. God knows what they all do, but it seems every one of them is necessary."

"If you don't know what they all do, how do you know they are necessary? Perhaps I will need to devote some attention to this soon after we arrive. It would be poor household management and reflect badly on me if we are spending money needlessly on excessive servants."

"I doubt the number of servants or what they all do is a matter of concern. Besides, Cecile keeps a close eye and tight rein on household matters."

"Who is Cecile? Is she the housekeeper?"

Robert almost rolled on the floor with laughter. Then reality dawned on him. Jesus, nobody even mentioned Cecile before now, let alone what she did there. It was a sobering realisation, and it took him a few moments to work out how to explain the situation.

"Yes, well, Cecile is a bit of a long story to tell in any detail, but I'll give you the pertinent facts.

Cecile is my sister. She and my brother, Cameron, also live in the house. Of course, each has their own set of rooms, a bit like their own apartments within the big house. Neither of them is married.

Cameron manages our other planation, which we acquired quite a few years after the home property. It's much smaller than the main one, but has its own factory and workers. The big difference is that Cameron's planation only produces juice from their crop. Then the juice is brought to the main planation for processing into sugar in our big factory."

"What about your sister, Cecile? Tell me something about her and how she comes to still live in the big house on the plantation."

"She is the middle one of we three Wallace offspring, and is a very attractive woman. Like Cameron and me, she was sent home to school and spent her teenage years in Glasgow. But, against my parents' wishes, she insisted on returning to the plantation, and then refused to leave with our parents when they relocated to Glasgow permanently. Both Cameron and I had to stay to manage the plantations.

Once mother left, Cecile decided it was her duty to take over running the household, and we two chaps were perfectly happy for her to do so."

"So, she became the de facto lady of the house?"

"Uhmm… yes, I suppose you could say that. There was no one else to take over mother's role."

"Right… and how do you think she will feel about my being there? Is it why there has been careful avoidance of any mention of her before this? Because you intend she should continue as the lady of the house, and I should just be there as a spare, or something decorative to be wheeled out at appropriate times?"

"What? No. Where did that notion come from? You are my wife. Of course, you are now the lady of the house. I don't understand why you would think otherwise. As for not hearing about her before this, I suppose it was because she didn't come up in conversation. There was no reason to mention her."

"Are you so sure Cecile will see things the same way? I'm not at all sure she will. She will likely resent my arrival and view my presence as usurping her position in *her* household. And it is quite likely the household staff will resent me as well for trying to topple their 'boss' from her position in charge of them."

"No-o, I don't foresee such a situation eventuating. In fact, there might be a few who would welcome such a change."

"Tell me about Cecile. Has she never married?"

"Ah well, Cecile never has had much luck in that department of life… not intentionally, of course. She became engaged to marry a young man when she was about nineteen or twenty, still young enough to require Father's consent to marry. Father did not think much of the man in question. During a casual meeting with his friend, the Governor, Father asked if the Governor knew anything about the chap."

"Oh, I sense this will not be a happy story."

"You guessed right. It appears the man was wanted for a number of offences on other islands, and the police were keeping an eye out for him. Needless to say, there was no marriage and Cecile blamed Father's interference for ending her romance. Later, we discovered he already was married to two women – at the same time."

"It's not hard to see how that experience turned her against marriage. I suppose her chances of meeting someone here who met with your father's approval were not great. All the more reason I would have expected her to return to Glasgow – and perhaps better choices."

"It didn't turn her against marriage, but it took her a while to find someone to replace her first love. By then, she was an adult and no longer required Father's consent to marry."

"But she didn't. What happened?"

"He was one of the overseers from a good, solid Scottish background who we employed on the plantations. They became engaged and planned to marry six months later. It was to be one of those major social events for the islands. Cecile was running herself ragged arranging every last detail of the ceremony and the subsequent reception. By the end of the week before the wedding, everything was in place for the big occasion. The day after the wedding, the couple were to overnight at the port before boarding a boat to whisk them away on their honeymoon.

Then, in the middle of that last week, the groom-to-be rode to the port to check everything was organised. When the groom didn't return after overnighting at the port as planned, I sent Cameron to investigate. Cecile was frantic. She thought he might have suffered an accident and be lying injured somewhere beside the track."

"Poor Cecile; I can imagine how distraught she would be. Argh, I suspect the rest of this story is not good news – not for Cecile anyway."

"Your instinct is right on the money. Cameron left for the port at daybreak. Instead of returning the following day, he returned late that same night. When he couldn't locate the missing groom, he spoke to the man in charge of shipping. He is a kind of harbourmaster who deals with all the manifests of ships in and out of the port.

He confirmed the groom-to-be had arrived at the port as intended, but he wasn't alone. A young woman, one of the household staff, accompanied him. She was an attractive young woman of mixed race. The same evening they arrived at the port, the couple boarded a ship that set sail early next morning. It was believed they were heading for America. Cameron and I had to break the news to Cecile."

"To be left virtually standing at the altar must have devastated her. The humiliation on top of the heartbreak must have been almost unbearable. What a callous man he was. If that is the stuff he was made of, perhaps it's as well the marriage never went ahead."

"True… but what made it more difficult for Cecile was that the staff knew about the two lovers the whole time. After they eloped and she was abandoned, Cecile found it difficult to maintain a position of dignity and authority in front of the staff. Although she has never said as much, I doubt she will enter another relationship."

"So, in effect, maintaining her position as the lady of the house and authority over the staff were all she had to shore up her dignity. All the more reason why she will resent my intrusion into her world, her last bastion of dignity and power."

"Let's not pre-empt what might never eventuate. But, I understand your point, and I can accept how much 'kid glove' treatment might be required as we install you in your rightful position in my house."

The young couple sat in glum silence for a minute or two before Robert's face lit up with excitement, and he leaned forward in his chair.

"All might not be as grim as we imagined. There is a way around this to avoid conflict between you and my sister and, at the same time, protect Cecile's dignity and her feelings. No, I won't explain now, but trust me. I believe I have the solution, but it will have to wait until we are home to be implemented."

A sceptical Sarah was less confident about this miraculous solution Robert insisted he could implement, but instinct told her now was not the time to push for further explanation. She hoped her wan smile reassured him she trusted his judgement.

For the next two weeks, at least part of each day was devoted to learning more about the island and the plantation. Nevertheless, nothing prepared Sarah for the reality of her new life.

*****

Fair wind and a following sea had the ship arrive at the island's port a little over two weeks after leaving Glasgow. Robert took Sarah up on deck as they entered its small harbour for her first glimpse of the island.

"I was about to say 'welcome home', but maybe I should save that until we are home. So, instead, I'll just say *welcome to our island paradise*."

Everywhere was green. As far as the eye could see, beyond the turquoise blue water, there was nothing but green, except for the small patch of infrastructure – grey and uninviting – that was the port facility. Sarah allowed her eyes to travel inland across the wide swathe of green until they encountered the first rocky outcrops poking through the jungle. Although she focused on them for a few moments, they told her nothing other than they were just the tops of grey and white mottled rocky outcrops.

Further beyond those rocks, her eyes travelled up to the top of a low rise in the distance. Was it the low hill on which Robert said their house stood, she wondered as she strained her eyes for any sign of a home. She couldn't detect any buildings on it, but assumed it was the house's location. After all, it was the only thing that rose above the surrounding landscape.

She focused on the port facility ahead of them as they neared the shoreline. Already, she was aware of ant-sized bodies scurrying about on the docks. Quite a bit of activity centred on another ship tied-up at one end of the harbour. But the ship she was on had started its tricky manoeuvring to come alongside the dock. Now they were close enough for shouts among those on shore to drift up to her on deck.

"Perhaps this might be a good time for you to return to our cabin. Make sure everything is packed, and keep those bags we want with us separate from the rest of our cabin luggage. Crew members will be along shortly to collect everything remaining in the cabin," Robert told her.

She wanted to stay on deck to watch everything happening, but instinct told her this was not the time to argue. Although Robert's words had been by way of a suggestion, their delivery indicated they were intended as something more definite. Still, Sarah was unhappy at being dismissed, regardless of how it was done. Lifting her skirt, she turned on her heel and flounced back to their cabin.

"It won't hurt to check everything is packed," she murmured as she stood in the centre of the cabin. Robert would not be happy if, after his instructions, she overlooked anything.

A few minutes later, Robert arrived, followed a moment or two later by two crew members. He indicated the luggage to be loaded on the wagon with the rest of their belongings from the hold. While he explained that, another two crew members arrived. They stood patiently outside the door until the first two, now loaded with small trunks, moved out.

Robert called the second pair into the cabin and gestured towards the two bags Sarah had set aside to keep with them. The men stepped forward to gather up the bags.

"No," Sarah yelped. "They are the bags we need to keep with us."

After directing a low growl at Sarah, he again gestured for the men to remove the bags. Sarah watched in disbelief as the bags disappeared out the cabin door.

"Don't ever do that again," he snarled at her. "Do not ever argue with me in front of the workers, or presume to countermand my orders. Is that understood?"

"How dare you?" Sarah hissed. "How dare you speak to me in that way? Perhaps if I knew why you saw fit for our bags to be removed when I thought we were keeping them with me, I might not have spoken out. Is this how I am to learn the *rules* that apply on this island? If it is, then when does the next ship return to Glasgow? I wish to be on it."

"What? Don't be ridiculous, woman. Why would you want to leave when you haven't even arrived yet? How can you want to leave when you still haven't had time to learn the first thing about the place?"

"It is not the place I wish to escape. It is you I want no more of after this morning. I expect respect from my husband and not to be treated like some lowly servant. Maybe for the first time, today I saw your true colours, and *those colours do not suit me*."

"Perhaps we might discuss this later – in the privacy of our hotel room. If you are considering staying on board until this ship sails again, that will be about a week away. So now, come up on deck with me to watch our ship tie up."

Confused and unsure, Sarah hesitated for a couple of moments to decide. It was obvious she couldn't stay on board by herself for a week… and Robert appeared to have regained his normal disposition. Perhaps she would accompany him to the hotel, but this matter was not over. He would hear more about his behaviour before the day was out, she promised herself as she followed him up on deck.

There appeared to be a small herd of dark-skinned locals hovering on the dock. Men in starched white outfits, whom Sarah assumed were the workers' overseers, were dotted here and there throughout. Then, pandemonium broke out – or so it appeared to Sarah.

The moment the mooring ropes were slipped over the bollards and made fast, the mass of bodies on the dock all surged forward, their shouting and wild activity creating something of a frenzy. Then amidst it all, a wagon inched through the crowd to come alongside the ship. Robert called a greeting down to the wagon driver. Moments later, Sarah saw the first of their belongings transhipped from boat to wagon. But it was time to go.

Robert took her gently by the arm and indicated the gangplank in place and ready for them to disembark. Sarah risked another look at the activity on the dock and hesitated. Was it safe? She feared she might be risking her life by descending into the melee below, but Robert was leading her to the gangplank.

That's when she noticed their two bags on the deck at the feet of the two crew members who collected them from their cabin. As she and Robert started towards the gangplank, Sarah saw the two men pick up the bags and stand ready to follow them. While picking her way gingerly down the gangplank behind Robert, she was surprised to see a carriage make its way through the crowd on the dock and halt at the foot of the gangplank. She couldn't help but marvel that it hadn't run over anyone on its way.

A couple of minutes later, Sarah, Robert, and their bags, were in the carriage and on their way to the hotel where they would spend the night.

Chapter 20

Welcome Home

Sarah deemed the hotel acceptable, if not palatial, but she suspected they had been provided the modest establishment's best rooms. Her suspicion was partly based on the manager's welcome extended to Robert when they arrived. Robert was obviously a frequent and treasured guest. Their late lunch surpassed Sarah's expectations.

After lunch, Sarah retired to their rooms. Robert left her alone to rest while he dealt with plantation business. It was wonderful to be on solid ground again, to lie on a proper bed that was still. She slept. Later, she would tell Robert it probably was her soundest sleep since departing Glasgow. And dinner that evening, while not lavish, left nothing to be desired. Dinner also provided another opportunity to expand her knowledge of the island.

"Robert, we appear to be the only guests registered at this hotel. How does it stay open for business if so few avail themselves of its accommodation?"

"Although there are no other guests now, all available accommodation is occupied at other times. The establishment welcomes a few guests during most weeks. Some only stay overnight, while others remain for two or three days. The hotel's trade depends almost entirely on its guests' business here at the port. It means that, at some parts of the year, the place is quite busy, while at other times, there are few guests."

"I notice there's another ship tied up further along the dock, but it appears no one from that ship is availing themselves of the hotel's accommodation or dining room."

"That ship belongs to a different plantation owner. The captain and crew probably spend their time here on board. Any passengers delivered to the island, or joining the ship early tomorrow morning, would be accommodated in the other hotel further along from here. Like the other ship, that other hotel is another plantation owner's property."

"Do I take that to mean that this hotel belongs to you?"

"Your assumption would be correct. The plantation needed accommodation at the port, not only for family, who might be dealing with business here or catching a ship, but also for important visitors and dignitaries who might visit the plantation. One of the other plantation owners, who doesn't own a hotel here, sometimes takes advantage of our spare rooms when he is in town.

Like the Wallace family, the owner of the other hotel has an extensive plantation and frequently needs considerable accommodation. It suits him best to have his own hotel."

"I see. Is the hotel the only business the Wallace family owns here at the port?"

"No-o; along with the men who run those establishments, we are part owners of a blacksmith's shop and a general store. Perhaps it is difficult for you to understand but, when lands were first taken up to establish plantations, there was nothing here. So everything – the port facilities, the roads, the factories, everything – had to be created from scratch for the plantations to succeed and people to live here."

"But, weren't people living here before the plantations were established? I mean, the locals, didn't they have villages here on the island?"

"Yes, but those villages were clusters of shacks and a few gardens growing a limited range of fruit and vegetables for subsistence living. They caught fish and other wildlife to supplement their diet and ate oysters and crabs, but there were no industries. There was no commercial endeavour happening here before the plantation owners arrived."

"I'm looking forward to meeting your brother and sister tomorrow and seeing my new home. Will the rest of our belongings be there when we arrive?"

"The wagon will arrive sometime before us and might be unloaded when we arrive. It will leave for the plantation at first light, whereas we will wait until after an early breakfast before setting off."

"If the two men from the wagon are spending the night here, where are they staying? I haven't seen them here at the hotel. And where will our wagon be tonight? Will our belongings be safe?"

Robert chuckled before realising Sarah was serious. "Sorry, I didn't mean to make light of your questions. The two men from the wagon are local plantation workers. Such employees are not provided accommodation at the hotel. They have other accommodation available to them. As for the wagon, it is safely locked in one of our warehouses, so no misfortune will befall our belongings before they leave for the plantation."

"It appears I still have much to learn about life on the island. Although, in some ways, I suppose it doesn't differ too much from the life I knew on the tea plantation. Even there, the plantation workers would not have been allowed to overnight in any of the guest accommodation."

"Do not trouble yourself about the intricacies of island life at this early stage of your time here. Allow yourself to learn things as we go along, and you shouldn't find it too unpleasant or difficult to become accustomed to our way of life."

*****

For much of the night, the heat and humidity were unbearable. It shocked Sarah. After their arrival yesterday, she had enjoyed the sea breeze coming in off the ocean. But, while they were at dinner, that breeze dropped, and nothing replaced it for the rest of the night. Between the heat, and insects that bit and made her itch, it had been impossible to sleep. Nothing had bothered Robert. He was asleep the moment he fell into bed and slept soundly all night.

Just before dawn, a light breeze sprang up again, bringing Sarah some welcome relief. Exhausted from tossing and turning all night, she finally fell into a deep sleep, only to be woken what felt like moments later.

"Come on, Mrs Wallace, it's time to be up and dressed. We need to go down for the early breakfast prepared to allow us an early departure for home," Robert murmured as he gently shook her awake.

"Go away; I was enjoying my first bit of beautiful sleep for the night. Do we have to be up at this hour? Can't we sleep a little longer now we have a cooling breeze?"

A grumpy wife accompanied Robert to breakfast, and then followed his instructions almost zombie-like until they were in the carriage and on their way out of the port. The place was well and truly alive as they headed out. The port area was a hive of activity as (mainly local) workers went about their jobs, and already the noise level was almost as she remembered it from yesterday. Above the noise of the horses and the carriage, shouted orders, babbles of a strange language, and even singing, assailed her ears.

Sarah sat statue-like next to Robert as he flicked the reins to urge the horses on. Later, she would recall the sound of the gravel road crunching under the horses' hooves and the carriage wheels, but it did not register with her then. And likewise, the motley cluster of rough, greyed timber buildings they passed, although imprinted on her memory, triggered no response at the time.

About ten minutes after leaving the port precinct, Robert felt compelled to break the prevailing silence in the carriage.

"What in heaven's name is wrong with you this morning? Are you ill, or have you been struck dumb? I know the scenery is stunning, but I did not think it sufficiently impressive to cause loss of speech. Talk to me! What is the matter?"

"Lack of sleep...."

"You were sound asleep when I woke you this morning, so how can you complain of a lack of sleep?"

"Biting insects attacked me all night, and it was too hot to sleep until just before dawn when a little breeze came up. I hadn't been asleep more than an hour or two when you woke me."

"Well, try to brighten yourself up as we go along. It will not do any good for you to arrive at the homestead behaving like this."

Although the temptation to bite back at him was strong, she couldn't muster enough energy. Instead, she maintained her rigid posture and kept her eyes focused straight ahead. But she knew he was right. It was up to her to create the best first impression possible, not only for herself but also for Robert's sake. What would they all think when they were introduced to some zombie-like creature Robert had married, and who would now live among them?

Her eyes slid to the hamper and the demijohn that Robert loaded into the carriage before they left the hotel. She knew the journey to the plantation would take all day. So, it was reasonable to assume the hotel had provided them sustenance for the trip. That explained the hamper, but what about the demijohn? She hoped it contained water and not rum. Heat and humidity seemed to have sucked the moisture out of her, and she felt her now soggy clothes sticking to her.

"Will we stop anywhere along the way?" she asked timidly.

"We need to cross a little creek up a bit further. It's a good place to stop to rest the horses for a while and to let them drink from the creek. As it is a pleasant spot – cool and shady – it's also a good place for us to rest and refuel. The hotel provided a hamper of food and a container of water. So, while the horses drink and rest, we will take in sustenance to keep us going for the rest of the ride home."

Relieved by the prospect of a rest stop before too long, Sarah settled back on her seat and took an interest in her surroundings for the first time that morning. Both sides of the track were cloaked in thick jungle from which some occasional large bird would fly out and squawk at them as it flew overhead. But she became aware of something else as well. At first, Sarah thought she had imagined it, but now she realised she was right: it had become cooler. Perhaps rain clouds had rolled in and blanketed out the sun. She looked up to check the sky but saw only the occasional patch of blue here and there through the overhanging trees.

After what felt like an eternity, they arrived at the creek where they would spell the horses. While Robert unhitched and attended to the horses, Sarah unpacked the hamper: slices of salt beef, cheese, pickles and freshly made bread. It was simple fare, but she felt her stomach rumble. Although she was not interested in food at breakfast, she discovered she now was hungry. Perhaps it was down to the air being cooler here than down on the coast.

For their lunchtime spread, the couple sat on a patch of thick, soft grass at the base of an enormous tree trunk. Sarah surprised herself with the quantity she ate and the copious amount of sweet water she drank from the demijohn. Then, lunch finished, and while she repacked the hamper, Robert attended to the horses. As she watched, Sarah leant back against the gnarly bark of the tree trunk behind her.

Although it felt like only a few moments, it was more than half an hour later when Robert gently shook her awake. He stood smiling down at her. Behind him, she saw the horses were hitched and ready to continue their journey.

"Come on, my dear. We must be away if we are to arrive home in time to rest a little before dinner." Reaching down, he hauled Sarah to her feet and, with his arm around her waist, led her to the carriage.

Revived by lunch and her nap, Sarah became more interested in her surroundings. They hadn't travelled far before she began worrying about the reception she might receive at the homestead.

"Robert, how long before we reach the plantation?"

"Oh, less than an hour until we reach the plantation's boundary and start on the long track up to the house. Off to your left, although you can't see it for all the trees lining the road, is our other plantation, the one Cameron manages." He was right.

She couldn't see beyond the jungle, despite keeping her eyes glued to the passing scenery.

A while later, they drove through a thin strip of scrub and came out on an open and orderly expanse of land. Workers seemed to be everywhere, and numerous horse-drawn drays moved through the rows of plants, which the workers cut down and loaded into the drays. Further up a hill, smoke billowed from tall chimneys, and as they drew closer, she saw a collection of buildings surrounding the chimneys.

"Is that the homestead over there near those chimneys?" Sarah asked as she sat forward. Her stomach started to tighten in response to a mixture of excitement and dread.

"No. Those are the factory buildings. The homestead is further on. You can't see it yet, but it is on the top of that rise over there. You'll be able to see it after we go around the bend up ahead."

Soon, a large, conventional building appeared ahead of them. Set atop a low rise, it seemed to command a view over a vast area of the land below it. As they drew nearer, Sarah realised the house she initially thought conventional-looking had grown and developed over some time. An original stone building now formed the nucleus of a final structure derived over time from many additions of different materials. Regardless of its development, it presented an imposing picture when viewed from down on the track. The wide verandahs encircling the house to catch every available breeze appealed to Sarah.

Not a 'new' building, it appeared to have evolved over many decades to meet the needs of the family, and using whatever materials (and money) were available at the time. But what would it be like inside? Would it be elegant but comfortable, or would she be confronted by a jumble of mismatched bits and pieces the family collected over the years? Then the reality of the situation dawned on her.

This was to be *her* home. *She* would be the lady-of-the-house. It would be up to *her* to turn this place into whatever she considered a suitable home for herself, Robert and the family they would produce. With that realisation firmly in her mind, as the carriage drew up at the foot of the front steps, she felt strong enough and ready to deal with whatever came next.

A young man, his coal-black skin in sharp contrast with his starched white outfit, rushed to meet them. He took charge of the horses as Robert climbed down from the wagon. Sarah remained seated until Robert came around to help her down. As she waited, three young women rushed down and stood clustered together at the foot of the steps to wait for Sarah to alight. As she went to take his hand, a movement on the stairs caused her to look up.

In sharp contrast to the three young local women in the grey frocks topped with white pinafores now standing near the carriage, an imposing figure stood at the top of the steps. Like a queen pausing for effect before coming down to meet with her subjects, the young woman swept out of the majestic front doors and adopted a haughty pose for a few moments on the doorstep, before sweeping down to meet them. The three young girls moved aside to allow the woman a clear path to the carriage.

No doubt, this was Cecile, Sarah thought as she watched the performance from her perch atop the carriage. She assessed the woman as overdressed for the occasion and the weather. Although Sarah didn't quite know what to expect, she was a little put off by Cecile's behaviour. Reaching ground level, Cecile adopted an imperious pose and … waited … without as much as a smile or hint of recognition, even towards her brother.

So, she expects me to scramble down and rush to greet her as some reigning monarch, does she, Sarah thought of Cecile's performance. Well, we'll see about that, she told herself. I wasn't brought up to be treated as some lesser individual. With her mind filled with such thoughts and her anger rising, Sarah took Robert's proffered hand and made the most elegant show she could manage of alighting from the carriage.

She did not rush to meet Cecile, instead remaining beside the carriage for a moment to survey everything before her. Then, she gave each of the three young women from the household staff a smile and brief nod of acknowledgement … before lifting her chin and turning to face Cecile. Sarah glimpsed Robert move as if to take hold of her and move her forward.

Without taking her eyes off Cecile, Sarah took an almost indiscernible sideway step away from Robert. Then, in a slow and measured gesture, she gave Cecile a half smile and nod of acknowledgement, before raising her outstretched hand to Cecile. Well-versed in such protocols, Sarah knew that, as the boss' wife (and the new lady-of-the-house), Cecile had no option for saving face other than to come forward and accept the hand offered to her.

Robert's timely intervention at that point probably prevented the situation's deteriorating into a complete disaster.

"Cecile, this is Sarah, my wife. I'll take her to our suite of rooms for her to settle in a little before dinner. There will be plenty of time to catch up on everything after dinner. Is Cameron home yet?" His last question was directed to one of the young girls.

"Yes, Sir. He arrived about half an hour ago to be here to welcome you both when you arrived. I'll tell him you are here."

The young woman started up the steps as a young man bounded out the front door.

"Robert, you've made it… and this must be Sarah, the new Mrs Wallace," he said as he bounced down the steps and nudged Cecile aside. "Welcome, welcome; I hope you have survived the transition from Glasgow to here without too many regrets."

Cameron was a younger-looking version of Robert, but with an added boyish impishness about him and a mischievous twinkle in his same intense blue eyes as Roberts'. He was someone who might prove a useful ally, Sarah thought as he shook her hand and then hugged her.

"Sorry I couldn't make it to the wedding or to be big brother's best man… to make sure he behaved appropriately and didn't bolt at the last minute," Cameron continued.

Sarah heard Robert give a soft growl as he fixed Cameron with a hard look. Looking awkward and suitably 'put in his place', Cameron stepped back, gave a low bow and gestured for them to head up the steps.

"Go and rest for a while. I'll see you both again at dinner tonight."

"Ah, no, Cameron, after I take Sarah up to our apartment, I need to talk to you. Allow me about twenty minutes, and then meet me in the office. Urgent news from home…," he added over his shoulder as he guided Sarah up the steps.

There was no opportunity to look around or inspect her surroundings as Robert rushed her through a large, imposing 'front room' and on to a sweeping polished timber staircase to the first floor.

"Our apartment is along here," he said at the top of the stairs and indicated a balcony leading off to the left. "It was the main suite of rooms when my parents lived here. Cameron and I had apartments on the other side of the house. After my parents returned to Glasgow, I took over their apartment. Since then, on the few occasions they visited, they stayed in the guests' wing."

Throwing open the door and leading her into a comfortable sitting room, Robert continued, "Welcome home, Mrs Wallace. I think you'll find your cases are already in your private dressing room. Freshen up and rest. I'll return as soon as I have finished talking to Cameron. Dinner usually is at 7.30 after pre-dinner drinks at seven o'clock."

After a guided tour of their suite of rooms, Robert left Sarah to settle in while he spoke to Cameron. Back on the ground floor, he was on his way to the office when Cecile stopped him.

"I suppose she will need a maid before too much longer." Robert noticed the definite edge to her voice as she asked the question.

"Yes, Cecile, *Sarah* does require her own maid. One should be appointed immediately to help Sarah with the unpacking and settling-in process."

"Humph… well, I suppose Elula could be made available after I speak to her tomorrow."

"No, Cecile, it will be Femi, and she should be sent up now to help Sarah."

"Oh, no, it can't possibly be Femi. She…."

"You must have misheard me, Cecile. I told you Femi is to be Sarah's maid, and she should begin her duties now. I would expect to see her going about her duties in our apartment when I return there after meeting with Cameron. Also, after breakfast tomorrow, please make yourself available for a meeting with me. Thank you, Cecile. I should go. Cameron will be waiting for me."

Cameron wasn't waiting. Although coming from different directions, the two brothers arrived at the office together. After pouring them each a measure of rum from a cabinet in the corner and taking a few sips, Robert began the conversation he had to have.

"What I am about to say will not come as any surprise, I'm sure, but you might find the new developments disturbing. We live here, so it goes without saying we are aware of the groundswell of opinion developing on these islands. And we know this island is not immune to, nor isolated from it."

Chapter 21

Imminent Changes

"As you say, Robert, I have noticed changes, though not so severe and widespread as I've heard about from other islands. But, even here, I have detected a degree of restlessness among certain groups of our workers. The overseers sense it too. A few left after citing concerns about their future safety. I managed to recruit a couple of replacements, but they don't have the experience of those we lost.

You called this meeting because you wanted to talk to me, so you have the floor. What is the news you wanted to share with me?"

"As a result of the changes occurring right through the Caribbean, Father is concerned about our situation. While his concerns cover both our plantations, his immediate thoughts are for the one you manage. Because nobody lives there, he feels it is in a vulnerable position, and could be a temptation. It is an ideal location for any unlawful activities the locals might be tempted to mount.

The former owner's house still stands, although unoccupied for nine or ten years. Father wants you to take up residence there to provide a full-time management presence on the property. It's to be expected the house will require work to render it liveable again. As of tomorrow, your first task is to inspect the house and identify the work required."

"Right; while I understand Father's thinking on the matter, I doubt I have the expertise to identify the work required. I can assess it in terms of my comfort, but I know nothing about the domestic side. Any work needed in the kitchen and laundry areas is beyond my ken. And I will need household staff. Again, this is beyond my existing knowledge.

And, as I mentioned earlier, we have lost good, long-term overseers. Despite a couple of new recruits, we remain short-handed. I have to undertake some of their work as well as my own. I won't have the time to organise the refurbishment of the house or recruit suitable household staff." Cameron shrugged and shook his head as he finished speaking.

"No, I agree with you. The long ride from the port gave me time to devote serious thought to the matter. I think I have a solution, subject to your approval, of course. I have to admit it is not entirely my thinking. Father also floated it as something to consider."

"I hope your solution also includes a magic wand, because I think I will need one."

"Not a magic wand, but an extremely efficient person to manage the whole exercise and ensure you continue to be well looked after: Cecile.

Cecile will have that place licked into shape and suitably staffed in no time, and she can then stay on to maintain your household."

"Do you think Cecile will welcome such suggestions?"

"Knowing Cecile… probably not. Anything that is not her idea is never welcomed. I suggested to Father that his daughter might not be happy about the plan. He left us little room to move on this one – even went as far as to insist on it.

Although he didn't dwell on it, he did mention that I now had someone to run my household and no longer needed Cecile. He also hinted that he believed Sarah would be relieved to have Cecile out from under her feet."

"And you agree?"

"After today's performance by Cecile… oh yes, I support his suggestion wholeheartedly. But, the question is, how do you feel about it?"

"Well, it's not that I particularly want to leave here, but I believe father's plan is sound. Cecile is perfect to lick that other house into shape and have it running like a top. We get on quite well, so there won't be problems there. It will keep Cecile in charge, and we both know how important that is to her. When is all this to happen? I mean, when do you tell Cecile?"

"We are meeting tomorrow morning. What I tell Cecile then depends on the outcome of our meeting. If you had vetoed Cecile's involvement in your move to the other plantation, it would restrict my comments to her behaviour now Sarah is in charge of this house. It would not have been an easy meeting. The conversation I now can have should be easier… but I don't doubt it still will cause arguments and a good deal of sulking."

"Either way, it always was a case of 'better you than me', big brother."

While Robert met with Cameron, Cecile dispatched Femi to help Sarah unpack. Once everything was in the cupboard, Sarah selected a dress for dinner and held it up for Femi to see.

"What do you think about this for my first dinner in this house?" Femi looked awkward and eventually gave a little shake of her head.

"Begging your pardon, Missus, but that is not for dinner. That is for dinner when we have guests – special guests." She rummaged through the dresses in the cupboard and withdrew one. "This is good for dinner tonight," Femi said as she held up her selection.

"Oh, I see. Thank you, Femi. It would never do for me to arrive at dinner overdressed on my first night. The atmosphere is bad enough already. Now, what about jewellery? My amber necklace would go with that gown."

Sarah opened her jewellery box and lifted out her amber necklace to show Femi… who again gave a negative response.

"No, Missus. Jewels are for wearing to Government house – for special occasions. This would be better for at home." She selected a small gold locket on a slender gold chain and held it up for Sarah to see.

"Ah, yes, that will do nicely. It's a family heirloom handed down through four generations. Thank you, Femi. I hope you can be patient with me while I learn the ways of life in the Caribbean. I will depend on you to help me get it right for some time." Femi beamed at her, and both women knew a certain bond had been forged between them.

When Robert's meeting with Cameron finished, it was time for the men to dress for dinner. Dressed and ready to go down to drinks, Robert stood in their private sitting room and called to Sarah. She came out of her dressing room and waited for his comments.

"You look wonderful; just right."

Beaming with delight, Sarah did a twirl in front of him so he could assess the full extent of her outfit. When her back was to him, and she faced Femi watching from the dressing room doorway, she dropped Femi an exaggerated wink.

"Yes, perfect," Robert said when she again faced him. "We should go down. The gong for pre-dinner drinks will sound in a moment."

"A gong! You have a gong?"

"Yes, it summons us to meals and drinks. Is there a problem with that?"

"Of course not, it's wonderful – but it might make me homesick."

"For Glasgow…?"

Sarah giggled. "No, silly, for India. The sound of our big old brass gong regulated our lives there. Aunt Bess had one in Glasgow, but it wasn't a proper brass one and made a funny sound, not a proper sound."

"Well, ours makes a proper sound that can be heard everywhere in the house, and it is about to be heard now. Come, we must go down. It would not do for you to arrive late." As they started down, the deep, resonant sound of the gong came up the stairs to meet them.

They weren't late. Cameron entered the small sitting room off the dining room a few seconds ahead of them. He gave Sarah a low whistle of approval as she entered.

"I can see why big brother snapped you up so quickly," he said as he approached her, hand outstretched. "Welcome to our island and your new home. I hope your settling-in process is as painless as possible." Cameron shot his brother a knowing look as he delivered his last comment.

"Cecile is not here. Doesn't she join us for drinks?" Sarah whispered to Robert as Cameron busied himself pouring drinks.

"Oh yes, she will be along shortly. She likes to arrive late to make a grand entrance… tonight, more so than at any other time, I should think."

Robert gave a little chuckle as he finished speaking. It was cut short by the appearance in the doorway of Cecile. She was wearing her most haughty countenance. Sarah realised her sister-in-law's mood was as black as hell.

At precisely 7.30PM, the dinner gong sounded. Obediently, everyone put down their glass and trooped into the dining room. Robert stood beside his chair at the head of the table. Cecile headed for the opposite end. But a footman took her arm and escorted her to a chair along the left-hand side of the table.

Unsure of the seating arrangements, Sarah held back until everyone else was in place. Immediately, Cameron came and escorted her to her appropriate place opposite her husband at the end of the table. While she knew that was her rightful position, she had witnessed Cecile's attempt to take that chair. Sarah had no doubts Cecile had sat there since her parents left the island. Relegation to the side of the table would embarrass her, a visible indicator of her demotion in the household. More than that, Sarah knew it would add to the tension and not help smooth the transition to the new order of things.

Could no one else feel it? The tension in the room was so strong Sarah thought she could almost chew it. Yet, no one else at the table seemed to notice the antagonistic vibes from Cecile. I suppose that's only right, she told herself. After all, it is me they are directed at. Later, as she and Robert climbed the stairs to their apartment, Robert seemed preoccupied.

"My Dear, you hardly touched your meal tonight. Are you ill, or was the food not to your liking? You know, your position in this house allows you to change whatever you wish, including the meals being served."

"There was nothing wrong with the meal. It was wonderful food. As for making changes, good God, I've only been here five minutes and still know nothing about how the place works. Please allow me time to become accustomed to the place first."

Alone in her dressing room preparing for bed, she murmured to her mirror, "I must make a stand. Starting tomorrow, I must make a definite show of my position in this house. If I don't, Cecile will win, and the rest of my days here will be hell. You are not a Shrinking Violet, Sarah Erskine. Round up your mettle and show them what you are made of before it is too late." Any further thought on the matter was cut short.

"What are you doing in there?" Robert demanded. "Are you planning on coming to bed at all tonight? After complaining of no sleep last night, I thought you would be first to bed tonight." Giggling, she rushed to their bedroom.

A cool breeze from the open window drifted across her as she snuggled into the soft, big bed. Her eyes felt heavy. She allowed them to close, before they suddenly flashed open again. Wide awake, she rolled over to face Robert.

"Are you still awake?" Sarah whispered. He grunted in response. "The hatred I felt in the dining room tonight was almost unbearable. Is it likely Cecile will continue to hate me, no matter what I do or how long I live here?"

"Don't worry about Cecile. She always is unpleasant to all of us, not just you. Although, I did notice she seemed to have something special reserved for you. But, as I told you before, I have a solution. Try to be patient with her for a little longer. Argh, now I think on it, prepare for things perhaps to become even worse after tomorrow morning. It should last only a few days though. So try to put up with it if you can. I know it's not easy, but try to ignore Cecile. That's what we do."

Moments later, he was snoring. Sarah knew his comments meant she would not fall asleep any time soon.

*****

Robert's words proved prophetic. For the next few days, Cecile was almost unbearable to be around. The only good thing was her need to spend most of each day at the other plantation supervising the work on the homestead and recruiting household staff, who she set to cleaning and polishing immediately they were hired.

By the end of the week, although work on refurbishing the homestead was far from complete, Cecile deemed the place liveable and with a functioning kitchen once more. She and Cameron relocated to the other plantation, and Sarah – and probably most of her household staff – breathed a sigh of relief. In the changeover, Cecile did manage to cause one final upheaval.

Near the end of the week, and just as Cecile and Cameron were about to move out, Femi reported to Sarah that the household staff were unhappy. After some encouragement, Femi divulged the reason – which Sarah duly reported to Robert. Cecile and Cameron were supervising loading the last of their belongings on a wagon when Robert stormed out and ordered them both back into his office.

"Perhaps you might care to tell me, Cecile, why you think you have the right to steal my household staff," he demanded. "They are my staff. They belong here in this house, and any you have installed at the other place had better be returned before lunchtime. Any others you had designs upon will not join you on the other plantation. If those already there are not returned as requested, I personally will take a wagon over and bring them back.

And, more importantly for you, if you create any problem about this, you will be on the first ship out of here for Glasgow. We have suffered your nonsense long enough and have tried to ignore it most of the time. Now you have gone too far to be ignored. Not only have you set out to make Sarah's life a misery and as difficult as possible since she arrived, but your behaviour regarding the household staff cannot be excused.

I'm sure Cameron will confirm that, as our father's representative here on the island, I have the authority to put you on a ship any time I choose. Here's a final warning: return my staff and do not try anything like this again, or I *will* throw you off this island. Do you need further explanation about any of that?"

Cecile drew herself up to her full height and glared at Robert. She was ready to unleash a tirade at him, but his stance and angry glare made her back down. There was no apology. She simply dropped her head, kept her eyes downcast, and nodded. He thought he glimpsed the glint of a tear on her cheek, but his anger prevented any sympathy for her.

A downcast figure was perched high on the wagon beside Cameron as the wagon left for the other plantation. From an upstairs window, Sarah watched it drive away. She felt a pang of sympathy for Cecile, but it was momentary at best. Then, the reality of her situation hit her. She was now in charge of this house and all its staff. Along with that realisation came the almost overwhelming belief that she was not up to the job.

It was as if Femi could read the turmoil in Sarah's mind. She came and wrapped an arm around Sarah's shoulders.

"Come away and sit down for a bit, Miss. I will set up a meeting with Delores straight after tea this morning. Delores was the housekeeper here before Miss Cecile decided she would run the place, and she knew this house better than anyone. All of the staff love her. She will understand – everything. Put your faith in her, and she will have this place running like a top in no time … and it will be a happy household again."

"What about you, Femi? Are you happy to stay with me as my maid? Would you rather go with Miss Cecile and Mr Cameron?" Sarah asked in a voice little above a whisper, and held her breath as she awaited the answer.

"No, Miss, I belong here with you. Besides, I was born here in this house, and it has been my home ever since."

Relieved, Sarah turned her attention to the proposed meeting with Delores. With Femi's help, she put together a list of topics to discuss and another list of the questions she should ask. When morning tea was served in her sitting room downstairs, Sarah felt relatively confident about the forthcoming meeting.

By the time Robert returned for lunch, a very different wife awaited him. The meeting with Delores was a joy. It achieved a better outcome than she had hoped for. It was a vibrant and happy wife who sat down with Robert for lunch. And it did not go unnoticed.

The speed at which everything seemed to fall into place afterwards surprised Sarah. The household was running well, and she had initiated a couple of small changes in how things were done. Everyone seemed a lot happier, including Sarah herself. But, while everything was going well at home, other more far-reaching forces were at work throughout the Caribbean.

*****

Sarah decided to devote the morning to catching up on correspondence. So far, she managed no more than a few hesitant, uninspiring lines of a letter to her mother. Pen poised to start a new paragraph, Sarah again hesitated. Should she share her concerns with her mother? After all, they were personal and not easy to document in a letter. She heaved a sigh, put her pen down and stared out the window as she gave the matter further thought. With her desk tucked in below the window in her upstairs sitting room, anything happening outside was a ready distraction.

1842 was fast drawing to an end. Soon, it would be Christmas, and then they would celebrate their second wedding anniversary… and her arrival on the island a few weeks later, almost two years ago. In some ways, a lot had happened over those two years but, in other ways, nothing much changed after the initial few weeks.

Nevertheless, she never tired of the sweeping views across the plantation afforded by this window. It was restful watching the workers in the fields, and the wagon loads of cut sugar cane stalks on their way to the factory for processing. If she allowed her eyes to roam far off in the distance, it was possible to make out the homestead on Cameron's plantation. Cameron had remained a regular visitor, coming to discuss plantation matters every couple of days or so. While Cameron managed the second plantation, Robert was responsible for both properties.

While the rhythm of life and everything about living here was sweet, a growing concern began consuming her. She wished her mother was there to discuss it with her: after almost two years of marriage, they remained childless. She reassured herself that it was a good marriage, and it wasn't due to a lack of trying that there were no children. The lack of an heir must trouble Robert and his family. But Robert never alluded to it and seemed happy enough in their marriage. Was she worrying needlessly?

It was thinking about Robert that brought something else to mind. Recently, she had noticed he had lost some of… some of what? It wasn't some of his spirit. He remained the same Robert she married. Was the lack of a child eating away at him too, or was he troubled by something else? Now she thought about it, he seemed more tense than usual. Even Cameron seemed preoccupied these days.

Abandoning the letter to her mother, she murmured, "It's no use today. But I must try to talk to Robert as soon as possible. Something is afoot. I can sense it."

That proved easier said than done. Robert seemed so busy, and tired at the end of each day. No ideal time to talk to him presented itself until a couple of weeks later. He came home early that afternoon and seemed more relaxed that evening. She decided to try her luck over pre-dinner drinks.

"Robert, would you feel up to a chat with me after dinner tonight?"

"Of course, my dear; after dinner, we should adjourn to my office where we can talk in relative privacy."

Right, I have until after dinner to work out how to broach the matters I want to raise, she thought as she sipped her drink in silence.

Chapter 22

Difficult Times

"Mrs Wallace, you have my undivided attention. What is concerning you that you wish to discuss with me?"

Thank you, God, Robert, or whoever, Sarah thought, encouraged by Robert's opening comments.

"I've detected a certain tension, not only in you, but in Cameron and others as well. I'm not so naïve as not to be able to work out that it must be something serious. If that be the case, perhaps I need to know about the situation. What is afoot to cause you and others such tension? Has something happened that I wasn't aware of?"

"Nothing recent, my dear. It's more about the state of the nation – or perhaps I should say 'the colony'. It's a situation that's developed over the last decade or so. I'm not sure how much you know of the history of this British West Indies colony and, more particularly, what you know about the establishment of the sugar plantations here."

"I admit to being ill-informed, but I understood that plantations were developed here towards the end of the last century. Can you share with me now that part of the history that relates to the sugar industry and, by association, this plantation?"

"As I said, it's not a recent development. The problem started back in 1830 with the abolition of the slave trade. The rot really set in with the emancipation of slave labour in the British West Indies in 1834. The situation for plantations worsened further in 1838 when the apprentice system was abolished."

"My God, I had no idea this place benefited from the slave trade. What about our current employees, including our household staff? Are they still part of the slave trade?"

"No, of course not. In this colony, slaves were emancipated in 1834. The workers on our plantations are part of the local population who were hired under the apprentice system."

"Does that mean our workers can leave whenever they feel inclined?"

"Yes, I suppose that is true. But you also have to ask yourself how they would support themselves and their families if they gave up their positions here. By continuing to work on the plantations, they continue to earn a steady income. There are few other opportunities for employment on this island, other than working on the plantations. And the plantations would cease to function if their workers chose to abandon their employment. We employ but a handful of white overseers to ensure proper order and function are maintained, and that a quality product is produced to ship to Glasgow."

"I see. Now I understand the interdependency between plantation and the local population, but is there any guarantee that situation will continue? Is it likely the local population might band together to take over one or more of the plantations, to run it themselves?"

"That is the real and present fear. It has happened in other parts of the Caribbean, and without too much effort from the locals. In the French and Spanish Caribbean colonies, many of the white owners abandoned their plantations. They walked off their properties because it became impossible for them to continue viable operations. There are no buyers. The locals do not have the money to purchase the plantations, and nor are they interested in buying them. They are prepared to return to living as they did before the advent of the plantations, and to maintain that lifestyle until the white plantation owners give up and walk off their land."

"Is that likely to happen here? Are there indications the people of this island might adopt a similar approach in response to a lucrative opportunity?"

"I can't claim there are definite indications along those lines. But, realistically, such an occurrence can't be ruled out. Having said that, we can do little to prevent such an occurrence. Our only hope of managing this as best we can is to keep an ear to whatever is happening throughout these islands. And for those in Glasgow to pay particular attention to politics both there and in other countries with colonies in this region."

"So, your father will be heavily involved in saving his plantations, although he is now far from here?"

"Aye, he is being kept busy and involved. After all, he has more than the plantations at stake. He also needs to think about his shipping operation. A downturn in his shipping operations resulted from the loss of sugar cargoes from some of those other colonies

The family has agreed we need to develop a strategy, if not for the protection of our physical assets, for the preservation of our enterprise's continued financial well-being. And that brings me to something I intended to discuss with you tomorrow. Father has requested that I return to Glasgow immediately for just such a purpose. I have booked a passage on our ship leaving the day after tomorrow. I doubt I will remain in Glasgow for an extended period, but it might mean I will be away for up to three months.

While I do not want to subject you to the prospect of facing a trip to Glasgow and back, I am also concerned about leaving you here alone. I would appreciate your honest thoughts on whether you wish to undertake the Glasgow trip with me, or remain here while I am gone."

"But, if I were to remain here, I would not be alone. I am surrounded by staff, and I have Femi to look after me as well. Apart from that, Cameron lives not so far away that he can't continue to visit regularly as he does now."

"Am I to take it that you do not wish to accompany me to Glasgow? I was almost sure you would want to return to the city to visit your family and renew acquaintances."

"It is a temptation. But, I fear that, if I return to Glasgow, I might not want to return here. And, before you ask, I am happy here with you and my life on this plantation. So, if it's all the same to you, I will remain here while you deal with whatever you must do in Glasgow, but promise me you will return here as quickly as possible."

Back in her dressing room, she felt uneasy as she readied for bed that night. Had she made the right decision in electing not to accompany Robert to Glasgow? What about all that unsettling news about the future of plantations in other colonies and perhaps on this island? Suddenly, while being childless remained a concern, it had somehow been pushed further into the background. She heaved a sigh and gave a little giggle.

"Well, now, what are you going to put in your letter to your mother when you sit down to finish it tomorrow?" Sarah asked her reflection in the mirror.

*****

Little changed after Robert left for Glasgow. On a daily basis, everything continued much as it had done previously. One noticeable difference was Cameron's more frequent presence on the main plantation. Whenever he was there, he always spent at least a few minutes with Sarah.

As Cameron confided to Femi on one such occasion, "Robert would never forgive me if I didn't keep a close eye on her and make sure she was all right." Sarah was touched by it when Femi relayed Cameron's comments to her.

Despite the sameness, Robert's absence did have her feeling something was missing from her life, as she explained to her mother in a letter early in 1843:

Robert remains in Glasgow as I sit down to write this letter. It feels he has been gone an interminable time. Christmas was spent without him, as was our wedding anniversary and Hogmanay. Somehow they seemed to lose much of their significance due to his absence.

Before Robert left, he had indicated that a worst-case scenario for his absence might be three weeks to Glasgow, a month spent with his father, and then another three weeks on the return voyage to the island: about ten weeks. He had written soon after his arrival in Glasgow, but nothing more since. It was now twelve weeks since she had farewelled him with a smile – and then cried her eyes out. Although she tried her best to prevent it, worries crept in and began intruding on her days.

She now anxiously awaited Cameron's every visit and, despite her best intentions, inevitably asked after any news from Glasgow. Yesterday, when she inquired whether Cameron had heard anything of Robert, his reply made her vow not to ask again.

Cameron had guffawed and said, "Robert…! He'll be too busy having a good time to write." Then, realising the insensitivity of his remark, he attempted to repair the damage. "I'm sorry, Sarah. I do not believe that for one moment. I'm positive he will be as anxious to return here as you are to have him back. Don't worry. Father will have him on the first available ship as soon as their business matters are done."

While she knew in her heart Cameron probably had given her an accurate summation of the situation, she lay awake a long time that night trying to still the myriads of doubts flooding her mind.

Even Femi felt the strain of trying to find positive comments to lighten her mistress' mind about the situation. It was four months, and Mr Robert still had not returned. Why had he not written to his wife occasionally, even if only a brief note to explain his delay?

Then, a few days before it was five months since his departure, Robert returned. Later, he explained how it had been a last-minute rush to grab a passage on the first ship to leave port, and there had been no time to advise of his imminent return. No one knew of it until the wagon loaded with supplies from the ship stopped at the front steps. Femi, watching from an upstairs window, screamed.

"Miss Sarah, Miss Sarah, come look… quick … look out the window."

Alarmed by Femi's behaviour, Sarah hesitantly made her way to the window and peered out. Then she was running to bounce down the stairs at a dangerous pace to reach the huge front doors as a couple of young staff lads flung them open. Without hesitation, she rushed down the stairs and threw herself at Robert, who stood beside the wagon, rubbing his backside and stretching after the trip from the port. Almost knocked off his feet by Sarah's impact, they fell back against the wagon in a laughing, tangled mass.

"Easy on, old girl; if we don't get our feet back under us, we'll end up in the dirt when the driver moves the wagon."

Remembering her position and the decorum it demanded, Sarah untangled herself from her husband, stepped back, and straightened her dress. After signalling the driver to move on, Robert stepped up and wrapped an arm around Sarah's waist. He planted a kiss on her forehead before gently urging her forward.

"Come, my dear Mrs Wallace, we have much to catch up on before dinner, and this is not the place to do it." Sarah blushed at the twinkle in his eye.

They had little time together before the gong for pre-dinner drinks. Sarah would have been happy to ignore it, but Robert felt in need of a drink after his long day. When the gong sounded, he rushed to open the door before holding his hand out to Sarah. Arm-in-arm, they went down to drinks and dinner, but they indulged in an early night as soon as dinner was over.

As he drifted off to sleep, Robert remembered something to tell Sarah. "I sent a message with the other wagon driver to tell Cameron to come in the morning. Perhaps, you might join us for at least part of that meeting." Of course, she would join them. Although she didn't know why, she felt a frisson of excitement ripple through her body.

*****

Cameron arrived a short while after breakfast. Robert asked for an early morning tea tray to be brought to his office. Conversation was light and of no particular consequence as they made themselves comfortable while they awaited the tea tray. Then it took a few more minutes before everyone had their tea and a scone, and the real business of the meeting could begin. In a voice that made Sarah's stomach tighten, Robert opened proceedings.

"As you are aware, Cameron, and as I outlined to Sarah before I departed for Glasgow, these are unsettled times in the Caribbean. So far, this colony has fared much better than most in the area, but we are unlikely to escape the winds of change sweeping the whole of the Caribbean. These are hard times for plantation owners, even on this island.

The political changes over the decade aside, the price of sugar is not in our favour. It has declined since about 1820. Some are now predicting that, by 1850, the sugar price will have dropped by fifty percent. Already, we are aware of its impact on our profit margins, and they are likely to narrow further in the coming years."

"Aye, as you say, we have felt the adverse impact of everything so far. Is there any good news to come out of Glasgow you might share with us?" Cameron asked.

"Only more bad news, I'm afraid, brother, and it will be *really* bad news if the experts are correct."

"Bad news for whom?" Sarah queried. "Are we talking about just the plantation owners, or everyone living here who isn't a local?"

"Well, the two go hand-in-hand, I'm afraid. Anything impacting the viability and continued operation of the plantations is likely to have catastrophic consequences for any colonials in the region. Most of them, and the colonial administrators appointed to the positions here, may well find themselves thrown out."

Robert spoke without lifting his eyes from the tea leaves he swirled in his cup. Sarah's heart went out to him. It was difficult news he had to share, and it was obvious to her that Robert himself struggled to deal with it.

"Right, big brother, give us the full story. Tell us about this next dose of bad news we are likely to be dealt. And is there anything we can do about it… like avoiding it somehow?" Cameron didn't sound at all hopeful as he asked his question.

"Talk about a Sugar Duties Act is gaining momentum in some quarters. Obviously, such an Act is seen by planters as a possible beginning of the end. In Glasgow, those with any affiliations or interests in the industry are lobbying support against such a move. Nevertheless, some insiders see opposition to it as a futile undertaking. It likely would open the door to free trade. Those with an eye to the future see it as the first step in colonial sugar ultimately losing its protection in the British market."

"Christ, where does that leave us? I suppose the big question is about timing. You make it sound as though there is little chance all this won't happen, but when is it likely to happen?"

"Father's connections in the political sphere suggest debate on a possible Sugar Duties Act will likely begin within the next couple of years."

"A couple of years….! Hell, that doesn't give us much time to protect ourselves. Does Father have a plan?"

"Well, a plan of sorts... Regardless of whether he can pull it off or not, it appears a safe bet our days on this island – on our plantations – are numbered, as is living the life we've known since we were born. With some degree of urgency, he is searching for a buyer for our properties here. So, how much longer we have here rather depends on how successful he is at finding a buyer."

"That is unlikely to happen overnight, and I suppose that is some small comfort. It would allow us a little more time here. What happens if Father can't find a buyer? Do we hang on to the bitter end before walking off as many have done in other colonies?"

"No, not exactly. There is an emergency plan. If, as in other colonies, the local population becomes restless and impatient to become 'entitled' to whatever is on their island, we will be forced to make a rapid and covert exodus."

"We'll still walk off. Doesn't that amount to the same thing but with a different timing?" Robert nodded, and Cameron continued. "So, in the meantime, we sit here with our bags packed and watching every move made by the workers in case it threatens our safety." Robert's response was a shrug followed by a nod.

"Does Father not have any suggestions regarding what we might do now?"

"Argh, yes, I was just coming to that. He has drawn up a realistic timeline for us to follow. He thinks he has all but secured a buyer for your plantation and that the sale might go through in the next couple of months."

"And what am I supposed to do then?"

"You will move back here to help run this plantation… until the end of the year. By Christmas, he wants you back in Glasgow to help run our shipping operations. That side of the company's business has expanded with a significant increase in cargo from the American plantations. As you are familiar with such operations, having overseen all shipping to and from here, he believes your expertise will be invaluable in running the entire shipping operations from Glasgow."

Having sat quietly taking in all Robert's news from Glasgow, Sarah could no longer remain silent.

"What about Cecile? If the other plantation is sold and Cameron has to move back here, Cecile will have to move back too." She didn't need to explain why it concerned her.

"It rather depends on what happens in the next couple of months. Until and unless the other plantation is sold, nothing will change. Once it is sold, Cameron will be living back here. Cecile's situation is a little different. Whether the plantation sells or not in the immediate future, Cecile will be on her way back to Glasgow. Father is adamant he wants her back in Glasgow by the middle of the year at the latest, and sooner if possible."

"I take it he means her return to Glasgow to be a permanent arrangement and not just a holiday?" Robert nodded. Cameron let out a low whistle. "Good luck breaking that news to her. I think I will spend a lot of time in the paddocks over the next little while."

"Probably the safest move…," Robert agreed. "I plan to ride over this afternoon to break the news to her, and try to negotiate a possible departure date."

"Robert," Cameron began hesitantly, "what about you and Sarah? What are the plans for your future?"

"Again, it will depend on whether Father finds a buyer for this plantation and how soon. He has suggested we might move to the sugar-growing areas of the Americas, where I could become involved in their industry. While I didn't reject the suggestion, I made it clear I wasn't keen on the idea. Then, just before I left, he came up with another suggestion: we could move to Java."

"Java…?" Sarah exclaimed. "Why the hell would we want to go to Java? I'm not sure exactly where it is, but I am sure I don't want to live there. Well, Robert, why Java?"

Before he could begin to explain, Cameron cut in again. "He's not looking to buy a plantation in Java, is he?"

"Let me explain, please, before you both shoot me. No, he's not buying a plantation in Java. I don't think outsiders can, anyway. But, the sugar industry in that country is forging ahead in a big way and is keen to embrace new technology. Much of the equipment they are interested in is manufactured in Scotland. Father's connections assure him I would be an asset on the ground in Java for those Scottish manufacturers keen to advise and supply the industry there.

They are prepared to wait for me to come on board, but not for too long. So far, they are servicing enquiries from Java by sending one of their engineers to the country every so often to talk to major players and explain the new technologies being developed in Scotland and England. Before arriving in Java, I would spend a brief period in Scotland to allow me to become familiar with all that's being developed."

When the gong sounded for lunch, a gloomy trio made its way to the dining room. Apart from whatever she might feel about the news Robert shared with them that morning, Sarah's immediate concern was for Robert and the meeting he was to have with Cecile that afternoon.

*****

At first, life seemed content to imitate Douglas Wallace's plan for his plantation ownership, the first stage of which was for Cecile's return to Glasgow. Predictably, she dug her heels in and accused Robert of concocting a vicious plan to remove her from the island.

It took a stern letter from her father before she accepted defeat and started packing her belongings. A little under three months after his return from Glasgow with the bad news, Robert and Cameron stood on the dock waving to their sister, Cecile, on the ship making its way out of the port.

On the way back to the plantations, Cameron dared to broach the subject of his future.

"The last letter I had from Father suggested a deal was all but done on my plantation, but that was more than a couple of weeks ago. Have you heard anything more recent than that? I guess I'm wondering whether I should be preparing to move back into the big house with you sometime soon."

"The letter I received three days ago said the deal had been finalised, but that further negotiations were underway. Although Father's information was sketchy, I understood it to say that the ongoing negotiations were for the sale of my plantation. There was no indication of a timeline or anything else. So, I don't know whether to sit back and relax, or if I should get busy packing.

I haven't shared that information with Sarah yet. She still isn't enamoured of the idea of moving to Java, but that's now becoming more likely to be where my future will be. I hope that whatever happens, it occurs before life gets too difficult here. So far, we are lucky the local population doesn't seem keen to exercise its newly granted freedom or power."

Everything followed the plan: Cecile arrived in Glasgow; Cameron's plantation sold a couple of months after Cecile left, and he moved back into the big house on Robert's plantation; Cameron was back in Glasgow permanently by Christmas 1843. The last part of Douglas Wallace's plan for his Caribbean properties was slowly taking shape.

A couple of big spending speculators had blown hot and cold over buying the last plantation. The continuing worrying feature for Robert was the prospect of the introduction of the Sugar Duties Act. His father's letters continued to mention increased support for such a move. In his most recent letter, he went so far as to suggest that whispers in political circles had the Bill likely to be introduced to Parliament for debate in the first half of 1845.

Nevertheless, the sale of the plantation went through in mid-1845… but only after it was agreed that Robert would stay on to manage the plantation for its new owners. How long such an arrangement should be in place was never discussed as far as Robert knew, but happenings beyond their control dictated when it ended.

In 1846, despite ongoing protests by planters, the Sugar Duties Act was passed by parliament and took almost immediate effect. The sugar price declined further. But, a further blow for the colonial industry was yet to come. Rumour had it that, by the early 1850s, colonial sugar would lose its protection in the British market.

Despite the declining profitability and increasing unrest on the island, the new owners of the plantation Robert managed carried on for as long as they could. But, early in 1849, they also succumbed to the worsening situation and called it a day.

So, in mid 1849, it was no surprise to Robert and Sarah when they were told the plantation had become a liability and the owners planned to abandon it. They recommended Robert and his wife return to Glasgow on the next available ship.

PART 4

Java 1850

Chapter 23

Jane

Sarah remained unhappy about leaving the Caribbean and even more depressed – if that were possible – about the prospect of moving to Java. Saying goodbye to Femi had been difficult, but breaking the news of their departure to the other household staff wasn't easy either. She tried putting a positive spin on it by assuring them a new lady-of-the-house probably would arrive soon after she left, but she could give them no assurances regarding their continued employment

Robert was relieved when, after a few days at sea, Sarah showed some interest in the next phase of their life. Sarah demanded information as they sat in their cabin sipping their morning tea.

"So, what happens next, Robert? I know we are expected in Glasgow, but how long are we likely to remain there?"

"It could be a couple of months. Apart from spending time with the suppliers I will represent to the Java sugar industry, there will be some business with Father to take care of first, and hopefully, a brief holiday for us. I have alerted Father that I hope to utilise the family's highland property for at least a week, so we can unwind a little before tackling anything else.

Then later, while I am busy with other matters, you will have ample opportunity to spend time with your grandmother and Aunt Bess. And, no doubt, there will be plenty of shopping you will want to do."

"Ye-es, there is that. But one of my priorities is to contact my friend, Jane McCabe. You might remember her. She was my maid of honour at our wedding. We corresponded regularly for a while after I went to the Caribbean, but she stopped responding to my letters. I was concerned she might be ill – or worse – and asked Aunt Bess if she had heard anything of Jane. She didn't know anything, but queried whether she might have married and moved away from Glasgow. As the only real friend I made in Glasgow, I want to catch up with her again."

A lack of response from Robert made Sarah look up at him. His furrowed brow suggested he was deep in thought. Perhaps he was thinking of some way to locate Jane, Sarah thought.

"What do you suggest I do about Jane, Robert? I doubt sending her another letter will help."

"I would be the last person best able to help you with this. Perhaps try Aunt Bess again. She might have heard something or be able to enquire after Jane among some of her friends. But, as you say, she is likely married now and living elsewhere – under her married name."

While his suggestions made sense, Sarah didn't find them helpful. But, while speaking of Jane, Sarah decided on a course of action. She would go around to where Jane had lived with her grandmother. Hopefully, she would find Jane there. If not, maybe Grandmother McCabe would tell her where her granddaughter now lived.

"Right, Robert, so tell me what happens after you finalise all your business in Glasgow. I assume we will head to out new life on Java." Robert confirmed she was correct. "So, tell me what you know about this place where we will live."

"I don't have details of our living arrangements to share with you, but I can tell you what I know about the island."

"Anything at all will be an improvement on what I know now. Please enlighten me."

"As you wish. In much the same way as our island in the Caribbean was a British West Indies colony, Java is a Dutch colony. The difference is that their sugar industry is relatively new compared to the Caribbean industry. On Java, until 1830, much of the arable land was under paddy fields, and rice was the main crop. Only small pockets of sugar cane were grown, mainly by the Chinese landholders, and only for local consumption. These were located on the capital's outskirts, and each had its own small processing factory.

The Dutch Government saw a lucrative opportunity and made sweeping changes under something referred to as The Cultivation System. Under that system, they moved the industry away from small plantations in urban areas to the more densely peasant-populated north-eastern part of the country where vast areas of land were also under rice. The local population grows the cane and processes it in factories on the properties that the Dutch Government helped establish. European or Chinese are contracted by the government to run such establishments.

Although I don't know too much about their industry, I understand it has flourished in the subsequent years and now boasts dozens of plantations and factories, and networks of roads and railways."

"So, those government-oriented factories will likely be your future customers?"

"I believe that will be the case. The plantations' products are shipped to the Netherlands, and the locals are paid in some way for producing and processing the cane."

"Are their factories similar to the Caribbean ones you are familiar with?"

"No-o, I think they are more advanced than ours were in the Caribbean. It appears Java is keen to adopt any new technology as soon as it becomes available. That's why British manufacturers need someone on the ground to service the industry there… and there are plenty of factories to service."

Sarah sighed and pondered Robert's words for a moment before asking, "How do you *really* feel about this job you're being offered?"

"What other options do I have at the moment? It will bring in income to support us, at least until something else comes along, and it is something I already know about."

"There is always the family business… Might your father be able to find you a position in his empire as he did for Cameron?"

"He might – but I wouldn't accept it.

His reply surprised her and had her intrigued, but some instinct told Sarah now was not the time to pursue it. After a brief pause, conversation turned to generalities until Robert remembered something he needed to discuss with the captain and went off to deal with it. Alone in their cabin, the solitude allowed Sarah to revisit Robert's strange comment about working in the family's enterprise.

Robert and his father always appeared to get on well and, whether he thought of it that way or not, managing the family's plantations in the Caribbean was, in fact, working for his father. Was it a case of her not being aware of something that happened between father and son to sour the relationship? While she would not explore it now, she knew she would seek an explanation sometime soon.

A mixture of excitement and dread helped the days fly past until they were only a day out from Glasgow. The prospect of seeing her grandmother and Aunt Bess caused mixed feelings. Her last encounter with those two dear ladies was when she bade them farewell before setting sail for the Caribbean at the start of 1842.

Now, she would arrive back in Glasgow early in the second half of 1849… and Sarah was still without children to show them. Although no mention of Wallace offspring was in any of their letters, Sarah knew the two women would be wondering about her health – and the state of her marriage. She also knew that assuring them her marriage was in fine shape would be useless. So, this would be the time, eh? The time she had to admit her inadequacies as a wife and woman, and accept the shame and scorn that would accompany it.

What about her best friend in Glasgow, Jane McCabe? What would she think? Would she expect to meet Sarah's children? No, perhaps she wouldn't, Sarah told herself. After all, they lost touch some time ago. Jane wouldn't know what had happened in the interim. It wasn't working. No matter what Sarah tried telling herself, she was not convincing. While Jane might not know if Sarah had produced children, Jane would expect she had. It was the natural assumption to make. So, how would she explain her childless state to any of those most likely to enquire about it?

"I'll deal with it as best I can, as and when the time comes," she firmly told the empty cabin. "In the meantime, this forthcoming Java thing is more than enough for me to worry about."

Dread was fast overcoming excitement until they turned into the port, and it obliterated any sense of excitement.

Cameron was on the dock with a carriage waiting. He had arranged a wagon to collect their belongings as they were unloaded from the hold. "We will store them in one of the warehouses until you are ready to leave," he told Robert as the two men stood supervising loading the wagon. Once the wagon was on its way, the brothers returned to the carriage where Sarah waited. Cameron took up the reins, and they were on their way into the city.

"Your rooms are ready for you," Cameron told Robert. "It's as well your ship came in early. It allows you a little time to settle in before lunch. Father asked that you attend a meeting in his office at three o'clock this afternoon."

"Which office? His office at the house or the one at the business?"

"At home… he plans to be home early to discuss several matters with you."

"Cameron, how have you settled back into life in Glasgow? And, how is the new job going?"

"Argh, it's a different life, but it is not unpleasant or difficult. I quite enjoy running the shipping operations, and Father tends to leave me alone to get on with it."

"What about Cecile? How has she settled in?"

"Detente prevails in the Wallace household. It has been an interesting time. Cecile and Father are two of a kind. Cecile did not want to be here and was determined not to remain here, while Father was just as determined she would remain here for the rest of her life. I think the sale of the last plantation helped achieve a tentative peace. It made her realise she had nowhere and nothing to return to in the Caribbean.

I didn't tell you this, but I suspect Father is trying to marry her off. There has been a line-up of suitable single men of an appropriate age invited to dinner of late, but she hasn't appeared tempted by any so far."

"Lord preserve us! Such a move on his part is bound to trigger an all-out war. I hope détente lasts at least until we are on a ship for Java. I do feel for you though, if the whole thing turns as ugly as I think it will."

"You are determined to go through with the Java job… even though Sarah does not want to live there?"

"Yes, quite committed. Sarah will have a choice when the time comes. She can either come with me, or remain here in Glasgow. I won't attempt to force her to do something she does not want to do."

"If she has to choose, it will be a big chance you're taking. I hope your marriage is strong enough to stand the test." Cameron cocked a questioning eyebrow at Robert as he finished speaking, but Robert did not rise to the implied question.

*****

The rest of her first day back in Glasgow went as expected. The one bright spot was that they were to stay in the same cottage on the grounds of the big house as they had occupied before their departure for the Caribbean. Sarah was concerned they might be expected to occupy rooms in the big house, where she would not feel comfortable, and they would not have the same degree of privacy as the cottage afforded.

In the afternoon, when Robert went to meet with his father, Sarah hastily wrote letters to her grandmother and Aunt Bess and had a driver deliver them. A message came back from Aunt Bess within the hour inviting her to spend the day with them tomorrow. Robert thought it was a wonderful idea when she told him of it later.

"They will be beside themselves with excitement at seeing

you again, and you could do with some fussing over. I'm sure it will be a most enjoyable day. And, as I will be away from the cottage all day, I am pleased you will not be spending it alone."

As anticipated, dinner that first night was at the big house. While the invitation was not a problem, as she dressed for the occasion, she realised she would again be seated at the table with Cecile. Nothing was resolved between them before Cecile left the island, and Sarah suspected that Cecile held her responsible for Mr Wallace's insisting on his daughter's return to Glasgow.

"Well, my conscience is clear," she announced to the mirror. "True; I was pleased to see her go, but I had no part in it." There was no time for further conversation with her mirror.

"Who are you talking to in there? Aren't you ready yet? It's time to go, or we will be late, and you know how Father hates tardiness." Picking up her stole, Sarah hurried out to join Robert for the short ride to the big house.

After dinner, while Robert and his father were organising drinks and cigars, Sarah found herself alone in a quiet corner of the sitting room with Cameron. After a quick look around to ensure nobody was within earshot, she asked her question.

"Cameron, since you've been back, have you heard or seen anything of Jane McCabe? Do you remember Jane? She was my maid of honour at my wedding."

"No-o… Well, yes, I do remember Jane, but I haven't heard anything of her since my return." While it was a simple enough question and received a straightforward answer, Sarah felt she detected a hint of discomfort in Cameron when he answered.

Later, in bed that night, Sarah replayed Cameron's response in her mind. It was perfectly reasonable for him not to have heard or seen anything of Jane, but something told her Cameron had been less than truthful. Why would he need to do that? She knew she could go back and question him about his response, but she decided to pursue the matter with Aunt Bess tomorrow.

With her stomach a squirming mass on the way to Aunt Bess's house, Sarah sat bolt upright in the carriage, her hands curled in tight fists. Then, they were at Bess's front door. A footman helped Sarah from the carriage, after telling the driver he would not be needed later as Bess would use her carriage to take Sarah home. As Sarah set foot on the bottom step, she was almost bowled over by Aunt Bess, who rushed down to throw her arms around her. Grandmother Mary was no more than a second behind Bess, and followed Bess's example. There, on the bottom step, three women remained wrapped in a tight embrace for a few moments before untangling themselves and going indoors.

Neither of the women asked the question Sarah had been dreading, but she noticed each eyeing off her stomach. She wanted to shout 'no, I'm still not pregnant', but couldn't utter the words.

An indulgent morning tea and nonstop conversation filled in the morning until lunchtime. Over lunch, Sarah seized a lull in chat to ask the question she had longed to all morning.

"Aunt Bess, you remember my friend, Jane McCabe, who you used to talk to at Kirk sometimes? Does she still attend Kirk here?"

"While I remember her well, I can't say I've seen anything of her in quite a while. As I recall, she lived with her grandmother while her parents were overseas. Her grandmother wasn't a member of our congregation, preferring to attend a different church closer to where she lived. I remember someone saying they'd heard the old lady had been quite ill, but that was some time ago, and I haven't heard anything since."

"I heard the same story," Mary added. "I knew Jane's grandmother when we were both young girls here in Glasgow, and I remember being concerned about her ill health. It was remiss of me not to follow up on it at the time – especially as Jane was your close friend. But, time got away and, when I didn't hear anything further about her, I assumed she had recovered."

"Would either of you know if she still lives in the same house? I still have the address and thought I might go around there to find out where Jane might be."

Both women shook their heads, but Bess suggested that, if Sarah could come again tomorrow, they could all go around to the address.

When Sarah told Robert that night about their plan to visit Jane's home tomorrow, she was a bit disappointed by his response.

"I'm not sure that is such a wise move. Perhaps it would have been better to send a letter around first. If Jane severed contact with you, for whatever reason, she might not be too pleased to have you and the others turn up on her doorstep. I think you would be wise to prepare for the possibility it might not go well."

Too bad, she thought. I will go to Jane's address tomorrow and put up with whatever happens when I arrive. But, Robert did have a point about the others accompanying Sarah to visit Jane. It might be better if she went alone. Now, how does she convince her grandmother and Aunt Bess that's how it will be?

In the end, it was not as difficult as she thought. Once she explained her concern about all three of them lobbing on Jane's doorstep, the other women agreed it might be better if Sarah went alone. Without wasting any time – and before the others changed their minds – Sarah suggested she should not delay any longer. Aunt Bess called for her carriage and, within twenty minutes, Sarah was alone and on her way to her last known address for Jane.

Sarah felt her resolve weakening when there was no response to her knock. She asked the carriage to wait, and was now inclined to bolt back to it and return to Aunt Bess's house.

"One more try," she murmured, "and then I'm leaving." She raised her arm and thumped on the door with all her might.

This time, she heard faint sounds of movement inside. A few moments later, a middle-aged woman in a stiff white smock and cap opened the door.

"Yes…? Can I help you?" she demanded in a none too

welcoming tone.

"I've come to visit Miss Jane McCabe. This is the address I had for her from some time ago. I had hoped she still lived here."

"Nah, nobody by that name lives here. You must have got it wrong. Now, if you don't mind, I have work to do." She stepped back and was about to close the door when a voice from somewhere inside the house stopped her.

"Lily, who is it, dear?" An elderly woman leaning heavily on her walking stick appeared in the doorway. Sarah repeated her reason for calling at the house.

"Thank you, Lily. I will deal with this. You may return to your duties." Having dismissed the first woman and watched her disappear from view, the older woman turned her attention to Sarah.

"My apologies for my housekeeper's lack of courtesy. Lily is a good worker but doesn't do well with visitors. Now, please refresh my memory. What was the name of the person you thought lived here?" Sarah repeated Jane's name. "McCabe… oh, a young woman was she; maybe about your age?"

"She was my age, but she lived here with her grandmother when I knew her."

"Aah, yes… now I remember. When the grandmother died, she left the house to her granddaughter. She was moving away from Glasgow and needed to sell the house. My husband had died. Our home was too big for me, so I bought this place."

"Oh, I see. I don't suppose you know where Jane went after she left here?"

"No, I can't say I do. Don't rightly remember her mentioning where she was going. None of my business, I suppose, so I didn't ask, and she didn't say. I'm sorry I can't help you."

"Thank you, but would you mind telling me when Miss McCabe moved away?"

"That would have been straight after the sale of the house. She was already packed and ready to go when I came to inspect the place before I bought it. Now, let me think… aye, that would have been late in 1843. Yes, 1843… my husband died at Easter that year, and I purchased this house a few months later."

"It was about then contacted with her ceased. I continued to write to her at this address but received no replies. I'm sorry if my letters inconvenienced you in any way."

"No inconvenience involved, my dear. I do remember a few letters arriving after I moved in, but I had Lily take them to the agent who had sold the house on behalf of Miss McCabe." She gave Sarah the agent's name, but warned she didn't think he was still in business.

A dejected Sarah returned to Aunt Bess's house. "Argh, we don't need to ask how your expedition turned out," Bess said as she met Sarah at the door. "Your face says it all. Come, I think this might call for something a little stronger than a cup of tea."

The three women sat in Bess's sitting room and sipped their drinks for a minute or so before Grandmother Mary became impatient.

"We know you were disappointed by what you discovered at Jane's home, but we would like to hear about what happened."

Sarah took a deep breath before launching into her report on her disappointing morning. As she spoke, tears welled up and, by the time she finished her story, they were rolling down her cheeks. Both women rushed to Sarah with their lace handkerchiefs at the ready. Sarah waved them away.

"I appreciate your kindness, but I am just fine. I knew there was more than a chance she would no longer live there." She recounted all the elderly owner told her before admitting there was nothing more she could do.

"You might be right about that," Bess agreed. "I know the agent she mentioned is no longer around. He was killed when his horse bolted in the High Street, and his carriage turned over. He was thrown out and died."

"So that's it then," Mary said. "Sometimes we do have to accept the way things are. And, if somebody doesn't want to be found, there's a fair chance they won't be. There is naught more you can do about Jane McCabe."

"While I know that's true, and I will come to accept it, I just don't understand why it happened… perhaps I did something to offend her."

"That's stuff and nonsense, Sarah. Give up and forget about her," Bess counselled. "I will ask at Kirk on Sunday in case anyone should know anything of Jane, but I think it unlikely."

When Sarah returned to the cottage that afternoon, she was relieved that Robert wasn't there. After holding her emotions in check after visiting Jane's former home, Sarah needed to give way to them. The tears came in great sobbing waves until there were no more to bring forth. Then, she took herself to bed with a cold, damp cloth over her eyes to lose their redness before Robert returned.

Chapter 24

A Job

Feeling dejected after her failed attempt to locate Jane the previous day, Sarah tried to sweep it from her mind as the carriage took her to the big house to meet with her father-in-law, Douglas Wallace, for tea that morning. Last evening, he had sent her a note requesting her company for tea in his office at ten o'clock this morning.

Unsettled by the invitation, and unsure of why she received it, she queried Robert about it. He was perplexed by it, but suggested it was his father trying to be hospitable and wanting to help entertain her while Robert was away all day attending to business. His explanation, while plausible, did not convince her that was the case.

Her stomach, a squirming mass when she left the cottage, had become a lead ball by the time she was being shown into Douglas's office.

"Ah, good – punctual; I like that and demand it of my employees." His welcome did nothing to ease her tension. A tea tray followed Sarah into Douglas's office and, as soon as the maid left, Thomas was straight down to business… while Sarah poured the tea. She surprised herself by managing not to spill a drop as he outlined his reasons for their meeting.

"What are your thoughts on this Java job Robert is taking?"

"He seems quite involved with the work he will be doing. I confess to knowing nothing about Java, but I am trying to learn as much as possible about the place before we leave here."

"Yes, yes… but I'll rephrase my question: How do you feel about going to Java?"

"I'm sure it will be fine once we are there. Of course, it will be strange for a while, but I'm sure we'll settle in without too much trouble."

"Right; now let's try again. How do you *really* feel about having to go to live in the East Indies? I don't want all the 'right' words. I want to know your feelings." Douglas fixed her with a stern gaze, a gaze that made her rethink the 'right' words she was going to say.

"If you insist. No, I do not want to go to Java. I never have and I still don't want to live there. But, I am Robert's wife, and my place is with him, wherever that might be."

"Now we are getting somewhere. Whatever we discuss from here on this morning needs to be open and honest – and not what you might think I want to hear. Are we both clear about that?" Sarah nodded, and noticed she had relaxed in Thomas's presence. "Good; how would you feel about remaining her in Glasgow?"

"Remaining in Glasgow…? I never considered such a situation. As I understand it, Robert is going to work in Java and, as his wife, I will be with him. If remaining here is an option, I am willing to consider it."

"Robert insists on taking this job and going to Java. I don't oppose that. His job there will not allow him to remain in any one location for any length of time. There are over 90 sugar processing factories in Java. Robert will be required to service all of them. That means Robert is likely to spend no more than a day or two at a time in any one location, unless they have a major project happening. In which case, he might spend a week or two there. He will not have a house in the capital of the colony, or anywhere else on the island. And that situation is unlikely to change for some years."

"Where will he stay? Where would I live while all this is happening? Would I have to travel around the island with him?"

"He will be accommodated in hotels and guest houses, or in whatever accommodation is available in some of the more out of the way places. No, you would not be able to travel with him. And, nobody wants you to have to spend long periods of time on your own on that island. Apart from travelling around the factories, from time to time, Robert will need to return to

Glasgow and parts of England to discuss specific issues relating to machinery requirements for some of the factories.

There is no place for a wife in that life… not for some time to come anyway. Your alternative is to remain here in Glasgow, either with your Aunt Bess or, as I would prefer, here on the estate either in this house, or in the cottage."

"What will I do all day without a house and staff to look after? That is not a life I am used to, and probably would not enjoy."

"You will have plenty to do. You will work for me. I was trying to train a young man as an assistant, but he was hopeless. I think he finally realised that, and chose to move on to other ventures. So, I am in need of an assistant – and one who also can manage this house for me. Robert has been generous with his praise for the way you managed the household and its staff on the plantation. It appears you have the necessary ability with figures and abundant business acumen for the position I have in mind for you."

"Yes, I enjoy working with figures. It's an ability I think I inherited from my mother. She occupied a position (similar to the one I think you are suggesting) in Aunt Bess's enterprise when we lived here for a while when I was a child. On our return to India, she took over much of the business management of the tea plantation."

"Excellent; so, will you at least consider taking on the position as my assistant? You don't have to tell me now, but I would like an answer in the next day of two. If you are interested, we will discuss details of what the position involves and how we will manage things between us. Do you have any further questions at this time?"

"Only one: does Robert know about this meeting and what you are proposing?"

"Uhmm… no, he does not, but he has expressed his concern about what would be best for you when he leaves for Java. Oh, and his absences begin earlier than you might imagine. He will be working for a group of manufacturers of sugar milling equipment located both here and in England. Possibly by the end of this week, he needs to spend time with those firms in England, and will be away for at least two weeks."

Over dinner that night, Robert dropped his first bombshell. "In two days, I need to visit equipment manufacturing firms in England. You need to think about whether you want to remain here in the cottage, or if you would rather stay with Aunt Bess while I am away. I will likely be away for at least a couple of weeks."

"No question about it; I would prefer to stay here. It's hardly worth all the fuss of moving in with Aunt Bess for such a short time. No, I'll be fine here. If for any reason I should need any assistance, the big house – and Douglas and Cameron – are close by. I'll be fine here, thanks."

While Sarah's answer pleased him, he felt taken aback by her lack of reaction to the news that he would leave her for a while. "It was almost as if she expected it," he told his father later.

Douglas nodded sagely before replying, "Good, good; it is much easier that way than engaging in a drawn-out melodramatic debate about it." Again, Robert was surprised by the response his news received.

As soon as Robert left the next day to finalise his travel, Sarah went across to the big house unannounced and asked to see Douglas. He came and escorted her into his office.

"I believe Robert already has informed you of his imminent travel to London and other parts of England?"

"He has. As I had already made my decision regarding your offer, his news caused me no discomfort or concern. If your offer remains open, I am prepared to begin working with you as soon as you see fit. As for my living arrangements, if it is all the same to you, I think I would prefer to remain in the cottage – at least for the immediate future. Of course, that may change after I've had some time to see how it fits with working here."

"Excellent news, my dear, and of course you may continue at the cottage for as long as you wish. Robert departs for

London sometime tomorrow. I suggest you might start in your new position the following day. That will allow you tomorrow to deal with his departure and perhaps see your family members before your time is taken up with working here."

*****

Everything went as if in accordance with some fully-scripted play. A couple of days later, Robert headed for London and other parts of England and was gone for almost three weeks. Sarah found herself a bit teary the morning of his departure, but not until after he left. Nevertheless, the moment Robert departed, she sent an early morning note to Aunt Bess asking if she might come to morning tea with her and her grandmother. Bess's reply arrived about half an hour later. Shortly before ten o'clock, a carriage took Sarah to Bess's house.

The fuss they created when she arrived for her unplanned visit almost started the tears again, but the two older women's company soon banished them. Sarah's news of Robert's trip to England and his likely absence for a couple of weeks caused the two other women to exchange looks.

Without missing a beat, however, Bess's immediate reply surprised Sarah. "Of course, you must come and stay with us. There is no point in your sitting at home pining for company. But, I do think it a bit remiss of Robert not to have made suitable arrangements for you during his absence."

"To be fair, Aunt Bess, he did suggest I might prefer to stay with you rather than in the cottage on the Wallace estate. I assured him I would rather stay at the cottage. You see, I have plans for while he is away now… and for all the other times he will be away in the future. Douglas Wallace offered me a position as his assistant. I will work in his home office alongside him while I am learning the business.

Then, once I am familiar with it, I will take over the running of his household for him. I'm quite excited about it, and looking forward to learning new things and gaining a better understanding of the Wallace enterprise's operation." The two older women exchanged another look.

"Hmm… it sounds much like what your mother did for me while you were here when you were a little child. She worked in my office in the city as an assistant to my manager. As there is a lot of your mother in you, I suspect you will enjoy the work even more than you anticipate," Bess suggested.

Mary's loud sniff suggested she smelled something foul. "And, exactly how long and how often does he plan to be away in future?" she demanded, her tone heavy with indignation and disapproval.

"I don't have details, but I understand it could be a frequent occurrence and for months at a time as he attends to his work on the island of Java."

"Java…!" both women exclaimed in unison, before Bess recovered sufficiently to request more information.

"And what is it you are to do while he is off on the other side of the world? Are you to join him there once he has established a home for you, and how long is that likely to take?"

"No, I won't be joining him, at least, not in the foreseeable future anyway. As for what I will be doing while he is away, I'll be working with Douglas on running his business and his household."

"And you are happy with this arrangement, my girl?" Mary asked in an incredulous voice.

"Oh yes, I'm quite looking forward to being busy. The only downside to it though is that I won't be able to spend so much time with you two special ladies."

The drama of Sarah's changed situation dealt with, the morning adopted its more usual format and the three women went on to enjoy each other's company until after lunch. Aware the two older women often partook of a post-prandial nap, once lunch was over, Sarah took her leave as soon as polite decorum allowed.

Back in the cottage, Sarah explained her changed household arrangements to her three household staff, before spending the rest of the afternoon sorting through her wardrobe to identify suitable 'work attire' for her new life. It felt strange having the whole bed to herself that first night, and she half expected another flood of tears as she slid into bed. The tears did not come. In fact, she was surprised when, apart from those first moments of realisation that this was how she would be spending many nights in the future, she didn't miss Robert at all.

She revisited that realisation at breakfast next morning, and spent some time examining it. Did it tell her something about the state of her marriage? Was this to be the beginning of the end? But, time was away and she did not want to be late for her first day at work. A mixture of excitement and nervousness accompanied her on the carriage ride to the big house.

******

Robert, on his return to Glasgow after his England trip, was none too impressed to find his wife gainfully employed as his father's assistant. He waited until Sarah had returned to the cottage to supervise dinner after her day at work before confronting his father about the arrangement… and immediately regretted his temerity.

Without wasting time, Douglas acquainted Robert with his many shortcomings as a husband and son. He left Robert in no doubt that, on his return from the Caribbean, Robert's refusal to accept a position in the Wallace operation still rankled with Douglas. His father also went on to question Robert's motivation in taking on a position that would see him abandoning his wife frequently and for long periods.

"I will be doing what I know; all I have known growing up, and I continue to be involved in an industry I love. Yes, I will be away from my wife a lot, but who knows how long it will be before Sarah is able to join me the East Indies. To date, I know nothing of what might be possible on Java."

Douglas's response is best left between the men involved. Suffice to say, the relationship between father and son did not improve during the three months before Robert's departure for

Java. Sarah, although ignorant of the situation between the two men, was aware Robert rarely visited the big house during those months. And, whenever he did, Sarah sensed a certain tension in the air while he was there.

By the time Robert set sail for Java, Sarah later admitted to herself the tension she sensed at the big house also had extended to the cottage. She and Robert seemed not as close as they used to be. Again, Sarah found herself questioning the true state of their marriage but realised such thinking could send her insane if she pursued it. Although she pushed it to the back of her mind determined to ignore such thoughts, they would not go away, not entirely. Over the next several years they would revisit. But, with the passage of time, such visits became less painful and less concerning.

Sarah's entry in her journal on that night in mid-June 1850 later proved prophetic:

Today Robert sailed for Java. How long will he be gone, and will I ever see him again? Is this the way Mr and Mrs Wallace are to spend the rest of their married life, separated and not knowing what the future holds? Perhaps I would do well to accept that might be the case and prepare myself for a lonely old age. I can't help wonder if our story might have been different if there were children. If I'm honest, I am the only one of us who appears to be concerned by our lack of ability to reproduce. Robert never spoke of the situation. I'd like to think he spared my feelings, but I'm not sure that is the reason. Did he never long for children?

Over the next few years, Robert's visits to Glasgow were sporadic and lasted not much more than a couple of months at best, and often only a few weeks. After his absence of about six months on his first trip, Sarah told Douglas she thought it would be easier for her to manage his household if she were a part of it, instead of residing in the cottage. Douglas was delighted, and immediately set the staff to preparing an apartment for her in the east wing of the house, similar to the one Cameron had in the west wing. Leaving the cottage was a wrench, but she knew in her heart it was the right move.

This 'occasional form' of married life continued for the next eight years, during which the periods between Robert's visits to Glasgow grew longer. On his visit home late in 1858, a monumental row occurred between Robert and his father. The afternoon Robert arrived home, Douglas sent a request for him to attend Douglas's office at ten o'clock the following morning. Sarah was unaware of the request until Robert questioned her about it.

"What does my father want to speak to me about tomorrow? I thought I should be allowed a day or so to settle in before being summoned to his office. What has he afoot that he needs to speak to me so urgently?'

"I'm sorry, Robert, but I was unaware he had requested a meeting with you. Perhaps it is something personal regarding the family he wishes to discuss, something that is none of my business."

While Sarah was unaware of the meeting request, it helped explain something odd that happened. As she was about to finish work for the day, Douglas had come into the small room she now used as her office. He looked distracted when he told her to 'take the day off tomorrow'.

"It's far too long since you have been to visit your grandmother and your aunt. Send a note around now to arrange a visit for morning tea tomorrow. No, don't argue. You are spending far too much time in this office. Take yourself out for the day. If you don't wish to visit your family, go shopping or something else – but stay away from your office for the day tomorrow."

At the time, she thought it a generous and kind offer, but since learning of Robert's impending meeting with Douglas, she now wondered about Douglas's motivation. Nevertheless, she had sent a note to Aunt Bess as Douglas suggested and her only two family members in Glasgow now expected her for morning tea tomorrow. Of course she would go as arranged, but whatever was to take place at the big house in her absence intrigued her.

The mystery was solved that evening when Robert announced he would be leaving for London in the morning.

"Oh, you're off again so soon. You only arrived yesterday, and I thought you were to be here for a few weeks this time. When do you expect to return to Glasgow?"

"I'm not sure, but when I do, I think it will be only for an overnight stay before I leave for Java again."

Sarah bit her lip. She didn't dare risk a reply as she struggled to control her almost overwhelming disappointment. And, that's more or less how it played out, except it delivered Sarah more hurt.

It was an established routine: when Robert was away, Sarah lived in the big house, but moved back to the cottage to resume married life whenever Robert returned. This occasion was no different. The day Robert left for London, Sarah moved back into the big house where she would stay until he returned, even if it was to be for only one night. But it didn't happen that way.

No word was received from Robert regarding his likely return. Sarah wanted the cottage to be just right when returned as it would be for only one night. She mentioned giving the cottage an airing and maybe a quick dust. The strange look she received in response intrigued Sarah, but no comment was offered by the maid.

At breakfast a couple of days later, Cameron looked surprised when Sarah came down to join him in the dining room. "Why are you here? I'm sorry, that didn't come out right. What I meant was why aren't you at the cottage?"

"Because I live here in this house while Robert is away. Haven't you noticed my presence here before?" Cameron just shook his head without offering any explanation for his question.

Straight after breakfast, he slipped into his father's office before Sarah came down to start work. "Father, Sarah was at breakfast here this morning. Has something happened that I don't know about?" Douglas reiterated Sarah's comments about living in the big house. "Yes, I know, but she was here last night … when I know Robert was at the cottage. He was dropped off at the cottage while I was out walking last evening. I had dinner in my room after I took a long walk around the estate. I know Robert – or someone – spent the night in the cottage because, from one of my windows, I could see a light there sometime later."

"Robert came home yesterday, but didn't tell Sarah?" Douglas asked.

"It appears that way. Should I check the cottage before she comes down to start work?"

Douglas told Cameron to go and to be quick about it but, should he encounter Robert at the cottage, he was to return and tell Douglas immediately. A little over half an hour later, Cameron slipped quietly past Sarah's office door and into his father's office.

"Well… were you mistaken?" Douglas demanded.

"No. Robert spent the night there. The kitchen maid confirmed he stayed the night, had an early breakfast and left an hour or so before I went to check the place. I asked if she expected him to return this evening. She said he told her he would not be back as he was leaving for Java today."

"So, this is the rotten son I have raised. Not a word to Sarah if you would, please, Cameron. I will check a couple of things before I have a particularly difficult conversation with her." On his way out, Douglas stuck his head around Sarah's office door to tell her he would be gone for the rest of the morning.

For much of the afternoon, Douglas was busy with meetings. It wasn't until just before the end of their working day that he finally had time to have a difficult conversation with Sarah. Striding resolutely out of his office he asked Sarah to join him in his office.

"Douglas, you look angry. Is everything all right? Have I done something wrong, or something to offend you?" she asked as she sank into a chair across the desk from her father-in-law.

"I doubt you could, my dear. But tell me, please, have you heard from that husband of yours about when he might be returning from his trip to London?"

"There is no word yet, and I am becoming anxious about what might be happening."

As Cameron walked past Douglas's office on his way in from work, he glimpsed Sarah sitting in there with her head in her hands. Cameron took a couple of steps back and directed a hard look past Sarah to Douglas, who gave a slight shake of his head followed by a little flick to tell Cameron to move on. The grave look on Douglas's face was sufficient to silence Cameron's questions, but they were questions he didn't need to ask. He knew the answers. Douglas had broken the news of Robert's night at the cottage to Sarah.

How Cameron wished Robert was planning also to spend that night at the cottage. Cameron would go there now and thrash the life out of his good-for-nothing brother for the way he was treating Sarah. He was disgusted by his big brother's behaviour, "And to think, as the eldest, one day everything Father has worked to build for this family will be his," he told his empty room as he threw himself down in his favourite armchair.

Robert was proving to be a thorough mongrel and there was nothing he, Cameron, could do about it. Although he knew there was nothing anyone could do about Robert, it didn't stop Cameron feeling frustrated and useless.

291

PART 5

Australia 1862

Chapter 25

A New Life

Christmas 1858 and her wedding anniversary a few days later were difficult times for Sarah. She had heard nothing from Robert since Douglas broke the news of her husband's overnight stay at the cottage without telling her about his presence in Glasgow. While she told herself she had written off her marriage, a small part of her still clung onto a skerrick of hope that she misjudged Robert and all would turn out well in time. While that wisp of hope remained, she delayed telling her family she believed her marriage had failed.

She continued to function, albeit in a daze much of the time, for months. Then, as Easter 1859 approached, one day, while strolling in the grounds as she had taken to doing daily now, the haze seemed to clear from her mind.

"Stop kidding yourself," she told the whole universe and anyone else who might be listening. "It's over. Your marriage is finished. Accept the truth. Move on. And be thankful there were no children to be hurt by what has happened." She found a new spring in her step as she returned to the big house.

She went in via the kitchen to ask for her dinner to be sent up on a tray and for Mr Douglas to be told of her intention to eat in her room. After dinner, on his way up to his apartment, Cameron knocked on Sarah's door.

"Apologies if I'm intruding, but I was concerned you might be ill when you elected not to come down for dinner."

"Thank you for your concern, Cameron, but no, I'm not ill. I had some serious thinking to do and had put it off for far too long."

"Is there anything I can help you with? I might not be good at advice, but I am a good listener. Sometimes that helps."

"That might not be a bad suggestion. Come in. If you have time for a chat, you might be able to help untangle some of my thinking."

As soon as they were seated in her sitting room, she launched into what she hoped was a reasonable overview of her current thoughts.

"Cameron, I have come to the conclusion I am the only person on this earth who hadn't realised some time ago that my marriage to Robert was over. Despite what I knew to be true, I held onto the hope it would come good in its own time. Today, reality visited me, and I now accept the truth of my situation. The question then for me is: what to do with the rest of my life?"

"You are an important part of this family and always will be. Why would your life not continue here as it is now? You know Father and I are fond of you, and Father depends on you more each passing year. Argh, I suspect you will tell me you have decided to do something different, haven't you?"

"I'm not sure, Cameron, but I think it might be wise to consider other options. After all, your father is not getting any younger. Although we hope he will go on for many years, sometime in the future, Robert will inherit all this … and presumably will return to live here. There is no room for both of us in this house and, more importantly, I do not want to share a house with him. So, while it is not urgent, I must plan a new life for myself."

Over a dram or two of rum, Sarah and Cameron talked well into the night. Although at the end of it, her future remained as much a mystery as beforehand, their discussions left Sarah feeling somehow unburdened. The only firm decision taken late that night was that Sarah promised not to rush into anything, to let life evolve around her but be ready to grasp the right opportunity when it presented. Exactly what that meant, Cameron wasn't sure, but he was glad Sarah would be staying for some time to come.

A few days later, at her early morning briefing session with Douglas, he told her an old acquaintance from the Caribbean was in town, and Douglas had invited him to dinner that night. He asked Sarah to alert the kitchen staff they would be one extra for dinner, and that something special be prepared for his friend. He did not enlighten Sarah about who the 'friend' was, but she figured he would be an older gentleman like Douglas.

When Sarah swept into the downstairs sitting room for a pre-dinner drink, she was surprised to see a familiar face engaged in conversation with Douglas and Cameron.

"Ah, Sarah, my dear, I don't know if you had the pleasure during your stay on the plantation of meeting an old family friend. Our guest tonight is Mr...."

"Jimmy Fraser! How wonderful to see you again, and what brings you to Glasgow? As I recall, you left the island a while before Robert and I did," Sarah remembered.

"Oh, I see," Douglas began. "You two have met. Of course, it makes sense. You would have met on the island. Mr Fraser… Jimmy is spending a couple of weeks here before heading off again, this time to Australia. It seems they grow sugarcane there now."

Once dinner was over, and the men adjourned to smoke and drink rum in Douglas's private sitting room, Sarah followed the age-old rule, and left them to their serious 'for men's ears only' discussions. But, as Jimmy was bidding her goodnight before following the other two men into the sitting room, she asked if he might have some time before he left Glasgow to come to lunch with her to share fond memories. A date was set for two days later.

The following night, at dinner, Sarah told Douglas that Jimmy would be lunching with her the next day. Douglas said he didn't think he could make it for lunch as he had meetings in the city. Cameron laughed at his father's discomfort at missing the lunch.

"Don't worry about it, Father. You weren't invited anyway. This is Sarah wanting to discuss her time at the plantation with Jimmy, and it's not a time for us to intrude."

Douglas, looking suitably embarrassed, apologised for his presumption, and Sarah thought that was the end of it. But, after dinner, Cameron followed her upstairs and caught up with her as she was about to enter her apartment.

"Sarah, please spare me a moment to talk with you." She ushered him into her sitting room. Cameron made a hesitant start on what he wanted to say. "Sarah, I just … perhaps there is something… Oh, Hell, I'll just come out and say what I want to tell you. Jimmy Fraser has come to Glasgow directly from Java. He has been working there for a while, but is keen to move on. The Australian sugar industry, in its infancy, appealed to him. So, he came to Glasgow to educate himself on the new machinery and processes now available and being developed for the future before he heads to Australia.

He has a wealth of industry knowledge and will probably have a big future there. But, I wanted you to be aware he has been in Java almost since leaving the Caribbean."

"I find that interesting, but not concerning. Is there something I should be aware of when discussing old times?"

"No, I don't think so, but I beg you to be a bit circumspect in what you say should your conversation move to his time in Java."

"Wouldn't it be surprising if we didn't talk about Java?"

"Yes, it is bound to be discussed. I only ask you not to probe too deeply into his time there. Keep focused on the state of the industry and the people, rather than Jimmy's experiences there."

Later, as she replayed Cameron's comments over in her mind, she murmured, "Intriguing that he felt compelled to provide such advice. I will heed it while talking to Jimmy tomorrow, but I will demand more information from Cameron as soon as possible."

Lunch was a wonderful occasion, the memories they relived were a pleasure, and all was going well until Jimmy mentioned Java's rapidly expanding industry and how he had become disillusioned with the place. Sarah faced a dilemma. Should she mention Robert's involvement in that industry, or not mention him at all? Jimmy and Robert probably had crossed paths at various times, so perhaps she should wait to see if Jimmy mentioned her husband before she said anything. But what should she do if he asked after Robert? Having decided to wait and see how the conversation played out, she settled back and relaxed.

It wasn't until after Jimmy left the house that Sarah had time to think about their discussions. Now, it did seem strange that Jimmy did not once mention Robert or ask after him. She stared out her office window as she pondered the lack of mention of her husband. Her thoughts were interrupted when Cameron knocked at her door. He looked on edge and unsure of himself. Sarah felt her stomach tighten. Had something happened to Douglas?

"Come in, come in, Cameron. What troubles you? You look so concerned."

"Did you discuss Robert over lunch with Jimmy?"

"No, Robert's name never came up in conversation at all, though I must admit I found that strange. Why do you ask? Or, perhaps I should ask what you know that I don't."

Although it took some prodding to get him started, Cameron opened up. "I met Jimmy at the port before he came to dinner with us. He was always a gentleman and would never share what he told me with you."

"Things about Robert...?"

With a little more encouragement, Cameron nodded, and the gist of Jimmy's information rolled out. Robert had been living quite the life while he enjoyed traipsing all over the island because of his work.

"I'm so sorry, Sarah, but your husband has not been going without all the ... Uhmm ... without all of the comforts of home."

"You mean women... other women, local women, I mean?" Cameron nodded. "And has any particular young thing taken his fancy?" Cameron shook his head. "Oh, I see. He has been sampling a wide range of the local produce, has he? If I'm honest, I'm not surprised. Cameron, please share whatever Jimmy told you. I do need to know."

"I don't know how to put this politely or less painfully, but it seems he has gained himself something of a reputation for helping to increase the population of Java. I suspected it was gossip and queried Jimmy for details. It appears he has fathered several children, although the exact number is unknown. When a young woman becomes pregnant, he pays her a sum of money to go away, and that's the end of it for him. The girls are from poorer families that welcome the money, and one more mouth to feed in an already big family doesn't create too much of a problem."

"Does Jimmy know this is true, or is he just relaying hearsay?"

"The same question occurred to me. So, this morning I took a look at Robert's bank records. I suspect when a girl finds herself in that predicament, he pays her £100 to see her on her way."

"Are you sure?"

"No. Of course, I can't be sure, but there are several payments – many payments – of that sum from his account over the years, and those payments tend to align with Jimmy's stories. Sarah, I'm so sorry I had to share this with you but, despite everything you've told me, I think you maintained hope things would work out for you and Robert."

"For a while, I did. But I gave up on that idea some time ago. Do you know where Jimmy is staying while in Glasgow? I would like to see him again."

"You won't tell him I shared all this with you, will you?" Cameron almost pleaded.

"Of course not, but I have a sneaking suspicion one of those opportune moments we discussed some time ago might be tempting me to explore it further."

*****

Next morning, Sarah sent Jimmy a note asking if she might meet him somewhere for lunch. He replied with an invite to join him for lunch in his hotel's dining room at midday.

While they waited for their meal to arrive, rather than waste time, Sarah explained her reason for requesting the meeting. "Tell me about this Australian sugar industry that seems to have caught your attention. Australia is a long way from anywhere. Surely sugar industries have been established in other countries closer to home. For that matter, why abandon the Java industry?"

"The Java industry is so well established now. The only improvements possible are through new equipment and technology as it becomes available. They don't need my expertise anymore. Local 'experts' now proliferate throughout the industry. If anything, what I know is of no use to anyone anymore. I also find not to my taste the ownership and involvement of the Dutch Government in that industry. Nevertheless, their industry has moved on with amazing speed and, in many ways, I've been left behind. That's partly the reason I'm in Glasgow now. "

"I thought you still had family here in Scotland somewhere."

"Aye, I do; my sister and her family. Of course, I wanted to spend some time with them. But, I wanted to become familiar with all the new stuff that I still don't know enough about, and to see what was likely to be available to the industry in the future. Before I leave, I will also visit those manufacturers in England working on new stuff for the industry."

"How established is the Australian industry at this time? I assume your thinking is that your expertise and experience have much to offer that new industry."

"After a couple of unsuccessful attempts, an embryonic industry is establishing itself in some of the coastal areas in the north of the Colony of New South Wales. The eastern part of the continent north of that colony recently became the new Colony of Queensland.

So far, much of that colony is pastoral land, but I suspect much of the coastal strip might be suitable for sugarcane growing. It's early days yet. I intend going to Australia to explore what opportunities are available to me in that fledgling industry in New South Wales. But my real interest lies further north, in the Colony of Queensland. If my assumptions are correct about the land and climate in that colony, it is where a *real* sugar industry might be established. And it is where my expertise might be worth something.

Now it's my turn to ask questions. Why are you so interested in this matter?"

"To be honest, I'm not sure. When I heard you mention an Australian sugar industry, my instinct told me an opportunity awaited me there. If you don't think it too presumptuous of me, might you find time to write me occasionally to inform me of what you have found and the state of their sugar industry?"

"I should enjoy corresponding with you on this matter. I suspect only a handful of us hold any interest in what might be happening in that part of the world."

Her main objective achieved, Sarah allowed conversation over the rest of their lunch to take them down memory lane. As she sat alone in her carriage on the way back to the Wallace estate, Sarah was aware of a frisson of excitement running up and down her spine. While she knew the reason for it, she would never be able to explain it to someone else, not even Cameron. But, even then, Sarah knew her destiny was in Australia, and she also knew that destiny did not include Robert.

Australia and its possible future sugar industry proved her preoccupation for the next couple of weeks. At first, it was no more than a jumble of wild thoughts and excitement but, as the days slipped by, her thinking became focused. There were questions. Of course, there were questions to which she had no answers… And probably Jimmy didn't have the answers either. She hoped Jimmy's agreeing to keep her informed wasn't an idle promise, because a definite plan was beginning to form in her mind.

A couple of weeks after her last meeting with Jimmy, a thought slammed in from nowhere, almost stunning her: what about her marriage? When was the right time to tell people it was over? How did you go about doing that? She giggled at the next thought that arrived as she strode along: did one take out an advertisement in the local newspaper? At least that way, everybody would know at the same time, and she wouldn't have to go around telling everyone individually.

Aunt Bess was the most worldly-wise person she knew, and Aunt Bess would know what to do. Besides, Sarah knew she would need Aunt Bess's support when she broke the news of the end of her marriage to Grandmother Mary. By the time Sarah was seated at her desk, she had resolved to visit Aunt Bess on Thursday morning when Mary was on her weekly visit with her old friend, Mrs Mackenzie.

The note Sarah sent Bess implored her not to mention Sarah's visit to Mary, as Sarah did not want Mary to cancel her visit to Mrs Mackenzie because of her impending visit. She need not have bothered with the subterfuge. From the moment she read the note, Bess guessed Sarah chose Thursday morning for her visit to talk to Bess alone. And, the ever-astute Bess was not at all surprised by the topic of discussion that morning. Once Sarah delivered her 'big' announcement regarding her marriage, Bess simply nodded and thought momentarily.

"So, Sarah, why have you deliberately come to tell me something I already knew, and when you knew your grandmother would not be here?"

"What do you mean by 'you already knew'? How could you?"

"Sarah, my dear, anyone who bothers to give you and your marriage a thought will know it's over. It has been over for years, although it now seems we all knew it while you didn't. There is no news in anything you've said today. And, unless I'm quite mistaken, it will not come as any surprise to your grandmother either. Still, Mary will be home for lunch, which will be a good time for *us* to tell her."

That's how it happened, and Mary reacted as Bess had predicted. Mary was surprised Sarah was acting as though she was delivering some great revelation, and went so far as to tell Sarah *anyone who mattered had known for ages.* Then, after a moment's thought, she asked if Sarah had told her mother, or even discussed Robert's long absence from their marriage bed with her mother.

"No, of course not… it would only cause her unnecessary concern. But, now that I've decided it is over, I shall advise her of it."

After sharing her decision regarding the state of her marriage with Douglas and Cameron, Sarah considered the matter closed. A couple of days later, Douglas summoned her to his office.

"Thank you for sharing your decision about your marriage. It would have been difficult to do. But, in all fairness, I wanted to tell you that I reached the same conclusion some time ago. Suffice to say, I believe you are better off without Robert. He was not worth the time of day. Robert was a disgrace and an embarrassment to this family.

I have ensured he does not benefit now or in the future by his name or association with this family or its enterprises. Cameron is now named as my heir. He remains unaware of the change, but will be advised at some appropriate time in the future.

My real reason for this discussion is to allay any concerns you might have regarding your future. You are a member of this family and shall remain so for as long as you choose. And this place will always be your home for as long as you wish. Do you have any questions or anxieties I can help you with? I'm here to reassure you the Wallace family will always care for you."

*****

A couple of years slipped by, with only a couple of events worthy of note: Cameron's extension of the Wallace's shipping routes to Australia, and Sarah and Jimmy Fraser's regular correspondence over that time. It was largely due to intelligence from Jimmy that prompted Cameron to look to Australia as a new source of cargo. Then, late in 1862, one of Jimmy's letters caused Sarah the most excitement she had experienced in years. It was the continuation of a story that began soon after Jimmy arrived in New South Wales.

At the end of 1860, Jimmy reported a local northern New South Wales newspaper had run a story of one (Scots-born)

John Mackay, who had been one of a party that explored new lands about midway along the Queensland coast. The land had great potential. At the start of 1861, Mackay applied for a parcel of land in that new area. He then began moving a large herd of cattle north to the new land. Jimmy was intrigued and, about a month after Mackay left with his cattle, Jimmy set out to follow them. He eventually caught up with the group near the Port of Rockhampton, and continued on with them.

After crossing the range to come down onto the alluvial river flats, Jimmy's letters became a little more erratic. But, one thing became clear to Sarah: the area's promise excited Jimmy. And news of the development of an embryonic settlement was equally exciting. Then, the letter that changed Sarah's life arrived.

Jimmy reported that, just off the boat in April 1862, the Barbados-born John Buhot had manufactured a little sugar from a small plot of sugarcane growing in the Brisbane Botanic Gardens. That news, coupled with Jimmy's comments about the land and climate in the area John Mackay had helped discover would be ideal for growing sugarcane, was a call to action for Sarah.

She discussed with Cameron the possibility of a passage on one of the company's ships to Queensland. A suitable opportunity would occur in about a month. Sarah dispatched an immediate note to Jimmy advising him of her potential arrival in the settlement in about five months. Then there was so much preparation for the voyage, including dealing with Douglas, who was unhappy about her impending departure.

Fate worked against her, and a couple of weeks later, she dispatched a follow-up note to Jimmy advising of some unforeseen circumstances delaying her departure. Later, she would thank Fate for its intervention. During the three months delay in her departure, Grandmother Mary McGowan died unexpectedly in her sleep. No illness or any other sign had forewarned them of the woman's demise. It was a sad time, but Sarah was thankful she was still in Glasgow when it happened.

For her mother, Flora Erskine, it would have been a particularly difficult time. As Mary's death was sudden and unexpected, Flora could not be with her at the end.

Then, less than a fortnight later, further tragedy visited the Wallace family. Douglas received word that his eldest son, Robert, had died when the ship on which he was a passenger went down in heavy weather off South Africa. According to reports, Robert was on his way to meet with Dutch Government officials to discuss future plans for the sugar industry in its colony of Java. All on board the Netherlands-owned ship were lost when the ship went down.

Although it took them all a while to cope with the news, a few days later, Douglas admitted privately to Sarah that the loss of Robert had simplified the company's future. Now, there would be no obstacle in the way of Cameron's taking over in the event of Douglas's death, no risk of a challenge.

With a heavy heart and mixed emotions, Sarah boarded the ship for her voyage to the new Colony of Queensland. Cameron refused to allow her to sail alone and insisted on accompanying her. She argued Cameron's place was in Glasgow to assist his father through the grief of his recent loss. She lost the argument. Both Douglas and Cameron were adamant Cameron would travel with her.

Chapter 26

A New Land

1862 was almost ended when her ship hove-to off the coast to await the tide. The ship's shallow draught allowed it to enter the tidal Pioneer River at high tide and sail on to tie up alongside the new settlement on its south bank. At low tide, the vessel sat comfortably on the sandy bed of the river. Unsure how long he might remain at the port, Cameron left it to the captain to allow his men shore leave. But he suggested the captain consider departing again on the next high tide to continue the remainder of the boat's scheduled voyage. They agreed the ship would return one week later to collect Cameron and whoever else wished to return to Glasgow.

Jimmy Fraser met them as they came ashore. Sarah's belongings were unloaded onto Jimmy's wagon as soon as the ship tied up. Once that was done, he took her and Cameron to the 'best hotel in town' in the developing settlement. After seeing Sarah safely to her room, Cameron and Jimmy returned to the horse yard behind the hotel where Jimmy had left his loaded wagon. Cameron insisted Jimmy also stay the night at the hotel as his guest, as it would allow the three of them to plan their next few days together.

Over dinner in what passed for the hotel's dining room, the trio agreed on plans for the following days. It would begin with a trip to a block of land Jimmy had applied to purchase. He had erected a rough makeshift building to store Sarah's belongings until she became settled. After requesting a hamper for early next morning, they turned in for an early night.

It was barely daylight when Cameron knocked on Sarah's door. She was dressed and ready, but looked haggard and admitted to a poor night's sleep. In the horse yard, the wagon was hitched up and ready to leave as soon as Sarah came down. The settlement was coming to life as the trio rode out through the cluster of shanties that comprised the township.

As they rode through open country following the river along towards its source, Cameron asked the question that had bothered him from the moment they left the hotel.

"Are you sure this is where you want to be, Sarah? Do you really want to try making a new life here where there is nothing?"

"Yes, I think I do, but I reserve my right to change my mind once I see what the country is like."

At about midday, Jimmy announced, "Yonder magnificent structure is *chez moi,* and where you will spend tonight. Impressive, isn't it?" he chuckled. "Aye, I know it is not grand, but it will keep the sun and the rain off us. Sarah, the small shack over there is where we will store your belongings … until whatever it is you decide to do about this place."

After Sarah's belongings were unloaded, they ate the lunch of cold cuts, cheese and bread, provided by the hotel, before leaving Jimmy's place to explore the land he wanted to show Sarah. Cameron sat quietly and observed as they headed further along the river bank lands.

"This is beautiful country, Jimmy. You did well in selecting your block. Who has selected this land adjoining yours?"

"Ah, well now, I thought it might be Sarah who would want it."

"But it has been staked out. Someone already has staked their claim on what appears to be a hefty chunk of land."

"Aye, they have… And, should you be interested in finding out who that was, you might find it is in the name of Mrs Sarah Wallace."

"I've staked… I mean, you staked it out in my name?" Sarah looked stunned as she ran her eyes over the land in question. "And it's registered in *my* name, Sarah Wallace, and not as Mrs Robert Wallace?"

"He's gone. No point in using his name no more. You are your own person now, so this land – if you want it – should reflect that it is yours and yours alone."

"Oh, I think I do want it, Jimmy. And thank you for looking out for my interests. What do you think, Cameron? Do I want this block of land?"

"There is no denying it is beautiful country and would be excellent for growing sugarcane, if an industry ever started in this area. But, Sarah, it is a long way from anywhere, and even the thought of you alone in that settlement worries me.

Jimmy, what is the size of the two blocks, yours and Sarah's, you've staked out? They look enormous."

"As well they should; there are a little over 1200 acres in each block. Of course, it is designated 'pastoral land' at the moment, but that can change later."

Cameron continued shaking his head in disbelief. "1200 acres...! I dread to think how much that will cost. Sarah, I know you inherited some money from Robert's estate, but I doubt it will be enough to purchase this land."

"No, I doubt it would be, but it is not the only money I have to invest. My grandfather left a sizable amount in trust for me when he died. Although I could access it from when I turned twenty-five, I've never needed to touch it. And now, my grandmother also has left me quite a substantial amount of money.

Perhaps, Jimmy, you might estimate what this land might cost me."

"Well, Miss Sarah, there are two ways of going about this business of acquiring land here. It can be leased over ten years and, at the end of that, with the added expense of a little more to cover the necessary paperwork, you own it." Sarah wrinkled her nose, and it was exactly the reaction Jimmy expected. He continued, "Of course, those with the ready cash don't need bother about such arrangements. Theirs is the land to buy outright from the outset *if they be allowed to buy it.*

I believe it would be better for you to take out a pre-emptive lease. You see, apart from the annual rental, various improvements are required each year, and there also is a residential requirement. We can go into the finer details later. But, if your application is successful, you will need to erect a certain length of fencing, stock it with the required number of cattle, and establish a residence on the property. The landholder is required to reside on the property. All of that costs money. Better to pay the annual rental and put whatever cash you have into making sure you meet the required improvements."

"Sarah, you can't live out here alone. It is not safe."

"Because I am a woman?"

"Yes, partly … oh, all right; yes, because you are a woman."

"Go carefully there, Cameron, my friend. You are likely to start a war with comments such as those. I have a way around it – if you decide you want the land and want to stay here."

"Of course, I want the land, and yes, I intend to stay here. So, what is it we need to do next?"

"You've made up your mind already; so quickly?" Cameron asked. "Do you not want to consider it at some length before making a decision?"

"Thank you for your concern, Cameron. But, no, I don't need time to think about it. I know what I want, and this is it. Right, Jimmy, what comes next?"

"We could head back into town and hope they still have rooms available at the hotel, or we could camp under less than ideal conditions in my shack tonight and head back to town tomorrow."

"What do I need to do in town?" Sarah asked.

"I'm pleased you asked," Jimmy said as he grinned at her. "There are men to be hired, and fencing materials to be purchased. No point in thinking about stock yet, not until the fences are up. Oh, you might need some equipment: horses, wagon, shovels, and a rifle."

"A rifle…?

"Yeah, if I remember correctly, you do know how to use one of those."

"Will she really need a rifle?" Cameron demanded. "Sarah, this is starting to sound like a very bad idea. I really would prefer you returned to Glasgow with me."

Jimmy, a mere spectator to the discussion, chuckled when he saw Sarah's jaw tighten as she pulled herself up to her full height. He feared Cameron had touched the wrong nerve to have any hope of persuading Sarah to leave. Jimmy wandered off a short distance to give the family members privacy while they settled their argument. Out the corner of his eye, he saw Cameron throw his hands up in resignation and shake his head.

"And the victor is… Sarah," Jimmy murmured as he turned and wandered back towards the others. "I assume it is now safe to approach?" he asked when again in earshot. Jimmy chuckled again. "Ah, Cameron, were you ever in any doubt you were going to lose the battle? But, all that aside, have we decided what we are to do tonight?"

"It sounds to me as though we have quite a bit to do tomorrow," Sarah began, "so it might be as well to try our luck at the hotel tonight. If we return tonight, we won't waste half the day tomorrow travelling back into town."

Without losing more than a few moments, the trio were back on Jimmy's wagon and heading back into town. It was dark when they reached the hotel, and Sarah was relieved to find the rooms they occupied the previous night were available. The publican made it clear that, if they intended to eat there, they should go through to the dining room now or they would be too late.

While dinner was nothing to write home about, it was filling, and they were the only diners. No one seemed anxious for them to leave, so they remained seated at their table and developed a plan for the next day. Jimmy insisted hiring a fencing gang was their priority. It resulted in a debate about how much fencing was needed, where it had to go, and the required materials.

"After the fencing is in place, we can start stocking the place," Jimmy continued. "That will take care of most of the improvements required for this year."

"Yes, that will be a good start," Sarah agreed. "But, where am I supposed to live? I refuse to spend my life in this hotel."

"And I would not allow it," Cameron added. "Sarah is right, Jimmy. Maybe her accommodation should be our highest priority."

"Well, if I might be allowed to continue with the list of things we must do tomorrow, we will come to that. Now, after we organise a fencing gang, we need to acquire a wagon and team for Sarah. I take it you still remember how to handle a team, Sarah?"

"Of course I do. And you are right. I do need my own transport so I can come and go as necessary."

"Right, then before the end of the day, we need to find Roddy McDonald and have a chat," Jimmy said before slumping back on his chair. It suggested to the others that tomorrow's plan had been completed.

"Uhmm, Jimmy, who is Roddy McDonald, and why do we need to talk to him?" Sarah asked.

"Eh, oh yeah, of course, you don't know. Roddy is the best carpenter you will find in the area. We need to establish when he might start building your house."

"My house…! We haven't discussed anything about a house. How can we talk to him about something we haven't even thought about yet?"

"We are not going to discuss the house. We are going to establish when he might be free to start building one. Then we will know how much time we have to draw up a plan for the house you want."

"These are all sound steps to consider," Cameron commented, "but aren't they a bit premature? You appear to be rushing ahead with everything, Jimmy, without knowing Sarah's plans. Having seen the place, is she interested in staying here, let alone setting up a whole new property?"

"For goodness sake, Cameron, of course I'm staying here. This place is all I expected – and more. I'm so excited to be here and making these plans for my future in this new place.

The only sadness I have is not having you and Douglas – and Aunt Bess – here with me. I will miss you all so much, especially you, Cameron. You have been my rock since I left the Caribbean." Sarah felt the tears starting to well up as she spoke. She swallowed hard a couple of times, before announcing she was tired and would see them both again at breakfast.

Alone in her room, she enjoyed her first moments of solitude for the day. As she prepared for bed, she let her mind return to the day's events. Everything was amazing so far, much more than she even dared hope. Yes, she could be happy here; this would be her new home and the start of her new life.

It was inevitable such reverie would bring her back to Cameron, and the pangs of sadness returned at the thought of being separated from him... maybe never to see him again once he sailed away in a few days. Cameron had always been there for her. How could two brothers be so different in every way? And, she marvelled at the poor choice she made in marrying Robert – not that Cameron had ever been a potential husband. Such thoughts led her to the tragedy in Cameron's life.

About a year after he returned to Glasgow from the Caribbean, he married Elizabeth. Their families had been friends forever, and Cameron and Elizabeth spent much time together when they were young. Reportedly, it was a good marriage, and their first child was due around the time of their first wedding anniversary. That's when Cameron's perfect life crumbled around him.

After a long and difficult labour, Elizabeth died in childbirth, but managed to give birth to a son. Stressed and weak, the baby lasted only a few hours, and mother and child were buried together. Douglas lost not only a grandson but also what he saw as the next generation to carry the Wallace name into the future. Robert and Sarah only heard of the tragedy by mail after the event. It always saddened Sarah that she hadn't been there to support Cameron.

Those tears that welled up in the dining room returned at the thought of their parting when Cameron rejoined the ship to return to Glasgow. This time, there was no controlling them. They tumbled down her cheeks for a long time that night.

*****

Sarah was amazed. The day had gone like clockwork and according to plan. The two men had engaged a four-man fencing team to begin in two days erecting fences. In the horse yard behind the hotel were Sarah's team of two horses and her wagon loaded with an almost unbelievable quantity of fencing materials and other tools.

They met with Roddy McDonald late in the afternoon and, over a drink, discussed the possibility of his building Sarah's new home. He had just accepted a contract for some new work on another property, but it would require no more than a couple of weeks to complete. After that, he would like a couple of days to attend to some personal business before starting Sarah's house.

If there was one thing Sarah was adamant about, it was the type of house she wanted. A shack like Jimmy's would not do. She wondered whether Jimmy's met the standard of 'improvement' required under the lease of his block. While Sarah accepted that stone and brick were out of the question and resigned herself to timber construction, she was determined the house should be as she wanted it. After all, this was to be her permanent home for however long she had left on this earth.

Such determination was the cause of much argument between Sarah and the two men over the next couple of weeks. Neither man could understand why she was so insistent about some aspects of the plan but, in the end, they had to accept that it was Sarah's house and Sarah would have what Sarah wanted. But, it would not be cheap, and the thought of the cost of erecting the house was an ongoing concern for Cameron. Ultimately, he adopted the bold move of questioning the state of her finances.

"Feel free to tell me it's none of my business, but I am concerned about the expense you've incurred since we arrived here. It will be some time before you have further income. In the meantime, there will be further considerable expenses. I don't mean to pry into your private affairs, but I don't wish to see you become financially embarrassed. I am willing to lend you whatever money you need to render your block a going concern. If you cannot accept it as a gift from me, please accept it as a loan that you can repay at some time in the future. I cannot leave here without knowing you are financially secure, and your hopes and dreams are safely assured of becoming a reality."

"Thank you, Cameron, for your care and kindness, but please be reassured that I am financially independent. Both my mother's parents left me substantial amounts of money, and I have the money from Robert's estate and a little of my own put aside over the years. I have not gone into this without giving it careful thought and much consideration. I will be fine… but … should I find that not to be the case at any time in the future, I will take up your offer."

Sarah's last thought that night before the amnesia of sleep intruded was that they had made no plans for the next day.

*****

At breakfast, the two men announced Sarah would have a couple of hours to herself before they headed out to their blocks. But, there was one thing that occurred to her last night that she needed to discuss with them.

She needed a good horse to pull a plough and another sound horse for rounding up cattle. The latter one wasn't necessary until the property was stocked, but she wanted the plough horse now. Jimmy argued that one of the wagon team could do the job, but Sarah wanted a separate horse for that purpose.

As soon as the men left to attend to whatever they needed to do, Sarah crossed the street to the general store. After buying a good supply of provisions, she told the storekeeper she would collect them on her way out of town. Then, with nothing else to do until the men returned, she explored the township. It presented a sad and sorry picture with its makeshift timber, bark and canvas shanties. Nevertheless, its appearance belied the hive of activity in the township. When she returned to the hotel, Jimmy and Cameron followed her.

Minutes later, all three were in the horse yard behind the hotel. Sarah stood staring at the sight before her. Her wagon was hitched and ready to go, but more material had been added since the last time she saw it. It now held extra timber and sheets of iron, and tied on behind were two new horses. She looked over to where Jimmy was hitching his wagon. Her mouth dropped open. Jimmy's wagon was loaded to the point of being dangerously overfull with various pieces of lumber and sheets of iron. There was no time to ask questions as Cameron hurried her onto the wagon.

"I need to call at the general store on our way out to collect some provisions I bought this morning," she told him as he flicked the reins and eased the team and the loaded wagon out of the yard.

"Where are we supposed to put this?" he asked as he carried the box of supplies to the wagon. We have no room for it, and Jimmy doesn't either."

"It's fine. It can sit on the floor at our feet."

Cameron dumped the box at Sarah's feet and climbed on board as Jimmy drove his wagon past them. As they followed him out of town, Sarah asked, "What does Jimmy plan to do with all that lumber?"

"Oh, I believe he has a couple of building projects in mind. I'm sure all will become clear in due course."

*****

Over the next few days, the two blocks of land on the southern bank of the river became a hive of activity. The fencing gang arrived. Their first task was to set up the large tent Jimmy insisted was necessary to provide them with accommodation while they worked on her block. Then, with surprising speed, fencing snaked its way around areas of her land.

Meanwhile, while Sarah was left to her own devices in town, on Jimmy's block, Cameron and Jimmy practised their carpentry skills. An extension was being added to Jimmy's shack in record-breaking time. By week's end, the extension was complete, and the two men stood admiring their handiwork.

"The new bit makes the rest of it look pretty sick," Jimmy commented. "Looks like I might need to rebuild it to match the new part. How long did you say you might stick around? I'll need an offsider to help."

"We have another building to complete before you start work on renovating your castle," Cameron reminded him. "When do we bring Sarah out here? Is tomorrow too soon?"

"If we don't allow her out here soon, she will come anyway."

Sarah was surprised and excited when the two men appeared at the hotel to join her for dinner that night. She had so many questions. They barely answered one before she fired the next one. Then, in desperation, Jimmy held up his hands and shouted, startling men dining at another table.

"Enough! That's enough with the questions, Sarah, but I will tell you Cameron and I are spending the night in the hotel. Now, it's my turn for questions. Do you have anything else to do in town?" Chastened, Sarah shook her head. "Good; can you be packed and ready to leave here after breakfast tomorrow?"

"Of course; it won't take me more than a few minutes. But where am I to go?"

"Just be packed and ready to leave," Cameron said. "The rest will be a surprise."

Her surprise the next day was to be installed in the extension to Jimmy's shack. "Welcome to your new temporary home," he chirped as he opened the door for her. "Cameron and I will be camped in the other part of the building should you require us for anything."

It was all too wonderful. The gang finished the fencing they were hired to do and were happy to stay to build a yard close to the site Sarah had earmarked for her home. After Jimmy's extension was finished and Sarah moved in, they began work on another building on Sarah's block. They refused to tell her what it was until it was almost completed.

"This is your new stables building, and that end bit is where you store your wagon," Cameron explained. "As soon as that's done, our next task is to mark out the site of your new home. Roddy McDonald will be here to start work in about a week. Jimmy and I will go tomorrow to discuss your plan with him and pick up the first of the timber for its construction."

Cameron would not see the house completed. He left for Glasgow soon after Roddy started work. It was a sad, heartbreaking time for Sarah. Not only would she miss him more than she could say but, to her dismay, she realised it was more than friendship she felt for Cameron.

"It's as well he'll be back in Glasgow," she told herself. "It will save me from making a complete fool of myself."

Chapter 27

Surprises

1863 was proving a year of progress and surprises. Sarah's block was stocked, and she was living in her new house. With Jimmy's help, she had employed a Chinese gardener and a young Irish lass as a housemaid. There was an abundance of eggs, milk and fresh vegetables, fresh meat from the occasional chicken and pig slaughtered on the property, and the chook house provided the Chinese gardener with a plentiful supply of manure for his gardens.

The Lands Board approved both Sarah and Jimmy's applications for their selections, and the Lands Board's inspector was suitably impressed by the improvements made on them. Separate from the house garden, an acre of ground had been ploughed and put under vegetables. Its crop, plus any excess egg supply, sold through the general store, brought in a small regular income.

Life was sweet, Sarah often told herself, but something was missing. Despite their regular correspondence since his return to Glasgow, Sarah missed Cameron. But then, the biggest surprise happened just before Christmas. Cameron would return to Mackay around the end of January. Unable to believe the news, Sarah read his letter several times before allowing herself to become excited. What prompted his visit? Various possible scenarios flashed through her mind, but were dismissed as unlikely.

Then it was late January, and Jimmy brought news from town of a Wallace ship arriving in four days. Although it was too early, Sarah booked into the hotel the next day to await the ship's arrival. She wanted, above all else, to meet Cameron as he came off the boat.

And then the next surprise happened. As Cameron stepped off the gangplank, a strapping young man followed him, carefully watching where he placed his feet. Cameron rushed over and wrapped Sarah in a hug. The other young man looked up at her. Sarah's heart missed a beat, and for a couple of moments, she couldn't breathe.

"I intended this should be different," Cameron whispered, "but what's done is done. Come, I need to introduce you to someone." He beckoned the young man to join them. "Sarah, meet Philip Robert McCabe Wallace. Philip, this is Mrs Sarah Wallace." She managed to extend her hand to the young man.

At that point, Jimmy Fraser made a miraculous appearance. Cameron introduced him to Philip, explaining, "Jimmy is going to show you around the settlement and, afterwards, you both will join us at the hotel." With Philip out of the way, he turned his attention to Sarah. "There's unlikely to be anyone in the hotel dining room at this hour. We should be able to speak privately there."

After booking himself and Philip in for the night, Cameron led Sarah to the dining room. "You noticed the resemblance…?" he asked as soon as they were seated.

"Resemblance…! Philip is the mirror image of Robert. I don't suppose there is any need to ask who his father was, but his name intrigues me – especially the inclusion of 'McCabe'."

"Sarah, please bear with me while I tell you this story. It may prove uncomfortable, but it needs to be told." She nodded, and he continued. "Although I was unaware, Philip worked in one of our warehouses before I came here with you. Then, soon after we left, he delivered a letter to Father. The letter was from his mother, Jane McCabe. In her letter, she admitted her indiscretion with Robert that resulted in the birth of his son, Philip. She had not intended to trouble the Wallace family with the story, but her circumstances had changed, and she felt compelled to do so. She did not know Robert was lost at sea when she wrote the note, but she was ill and with not long to live. Her intention then was to introduce her son to his grandfather in the hope Douglas might take an interest in his future."

"All this would have happened in 1843 when Robert visited Glasgow to discuss the future of the plantations. That's when Jane ceased corresponding with me. So, that makes Philip about nineteen, going on twenty."

"Yes, she was so ashamed. She could not, in all good faith, masquerade as your friend any longer. Anyway, she found herself pregnant and desperate. Her grandmother had been ill. Fortunately, before Jane's condition became obvious, grandma died, leaving her house to Jane.

Then Jane's mother stepped in. She contacted her cousin, who owns a considerable estate up north and secured Jane a position as a nanny, or governess, to the herd of children the family was producing. Jane's condition wasn't a problem, and one more child on the estate wouldn't make any difference. Jane stayed with that family to the end. Jane used the money from the sale of grandma's house to educate Philip, who is a bright lad."

"What about his Wallace surname? How did that come about?"

"Father accepted Philip as his grandson – and probably his only grandson – to continue the family into the next generation, but he also wanted the name to continue. By whatever legal process, Father succeeded in having the Wallace surname tacked to the end of the lad's name. He has been taken under Father's wing and is being trained for his future position in the company.

Father and I felt you should know about Philip and be allowed to meet him. He knows nothing of this story, and it is up to you whether he learns of his connection to you or not."

"I hold no grudge against Jane. She was just another of Robert's unfortunate conquests. Philip represents the son I could not give this family. Despite the doctors' assurances there was nothing wrong with me, it just never happened. His parentage is through no fault of his own. I would like to get to know him. After all, he is part of Robert and looks identical to his father. Perhaps you should seek a quiet moment to tell him of my connection.

But, tell me how long you will spend here with me, and is it your intention to stay at my house while you are here?"

"I had hoped we might stay with you, so thank you for the offer. As for how long I will be here, that involves another story. You might have time to hear it before the other two join us." Of course, she wanted to hear it.

"Right, I'll be as succinct as possible. We have made some major changes to how our enterprise operates.

Shipping to America is reduced to almost nothing, while the number of our ships servicing this colony has increased. Some of the import/export business previously carried on has been curtailed or dropped entirely from our operations. No need to look alarmed, Sarah. This is not bad news. Our operations are changing to suit the times and how world trade is evolving.

The good news… well, I hope you consider it good news… is that I will remain here in Mackay when Philip returns to Glasgow. More importantly, if you don't think me too forward in saying this, I would hope to stay here with you. Have I shocked you?"

"Not at all… I could not be happier if you did stay with me. But what about your position in the company and your work in Glasgow?"

"Philip will take over the Glasgow end of the shipping, while I manage the rest from here. I will also look to source additional trade here for the company. But, above all else, I want to be your husband and be involved in the new life you are forging for yourself here in this new colony.

Sarah Erskine Wallace, will you marry me?"

"Cameron, are you sure about this – really sure?"

"I am both sure and determined."

"Then, yes, please, I'd be proud to be your wife."

Confronted by the couple in a tight embrace as he entered the dining room, Jimmy made a great fuss of wiping his boots and clearing his throat. The couple sprang apart, Sarah embarrassed and red-faced, and Cameron smiling wide enough to split his face.

"Aye, aye, what's afoot here then?" Jimmy demanded, grinning and with a glint in his eyes.

"We have a wedding to organise. How do you do that in this place?" Cameron asked.

But Sarah saw the look on Philip's face turn from surprise to disapproval, and he stood there shaking his head in disgust.

"Don't judge us too soon, Philip," Sarah counselled. "I have a story to tell you. Please wait until you hear it before you pass judgement." Philip looked unsure, so Sarah continued. "Not now; I will tell you tomorrow when all of us are more settled again." He shrugged but reluctantly agreed.

"It's still early enough. We could go to our blocks instead of spending the night in town," Jimmy suggested.

Everyone agreed it was the right thing to do. Soon, the two wagons left town with Cameron driving Sarah's wagon, and Philip riding with Jimmy. They congregated at Sarah's house, where her housekeeper was advised there would be four for dinner that night.

Straight after breakfast next morning, Sarah sat with Philip in her dining room and told him the story she promised him. Before she finished, he was moved to tears. Then, when the story ended, he sat with his head in his hands for a moment before looking up at Sarah.

"Where does that leave me now? I mean, other than as an orphan with an assumed name?"

"It leaves you with what is your rightful name by birth and, more importantly, it means I have now met my stepson. You are the child Robert and I never had, but you are Robert's child with my best friend in Glasgow. That makes you so special to me. And I know you are special to Cameron and his father too. You are a part of the Wallace family, and there is no question about our wanting you to be and to be happy with us.

I hope, if not immediately, then in time, you might find it in your heart to be happy for Cameron and me in the new life we will make together."

He stood, hesitated a moment, and then rushed forward to hug her tightly. "Thank you. Thank you… but what do I call you now?"

"I'm Sarah. The same as I always have been… and you will remain Philip, just as you always have been. Now let's join the others and ask Jimmy how people go about getting married in this part of the world. It would be wonderful if you were still here when it happened."

"What will you do afterwards? Remain here or return to Glasgow? Cameron has hinted he might not return home. But, if you both remain here, what will you do?"

"We will continue to live here on my land. I will continue to work it, while Cameron continues to look after the family's shipping interests in this part of the world. The exciting news is that we intend to plant sugarcane in the early part of next year. Soon after New Year, Jimmy will return to Java to secure a quantity of cane for us to grow and use as our plant stock for the next year.

Rumour has it a new Regulation will be introduced to Parliament next year. It is likely to make it easier to obtain additional land. I have my eye on the block across from mine. The current lessees are not doing so well, and may be forced to walk off it. If things transpire as gossip has it, I should be able to purchase it cheaply – to grow coffee and sugar.

So, Philip, there are exciting times ahead for us here in this young colony, and you will always be welcome here anytime you wish to escape from Glasgow."

That night, after recounting to Cameron her earlier conversation, Sarah lay awake for a long time. She decided, while her life had not been unhappy – not really, neither had it been particularly happy. Now that appeared about to change.

Taking that earlier advice to 'seize an opportunity when it presented' was about to pay dividends. Her every instinct insisted her new life here with Cameron would bring the happiest time of her life.

The End

Also by the Author

Revenge is not Enough

Harbour Plaza: built on dreams

On the Way to Istanbul

An Unsuitable House

A Land Too Far

Paradise Interrupted

Unwelcome Mail

By Any Other Name

House of Secrets